To Richard, my

BLOOD WILL OUT

(With the Proper Solvent)

Thanks for joining my fang club!

Lauren Stoker

Blood Will Out

(With the Proper Solvent)

Lauren Stoker

Blood Will Out (With the Proper Solvent)

A Crowe & Thistle Book

For permissions contact:

Crowe & Thistle Books
99 Rocky Hill Road
Plymouth, Massachusetts 02360
(508) 746-5725

Hardback ISBN: 978-0-578-92453-3
Paperback ISBN: 978-0-578-96433-1

Library of Congress Control Number: 2021914638

The wolf's tale in Chapter 3 of *Blood Will Out* was originally published by Thurston Howl Publications' anthology, *Difursity,* as a short story titled, "No Substitutes Allowed." Copyright© 2020, Lauren Stoker.

Dedications

To Sir Terry. I very much minded how you went.

And to Ruth-Without-Whom Haber,
without whom this thing would never have taken off.

So much thanks to you both, *when*ever you are.

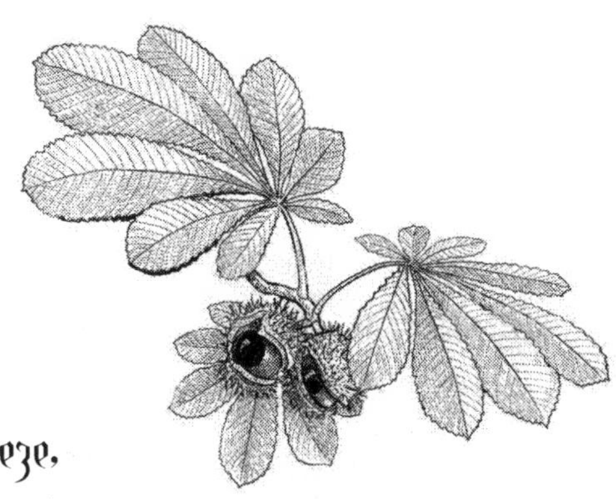

She swoops to conker,
Who rides upon the breeze,
And hurls her furious missiles,
Astride avenging bristles,
O'er chestnut boughs and thistles,
At those who dare to harm the trees.

She swoops to conquer,
Who descends upon the night.
From darkened room
To dungeon's gloom
She renders doom,
Securing justice with a bite.

Prologue

There were strangers in her forest. Even from inside the thick, white-washed walls of her cottage in the woods, even under the heavy thatch, Granny could feel them. And she didn't like it. Not one little bit.

She'd been feeling the pressure of their presence for days, like a storm building up. Or a sewer overflowing after a deluge. But she couldn't quite see or feel who they were or why they were here. She just knew they weren't up to any good.

The gaudy, purple-striped stockings on her feet, propped up on a hassock, belied the seriousness of her role in this land, her charge to protect. Granny leaned back in her chair, sucking on her clay pipe, trying to settle her nerves. She'd lit no lamps, preferring only the light that came from her hearth. As she smoked, she studied the rings she blew and the patterns of light and shadow the firelight threw on her walls, seeking answers and omens.

She sighed, worrying that she'd have to take her broom out of mothballs. The last time she'd been forced to use it had been decades ago, after she'd left her old life behind. Granny really hoped she wouldn't have to resort to all that again. She wouldn't have thought she'd ever have to—that lot had learned their lesson good and proper. But this felt just like the last time, only with a new bunch of players. It seemed that there was just no stopping stupidity.

The sound of soft scratching at her kitchen door penetrated her thoughts. She wasn't surprised at company, even this late. Laying down her pipe, she settled her black skirts and stuffed her feet in her clogs, then trudged to her back door. Opening it, she saw a wolf sitting on her mat, his trusting amber eyes gazing up at her. She knelt down and gave him a scratch behind his ears. “Come for a nibble, have you?” she asked, hoping it was only that.

He shook his head then laid it on his front paws and whimpered. The wolf was one of “her boys,” as she called them. They were her eyes and ears in the forest when her inner sight was blocked. It paid to have a fallback plan. The forest and its creatures depended on her.

“Ah,” Granny responded. “You’d best come in, then, and tell me about it.” She held the door open and the wolf padded over to her chair. She closed, then bolted the door.

As the wolf told his tale, the flame shadows threw images of two wolf shapes across the wall. They weren’t his clan—her wolves—and they weren’t natural. Mixed with shadow-grey, their images bore streaks of a poisonous yellow: the colour of greed.

CHAPTER 1

Not the Best Year

A ***Saturday Night in October up at ze Schloss on ze Hill.*** "Oh, darling," she sighed, cradling the Princess phone under her chin as she filed her crimson nails, "it's not that I don't appreciate blood. I mean, I have to, don't I? It's just as a beverage, it's beginning to pall. After three hundred years I should bloody well think it would! Am I right? And this stuff we're getting lately, absolute swill! Yes, I know the peasants can't help it, their poor diet, having to sleep with swine, blah, blah, blah. But you know what *grand-mère* always said, 'You lie down with hogs and you wake up with . . .' Oh, drat. What was that word again? *Trichinosis!*

"And anyway, it's not like we could charge down there unannounced, like Ladies Bountiful, overflowing hampers of victuals in hand, to ease the suffering of the unwashed. They'd be on us like stink on a corpse with torches and pitchforks! I for one don't appreciate being punctured."

The voice on the other end continued its gnatty buzz while she filed.

"I know, I know. It's much the best if they come to us for our . . . er, *their* needs. Anyhow, these days I'd as soon have a nice espresso. It does leave you a bit peckish at times, but I find just a teensy thimble of haemoglobin does the trick and sweetens it right up. But take my advice, go for the Fair Trade goods: none of those nasty chemicals and undertaste of stainless steel and polymers. Instead, you get that delightful hint of the true Central American *campesino*: sweat, fingernail dirt, tetanus—giving it that, oh, *je ne sais quoi. So* delicious, darling! And you're doing your good deed for the planet, don't forget.

"What's that? Yes, I did actually serve a very nice pinot noir at the last candlelight supper. Why do you think I insist on candle light? Much more flattering and in the gloom one can't tell even a mediocre red blend from the blood of your uncle, speaking metaphorically, of course. And every time the count waves his bloody hands making some bloody point or another, he spills the bloody plonk. It's damned hard to wash out, I tell you. Wine is much easier. These days, I'm leaning more toward a good cabernet. It's that wee bit more viscous. And as I said, if anyone starts getting suspicious, the old thimble trick will do."

The nasal buzz on the other end indicated agreement.

"But it's all getting to be such a drag. Oh! And then there's that wretched, tired old joke the count trots out at every single dinner for the past 200 plus years. Here she mimicked a heavy Slavic accent: 'I do not drink (long pause) wine.' Oh, oh—and then . . . *wait for it* . . . eyebrow raised. Leer."

Her listener's snickers blossomed gratifyingly into an unladylike snort.

"Gods' truth," she continued, "next time Vlad pulls that dead and stinking rabbit (I mean the joke, of course) out of his sad, sad hat, I fear I truly will forget myself and scream, 'Yes! We know!' I mean, considering the usual guest list, it goes without bloody saying it. And it would serve the old bore right to test that statement by serving him Hearty Fucking Burgundy."

A scream of laughter streamed through the receiver. Just as she was reaching her ribald stride, there was a knock at the door. Naturally.

"Oh, hang on a mo'." She laid the phone down on the dressing table and craned her neck, with a sharp report of cracks, around at her servant.

"What *is* it, Cedric?" she spat at the rustic retainer lurking on the threshold. "Speak up, man!"

He mumbled his message with apologies. "Someone at the door."

"Damn and bother! Well, go see who it is and tell him he's got to come back later."

Mumble, mumble.

"Oh, honestly! Now that I'm chairperson of the Intra-Species Coalition, these creatures think they can just drop by any old time of the day. Of all people, Count D. should know I never see anyone until after sundown!"

More apologetic mumbling and shuffling of bunioned feet. He was joined by her dogsbody, Karloff.

"Oh, all right, Cedric. I'll be down presently. Show him into the castle darkroom and make sure he doesn't mess about with the black-out curtains. Karloff, could you please pat him down for silver bullets and those infernal infrared laser thingies? He thought *those* were such a scream last time. Not!

"Ronny, dash it, I shall have to go. Count D. is 'begging' another audience with me. Yes, the very man. His ears must have been burning. If only. Oh, I don't know. Something to do with the dwarf problem, I suspect. But the man is always begging. I ask you, what is *with* that? He's like a damned dog. Perhaps I'll throw him a bone, if I can figure out whose. Well, ta, ta. I'll ring you back later."

The baroness rang off, slammed her bedroom door upon further intruders and wrenched her gold silk dressing gown off its hook. One had to make an effort, after all, and look one's best, she supposed. Although what that was she couldn't exactly remember. Three centuries tended to make recall a bit of a blur.

She hated seeing people during the day. Even in the red, stygian dusk of the darkroom, she never looked fit—so drawn out and positively shrunken. Well, skeletal, really. After sunset she plumped right up. And Count D. knew that, she pouted. But now that he'd gotten that new, hermetically sealed, light-proof carriage, he was popping up everywhere, sod him!

A quick glance at the double-refracting mirror (one couldn't be too careful) told her she'd done the best she could. At least her hair was presentable. Although maybe a touch dry. Note to self: more conditioner. Still, it was fully black, like her mamá's before she was lynched with a stout stake to the heart. Poor Mamá. Just short of her 400th birthday, too. The irony was Mamá really had been making an effort to cut back. It was so typical of her mother that, what with her vanity about putting on her specs or even reading the ruddy label, she never caught on that "plasma *Homo sapiens*" advertised in the mail order "blood substitute" was the same bleedin' thing as human blood. Well, that's what comes of cheating on one's Latin exams, she sighed.

The baroness stomped down the grand staircase in a bloody mood.

Silently, the door to the darkroom opened from its antechamber, permitting only the smallest gleam of hellish illumination. The baroness couldn't abide screeching hinges, so her staff kept them all well oiled, except for the front door, of course. A dark, caped figure emerged, hair product glistening in the gloom, and genuflected gallantly before the baroness as she sat on the requisite "throne" to receive him. Really, it was just a gilded Louis XIV-ish chair with curvy legs she'd picked up from Rack, Bog and Beyond. There was one in nearly every room. Of course, only royalty were meant to have them. Yet her people expected them: she might be a bloodthirsty vampire, but by gods, she was their baroness so there'd better be thrones. Like squeaky front doors, it kept them happy, but what a damned nuisance all the same, especially as one had to elbow aside the developing pans and the 8 x 10 glossies of screaming victims pegged up to dry in order to make room to sit down.

"My dear Baroness, you are looking vell, although perhaps a bit too zkin und bones, eh?" The count bowed with mock concern.

The baroness arched an eyebrow at his mean wit. "Yes, yes, Vladimir. Fabulous to see you, too. But you know how I feel about receiving visitors before nightfall. So I'm presuming this was urgent, yes?"

"Yes indeed, *meine Liebchen*. Zer is not only ze problem mit ze dwarfs, but now zer zeems to be zome zort of inzurgency among ze vervolves, as vell."

This touched on a sore subject. The baroness, as a debutante weary of the unending array of sycophantic bloodsuckers surrounding her, had opted, against Papá's entreaties, to marry just a bit outside her crowd. And such a handsome and charming man he was who, because he was so very handsome and charming, could be excused for turning extremely hairy and loping off on all fours once a month. After all, he put up with her . . . er . . . restricted diet. At least Heinrich didn't have that annoying speech impediment (or was it affectation?). Honestly! Could the count never learn to pronounce his "th's," "s's" and "w's"? He'd only lived in this country, what, 400 years? At least.

"May I remind you," the baroness replied, "that my dear husband, Heinrich, is also a verevolf, er, werewolf? And that he and his cohorts have no choice but to rise up, as it were, on a monthly lunar cycle." Here she cocked a coquettish eyebrow as she fondly remembered several "cycles" of theirs that had happily coincided. . . .

"Vat is zat? Heinrich is riding ze unicycle?"

The baroness struggled for patience. "No, I said 'lunar cycle,' Count. You know, the moon and all that?"

"Ah, I zee," zaid ze count.

No, you don't, you stupid, bloody Kraut, thought the baroness. Okay. Not technically a *Kraut*, mental apologies to her German cousins. No, Count D. was from one of those silly, damp little countries that kept changing their names as often as socks. Trans-something. What was it? Trans-Siberia? No, that was a rock band. Jolly good, one, actually. Whatever. If it hadn't been for Vlad and his blasted "pointed sticks," her cousins would have had that pitiful place under control eons ago.

She roused herself from her reverie and smiled disingenuously at Vladimir in his shoe-blacked, pointy toupee. "So what *is* the trouble with our shifty furry friends? We must all get along these days, you know. No more sampling another species' fluids, at least not without an invitation."

"Und zat is eggzactly ze problem: ze invitation!" glowered the count. "Always it is I who must vait to be invited, patiently in ze cold und dark, in ze zoggy cape outside ze bedroom vindow, vondering vhen ze hell ze *Fraulein* iss going to vake up und smell ze pheromones! But zese bounders chust jump right in zere und gobble up ze goodies zen claim temporary instinctivity, on account of ze looney cycle! And zey get off, vizout zo much as a zitation! Just like zat!"

The baroness murmured her commiseration, but golly, these "z's" were really getting to her. Her mind was crossing its eyes, struggling for translation.

"It's not fair, I zay!" the count harrumphed. "And zer number iss legend! Or vas zat 'legion'? Anyhow, zere's a whole lot of zem now."

Zere he goes again! "How many of them do you think there are?" the baroness queried. "Last time I checked, there was just Heiny and his old school mates, well and poker pals, but surely not more than a dozen or so. And they've always had impeccable manners, at least in their human shapes. You know," she laughed girlishly, "wolves will be wolves!"

"All zis I know," the count admitted. "Your husband und colleagues have been most gracious. I do not zink it is your husband's crowd. It appears to be some new gang zat's come into ze neighbourhood."

Now *that* would bring new meaning to gang graffiti. Considering it, she resolved to order more air fresheners. "But where would they come from, dear Count?

Her mind now ground its teeth, chagrined by the influence of illiterate visitors' dangling whatsits.

Soldiering on, she elaborated. "We have been most careful to keep the remaining few within these mountains, and they are all under strict decree not to 'turn' any further victims to increase their gene pool. What's more, they've happily agreed, since my fortunate marriage to Heinrich, that marital bliss can as easily be obtained within a mixed-species affiliation."

"Ah, but perhaps, dear Baroness, zey vere only giving you ze lip zervous. Or more likely ze znout zervous," he chuckled, slyly.

"Oh, droll, Count! Very droll. Well, I shall have to look into it, obviously. Perhaps Heiny can sniff out what's going on."

She caught the count's smirk at her unintended pun and reddened, which luckily went unnoticed under the darkroom's red glare.

The sun, at last, was going down, so she arose from her throne, more limberly than she might have an hour ago, her patrician features now properly capable of revealing haughtiness in all their haughtitude. The effect made its point upon the count. He'd forgotten how formidable she could be, when properly **. . .** refreshed.

"We shall get back to you when we know more," the baroness assured him.

The count bowed and backed out, being careful this time not to knock over the umbrella stand. What *was* an umbrella stand doing anyway outside a darkroom? One shuddered to think, even one used to impaling.

Well, that's put a dampener on my evening's plans and the next night's as well. Baroness Elisabetta Hermione Ermintrude von Intermittierend Allianzen unter Landadels (VIAL), or "Betty" to her darling Heiny and peers, strode into the Great Hall of the VIAL castle and yanked on the bell pull. (Behind closed doors, she was "Betty" also to her disgruntled staff, although they tended to change the interior vowel.) With satisfaction, she heard the dim sound of duelling gongs that would summon back her "man," one of them anyway. Hard to tell who might show up these days. Staff kept dropping off like flies bled dry by spiders.

As she was waiting, she reminded herself that she still had to call poor Ronny back. Ronny (more formally Veronica von . . . oh, never mind) had been her best chum from finishing school. They had always finished first, though how they kept their figures, no one knew.

She heard a phlegmy cough at the door. *Please don't let him spit on the parquet*, she prayed. The same grey-hair appeared as before, bowing. (Sometimes ducking was called for.)

"Ah, Cedric!" the baroness smiled encouragingly. "It *is* Cedric, isn't it?" She tended to assume her main manservant would be a Cedric, there had been such a long line of them through the years.

"Yes, Your Suckulence."

This got a stern look from the baroness.

"I'm Cedric the XLIXth," said the man in gravy-stained livery, "my old dad being the XLVIIIth."

"Of course," the baroness murmured, already sorry she asked.

"See, my old dad and my granddad before him and his granddad before him . . ."

She could see where this was going. "Yes, yes, I know." But there was no stopping him.

Cedric continued implacably. "See . . . " As he paused a long moment to recapture the thread of his narrative, Betty grabbed her nail file and resumed filing. "Us Smallbits been with your family for many years. Many, many years. I'm tryin' to recollect just exactly how long."

"Yes, dear Cedric. I *know*: 279 years, to be exact." *And 7 months, 11 days* . . . she thought to herself. "And we appreciate your family's loyalty, count on it, in fact."

At this, Cedric beamed, if that's what you could call what was happening to the creases in his ancient visage. All in all, she preferred either the scowl or wide-eyed panic.

"So I would like you to handle a new mission of mine, something that suits your . . . em, skills."

Cedric regarded her warily, remembering the last mission. "And what would that be, Your Incisiveness?"

Now that was pressing things a bit, but she decided to ignore the remark, as it was anatomically relevant.

Cedric performed many duties for the baroness, having worked his way up (or to his way of thinking, down) from gardener. Among them were butler, valet, official trusser, and castle spy/messenger (who at times was shot at). It was this last duty he dreaded most.

"I need you to summon all the members of the Order of Lupo to ze *Schloss* (blast this Teutonic influence!) the *castle,"* she amended, "and as soon as possible."

" 'Order of Lupo,' you say?" Cedric scratched his thinning pate. "You mean your wolf gang?"

"No, not Wolfgang. He's that wolf who pretends to eat grannies. . . . Oh, I see. Ha, ha! Good one, Cedric. Yes, in fact—the 'wolf gang.' But you *do* understand the 'gang' I'm referring to is our own bunch of occasional canines to which my dear husband belongs, correct?"

"Oh yes, ma'am. Them hairy blokes with the busted seams in their jackets. Hard to miss 'em, 'specially in a graveyard under a full moon, mouth full of vicar. . . ."

"Yes, quite," the baroness replied tersely. "But I am confident our werewolves don't do that sort of thing since the treaties."

Cedric kept his thoughts to himself and, instead, daringly inquired, "Whadya want with 'em, then?"

"There have been reports lately that a new gang or gangs of werewolves, complete outsiders and bounders by all accounts, have recently shown up on the scene and are poaching the 'wildlife,' as it were. So I've decided to round up all our local hirsute horde. I intend to cross examine them all, tooth and nail, to see what any of the order members know of this."

She had to wait while Cedric controlled himself after her last remark.

When Cedric had straightened his face once again, he commented, as solemnly as possible, "No disrespect ma'am, but you'll need to include your hubby, or it won't go right with the others, if you understand my meaning. And where shall I put them, Your Denticlity?"

Gnashing her denticles, she replied, "Naturally, I shall include His Heinous, er Highness. I'm putting him in charge of the proceedings. In regard to the location, put them all in the drawing room, where else?"

"And when's all this happenin'?"

"Tomorrow actually."

"What, tomorra? But it's not Thursday."

"Yes, well, it will have to do. We won't need the usual equipment. In fact, why not cover it or remove it for the time being? It might make our guests a tad nervous."

The baroness kept Thursdays as "Prey Day" in accordance with civic tradition and used her drawing room in a rather literal fashion for her supply and demand, *per se*. Her staff, when they weren't praying it wasn't their turn, derived much mirth from just how literal it was. Still, it wasn't like the old days. They had proper gurneys now, with sheets on (usually clean), IV tubes, syringes, the lot. No more ropes and chains (regrettably). And normally, her vassals could rely upon Karloff to use virgin, or at least, new-ish needles. Asked their preference, they'd enthusiastically agreed to "donate" the odd pint or two a month in lieu of her grandpapá's onerous taxation. That really had bled them dry. Lucky for them the baroness was a bit more kind-hearted, or at least canny about leaving something in reserve. Moreover, they believed it was all to a good cause, which made them feel helpful and proud. Well intentioned oafs that they were, they honestly thought that The Order of the Red Cross was getting it, poor lambs. *That was quite a good ruse,* she thought.

So the meeting of the wolf gang would mean having to move some of the bulkier equipment to accommodate her guests and to avoid getting their hackles up. She could use the parlour instead of course, but she couldn't tolerate all the hair they shed on the carpet, not to mention the velour settees. And then there was all that irritating nail-clicking on the polished floors. Her staff would positively riot if she allowed more quadrupeds in the parlour.

She heard the rumbling that meant the ignition of one of Cedric's witty asides, and glanced up at him.

"Funny how tetchy some of them wolf boys can get about a little vial of blood or two, when they're not tearin' out folks' froats. With a permit, naturally," he added diplomatically "Bunch of sissies, really."

The baroness glared at him, counting mentally the procession of Smallbits: *279 years, 7 months, 11 days, 15 hours, and 10 minutes too bloody long!* Cedric missed her disapproving glance and grinned with glee at his broadside. *What* can *one do with these people? At least Cedric is one of us, more or less, a vessel half full in any event. You couldn't question his loyalty. Or you could, but you'd get nothing intelligible out of the exercise. Although I do think his forbears lasted a bit longer. Cedric's barely pushing 90. Perhaps I should give him a vacay. At his age, he's probably overdue.*

"So, put the word out, please," the baroness resumed, "that I shall expect them all tomorrow night after sunset. You'll need to check the almanac to see when exactly that is, of course. We don't want any accidents. It's difficult enough to keep up with the dusting. And make sure to have individual shaving kits at the ready, if it's going to be a full moon. Chains, too. That will be all, Cedric."

Cedric bowed and shuffled away muttering, clearly not happy with his new "mission." How the hell he was going to round up a bunch of fellas who kept shifting from two legs to four and back, he had no idea.

Just as you were certain you'd collared one, he either turned out to be somebody's Fido, or suddenly rose up in his bleedin' pantaloons and clouted you on the ear for actin' above your station. 'Struth!

The baroness arose from her divan and moved purposefully to her escritoire. She regarded poor Cedric's plight and decided with uncharacteristic sympathy she would aid him as she could. She was not without heart, after all. Well, technically . . . But she committed herself to writing the various invitations in her own flowing hand so that, this time, Cedric could merely make the rounds handing out invitations, instead of playing dog catcher. Given the time constraint, it would be far more effective and get prompter results. Less wear and tear on the nets and stun guns, she should think.

A timid pawing at the door and just a whisper of a whine caused her to turn round from her writing.

"Ah, Heiny, my love. Did we have a nice nap? I see that you've forgotten your trousers again. Your tail's showing."

Abashed, Heinrich looked down to see that he hadn't quite completed his post-siesta transformation. Near the full moon, he had a tendency to morph into wolf shape while sleeping. "Oh, dash it all, Betty, I always seem to forget some detail or other."

"That's all right, my love. We all have our little faults. Come here, my pet, and let me give you a little cuddle."

Heiny loped over obediently, sitting adoringly at Betty's feet. She adjusted his cravat and scratched him behind his ears while he forced his hind leg to remain still.

"I really don't know what I'd do without you, Betty. I truly don't."

I'll bet you don't, she thought, *seeing as how no one else can afford Fangy Feast at these prices, not to mention keeping you out of trouble when you forget to keep track of the calendar.*

"I know, *mein Hündchen,*" she murmured affectionately. Heiny absolutely loved it when she spoke German to him. His own people came from Basingstoke, the aristocrats among them at any rate. The commoner kin were mostly from Wolverhampton. "But darling, please don't drool on the Bokhara."

Heiny ducked his head in shame, and reeled in his tongue (a skill that, when reversed, had its other uses), then shed a bit on the carpet.

The baroness, absently patted him and gazed out the French doors of her study, considering the suitors she once had had. No, she'd chosen right. Despite the housekeeping issues and the monthly aberrations in cuisine and physiognomy, Heinrich really was a love and true blue. Even in his wolf shape, he'd never dream (or dare) to run off with another bitch. She corrected herself, ". . . run off with a she-wolf." And he did have his uses, several of them in fact, she remembered fondly.

"So, my love, the doddering old count came calling today to alert me to the rumours of some new wolf gang prowling our villages and generally making nuisances of themselves, etc., etc. Have you heard anything about that?" Betty held up a palm. "Before you say it, no I'm not referring to Wolfgang, the foreign wolf who hangs out with Granny. I'm referring to an actual gang of wolves. That was just Cedric's little joke."

"Oh, bloody good! 'Wolf gang!' I shall remember that one."

"To continue, I need your help and that of your other 'kennel mates,' shall we say, to sniff this rumour out and see if there's anything in it. The count was most annoyed that these interlopers were snatching our local 'vixens' from the jaws of his defeat, and not waiting upon ceremony to do so. Sounds quite thuggish, doesn't it?"

"It certainly does! We made it quite plain when you inherited the title, well *you* did, my dear, that we (meaning you) would no longer tolerate newcomers who wouldn't stay in their own skin and went about dining on folks without permission just because the moon was full."

"Exactly. The lack of permission is what has him irked most, I think. But he has to be realistic. Now that plague, distemper and most other noxious diseases are in abeyance, you cannot expect people to just go belly up and beg for euthanasia at the slightest threat.

"It's not like it was in Papá's day," she reminded him.

"Damned pity," grumped Heiny. "Things were a lot simpler then."

"True, but so much messier. And I'm quite happy to no longer worry about guests' noticing a reddish hue coming from the tap, the water table was that saturated. Besides, we must move with the times."

"Still," Heiny continued, "I remember many an enjoyable roll in the stuff after . . . it was all over. Oh, don't turn up your nose. I caught you licking the faucet a few times."

The baroness looked away, peeved. "Well, that's behind us now. Anyhow, it always seemed to me to be such a waste of good protein, simply lolling around in it."

"Now, Betty, it was all in good fun."

"I suppose. But if there's anything in this rumour of a new pack of lobos amongst us, that won't be fun at all. It would be naïve to assume the outsiders would comply with the new stipulations. And think of their influence upon our current contingency of shape-changers. We've only just got them going along with our restriction program over the past decade or two. Instincts do die hard."

"You leave it to me, my dear," Heinrich replied resolutely. "I'll get to the bottom of this."

The baroness wished she could be sure which bottom he would be getting to. She really did prefer his human shape for the most part. That beastly olfactory fascination with everyone's private parts was so tiresome.

Alone in her salon, Betty drew the heavy, room-darkening curtains apart and checked the sky. She took an appreciative sip from her nightcap, the bright red liquid flowing slowly down her throat. *Ah! Good batch, that. Must make a note of the donors.*

Just then, a beautiful, round moon sailed right on cue from behind a cloud. *Rats*, she thought. *That will make tomorrow's meeting difficult. Perhaps it will rain and no one will notice.* She could only hope. Rowdy canines with bad haircuts weren't her idea of a good time.

She closed her curtains and returned to her vast, full tester bed, evicted a spider that had swung down from the draperies expecting a meal, and popped him absent-mindedly into her mouth. The spider's last surprised thought was, "WTF?" Then a pop and a crunch.

Once she was comfortably settled, Betty tried to cast her thoughts out across her lands, to her people, her creatures. But nothing alarming, or at least new, came up on her radar. *I wonder if these alleged interlopers are merely traveling through, assuming there's any truth to the rumour. If it* is *true, from where* have *they come and* why*?* The last MBS (Mythical Beast Survey) stated definitively that werewolves were extinct, outside of the small, select cadre they had managed to protect here. Even in Heiny's Basingstoke branch of the family, that gene had died out. Say some outsiders survived undocumented, why come here where they must compete with the resident pack for dinner or amusement?

Oh, gods. Please don't tell me it's a reunion and more are on their way. She could imagine the sheer volume of carrion, the maggots and beetles, the escalating murders of crows, the unbridled roughhousing. Why, the place would be turned into one big chew toy. And the poop to be scooped! The community disposal crew would probably strike.

She knew Pedigree.com had a very thorough database, when it came to humans. . . . Well, werewolves were human up to a point, so could one of their kind have developed a special search filter, maybe even a special MugBook page, to locate those with intermittent snouts?

She supposed it might be possible that could mean that some pal of her Heiny had defected and was even now gathering his undocumented clan to her realm. If they gained power, that could really take a bite out of her system, as well as her security budget. And that would not do!

It was nearly curfew: 5:00 a.m. or thereabouts. That noxious twitter chorus was about to start up. Betty tugged the crimson Damask drapes closed around the bed, then pulled the lid shut with a bang on the queen-sized coffin that served as her baronial mattress, tossing to and fro on the pink satin pleats, trying to evict worry from her mind. She was beginning to feel the sum of her centuries. *And I never called Ronny back! What* she's *going to make of this, I really don't know. Careful*, she cautioned herself. *It's no good getting your blood pressure up, especially while you don't have any.* Eventually, when the sun came up, she would drift off.

CHAPTER 2

The Rider

The Same Night. In the evening shadows, on the top of a hill looking down upon the crenellated battlements of the castle, a lone figure waited astride a dark horse at the edge of the forest, his features hidden by an overly deep hood.

"There's always a bloomin' 'lone rider on the hill' in these things," a voice complained from beneath some ferns.

"'Course there is. It's expected, innit?" replied a second.

"Yes, but you wait, that horse will turn out to be magical, can probably talk and all. Can't just leave it as a regular horse, can they?" whined a third.

"Shut up, you," hissed the second one, "I'm tryin' to follow the scene."

"And I'll lay you ten to one what that bloke's bleedin' name is," continued the first.

"What's that, then?" asked the second.

" 'Rider'!" the first and third ejaculated in stereo.

"Is that with a 'd' or a 't'? 'Cos, see, if it was a 't' as in '*Writer*' we could call him 'King Author.' " He had a thing for screen writers.

A groan and rolled eyes. "Don't encourage him," said the first to the third.

Three small, glowing lights, like fireflies on steroids, floated along the verge, unnoticed by their quarry. They were a species of fairie known as *Léirmheastóirí* (Gaelic for "critics"). But they preferred to be known as "Sprites," as they were fond of the fizzy drink. It was easier on the larynx and more dignified than "Orange Crush." That sounded too much like a punk rock band.

As the rider shifted in his saddle, the full moon helpfully slid back behind its cloud when he came out from under cover of the forest.

"And just in time, too," the rider remarked to his horse, watching with relief as the heavens darkened. "A tad close, that." He'd forgotten that wolves could sweat, at any rate a half-wolf could.

His horse looked up. *You forgot your shaving kit again, didn't you?*

"As my '*pack* horse,' I rather thought it was your job to remind me, Ed," the rider retorted.

The horse's chestnut withers rose with annoyance. *I thought we had agreed not to use that ridiculous moniker. It's "Eduardo," remember, compadre? I am not that imbécil, the talking horse on the telly.*

"Told you there'd be a talkin' horse 'fore we're through!" Sprite 3 triumphantly elbowed Sprite 2.

"Well," the rider parried to his *caballo*, "you *are* a talking horse, more or less, and it's so amusing when you bridle."

Oh, ha bloody ha, said the horse. *And anyway, technically, seeing that my voice is all in your head, I'm more of a horse whisperer.*

Naturally the three sprites, being magical, as well all beasts could also "hear" Eduardo. But the rider wasn't to know.

"Thank God for that," his rider replied. "I need to keep a low profile here, and approach the enemy as silently as possible."

In response, a long, reverberating fart broke the intended silence.

"Oh, thanks SO much for that!" The rider fanned the fumes frantically, eyes watering. "I must remember to inspect your fodder in future."

In the underbrush could be heard the frantic scampering of unseen small feet.

"Not to mention that now, thanks to you, the entire neighbourhood has been alerted, at least anyone with a sense of smell."

Blast from the past, the horse couldn't resist.

"I guess I deserved that for calling you 'Ed.' "

Sí. But we're probably safe in this "neighbourhood," the horse continued casting an eye around at the odiferous hovels and sties nearby. *Doubt this lot has anything left to smell with.*

"Good point. Just keep your flatulence to yourself when we get near the castle, okay?"

Como no.

The rider was about to spur on his steed when he caught the challenge in the eye rolled up at him. "Quite right. I am forgetting myself. No spurs." Once he could make himself understood, Eduardo had forged a firm treaty with his rider friend over that. Bad enough with the pointy silver bits poinging his sensitive areas when the moon wasn't full. But come the "change," he'd be hanged if he would put up with getting gouged by dirty claws. That was right out.

"Shall we proceed, then?" the rider inquired mildly?

You've only to say the word.

Groaning, the rider settled in the saddle and commenced as silently as possible down the hill, making sure his taser was at hand in case of trouble. Seated behind a pommel and surrounded by yards of cloak, a sword took far too much time to draw.

Above the village of Schlachtungunterburg (literally "slaughter-under-castle," but simply "Slaughter" to the locals), our Ern was just settling down for a snooze in front of the castle gates, when he heard the distinctive clop of a horse's hooves. *That's a bit of a throwback, seeing as how most folks pulled up in Porsches and such.* As the rider and horse approached, Ern's olfactory senses showed him the benefit of switching to four wheels from four legs.

"Halt! 'Oo goes there?" challenged Ernie.

Rats! There goes plan A: a quiet reconnoitre. "And who writes your scripts for you?" the rider jibed acidly.

"It's just what you say, innit?" returned Ern, defensively.

"Look, my good man, the 'good' part being presumptive, I'm in need of lodgings for myself, and my mount needs bedding down." The cloaked disguise tended to bring out the Regency romance in his dialogue.

"Now 'oo's talkin', speakin' of bad scripts and all?" said Ern. With all his free time in front of the gates, he'd been able to stream the latest flicks and the crime dramas on his UPad.

"Whatever. We need a place to sleep and eat, okay?"

Speaking for myself, the "bedding down" part sounds far more enticing, Eduardo interjected. He couldn't remember the last time he'd been a 'mount' to a filly.

Ern shrugged, "There's only the one place: the tavern on the square, 'cept it's more of a trapezoid, actually."

The rider breathed heavily. "Would you mind telling me where this tavern is?"

Ern pointed a mailed arm in the direction of the valley below, scratching absent-mindedly under his chain link vest with his left hand. "Be that way."

"There's no need for surliness. I assure you I *will* be that way, if it suits me."

"Eh? No, the tavern. It be that way."

"Oh. Right." The rider turned and headed down hill to the valley. "If I hear one snort out of you . . . ," he addressed the horse.

Moi?

Ern studied the duo as they rode away. The three dim lights following at a prudent distance went undetected. "Something about that fella," he ruminated. "Too many teeth, for one. But that's the trouble with your National Health. Don't run to decent orthodontia." He shook his head. *Maybe he was some kind of monk, with that deep hood and all? Bloody rude one, if so.* He sat back down on the stone steps and plugged the ear buds back in. *Nothin' like Smashfest Drummies to help you off ta sleep.*

The Bat and Whistle was jammed that Saturday night, but not much more so than it was any night in the week. Besides being the only tavern in Slaughter, it drew in trade from a dozen of the surrounding villages, thanks to its interspecies tolerance policy. It also helped that the kitchen was the size of a small hockey arena, so that Cook was able to cater to all the varied gustatory requirements of the clientele. There was an inn and convention centre attached, a beer garden for the odd occasion when it wasn't pelting down rain, and stables that were actually a while-you-wait car repair shop. Come the weekend, there was even valet service for the car park in the back field.

But you'd never know all this from the outside. The baroness up on the hill preferred everything to appear just as it did in her granddad's day, so tourists were treated to a view of wavy thatch and half-timbered walls, as expected from the guide books. With the advent of the larger ATCs (All Terrain Carriages), the narrow, cobbled street by the inn had to be made one way. To anyone driving or walking down the hill from the castle, the inn's ornate, painted sign showed bare trees against an indigo night sky, a *Fledermaus* silhouetted against a full moon and, inscrutably, a man tootling on his fife below. Happily, as the baroness was never on foot, this presented an irresistible opportunity to display a very different image on the sign's opposite side to those who were. The townsfolk therefore took full advantage by doing a "much-needed" repainting of that side of the sign. The baroness never questioned why only one side needed repainting. She put it down to prevailing winds. Driving past, she therefore never saw that, on the downhill side, the sign displayed the baroness herself, vampire wings outspread, with a dog whistle around her neck and her hubby sitting adoringly to heel.

Leaving the rider and horse to find their own way from the castle gates, the three sprites had swarmed on a mission down the hill to the pub. A light wind was up so the sign creaked satisfyingly. The baroness insisted on a good creak: the firm of Rustoration Inc. came by monthly to squirt a saline solution on the hinges so that the sign was never silent. Expectations must be served.

"Nice touch, that," one of the sprites said, pointing at the screeching sign swinging to and fro.

"Aye. I can't be havin' with all that neon and chrome," agreed another. "Nothin' like a creakin' sign with a grand pitchur on it outside the pub on a blowy night. Can't beat it for atmosphere."

"Fair gives yer shivers, don't it?" sighed the third happily. "Talkin' o' that, let's get out of this flippin' gale and have a warm-up inside, boys. I'm parched."

Inside, the antique theme continued, though the landlord made sure, when the baroness wasn't around, that the patrons had the benefit of all the latest technology as well. Against the rare occasion when the baroness paid a visit, there was a doorman stationed outside who would give a warning whistle, so that all might return in a flash to a previous century or three inside, with Herself none the wiser.

The three sprites sat themselves near the fire at a doll's table that had belonged to the landlord's daughter, pulling up the marmalade pots that served as stools, and commenced to nurse their thimble-sized beers.

Sprite 1, whose mother had named him Elmo, took a long swig and pronounced, "Ah, that's more like it, lads." A nodding of heads concurred.

On the other side of the fire, at a long, professionally-scarred table, sat a large, grey wolf holding forth to his audience: a pipe-smoking crow, a snowy owl with boots on, and a rat in a tartan scarf. Each had a brew in front of him and, though a bit squinty-eyed at this stage, they were nonetheless striving to follow the narrative. From the wolf's accent, it was obvious he was not from around those parts.

"Ooh, 'e's got a lovely twang," admired Elmo. "Reminds me of that bloke what was in *Super Fly.* Loved that filum."

"I heard tell this wolf came from a long way away. Maybe even across the pond," interjected Sprite 2, whose mother had named him "Dim," and never had the heart to tell him it wasn't short for Dimitry.

"Wot, the duck pond down the road?" sneered Sprite 3. *More like the bleedin' ocean.* Among the three of them, he tended to be the leader, probably because he'd been christened "Brain." *His* mum had been a bad speller. "What I heard was that this fella got here as a stowaway on a cargo ship," Brain said.

In actual fact, the wolf calling himself Wolfgang had left Brooklyn as "Bob" on a Carnival Cruise ship, disguising himself in a Burberry overcoat, Russian fur hat with ear flaps, and a muffler wrapped round his face. It was a Christmas cruise.

"Well, one thing's for certain, 'e's not from around here," Dim concluded, with a big swig.

"True, true," the others agreed, settling down to a pleasant eavesdrop.

CHAPTER 3

Big Bad Wolf

Wolfgang leaned forward, his forepaws on the table just getting into his yarn, his new companions sitting back with their draughts.

"So there I was, amblin' through the forest, mindin' my own bidness, headed for Granny's house like I always do on a Wednesday. She makes the finest roast pork every Wednesday and always invites me over on account of she don't have many visitors out her way no more. That uppity little princess of a granddaughter, Red, too busy impressin' business managers and potential entrepreneurs to come by and check on her granny.

"'Sides, I gotta keep up the image, you know—the 'big, bad wolf' and all that. Traipsin' up to Granny's once a week keeps folks believin' I'm still terrorizin' villages, shakin' down ol' ladies and eatin' up chil'ren. Gotta keep 'em in line. Plus they jes' not happy without they conspiracy myths.

"Truth is, I ain't fond of eatin' stringy ol' humans anyways. The stuff them folks eat! Might as well stick you snout in a cesspool. And turns out it's true, human do taste pretty much like pork, 'cept pork's a whole lot sweeter.

"So Granny and me have us this deal: I come over for her mouth-waterin' pork roast once a week and leave the villagers alone. And neither of us ever mention the 'm' word. Why anybody would want to put one of them fuzzy ol' sheep in they mouths, I can't figure. Like takin' a bite outa dust bunnies that smell like wet dog and old tennies.

Takes weeks to get the stink out. So this arrangement suits me jes' fine and saves my taste buds from cruel and unusual punishment.

"Oh yeah, to get back to the story: so there I was, boppin' down the path, *re*markin' on her primroses along the way. Granny and me been doin' this so long, I don't bother no more with the damned cape and basket. Ain't nobody but us out this way anyhow. 'Least not usually.

"I'm jes' about to her door what's got all those curlicue doohickeys on it, up on my hind legs like you do when you about to knock, when I hear this snotty little nasal shriek: 'Oh My God! Who is that atrocious hairy *Neanderthal* about to go into Granny's house? Brie, take a look. Isn't he the most dreadful creature you ever saw?' (Tee hee.) 'He can barely walk upright! Granny must be totally desperate for company these days or blind as a bat! Honestly, the people you get out in the sticks!' (Har, har.)

"This Brie, she reply, with sublime originality, 'For sure!'

"I turn around and damned if it ain't little Miss Red herself, finally condescendin' to give her granny the benefit of her presence, along with some other uppity lil' coed, jes' a sneerin' and snickerin'. And that made me mad. I mean, I wipe my feet on the mat and act respectful. Don't have them opposable thumbs so the cutlery thing presents a bit of a problem, but Granny don't seem to mind. She always wipes my muzzle after with a napkin, a real linen one, and gives me a scratch behind the ears. See, Granny and me is friends.

"So I turn to Red and say in my best uppity manner, 'I'll have you know, my deah, that I am here by invitation from your august grandmother herself and have accordingly brushed my fur and clipped my toenails in anticipation of her kind hospitality.' There, I says to myself, that should put her in her place.

"But no, she jes' laughs that silly little trill those hoity-toity girls do in all the fairy tales, Cheese Girl joinin' in with a snort.

" 'Well,' Red says, 'if that's the best you can do!' and commences to titterin' again.

"Right about now I'm startin' to work up a jones for some girlie flesh, 'cept I can't let her granny down. So I take the high road and only growl at her, 'Hey. I a wolf. Git over it. This as good as it gets.'

"At that she starts to shriekin' as the realization finally trickles in. I mean, three diplomas and she can't figure *that* out? Course, all that high-pitched screechin' brings the woodsman over with his ax.

"*Man!* I think. *We all know how* this *goes*. So I beat it and give up on my pork dinner.

"After I run a ways, I stop and peep out from behind a tree, eyein' Granny's front door. The two Miss Prisses patter on in, Granny holdin' the door for them like they was royalty. Guess she was expectin' them, too. And that gets me to thinkin'. . . .

"So I creep up to the window and take a listen.

" 'Granny,' says Red, outraged, 'did you know there was a smelly old wolf lurking around outside?'

"Granny says, 'Sure I did, child. I invited him.'

" 'Seriously? I mean, a mangy wolf? Do you know how many diseases they carry?' Red demands.

"Granny tells her calmly, 'I invited him for dinner as I do every Wednesday.'

"I grin to myself, feelin' whatchacallit—'vindicated.' That's the word!

"Red's mind is clearly blown. She sputters angrily, '*Really*? Well, what were you planning on having for dinner?'

" 'Wolf,' Granny says and shrugs. 'I was getting tired of pork, and the African grey wolf is no longer on the endangered list.'

"Man, I legged it out of there lickety split. Think after all I'll develop me a taste for *Homo sapiens*."

Wolfgang sat back, grinning toothily at the pounding of tankards and round of caws, hoots and squeaks (roughly, "Hear! Hear!") from his audience. The muted thump of tiny tankards joined them from the three critics on other side of the fire.

"And 'that,' as they say, gentlemen, 'is a wrap.' " The three sprites drained their tankards, slapped down their payment on the table and, donning their macs, headed for the door.

"Nothin' like a good tale with a great punchline," says Elmo. "How would you rate that one?" turning to Brain.

"Dunno, really. Wonder if 'e's got an agent."

Just then, Wolfgang felt a furry paw descend on his shoulder and looked around at one of his wolf buddies, who'd overheard his story.

His buddy grinned at the audience of newcomers, "I hope you blokes didn't believe all that malarkey. He does like to tell some tall tales. Red's actually a great gal, and Granny would never have a friend as supper. Right?" He cocked an eyebrow at Wolfgang.

Wolfgang had never actually met Red, but shrugged, caught out. "Yeah, you right. But it made a good story, right?" he winked at his audience. "I had y'all goin', ya gotta admit."

His audience chuckled and admitted he had.

"Anybody for another round?" Wolfgang asked.

"Thanks, but it's time we got back to our missuses," came the consensus. The group arose and took their leave.

The barman came over to wipe down the table, eyeing dolefully the three acorns and one bean. That was what came of all this tolerance, he considered, when too many of your regulars didn't have pockets. Next it would be wampum, he supposed. He scooped up his remuneration. *Well, knowing them fellas, these will most likely be magic. In that case, the acorns would greatly help with her ladyship's reforestation projects. Must remind her to space 'em a bit further apart this time or it'll be saplings up our arses.* The bean, he pocketed as his tip. The last one had given him quite a nest egg.

CHAPTER 4

A Horseman Cometh

Still Saturday Night. The cloaked rider and his horse approached the double doors of a cobbled innyard and peered in. Light spilled out the lead-paned windows of the Elizabethan public house, illuminating the old bat on the squeaking sign. The rider turned and looked around the outside of the inn, puzzled, searching for the aforementioned "square." All he saw were narrow streets and alley ways, overhung with cantilevered casements. He'd been expecting the usual expanse of grass bordered by the edifices of various shops and possibly a vicarage. Then he took in the layout. The guard's description had been literal: the tavern and the inn were built *on* the square. All that remained of the original square was a tiny bit lawn.

"This must be the place."

Ya think?

"Quaint."

Sehr Gemütlichkeit, Eduardo agreed. Eduardo prided himself on his linguistic talents, a genetic throw-back to his stud. His *papá* had travelled a lot, hanging with some Lipizzaner *muchachos*.

"At any rate," said Rider, "judging by the rustic architecture, I very much doubt there will be any mod cons laid on. Wonder where's that fellow who's supposed to run out and to see to one's horse."

'Ostler' I presume you mean?

"Yeah, that one."

Eduardo had, in fact, noted that the alleged stables did not smell of horses, at least the four-legged ones. He'd gotten a strong whiff of petroleum products. *At this time of night, I'd say he's probably tucked up watching a re-run of* East Enders*, if he isn't under a car with a spanner.* He jerked his head at the sign that read, "Mechanic on Premises."

"Where's the romance, where's the magic?" the rider rhetorted in mock outrage.

Oh, I dunno. Dizzyworld? By the way, you should be scouting around for a razor very soon. Lookin' a bit whiskery.

As the moon threatened again to sail forth from behind its cloud, the rider's mandibles did appear to be elongating more rapidly and sprouting a thickish thatch of fur.

"What *have* I been thinking? I must have completely missed the turning for the nearest Boots," he said, looking pointedly about him. The town was beyond quaint. More like an after-hours Diagon Alley. So an open chemist's was out of the question. He desperately hoped that, shaded by his hood, the locals would just assume he had a serious three-week shadow.

And anyway, the horse continued*, I'd have thought you'd had your fill of magic, looking at the state of you. Although, personally, it has come in handy, being able to make myself understood at last without having to pitch you off. You just need to find that meddling wizard is all. Given the right persuasion . . .* Here, Eduardo demonstrated with his hind hooves his best swift kick.

"Oh, good grief. If he's any kind of decent wizard, he'd see *that* coming. That great rump of yours telegraphs a block away. With all your faults, I would be sad to see you turned into a stoat or such. Hard to saddle—short stirrups, boots dragging on the ground."

Eduardo snorted at that.

"On the other hand, you do possess one lethal weapon that would blow his mind, or anyhow his sinuses. That could be quite persuasive, but I'd appreciate a warning so I can stay upwind."

Glad to oblige, when I can. Eduardo refused to be goaded. *But I can't always just work up an SBD on cue, you know.*

"Can't you? Gosh. Always seems well timed to me, if not particularly convenient."

Says he who will NOT leave the hard boiled eggs and beer alone.

"Any road, I need a shave, a shower and a . . . sit down. Also some nosh and a kip. I'll leave you here and suss out the possibilities, shall I?"

Oh, yes, do.

"Let me know if you see an old duffer in a pointy hat lurking about, will you?"

The rider slid none too gracefully down from the saddle and stalked toward the tavern door, his tall boots ringing on the cobbles. He pulled his hood closer about his visage. The inside of the tavern came as a bit of a surprise. It had all the requisite smoky old beams, tankards and copper pots hanging from the rafters, roaring fire in the inglenook, but above the scarred top of the oaken bar, there blazed a 40" plasma widescreen. Chelsea was losing 10 to 23 to Liverpool. *Well, that's a bit more like it,* thought the rider, and just stopped himself from tossing back his hood for a better view of the game.

He turned and looked around him. Aside from the telly and the omnipresent fruit machine in the corner, you'd never know you weren't back in the 17th century. *Remarkable.* He turned back to the bar as the barman approached . . . in a jerkin and flowing Jacobean shirt, rolled up at the sleeves. Of course. He prayed the beer was not likewise "authentic."

"What'll yer have?" the barman asked.

"Pint of best? Um, bitter?" Taking a gander at his surroundings, Rider thought it best to clarify.

"Tenant's all right?" The barman reached for the tap.

"Most certainly," the rider replied with relief.

"Good. 'S'all we got. The brewery's got a monopoly here. Result of her ladyship's sense of humour, I reckon. Two and six, then, please." The bar man slid a foaming pint across toward him.

The rider reached for his money, fumbling about the stupid cloak. *Bollocks! Why are there never any ruddy pockets in a ruddy cloak?!* A week or two ago, he could have simply reached into his suit jacket and pulled out a wallet like any other man. He grinned deprecatingly at the barman, “So sorry. Seemed to have left my *argent* outside. Won’t be a mo’.” The barman reached out a beefy arm and drew the pint back across the bar, scowling.

Outside, Eduardo was waiting. *You’ll be needing some lucre, won’t you?* He indicated the saddlebags with a toss of his head. Because of the waxing moon, the rider couldn’t trust his breeches to stay either together or on. So he’d had to rely on size XXL boxer shorts under his cloak and substitute saddlebags and a leather purse for pockets.

“Yes, thank you. Good job there are no thieves about.”

Good job you’ve got me, the sentient beast, to watch your back when you’re witless.

The once-and-future human stomped back into the tavern, fishing out the appropriate coins from his drawstringed purse. The pint slid back his way.

The rider glanced over his shoulder then leaned in. “By the way, you haven’t by any chance seen a short, bearded fellow in a pointed hat come in recently, have you?”

“A wizard like?” The barman scratched his chin at the rider’s nod. “Nay, can’t say as I have. Don’t have any in the village, ’less they’re passin’ through.”

“Just a long shot. Thanks.”

“You want chips with that? Kitchen’s closed but I can do that much fer yer.”

“Yes, please, if it’s not too much trouble,” the rider replied sheepishly and slid some more coins across the bar.

“Lovely,” said the barman, glancing at the denominations and grinning.

“Be back quick as Bob’s your uncle.”

“Ta.” *Paid him too much, obviously.* Tugging his hood further over his face, the shaggy outsider brought his pint over to a dark corner table, and took an appreciative swallow. Now that his sight had finally adjusted to the smoky murk, he was able to take in the local patrons more properly. His eyes widened at what he saw. *Good God!* he thought. *Help! I'm trapped in a Gothic film set and can't get out!*

Then he remembered his own appearance and thought perhaps, after all, he'd fit right in.

Just then, he heard a scuffling of boots on the flagstones approaching his table. *Oh, here we go;* he turned toward his inquisitor.

"Arr, me lad," said a tall, red-haired beardy person in a striped shirt, eyepatch and headscarf. "You be the new cabin boy? You be a bit hairy for it."

The rider sighed and pulled his hood forward more, greatly regretting he'd forgotten his kit. "Not really."

The "pirate" reddened. "Oh, sorry mate. Thought you was with Central Casting. No offense meant."

"None taken. But tell me, what exactly is this place? I mean, they've taken the 'ye olde' concept to a bit of an extreme."

"Oh! Yer mean yer don't know?" asked the 'pirate' excitedly, dragging up a stool.

The rider took a long pull from his pint and resigned himself to a garrulous explanation. *Please God, let there be malt vinegar and salt with the chips.*

"Well, yer see," said the pirate, "the baroness up in the castle yonder never was much fond of change and likes things traditional, which luckily brought our little village to the notice of one of them big film studios. So now there's this television crew in town making a documentary about the old way of life and all. Kept goin' on about findin' this 'precious pocket of peasant life' still surviving up here after all this time. They reckon it must look just the same as it did centuries ago in the old baron's day. Only problem is, time marches on, don't it? We like to keep up with things same as anyone, so we have to hide our electronic devices and such like when She comes round. That plasma TV up there? Got a hinged door that swings down over it when we get the alert, with a picture of her ladyship and consort on the other side. Clever, innit? She don't come by all that often, on account a she don't drink spirits much. Tends more to the red stuff.

"Wine?" the rider asked.

"Sure," evaded the pirate. "So anyhow, folks bein' that excited to get onta the telly, everybody's stowed away their Doc Martins and jeans and been rummagin' about in their grannies' drawers (*interesting image there*, thought the rider) for the old pantaloons and petticoats, three-league boots and tri-corner hats. The girls have even come up with some very tasty-lookin' bodices, ones that wasn't already ripped beyond recall."

"No doubt."

"Any day now, we're expecting the talent scouts to sashay in. There's only the one place any road to sashay into, which is why pretty much everybody in the area is holing up here in their best vintage dress. The landlord's dead pleased about it. This filum stuff is great for business. What'd you say your name was again?"

"Actually, I didn't. But you can call me 'Rider.' "

"Oh, you'll fit right in, you will. Central Casting will probably pick you up in a flash. Was that with a 'd' or a 't' "?

Another sigh and a long swallow. "R-I-D-E-R."

"Cos, otherwise, you could audition as 'King A—"

"Heard it," Rider interrupted.

"Just makin' sure. My name is Eric. 'Eric the Red,' " he added, expanding on the pirate approach.

"You get a lot of pirates up in these mountains, do you?"

"More like the odd Visigoth back in the day. I didn't have the helmet, you see." He hung his head, then brightened. "But for action, you can't go wrong with a pirate! And there is a lake up the way—the Boding Sea."

"For boding, I take it?"

"If you're a fish."

Well, I hope it bodes well for you, Eric."

"Thanks!" said Eric as he rose and lurched off to sit with his mates.

The lovely smell of hot, greasy potato and malt vinegar reached his nose as a blousy arm placed a trencher of steaming chips on his table. Plenty of salt, too. At this point, who cared if the old arteries choked up?

Rider reached for a succulent, bendy piece of carbohydrate but before he could quite get it to his mouth, he heard a scritchy treble address him from beneath the depths of a drooping, wide-brimmed hat.

He dropped the chip in irritation. *Now what?*

Rider looked up at ratty facial hair waving un-hygienically over his plate. Above the Rastafarian grey beard was a pointy hat, two sizes too large for the creased face in between. The irises were unsettlingly different colours: the right a bright green, the left a tawny gold. A liver-spotted hand crept out from the person's crusty robes, something squirming slightly in its clasp. In a voice that could do with a squirt of WD40, the hand's owner wheedled, "May I interest you, kind sir, in a radish? Goes down a treat with chips."

"What?" Rider asked, eyes locked in fascination at the struggles and muffled oaths coming from the codger's closed fist. "No! But what in God's name is in there?"

"What about some nice parsnips, then?" The hand dipped back into the vast recesses of the robe, replacing the struggling tuber with a handful of white, carrot-shaped things with glitter on and identical double roots . . . that appeared determined to dance, Rockette style.

Rider stared mesmerized, his chips cooling rapidly, as the parsnips broke into a synchronized can-can. No one but Rider took any notice. Something about this geezer was niggling Rider's mind. Then the loud babble of pub patrons abruptly stopped as Rider's hood fell back. The locals were fine with the occasional wolf, as long as he didn't eat your best mate, but this fella was a wolf of a different colour. The Rolex and riding boots were a giveaway, for one thing.

"Shaving kit?" The old geezer began backing up nervously, noting his sales pitch had fallen flat, then turned and scuttled away. The penny finally dropped in Rider's memory bank.

Rider rose like a shot, nearly dumping his pint. "Wait! I know you!" and made a grab for the back of the salesman's collar, just missing him because he was distracted by a small voice coming from beneath the table: "Wouldn't touch that, if I were you. Don't know where it's been."

Apparently, Rider's fingers had come to the same conclusion before the thought had reached his brain. His instinctive revulsion had worked to the old coot's advantage. It was absolutely amazing how fast a body of advanced years could move. In a flash, the geriatric git was out the door. When Rider burst out of the tavern close behind, the innyard was empty, save for his horse.

"Eduardo! That was that blasted wizard we've been following! Did you see which way he went?"

Sí.

"Well . . . ?"

He went thataway, señor.

"And you didn't stop him?!"

I wasn't about to touch that. You don't know—

". . . where it's been," Rider finished, fuming. "Damn! Three days of tracking and we've lost him. Actually," he turned meaningfully to the horse, "*you've* lost him."

I haven't lost him, amigo. As I said, 'He went thataway.' The horse indicated, with a casual hoof, the opposite doorway leading into ye olde stables. *Right about now I suspect he'll be in the grease pit beneath the Ferrari. I took the precaution, you see, of positioning the mechanic's creeper in the threshold in the anticipation of such an event.*

"You know, I think I liked you better when you couldn't talk."

Rider headed off into the auto shop, ignoring Eduardo's whicker (which, as you must know, is horse for "snicker"). When his eyes adjusted to the dark, Rider noticed three glowing lights at the edge of the grease pit. On closer inspection, these turned out to be, impossibly, three tiny, brown, wizened men in tweed vests and knickerbockers, gazing interestedly into the pit. A glurpy thrashing could be heard from within. The voice he'd previously heard from beneath the pub table now inquired about the wallowing figure, "That the bloke you been after?"

"Yes," Rider replied weakly, lowering himself onto a bale of hay that disguised a chest of metric sockets. This had been one hell of a week: first the bristly growth spurt and now this.

"I suppose you'll be wanting to get him out of there," commented Sprite 2.

"Yeah," said Sprite 3, "but we'd suggest using that pulley and winch affair over there. You don't want to be touchin 'im, 'cos—"

"Yes. I *know*." Rider gritted his incisors. ". . . 'I don't know where he's been.' "

"No, actually. He'll be that slick you can't get a purchase without some kind of tackle. Stands to reason." Sprite 3 fist bumped Sprites 1 and 2.

Rider grunted, then stood and whistled to his horse. "Eduardo, can you give us a . . . hoof, here?"

No hablo ingles.

"Oh, bloody typical." Rider marched across the shop and started to reach for the winch.

"No worries mate," said the sprites, "We gotcher covered."

At this, three lights swarmed up the tackle, lowered the hook, engaged the wizard's hood and hauled him up, plopping his sodden hat on his head.

"There you are!" chorused three voices. "No charge."

"By the way, mate, you could really use a shave," Sprite 2 added.

His hood restored over his head, Rider hauled the abashed wizard back to his dark corner table, leaving a greasy skid mark behind, and plunked the culprit down on the opposite stool, daring him with blazing gaze to even think of taking a runner. His stomach rumbled, itself running on empty. Glancing down at the congealing platter of spuds, he muttered, "Fantastic. My flippin' chips have gone stone cold." He slapped away the dirty hand that crept from the wizard's robes, trying to sneak one. "I didn't say I wasn't going to eat them, did I?" he snarled. The wizard made himself as small as possible, trying to remember that spell for disappearing and devoutly wishing he hadn't dropped his wand in the pit. The contents of his pockets seconded the notion.

"Look, I know you're unhappy," began the wizard.

"Unhappy? Just 'unhappy'? Like, 'Oh, bother, I missed the 10:38 to Cheltenham'? Not self-bloody-righteously pissed, enraged, ready to rip your throat out?" Rider inquired in a deceptively quiet tone.

"Yes. All right. Can't blame you. But I can explain. I think."

The wizard looked up, cringing, as a set of furry paws stuffed cold chips down a furiously masticating maw. The jaws continued to chomp. The beady, lupine stare stayed locked on the wizard. Silence, except for loud swallows.

"You see," wheedled the wizard, "it was an accident. Truly. I never meant to turn a fine gentleman such as yourself into a werewolf. I was only trying to help."

A pair of hirsute eyebrows shot up, boggling, then lowered accusingly.

"What with the dearth of dentistry in your country," the wizard continued, "malocclusion is practically epidemic and orthodontia's so dear a man has to take out a third mortgage."

"If you're objecting to my overbite," Rider growled, "I have *you* to thank for that."

The wizard hoped he didn't appear as sheepish as he felt, considering his audience. "It's this genetic engineering that's all the rage that got me thinking on the matter. I mean, if those scientists can make corn and peas so they won't get blight, well then, why couldn't you also alter someone's genes to fix their buck teeth?"

A sharp retort and a scuffle issued from within one of the wizard's pockets. Rider eyed the interruption pointedly. "Pray, continue."

"Yes, well." The wizard cleared his throat, which had become a bit froggy. Happily, the frog bounded away unharmed. "I guess it all went wrong."

"I'm guessing you started with, what, your basic leafy greens or courgettes, perhaps?" Rider suggested, fascinated by the continuing mayhem within the robe.

"Legumes and root veg, mostly, with the occasional brassica. Courgettes can get a bit slippery. And at first everything seemed to go quite well, until I tried to pop some Brussels sprouts in a pot, and they came up swinging at me. Must have gotten one of the words wrong in the spell I was using. My dentures *have* been giving me hell, lately. Either that, or they took 'bubble, bubble, toil and trouble' in the imperative sense. All those GMOs became sentient, you see. They're hard workers, I'll say that, but a pain in the arse. Cursed gassy, too."

"I must say I'm intrigued, but what has that to do with my finding myself suddenly busting out of my clothes and howling in the moonlight?"

"I was getting to that. See, I was already onto experiments on mammals before I realized the veggies had gone wrong. I don't cook much since Mother died."

"And let me guess," sneered Rider, "you skipped the lower orders like, oh, voles or even monkeys, am I right?"

"If I was going to beat the other wizards to a patent, I had to get a move on. No sense messing with success, says I, or wasting my time with rodents and their fleas. You should see the rates your average biological supplier charges for a measly sack of gerbils. Online robbery! 'Sides, I needed to work out the doses right, and you just try extrapolating the milligrams for a mouse to what you'd give a ruddy great horse."

"Ah, that must explain Eduardo."

"That your horse?" the wizard asked.

"Yes, my telepathic, four-legged friend in the courtyard. He thinks he's a stand-up comedian. I think he's damned annoying."

"I am sorry about your horse but I won't take the blame for *him*, at least. Caught him nose down in my auntie's rubbish bin in the mews behind her flat right after I'd pitched out the sprouts."

"That also explains the exceptional flatulence, I suppose."

"It would, that," the wizard agreed. "But now, with you I can't honestly say how it happened. I was aiming at another fella entirely, one who seriously needed a mandibular alignment. Then some cretin bumped my wand arm. I thought I'd just missed, so 'no harm, no foul.' But I suppose you could say that backfired."

"Indeed. I could say that."

"But any road, I was just putting a spell on his jaws. Shouldn't have caused any kind of lupine anthropomorphising or accelerated hair growth. Come to think on it, though, it did seem like I noticed a nick in my wand when I turned back round. If I could just find the blasted thing, I could probably sort this out for you."

"You. Lost. Your. Wand?" Rider asked acidly. "A flippin' wizard and you lost your flippin' wand? Tell me, . . . What was your name?"

"Herald."

"Herald. Right. Tell me, Herald, did you graduate top of your class?"

"No need to get snarky," objected the wizard.

"Really? And why is that? Why shouldn't I be THOROUGHLY AND COMPLETELY RAVING SNARKY RIGHT ABOUT NOW?"

A hush once again came over the pub. The match was over anyway.

"Everything all right?" asked the barman. "I can heat those up fer yer, if yer want."

"No, thank you. Everything's fine." Another pawfull of chips was crammed between Rider's chops, washed down by a prolonged swig of bitter. The barman retreated and the dolt at the fruit machine resumed his jabbing.

"Okay, okay. Don't get yer knickers inna twist. I didn't actually lose it, *per se*."

"No? Wonderful. Then where is it?"

Pause. A mumble.

"What was that?" Rider asked.

"It's in the pit. The grease pit under the Ferrari. Fell outa my cloak when I slipped in."

"Well then, let's have a look-see, shall we?"

The wizard hung his head. "It won't be there now."

"Really? Hmmmm . . . Dash it, I must have missed the stampede of treasure hunters across the way. Try the other one. I really doubt any of this lot carry a spare set of rubber gloves and have a yen to go diving in post-Jurassic goo."

"It'll be those three sprites. They'll have taken it and probably be in the next county by now. That's why they were being so helpful. They're little buggers, they are, especially if they get bored with the way something's playing out."

"And you're just mentioning this now?"

"Well, I might have brought it to your attention earlier 'cept that my mouth was full of sludge and transmission fluid. Not what I'd call a decent mechanic, judging by all the bolts I was spitting out."

Rider slumped in defeat. "It's probably just as well. You'd most likely make matters worse, although how worse they could be I can't imagine."

"So I'll just be going along then, now, shall I?" asked the wizard, beginning to slide away.

"I don't think so."

"Rats. I was afraid of that." The wizard crumpled and sat back down.

"One good 'turn' deserves another, don't you think? I've been turned into a flippin' werewolf without so much as a playful nip. So, just in case you're wrong about the whereabouts of said wand, I believe I'll turn *you* into a grease monkey. Come along. I'll show you the ropes."

"Oh, not again!"

"Practice makes perfect," said Rider cheerfully as he hauled the dejected mage across the courtyard.

CHAPTER 5

Home Boy

Back home in Brooklyn, Wolfgang (formerly known as Bob), had been used to getting most of his meals from a dumpster, lurking around after hours behind restaurants and diners. In desperation, he'd had to resort to chowing down on the occasional OD'd junkie lying beside the dumpster. But he didn't care for the taste, and it always left him feeling strung out. If he was lucky, he'd help himself to one of the bags of leftovers cooks put outside for the homeless. It was when he was licking up the last of a Big Mac about to spoil that he had an epiphany. There must be more to cuisine than this. He hadn't yet encountered Granny's pork roast, but he could dream. Living on the streets was hard for a guy like him. Aside from the ass-kicking rats, there was too little live prey that couldn't dial for the dog catcher for a single predator to take down on his own. And he didn't trust working with the local gang of bow-wows.

He'd gotten the idea for relocation from a travel show on a TV he'd taken to watching through a bar's side window. Doing a feature on cruise ship companies, the narrator mentioned that, though people often weren't aware of it, most companies also carried cargo to offset any loss from cancellations and underbookings.* The camera shot panned to the ship's hold, displaying crates and crates of exports, including a few containing exotic livestock.

Bob was amazed how easy it had been to get on board. His buddy,

---

* And now you know your doggy understands your commands perfectly well, but opts for selective listening.

Frank, like the weasel he was ran interference by scampering up the purser's pants as the purser was checking the passenger manifest. In his overcoat and fur hat, Bob simply sauntered past the distraction, waving a counterfeit passport in a gloved paw. After that, it was just a matter of locating the hold and hoping for an empty cage. All the TV viewing had given him some passable reading skills and his expert skulking finally paid off. All of the doors were conveniently labelled. The international symbols were a little puzzling, but he did okay with the English. The icing on the cake came when he discovered there was a luscious Siberian she-wolf down there in an animal carrier much too large for her. The poor girl was being returned to Russia, in hopes she'd increase the gene pool. In the meantime, she made it plain she wouldn't mind this handsome African getting in her genes. It was a bit lonely down there, and there was plenty of grub to share. This was Bob's lucky day.

"Vun problem," she asked in a throaty accent, "how ve get you in?"

"Babe, you don't need to worry about that. I a city boy." Bob knew his way around a simple carrier latch. In the spirit of *glasnost*, the two cuddled up, looking forward to a *perestroika* of their own.

Come dinner time, the approach of the handlers could easily be heard before the heavy steel door opened. By then Bob would be well hidden behind a giant pod of PVC pipe headed for Slovenia. The men did wonder, considering the lone inhabitant, why the bitch was increasingly ravenous. Chef might have to cut back on the Chicken Kiev, the way this was going.

Those were good times. It had been hard to say goodbye to his little Nikita, but Freedom called to him. And said, "Get the hell out before those guys with the whips and cranes come!"

The crew never noticed the bushy tail wagging underneath the Burberry trotting past, their attention being diverted by the heartbroken howls of his beloved.

He'd been only a pup the last time he'd seen any wide-open space with any real plants. That had been right before his mom was hit by a Good Humor truck. They'd escaped from their pen at the Brooklyn zoo but his mom didn't make it. He still missed her.

She'd told him their people had come from a vast expanse of grasslands called a savannah. Somewhere in Georgia he thought. Her stories had filled his head with visions of glorious scrimmages with squeaky toys that ran like hell before becoming hors d'oeuvres. Those memories turned out to be quite helpful. Because in his new country, with all those tall, pointy buildings and dark, pointy trees, it didn't seem like there'd be dumpsters around.

Once disembarked, his predatory skills, though a tad rusty, had brought him, after a few days and many miles, to a clearing in a forest enfolding an odd, detached dwelling that a building inspector would have condemned. Footsore and famished, he sidled up to the back door. Maybe there'd be at least a rewarding rubbish bin. Beggars couldn't be choosers. No luck. He wasn't to know that the zoning codes the baroness had imposed prohibited the use of outdoor rubbish receptacles. Compost bins were permissible, however, so a browser could get his daily ration of veg, *sans* protein. A bit rough on a carnivore, which was the idea. Figuring take-out was out of the question, Bob slunk over to the compost. Just as he was skulking past, a chintz curtain twitched aside.

"You poor thing," he heard from an elderly human, slowly opening her door. "You look absolutely starved!"

That was when he'd met Granny.

She smelled friendly, so this was lookin' hopeful. And he'd seen those brainless squirrels in parks coaxing folks to share their popcorn with that nauseatingly cute pose. So, hey, if it worked for them . . . He sat down, gave her his best puppy eyes, and raised one paw. A sad whimper sealed the deal.

"You wait there. I'll be right back," Granny told him.

He smelled something delicious and hoped it came his way. And it did! She set down on the back step a dinner plate loaded with some serious protein covered in heavenly gravy, and tactfully closed the door.

Mmmmmm, mmmm! Boy howdy, this was gettin' good! No wonder them squirrels is so eager to debase theyselves with that silly little act.

Bob decided it was such a good gig, he might as well settle down.

It was Granny who named him Wolfgang, 'Wolfie' for short, which was fine by him. He was nothin' if not adaptable. 'Reinvention, thy name is Wolfie.' Being a city boy, he'd only seen meat pre-packaged so he never made the connection between the fat, ugly critters with the twisty tails, snortin' over their slop out back, and those tender chops on the Staffordshire plate.

Sometimes he wondered if maybe Granny wasn't one of them witches. He'd heard some stories about her. Sure seemed like she could read his mind. And by and by, he felt pretty positive he could read hers, too. Soon, he found out he could actually talk and so could the other creatures. There was something in the water, folks said.

Granny'd made it clear to him, that so long as he didn't eat any of the forest creatures, be they four-legged or two-, she'd keep on feedin' him. She had no truck with violence, unless it came from her and it was good and necessary. Plus, she enjoyed the company. And he was grateful. He paid her back by fetching those weird weeds she collected and that funky stuff that grew under trees in a ring. She put those in a big black pot she always kept on the fire, mumbling over it when she stirred. Whooee! *That* did *not* smell delicious. He just hoped whoever had to eat it deserved it.

Yep. Life was good with Granny. Which is why he felt kinda bad makin' up that story about her havin' him on the menu. But she'd understand it was just to see if he could fool those new boys in town and get a laugh.

Thinking about newcomers, he felt the hair on his spine stand up and he turned in his chair back to that fella with the hoodie who had recently come in. At first glance, when the hood came off it was obvious it was some sorta relative. But now he took another sniff and even with all the other competing scents, of which there were plenty, he smelled that there was something wrong about this guy. Then he took in the expensive watch and the fancy footwear.

Now, that ain't right, he thought to himself. *What self-respectin' wolf would wear all that yuppie crap? 'Less he was pimpin'.*

Then he noticed that in the last hour the newcomer had grown increasingly wolfish and seemed to be havin' trouble stayin' inside his own clothes. Could definitely do with a manicure, too. *I think he one of them werewolves Granny's tole me about. She said they's two-legged humans most of the time, then when the moon's full, turn into one of us, minus the manners. Seems like she said there was some new ones in town, annoyin' the baroness no end on account of she liked to keep strict control of the wildlife. Not to mention, they put a damper on tourism. I better keep an eye on him. I always did want to see how that changin' thing worked out, goin'* and *comin'.*

When Rider marched back to the stables, the wizard dangling aloft, Wolfgang slid out the tavern door a trot behind to observe.

CHAPTER 6

Bros

B*ack at the Tavern.* An hour later, Rider and his recalcitrant perpetrator returned to the tavern after several unsuccessful laps in the pit. The landlord was eyeing the new oil slick, planning on upping the bill. At one point, during the dive, Rider had allowed himself to get excited when the wizard dredged up something encouragingly thin and pointed. This turned out to be, disappointingly, a wiper arm.

Back inside, Rider said to the landlord, "I'm very much hoping you have a room vacant."

"We do, in actual fact," said the landlord. "The film crew isn't expected back tonight, so I could do yer a comfy double room, with a bath en suite. There's even a shower attachment to hose yer . . . friend off."

Rider looked down at the oozing wizard. "He's not sleeping with me!"

"Only," the landlord pointed out, "'e's leaving a bit of a stain on the floor. So where shall I put 'im?"

"Have you a janitor's closet? With a large bucket, perhaps?"

"I've just the thing. Will save followin' 'im about with a mop and cleansers."

"And what would be your rate?" inquired Rider, feeling about in his purse, hoping he had enough cash. He sorely missed his charge cards, but they were too traceable.

"Oh, don't you worry about that, sir," said the landlord, figuring on doubling the rate.

That's exactly the time to worry—when a landlord says that!

After rolling the ambulatory oil slick up in the full edition of the daily news, Rider followed the landlord down a hall to the broom closet. The luckless wizard was deposited unceremoniously in an industrial-sized yellow floor bucket and spritzed down with solvents. Rider quickly closed the closet door before the landlord could see the pattern of stars emerging from the wizard's robes. No sense worrying him. (An unnecessary precaution, as it happens.)

In the dark, the wizard sulked and did his best not to breathe in the offending chemicals. Having wiped the worst of them off, he reached, with a sly grin, inside his deepest pocket. Good job he'd put a spell on that wand to make it unrecognizable. Time to see if all that goop had made it totally inoperable. He waved the windscreen wiper and disappeared.

Upstairs in his room, Rider removed his oil-spattered boots and cloak, and attempted to pull off his trousers. They weren't budging. *Oh.* Thinking further on the matter, Rider didn't remember putting on fur leggings that morning. Or a hair shirt. *This is getting to be really annoying.*

He peeped briefly out his window at the night sky, which was becoming alarmingly brighter, then snatched the curtains closed. Something quite disturbing was happening to his limbs, and then his jaws, in the manner of a monster growth spurt thrown into fast forward. The worst part was the hideous noise of internal stress on the engineering he heard inside his head. He sprinted to the bathroom mirror and saw with dread that his "whiskers" had grown considerably lusher and his lower lip was overhung by cosmetically-whitened dog teeth. *Whoa!* He was going to need orthodontia if this kept up. Perhaps if he kept the curtains closed, it wouldn't get much worse. He definitely could use a shave. Sometimes these posh B&B's offered guest soaps and razors. Worth checking at any rate. Nope. Hopeless.

Before he could quite panic, he heard a tap at the bedroom window. *What next?!*

Creeping up to the glass, he cautiously pulled a curtain aside then shrieked in a most unmanly way. On the other side of the glass a wolf face looked in on him. Assuming that his worst fears were confirmed and it was his own reflection, he fainted. He hadn't seen the ladder.

Rider came to, gazing again into a concerned grey wolf face with curious breath. It smelled remarkably like hard cider.

"Now don't be passin' out on me again, buddy," said this wolf. "I here to save you ass. Us wolves gotta stick together."

At this, some noxious herb was waved under Rider's snout and he shot up into a sitting position.

"I'm not normally like this," apologized Rider.

"Yeah, sure. That what they all say," chuckled his champion.

"And what the hell was that stuff?" Rider asked, his eyes still watering.

"What, this? Oh, this jes' some ol' mixture o' Granny's. Think it got some horseradish in it. She put it on her prime rib. Clears up you sinuses, don't it?"

"That it does. Do you mind my asking, do all the animals around here speak?"

"Yeah, most of 'em. It pretty cool. They say it somethin' in the water up in the mountains."

"And are you a real wolf or a . . ." His voice dwindled thinking of the alternative.

"You mean instead of somebody like you? Yep. I am. I mean a real one. And don't worry, I jes' ate."

"So you know what I am, then. I was so hoping that this phase would pass and I could exit before anyone noticed."

"See that's how these extrasensory smellers we got come in handy. Guy like you who don't smell like used wool or chicken poop kinda stands out, 'specially if he be wearin' clothes and a fancy watch. But you jes' wait and see how handy that nose's gonna be. So that's why I brought you something." Wolfgang went back to the window, hauled up a heavy sack by his teeth and dumped it on the floor. From the bag he dragged a set of chains and manacles. "Thought you might be needin' a good night's sleep, along with the rest of us." Wolfgang's eyebrows waggled suggestively. "Didn't think a place this swanky would have a set in the room."

"Good planning. I am greatly in your debt. But, when you're not . . . um . . . vocalizing, how is it I can still understand you?" Rider asked.

"'Cause we brothers."

Rider grimaced. *How long is this nightmare going to last? I just want to go back to the office.* "What's your name, then?"

"Wolfgang," the wolf said proudly.

Rider laughed. "What else could it possibly be?"

"Well, I used to be known as Bob, but that was back in the 'hood."

"I used to be known as a barrister, back in my 'hood."

"You don't say." Wolfgang's eyebrow arched. "You gotta name?"

"I had quite a good reputation, actually."

"No, I mean, you actual name, you handle. What folks call you back there?"

"You may just call me Rider."

"Rider, huh? I saw some initials on you saddlebag: 'ER'. The 'E' stand for 'Easy'?"

The conversation was becoming increasingly surreal. Rider felt a fit of giggles coming on.

"It was, *is,* Esmond. Esmond Rippon. The Third, in fact."

"Well that figures. I may be jes' a chump from Brooklyn, but I been here long enough to know 'barrister' is jes' you fancy word for attorney. You family name sure fits, since you lawyers so good at rippin' folks off. Maybe I change my mind about heppin' you."

"Wait!" Rider pulled himself together. "My family—we're actually the good guys. We're not ambulance chasers."

"Hunh. At least you got some sense. Could get youself flattened, chasin' them things. But what you mean, you the good guys? Didn't think there was anything good amongst your kind."

"We do tend to have what you'd call 'a bum rap,' " Rider conceded. "But I'm an environmental attorney."

"You some kinda snobs, only show up in the right 'environment'?" Wolfgang crooked a pinky.

"No, that would be the gentry. My firm and I plead cases on behalf of the *natural* environment, you know—forests, wildlife, clean water. Thanks to all the obnoxious, dishonest and greedy global corporations, not to mention the local developers, we have a constant caseload. I make it my business to take down as many of the bastards as I can."

"Now you talkin'! So what happened to you then?"

Rider shook his head. "I was on my way to deliver a rider we'd drafted to some new legislation prohibiting the local utility company from clearcutting virgin forest wherever it chooses."

"Why couldn't the rider jes' deliver hisself?"

"It's just a term for a bit that's being added on to an existing legal document."

"That where you came up with the name, I bet."

"It was a spur-of-the-moment thing," Rider admitted.

Wolfgang howled. "See now, I 'preciate a good pun."

"It was unintentional, I assure you," Rider laughed. "So, as I was saying, I was on my way to court when this fellow you probably saw me . . . er . . . interviewing downstairs bumped into me and I found myself flat on the pavement."

"You must be talkin' about the guy in the greasy robes and pointy hat."

"The very one."

"You know he a wizard, right?"

"I do now. When I came to, the air around me was shimmering and my briefcase was trying to walk off with my court papers. On six feet. Wearing Reeboks. I looked up in time to see the perp legging it up the road."

"Uh oh."

"That's what he was saying."

"So then what?"

"When I caught up to my briefcase, I wrangled it under my coat and sprinted to court."

"Lemme ax you. This your first full moon?"

"No. Second. The change came on gradually, maybe because I was in extreme denial."

"Yeah. I can imagine it take people that way."

"I had to give the case to a colleague and make up excuses. I couldn't appear like that, after all, could I?"

"No," agreed Wolfgang. "Coulda turned the jury."

"Well, I didn't think it would come to that, as we were seeking settlement without trial. So, after a lot of research and somewhat inept sleuthing, to my joy I accidentally stumbled across the trail of the wizard in Islington. He was trying to offload some animated produce, I'd heard."

Wolfgang chuckled. "Yeah, I saw some of them things. If he'd been smart, he coulda got on some talent show with them high-kickin' carrots in they rhinestones."

"Parsnips, actually."

"Same difference, only white."

"I assume he had too many aggrieved 'consumers' on his tail. He left town somewhat hastily."

"Wonder why he didn't jes' disappear hisself or something?" Wolfgang pondered.

"He doesn't appear to be the brightest bulb on the magical marquee."

"True 'nough. So then, you hopped on you horse and tracked him here through the forest, right?"

"Right. My estate wagon wouldn't fit between the trees, and the bugger wouldn't keep to the road. I hope, if this ever sorts itself out, there's a still a job for me at my firm. I had to take a medical leave of absence: 'chronic sinusitis, complicated by an abnormal increase of hormone growth factors and myogenic differentiation.' "

"Say what?"

"My face kept morphing into a muzzle."

"I see that. So what you plan?" asked Wolfgang.

"No idea. You?"

"I'm thinkin' on it. That wizard, you got him locked up in the broom closet right? So, if you gave 'im the right kinda persuasion, couldn't he jes' turn you back to normal, you know, reverse that spell or somethin'?"

"That was my hope," Rider said sadly. "It's why we tracked him up here, to get him to undo it."

"When you say 'we,' you includin' you horse down below you was talkin' to?"

Rider nodded. "We've got an . . . understanding, you might say. Turns out he's quite the articulate wit and not afraid to share his opinions."

"The wizard again, I'm bettin'."

"Yep."

"'Cause see, up here only wild creatures can talk, not farm or service animals. 'Least as far as I know."

"My impression," Rider said, "was that he was merely telepathic."

"To you, maybe, but all us critters can hear each other with our minds, even if it not out loud."

"I did always wonder. Our family dog always seemed so much brighter than my brother."

Wolfgang chuckled. "Hell, that ain't no stretch, no offense to your bro. So, dude, you gotta do some serious negotiatin' with this magic man. I mean, you gotta get tough and lean on him to do the right thing, know what I'm sayin'?"

"Problem is," replied Rider wryly, "he's a slippery character, especially at the moment."

Wolfgang snorted out a chuckle. "But seriously, you gotta be layin' down the law to this wizard, man."

"One: I don't believe he's under the jurisdiction of even the laws of nature, and two: the idiot has lost his wand."

"Okay. You're screwed."

"Yep."

CHAPTER 7

Strange Booty

S*unday Morning.* The following morning, as dawn stained the sky an anaemic red, two old women with shawls pulled over their heads trekked along the trail in the forest, bent over by their burdens. The first one stopped suddenly and exclaimed, "Ooh! Look 'ere, Doris, wot I just found!"

"What's that then, Hazel?"

"It's a lovely man's suit. Could be Savile Row. And there's a shirt and tie and all!"

"Pity about them rips in the armholes," Doris commented.

"Oh, I can stitch 'em up easy. My Darrell will look quite handsome in that when I'm finished, sayin' there's a weddin' or a funeral to go to. This will just do the trick." Hazel stuffed the clothes away in the bundle on her back.

"Wonder 'oo dropped it, though. And why . . ." Doris glanced around her warily.

"Come to think on it," Hazel mused, "that's the fourth lot we've seen in a couple of fortnights just lyin' by the wayside. But them others weren't so smart as this."

"Yer suppose there's some sort of nudist colony up here?"

"What? Inna forest? You'd get yer tackle caught on a twig. Or worse."

"I reckon you're right, Hazel. Still, it is odd. Let's get outa these woods before anybody gets a notion to flash us," said Doris.

"Right you are, luv. I'll put a kettle on when we get home."

And the two tramped down the path to the village with their booty.

Down in the valley, in the dim light of dawn, a bedraggled, oily figure trudged down the road away from the village, muttering to itself. Every once in a while it would wave a windscreen wiper and exclaim something nonsensical. "*Aloha Oi!* No, sod it, that's not right. *Alottamora!*" The windscreen wiper remained the same. "Well, at least it got me out of the broom closet. The range isn't what it used to be, though. Ever since I ate the dratted GMOs, just can't seem to remember the words anymore, and now I've got me a dodgy wand. Maybe it's time to hang the hat up," the wizard sighed woefully.

Mist was covering the farmlands that stretched away on both sides of the road beyond the hedgerows and twisted hawthorns. From underneath the hedge, three sets of snores could nearly be heard, a mini-symphony of wheezes and tootles. As the wizard drew closer, the snores stopped abruptly and three lights glowed with interest at the pedestrian going past in the semidarkness.

Brain elbowed Dim and Elmo awake. "Hey, you two, look 'oo's leavin' the scene of the crime."

"That be that wizard, I reckon," said Elmo. "I think 'e's takin' a scarper. Let's follow 'im and see what 'e's up to."

The three sprites clapped their caps on and floated off down the hill after him.

The wizard sneezed and heard three small voices say, "*Gesundheit!*" Automatically, he thanked whoever had blessed him, then turned slowly and surveyed the empty road which, oddly, was being spotlit.

"It must be those three little buggers, up to some mischief." As he turned back around, he saw that his windscreen wiper now glowed. And it appeared as a proper wand. Delighted, he exclaimed, "That was the undo word—I remember now! '*Gesundheit*'!" And the wand went dark again. He heard snickering from nearby. "All right, you lot! What did ya do?"

"Us? We didn't do anything, but it were right entertaining." Sounds of guffawing.

Dim offered, helpfully, “It must be one of them toggle words, you know, works both ways.” Dim did know his spellware.

The wizard eyed them suspiciously, but tried it out. “*Gesundheit*!” he exclaimed, brandishing the windscreen wiper, and it was restored once again. “Okay. I suppose I have you to thank for that.”

Elmo replied, “That *would* be proper *and* for hauling you out of the grease pit, too, don’t forget.”

“You just did that because you were hoping to pinch my wand.”

“Call that gratitude?” Brain demanded. “Should have left ’im to drown in the goop. Who’d want that wonky ol’ wand anyway? Look at the state of it. Pathetic.”

“True,” Elmo said. “And just look at the mess he made of that spell he put on that poor bloke. And he didn’t even magic the right fella!”

“I think you might want to get that thing repaired before you do more harm,” Dim admonished.

“Yeah, we can’t always be haulin’ you out of the muck. We’ve got places to go, people to see,” said Brain grandly.

“And just where might I find a wand repair shop in these parts, pray?” sneered the wizard, who’d never bothered to explore the local villages.

“Yer mean you don’t know the Wands R Us?” Elmo asked. “I’m shocked, I am, and you a wizard.”

“It’s just down the road,” said Dim. “Go past the stile on your left, the stone one, not the wooden one, take no notice of the bull in the pasture else he might romance you, then take the fork to the left just past the fifth twisty tree—be sure to dodge that bear trap the farmer leaves out—go about a mile more and you’ll see another fork where that old barn used to be, take the right one this time. Don’t take no notice of the enchanted cottage, if it happens to be there, . . .”

They could see the wizard was getting muddled. “Oh, all right. Boys, it looks like we have to do everything for this bloke. We’ll show you the way, Wiz. Mind how you go,” Elmo said, just as the wizard stepped in a steaming pile of digested vegetation.

The group set off, the wizard making a new glurping sound and trying to fling off something smelly every fourth step, like a spastic conga dancer. After several miles, they came at last to Otternought, the next village, which looked pretty much the same as the last, except it wasn't one-way streets, and there was a properly shady alley that ran diagonally to the main street. The alley's shops had opened for business and there could be seen browsing a few more folks in pointy hats, most of them considerably cleaner.

The group stopped in front of a storefront that was painted a livid purple with a neon sign blinking "Wands R US" in hot pink. The wizard stared, aghast, at the shiny, modern store and shook his head. As the rest of the stores around it looked quaint and cosy, the wand store stuck out like a glowing wart.

The sprites chuckled at the wizard's consternation. "There yer are! All the modern conveniences, *and* they're open seven days a week. They'll fix you right up. If they don't have it in stock, you can order online. They even have their own web site, yer see. Gotta keep up with the times."

The wizard turned wearily to thank them but they were gone. With great misgiving, he entered the store. A gleaming stainless steel coffee bar with pastries was set up next to the left-hand window. The wands were displayed on white steel racks that ran the length of the store under bright fluorescent lights. A teenage girl with blonde pigtails and a fuchsia fringe bounced up to him perkily, her pink, checkered mini-skirt matching her go-go boots.

"Hi! What can I help you with today? We've got oodles and oodles of stuff. I just know there's something here that will make your day!"

He stared at her grumpily and held up his wand. The tip was slightly bent and creaked a bit.

"Oh, you poor thing. Has your wand got a boo-boo?"

The wizard rolled his eyes and turned to leave.

"Wait! I'll just go get the owner, shall I?" she said, then disappeared through a beaded curtain that led into the nether regions of the store. The wizard plopped himself down on a purple vinyl sling-back. Presently, he heard the slap of worn carpet slippers and a polite cough, and looked up. With relief he saw approaching him a spry, elderly body with wispy grey whiskers, a skull cap and dark green, velvet smoking jacket.

"Rumpbuckle, at your service." The distinguished gentleman bowed to the shabby wizard. "I am the proprietor. How may I help?"

Herald again held up his wand. "Havin' a bit of trouble with it lately. It's had a few knocks. Can you fix it?"

The proprietor took the wand gingerly in his hands and peered up and down its length, rolling it between his fingers. Then he put the wand up to his left ear and listened carefully, nodding once. "Yes, I'm quite sure I can repair it, but you've come just in time. That newt's eye and frog's toe were soon to part company. Come this way."

The wizard followed the proprietor through the beaded curtains. He found himself in a wonderfully masculine, old-fashioned study: bookshelves with dusty books climbing each wall (some using miniature grappling hooks), a crackling fire in the grate with two wing-backed chairs pulled up to it, boxes of wand stock in piles here and there, and an enormous work-bench strewn with tools. In the corner was a deal counter with a two-burner hot plate and a kettle. Above it, a shelf held Spode mugs, a battered tea tin, a sugar bowl and a small blue jug of milk.

Now that's more like it! Feeling at home, the wizard smiled. His host gestured for him to take one of the chairs by the fire. "Fancy a spot of tea, good sir? I've just put the kettle on."

"Wouldn't say no to that!" beamed Herald.

Rumpbuckle poured the tea into two mugs and brought them over to the small table between them with the sugar and milk. He sat in the chair opposite Herald and the two sipped companionably, toasting their toes by the fire. "Don't get many visitors these days, so it's a pleasant change to share some tea with one such as yourself."

"Business slow then?" asked the wizard.

"Not really, just not the sort of business I'd prefer. All that . . . bright and colourful display out there," here, the man shuddered, "is my granddaughter's idea. She's helping out and insisted that I smarten the place up, attract the young crowd and all."

"Ah. I did wonder," commiserated Herald.

"Yes, it's quite dreadful, at least it is to me. But the young crowd seem to like it. Most of them come in, however, solely for souvenirs. Tourists, usually."

"What, you mean all those wands out there are just toys?" the wizard asked, appalled.

"No, no," the man reassured him. "They're the real thing, but the customers don't know that, and I don't give them the instructions, either. Unless, of course, I sense that they've got proper wizards' heads on their shoulders. But that almost never happens."

"Couldn't that be asking for trouble, in case one of them gets it to working, say by accident?"

The proprietor shook his head, "The wands all come with an anti-ignoramus spell installed. Saves a lot of bother."

"Jolly good idea, that!"

"And when my granddaughter finally goes off to college, I can restore the front part of the store to its previous dignity. At least until after I'm gone."

"Anti-tackiness spell?" ventured Herald.

Rumpbuckle winced. "Perhaps a better term is 'anti-upscale.' "

"So, how long do you think it will take to repair my wand?"

"I believe I can have it ready for you within a few days, a week at most. Getting the condor feather and wombat adrenal glands is easy enough. It's the industrial strength Wand Glue® that's the tricky one, as I've just run out."

The wizard appeared uneasy. "You see, I'm in a bit of hurry."

The proprietor chuckled. "Let me guess. From the state of your wand, I'm thinking that perhaps some of your spells didn't go exactly as planned, eh?"

"You could say that. I've got this fella I accidentally altered on my trail, and he's not pleased at all." The wizard didn't feel called upon to expand on the theme.

"Well, in that case, I can offer you a temporary replacement." The proprietor handed him a bright red wand imprinted with the 'Wands R Us' logo. "I've installed a mind-reading spell in it, so if you temporarily forget the command words or misspeak, it will know your intentions."

"You can do that?" Herald asked incredulously.

"Of course I can. I *am* Dr. Rumpbuckle, after all.* Our family goes back centuries in wand making. We weren't always known as 'Wands R Us,' " he added dryly.

"You think you could mebbe add that mind-reading spell to my wand?"

The proprietor smiled. "Of course, for a small extra fee. And what was the name, sir?"

"Um. It's Harold. With an 'a'. And an 'o'."

"Ah," said Rumpbuckle. "Well, Harold, I must caution you, I cannot take magicked constructions as payment." He had observed the ongoing hub-bub within the wizard's pockets. "It will need to be gold coin, *real* gold."

Herald (with an 'e' and no 'o') had the grace to look sheepish but, when they had settled on the rate, promised he would deliver as demanded. It would be more than worth the fee to get his old wand back and not have to worry if his dentures slipped mid-spell or he muddled the words. They shook hands, then he took the loaner wand and left the shop, whistling. This called for a pint.

Sunday Lunch. Before Herald entered the Otter and Hare ("Outa Here!" to disgruntled customers), he looked sadly at the state of his attire and tried an experimental wave of the new wand. Instantly he was arrayed in a lovely new robe—a regal midnight blue—embroidered with a pattern of silver stars and golden moons and trimmed with ermine, all without a trace of petroleum products. "Brilliant!" he chortled. He waved it again, bent on improving his headgear. His hat now sprouted peacock feathers and rhinestone medallions, the brim trimmed alarmingly with pulsing red and purple lights. "Ah. I see. Must be more specific." He waved the wand again, envisioning his old hat with just a brush-up, and his hat was restored more or less to his accustomed level of decorum.

* An unfortunate bastardization of the ancient and venerable surname of *Rompu la Boucle* ("Broke the Loop")

Swaggering a bit, he entered the main lounge and approached the landlord. “A pint of Old Peculier, please.”

“I’m afraid we don’t have that one at the moment,” the landlord apologized. “We’ve had quite a run on it lately. But I could do yer a Bishop’s Finger.”

“Right then,” said the wizard. “Lovely. Ta.” Herald gazed about him while he waited. He could see why they’d run out of his favourite brew. The place was jammed—mostly with wizards and quite a few witches, as well as some not quite identifiable but presumably magical creatures. “There some kind of convention goin’ on?” he asked a rotund fellow in scarlet robes and hat, just lifting his knee-length beard out of the way of his ale.

“Nope. Sunday’s bingo.”

“Wizards’ Bingo?”

“What else?”

“Count me in, then!” Herald rubbed his hands greedily. With this loaner, he was bound to make a killing and procure the coin for fixing his own wand. Things were really looking up.

Sunday Morning. That same morning, a different timbre of snores came from a room upstairs in the tavern in Schlachtungunterburg. One percussive issuance sounded very much like its owner was having a happy doggy dream. The other belonged to Esmond Rippon, III, who presently awoke, and felt his face automatically for . . . stubble. No worse than usual. Then he sat up abruptly in bed, or tried to, before the manacles jerked him flat again. It all came back to him: the night before, the escalating hairiness, the nausea when the change came over him, stretching his limbs with alarming popping sounds, his toenails snagging the sheets. He felt his face again. It wasn’t smooth, but it felt human, no elongated jaws or jagged overbite. His ordeal must be over, at least for a month. Lifting his head from the pillow, he inspected the room. The yellow chintz curtains were still drawn. Aside from the manacles and chains and the presence of his shaggy visitor snoring at the foot of the bed, the chamber didn’t seem to be in any particular disarray. That must mean he'd survived the night blameless, thanks to Wolfgang. He raised his arms and saw there were hands at the end, not paws—another good sign.

"Wolfgang, are you awake?"

"I am now. Man, I was jes' havin' me a good dream. Whatdya have to wake me for?"

"Sorry about that, but I desperately need to see a man about a horse and I'm a bit tied up."

"You horse okay—he prob'ly downstairs chattin' up that little filly who came in last night."

"No. I mean I need to use the facilities. The WC. The loo," finally when Wolfgang still looked puzzled.

"Oh, yeah. Gotcha. I'll get you out in a jiff. Lemme get the keys. You'll have to do the actual unlockin', of course."

"No problem."

Once Wolfgang had brought the keys over in his mouth, Rider unlocked his restraints and climbed out of bed. Pulling the curtains aside, Rider looked out the window at the view. The sun was well up now and sparkled on the dew-covered hemlocks and on the grass below. He checked the window: still locked with the ladder outside, undisturbed. Reminded by his bladder that there was a more pressing matter, he disappeared into the loo. When he'd flushed, he peered in the mirror. Rider had never thought of himself as handsome, but he was very happy to see his old face again, even with a dark, ten o'clock shadow. His green eyes looked clear once more, and his smile displayed mostly white, straight teeth. No fangs and only moderately bad dog breath. He wrapped a towel around his naked form and returned to his room, beaming at Wolfgang. "I don't know how to thank you! It appears I made it through the night without resorting to slaughter and I'm more or less back to normal."

Wolfgang wagged his tail. "Happy to help, bro. But remember you still only 'more or less' normal. This only a temporary fix."

"You're quite right. Still, I'm glad I didn't maul the natives. Let me wash and get dressed. Then we'll go downstairs and get some breakfast. I'm ravenous. And I'm buying."

"Much obliged. You better stow that hardware somewhere outta sight, though, in case housekeeping walks in while you in the bathroom and comes to some inconvenient conclusions."

"Good thinking. You go down and get us a table while I shower, shave and pack up. Won't take me more than ten minutes, I shouldn't think."

"See ya downstairs. Decaf or regular?"

"Oh, I think a couple of espressos would be in order after last night. Ta."

The shower was bliss, and he was careful to fish any hair he'd shed out of the drain. Pulling on his normal clothes, Rider felt like a new man. Hope seemed to be tap-dancing her happy little feet on his horizon. So that the landlord wouldn't be drawn to scrutinize the change in his appearance, Rider put his cloak back on and once more pulled the hood over his face. He then stowed the chains and manacles in the saddlebag he'd brought up with him, buttoning the keys carefully into an interior coat pocket. Last, he pulled on his boots, which no longer pinched, checked the room for stray items, grabbed the saddlebag and jogged downstairs in high spirits.

As Rider settled up with the landlord, his eyebrows rose at the reckoning, recalling the landlord's breezy imperative not to worry. Rider could see his point—worry was a useless exercise: out this way, without any standardization of custom, the man could charge what he liked. Rider sighed and fished out the required sum.

"Everything all right?" the landlord beamed.

"Fine, thanks. Very comfortable."

"Didn't hear a peep outa yer friend in the broom closet."

"Not to worry. I'll fetch him after breakfast. I saw that the door only had a latch on the outside, so I think I can manage on my own. I do appreciate your assistance last night."

"Oh, don't you worry about that." Clearly, the landlord had adopted this phrase for all over-charged occasions.

Rider smiled thin thanks at him and walked toward the lounge.

Wolfgang sat at a table by a courtyard window muzzle down, slurping his cappuccino. Outside, Rider could see that his friend had returned the ladder to its brackets next to the "stable." No one else seemed to be about, which was good. The landlord came over and took their orders. Rider stirred some brown sugar into his first espresso and took a sip. Rapture. Two heaping plates of bacon and eggs, fried bread and mushrooms arrived soon after, and the two happy mutts chowed down.

Finally wiping his mouth with his serviette, Rider asked, "Have you talked to Eduardo yet?"

"Yep, when I brought back the ladder. He said it was pretty quiet last night here at the inn, but sometime after sundown he smelled some peculiar canines passing, going up toward the castle. Said he didn't think they was dogs, on account of they used deodorant and talked human, only with a posh accent. Oh, and they was drivin' cars."

"Toward the castle, you say? And *driving cars?*"

"Mmmmhmmm. Musta been guests of the baroness. Maybe she havin' a ball or somethin'."

"Strange. I wonder what this means."

"Offhand, I'd say it was a bunch of them aristocrat wolves that her hubby pals around with."

"Wait! As in werewolves? There are others in this area?" Rider was astounded.

"Hell yeah. The baroness, she real open-minded. They say her own husband's one."

Rider boggled at that.

"You know she a vampire, dontcha?"

Rider laid down his cup of Joe and stared.

"Yep. But she makes sure they don't get up to mischief and deplete the working class stock much when the moon's full. Hard enough to get good help as it is. Partly why there's only one pub in town. Well that and her monopoly, 'course. The castle labs have developed some kinda blood substitutes that seem to be doin' the job and keepin' them folks civilized. 'Course, there's always coffee, if that don't work."

"Fascinating. I wondered why even the thought of coffee was so calming."

"Yeah. Somethin' to do with changin' the blood chemistry and enzymes and all. You don't want to see one of them guys goin' through a caffeine withdrawal, that's for damned sure."

"Have they been . . . er . . . shape-changers for long?"

"This high and mighty bunch has, or so I hear. They even proud of they wolf ancestry. Goes back centuries, some of them families. Take her Heiny for instance."

"Her hiney?" Rider's mind guffawed at the implication.

"Yeah, her husband. Name's actually Heinrich but Heiny her pet name for him."

"Oh, I see." Rider pulled in his lips, stifling a snort.

"Heinrich supposedly head of The Order of Lupo, the group of these here aristocrat werewolves started way back. The baroness makes him keep tabs on the other ones so they don't change they ways and go back to huntin' more 'n grouse and debtors.

"But I also heard somebody say they was some new ones in town. Folks is gettin' nervous because this new bunch not mindin' they manners and be bitin' whenever and whoever they please, 'specially the gals. 'Least, so they say."

"Did anyone mention how long they've been around?"

"Seem like maybe three or four weeks. Not that long."

"Since the previous full moon, then."

"'Spect you right. 'Spose this could be that wizard's doing? Like he done to you? He don't seem to have either good aim or trusty eyesight."

"I wonder. And speaking of the blighter, I think it's about time we let him out of the broom closet and had a little chat, don't you?"

"I surely do."

Rider rose and paid their egregiously padded bill, then followed Wolfgang down the hall to Herald's broom closet lock-up. Wolfgang put his ear to the door. "Must be sound asleep. Don't hear a thing in there."

"Oh no." Rider wasn't getting a good feeling about this. Cautiously, they opened the door to a distinctly wizard-free collection of cleaning implements. "Bugger."

"I'll second that!" said Wolfgang. "Now what you gonna do?"

"Looks like we'll have to put our noses together and see if we can find his trail."

As they went back down the hall into the main lounge, they saw a convoy of equipment vans and trailers rumbling through the main courtyard gates and out the other side into the car park behind the convention centre.

"That must be that TV bunch arrivin' to set up for the shoot."

"I think I'd better make myself scarce in that case," said Rider.

"No, man. This the perfect opportunity to mingle incognito. If you start gettin' bushy again, they'll jes' think you're in costume. Hell, you might even get a part!"

"Very funny. Damn."

"What?"

"With that wizard possibly still in the neighbourhood, I need to stick around. But I've already vacated my room and I heard that the inn's full up."

"That okay. You can bunk with me."

Rider was dubious, thinking, *smelly den filled with crawling things*. Eduardo could hang out pretty much anywhere as long as there was food and water and a good book. As if Wolfgang were reading his mind, he said, "It not far from here. I'll show you. Don't worry, ain't no hole in the ground. I got me a condo. The landlord said he needed some extra security so he set me up with my own place in exchange for 'services rendered.' I keep an eye on things for him."

"A watch dog, in fact?" Rider couldn't resist.

"Oh, har, har. You comin' or not?"

They picked up Eduardo, who had finished his repast, and set off down the hill through the village into the town proper below, Slaughter's End. Here things were a bit more modern with a supermarket and cinema. Wolfgang's "condo" turned out to be a modest two-bedroom flat with kitchen, bath, and den. The den had a couple of comfy brown chairs bracketing an electric fire, a few books (mostly cookbooks, like *The Compleat Carnivore* and *All About Meat*), and a TV and play station set up on an entertainment centre. A regular wolf-man cave.

Out back was a sunny paddock with a water trough and some hay where they left Eduardo under a shady oak. Wolfgang also had an arrangement with the farmer next door: keeping the foxes out of the hen house earned him grocery privileges. And as long as the livestock weren't bothered, he could use the paddock as visitor parking.

"Toss your kit in here." Wolfgang motioned to one of the bedrooms.

The room was furnished with a double bed, a white-washed nightstand with a brass lamp, and matching cerulean curtains and duvet with fluffy white sheep on them. As long as he didn't have to eat them, Wolfgang thought they were kinda cute.

"Nice!" Rider was surprised. "You did this all yourself?"

"Well, with a little help from Granny."

"Your grandmother lives here as well?"

"Nah. She jes' the old lady I have Wednesday dinner with each week. Lives out in the forest in a funny lil' house. She like the company. She sewed up them curtains and duvet herself. I picked the material, of course."

"Of course. Well, again, I'm obliged to you, my friend." Rider set his saddlebags down by the bed and dragged back his hood. "I don't think I'll be recognized down here. And I'm anxious to stay on the trail of this wizard. Did you sense anything down this way?"

"You know, I thought I smelled somethin' rooty and rotten right before that last fork in the road, the one that went to the left. But it was kinda mixed up with some other smells, so I couldn't pin it down."

"What's down that way?"

"Otternought, the next village. It where the camera crew and talent scouts be stayin', seein' it's got more to entertain 'em there. Got a sportsplex, arcade and a mall. 'Course, the network bigwigs and actors be usin' the convention centre up here, hopin' to rub elbows with the gentry. Plus, they be gettin' some righteous comps from the baroness."

"I noticed a lot of people in fancy dress in the tavern last night, among the human clientele, I mean."

"Yeah, they a whole lotta folks here hopin' to be picked as extras in the show they gonna tape about this place. So everybody been dressin' up and prancin' about 'in character.' Didn't know there was so many pointy shoes and frilly shirts, not to mention big-ass petticoats and hoop skirts. Gettin' hard to navigate with all them big booties collidin'. Like bumper cars. But it even worse down in Otternought. Poked my head into the Otter and Hare the other night and thought I'd landed myself at Hogwarts, they was so many witches and warlocks in there."

"So that might be a very good place to conceal oneself, if one were a wizard on the lam."

Hunh. I thought only us predators hopped on a lamb, Wolfgang cogitated, then dismissed the alternate image with a shudder. "So . . . regardin' that wizard's whereabouts, you thinkin' what I'm thinkin'?"

Rider grinned evilly. "I believe I am, my friend. First, let's go back to Slaughter just in case anything new has turned up, then see what's cooking in Otternought. Unless, you think we oughta not?"

"Oh, I think we definitely ought."

Sunday, back in Slaughter. Outside the Bat and Whistle, two men—a thin, dark one in a captain's cap and a pudgy one with a clipboard and sunglasses—accosted Wolfgang. "Say! Would you be interested in doing a screen test for our film?" asked the man in the captain's cap.

"Who, me?"

"Yes, in fact." The man turned to his talent scout with a cocky smile. "Told you the animals can talk here. Marvellous, isn't it?" He turned back to Wolfgang, offering his hand. "Name's Nigel. I'm the director of the film we're doing here. And this is my talent scout, Winston. You see, we've heard there have been sightings of werewolves in this area recently. I've even been told that there's a long history of werewolf activity here, and you look just the part."

Wolfgang withdrew his paw. "Nah, I jes' a regular wolf. What you want is . . ." and he started to gesture toward Rider, who was frantically waving at him to shut up.

Nigel and his talent scout caught the interchange and looked Rider over. "Nope. Don't see it," said scout Winston. "Sorry, my friend, but you just don't suit the type. This wolf here would be a much better fit."

Rider sagged with relief. Wolfgang just waggled his eyebrows at

Rider and grinned, then told the scout, "Well, that real flatterin', 'cept I got bidness in the next town so I don't know when I'll be available. But give me you card and I'll see what I can do, next time I'm back."

Winston pursed his pudgy lips and grudgingly handed Wolfgang his card. "I'm afraid we're on a tight schedule. I need to line up the actors and extras right away." Nigel shrugged and walked off.

"You might ask Ern, the guard up at the castle, about them werewolves. He can probably steer you to the real thing," Wolfgang suggested to the scout.

"Thanks for the tip. I'll do that." The scout donned his shades and trotted off to round up some crew.

"See, you got nothin' to worry about, 'specially now you shaved," Wolfgang said to Rider.

"That was a closer shave than I would have liked."

"Relax, bro. You secret's safe with me."

"I8. O50. B9," boomed the bingo caller.

Pieces rustled on their cards. "Call that benign? Would have gotten bingo, if it had been B*19*," muttered a disappointed player in forest green robes and hat.

"You ate, did yer?" someone else joked.

The bingo caller replied, stonily, "That was the letter 'I' as in 'ignoramus.' "

"No sense of humour on that one," the joker whispered to his mate.

In a poorly lit corner at a table to himself, Herald was surreptitiously trying out Rumpbuckle's wand on his card, waving it under the table. Being Wizards' Bingo, a certain amount of light spell magic was expected, just for show and bragging rights. But wands were banned, as changing the numbers on one's card could only be done by the deeper sorcery of a wand. Herald knew of the ban, but was desperate for cash. His shifty eyes kept scanning the room to see if anyone noticed his numbers subtly morphing into the ones called. So far, everything was working wonderfully! He hunched over his card, the better to shade it from view.

"N46. G19."

"B19?" asked the wizard in green excitedly.

"No, that was *G*19, 'G' as in 'gerrymander.' "

"Damn."

Lemme see, thought Herald. *If I change that one it might be a bit too obvious. Best leave it 'til the next number or so.*

The numbers droned on. "I65. And, no, it's not my age," today's caller quipped acerbically, heading off further humorous attempts. It was always the same in every town: the same old jokes, the old lads and blue-haired females.

Still, he preferred it to the Trivia circuit. And at least this lot was a bit of a change with their wizards' and witches' gear. He assumed the fancy dress was on account of these television blighters scouting for non-union talent.

"N72."

"Bingo!" shouted Herald, brandishing his card . . . which was now glowing with a strobing neon flash and emitting a tune that sounded very much like the cannon section of the *1812 Overture.*

The caller had never seen *that* before. One of the players leaned over to him and said kindly, "It *is* Wizards' Bingo, don't forget. They can't help showing off a bit. Last week, Ashburton over there had his card doing cartwheels across the bar. We don't get that many outlets for amusing ourselves."

"So you're not all in fancy dress, then?"

The wizard in green drew himself up to his full 5'2" height (6'8" with the hat). "I should say not. Abracadabra University (tagged 'Voodoo U.' by the students) is just down the road, of which most of us here are alumni."

"My apologies. Thought you were all hopin' to be cast in the telly show."

"Oh, we are. They'll be wanting the real thing, not just some blokes in bathrobes with stars on."

"Well, as long as you lot don't use your wands to cheat." The bingo caller then shouted over to Herald, who was wiggling in his seat like a school kid needing a wee. "All right. Bring it over and let's have a look-see."

Everything checked out and the caller pushed over to Herald a tidy pile of gold, which disappeared speedily into the folds of his robes. "Think you could turn it off? Your card?" the caller inquired wearily.

"Oh, sorry. Right you are." Herald started to reach for the loaner wand, then thought better of it. "Er, I seem to have forgotten the undoing spell. It's me age."

"More like his mind," muttered a nearby player. "Give it here." Harold surrendered his card, praying nothing moved about on it. The wizard player murmured some quick words and the *son et lumiere* desisted. The numbers mutely stayed put.

"There. That's better." The player handed Herald's card back to the bingo caller.

Herald thanked the caller and the player who helped him out and went back to the pint at his table, counting his swindled lucre. That would more than cover the fee for fixing and updating his old wand. A rare steak and fixings would go down a treat. He wondered if maybe he could accidentally forget to return Rumpbuckle's wand and just follow the bingo games from town to town. Abruptly, an ear splitting klaxon began blaring from his wand pocket. All heads turned toward him, eyes narrowed. Herald shook his robes and rethought his situation. The alarm ended.

"That had better not be a wand in your pocket," warned the wizard who'd reset his card. "We're meant to leave 'em by the door. Didn't you see the sign? Usin' wands is right out. We play fair here."

Herald ducked his head, smiled ingratiatingly and took out his leg-kicking parsnips, which energetically tapped out a choreographed arrangement of "Girls Just Gotta Have Fun," whistling the tune in three-part harmony.

"Somethin' musta set 'em off. I can't seem to stop the perishin' things. All they want to do is dance, dance, dance."

There were a few harrumphs, but the crowd seemed mollified and turned back to their new cards. Herald downed his pint, doffed his hat, and walked calmly out the door.

Then looked both ways and took off like a hare. He would have to find a meal elsewhere.

Wandering down The Mall, he stopped at Ye Olde Food Court and bought himself a ham ’n’ cheese bap and chips. Not the same as a juicy porterhouse, but he could wait to celebrate until he was clear of the town.

He just had to pick up his old wand first. It was certain that he couldn’t keep the loaner, not with the alarm installed. That Rumpbuckle was a canny one. A bloke couldn’t stay in the wand business otherwise, Herald conceded.

CHAPTER 8

The Council Comes to Order

S*unday Night.* At the top of the second highest hill in a fortress with far too many turrets and a hard-working portcullis, the baroness's servants were bustling about, readying the castle for that night's meeting and the banquet that would, naturally, precede it. It was Sunday night and the moon was still full.

"She always springs things on us at the very last minute," Cook complained.

"That be our ol' Betty," the scullery maid agreed.

"Ol' Bitey, more like. Or 'Batty.' Take yer pick."

Life could be a bit grim at ze *Schloss*, but it beat muckin' out sties or bein' one of them bleedin' "taxpayers" down below.

Cedric and Fred, the footman, grunted as they hauled the heaviest of the equipment out of the drawing room. The small stuff and sharp instruments had been tactfully covered or shoved into cupboards. "Here, where we gointer put this lot, Ced?" asked Fred.

"Buggered if I know. Mebbe the Pool Hall, as it's been drained."

"Right. Let's give that a go. We can use the elevator. Only mind the veneer inside. Herself wasn't half ticked when we scarred that imported teak."

"These sheets and rubber things oughter help," said Cedric. "Good job we have a few days before we have to haul this lot back." As they trundled away, a feline scream echoed through the hall as Fred trod on the castle cat's tail. Fred lifted his foot, apologizing. To Cedric he commented, "You just never see the sneaky blighters, do yer?"

Right after sunset, the guests began to arrive, looking sheepish as they began to grow woolly. Most had taken the precaution to wear their expandable tuxes, thankfully, to avoid that awkward moment they all dreaded. For the few who hadn't thought to do so, loose mandarin-like robes were provided. And shaving kits, as requested. An offer to freshen up before dinner was received gratefully.

A half-hour later, they gathered for drinks in the drawing room. In the centre was a damask-clothed table of an unusual height. The aspirator with suction hose and bottle, body support slats, and instrument tray that usually resided there had been tastefully hidden beneath the skirting. An enormous bouquet of highly fragrant lilies, imported from the southern hemisphere, dominated the table. Arrays of fodder-free hors d'oeuvres and cheeses were arranged on silver salvers, along with crackers and artisan breads to soak up the juice. Cedric and Fred circulated the room with trays of wine and wine substitute in stemmed crystal. As a precaution, the heavy gold drapes had been closed and secured firmly with heraldic pins to forestall further transformations.

They were a close society so pretty much everyone knew everyone. There was a lot of back pawing and risqué innuendo, loud barks of laughter punctuating their entitled blather. The baroness entered the room with her consort and all eyes came to attention, more or less. She was looking magnificent in her ruby velvet gown (displaying just enough cleavage not to be off-putting) and her garnet and diamond torque. Heinrich also looked handsome, if hairy. He wore the House of VIAL official raiment: loads of gold braid down the front and the satin pantaloons that so generously accommodated sudden limb reconfigurations.

Then the gong sounded. Betty and her Heiny preceded the crowd grandly into the Great Dining Room. Gazing around at the mahogany table, polished to glass-like brilliance, the snowy table linen, the crystal, fine bone china and flowers in the candlelight, Betty thought to herself, *We really must use this room more. It is so very beautiful. Perhaps after all this fuss is sorted, we can have some jolly balls like Papá used to have.*

After the borscht (her own recipe) came the *Boeuf Tartare*, a favourite which was wolfed down by her guests. Next came Fruit Bat with Plum Sauce. (This caused an epicurean sensation.) Then the terrine of hare, prime rib (no one's they knew), and shank of venison made their rounds. Vegetables were noticeably absent. Finally, for pudding was one of the baroness's favourites from her nursery days. It was a kind of pancake or flapjack, drizzled with a raspberry-flavoured tapioca. In the kitchen, it got dubbed "Flapioca."

Sir Rudyard pushed back his chair at last, easing the cummerbund over his paunch. "Damned fine feed, m'dear!" said he, beaming at the baroness. "You've really outdone yourself. No need to go on the prowl tonight for a late snack, eh?" Barks of "Hear! Hear!" seconded him around the table.

"You're too kind, Ruddy. One doesn't want one's guests to go away unreplete. But the mention of 'snacks' brings me to the issue I've called you all here for. Gentlemen, shall we return to the drawing room? You may smoke there, of course."

With a scraping of chairs and more surreptitious adjustments of waistbands, her guests followed the baroness back to the drawing room and took up comfortable chairs near the blazing fire in the hearth. Brandy and "port" were passed around. Glancing about her, Betty reminded herself that much of the dated facial hair, mutton chops and huge mustachios was merely a temporary outgrowth and that she wasn't really caught in a Victorian drama.

"So what's all this I hear about brazen interlopers amongst us, Betty?" asked Sir Terrance.

"Count D. came to me just yesterday complaining about some sort of gang of shape-changers that has been seen in our area recently. Werewolves, to be exact, who have been upsetting the *status quo*. I thought perhaps one of you might have heard or seen something and could enlighten us. According to him, they're not playing by the rules."

"I haven't seen anything. Have you, Stinky?" Sir Terry addressed the fellow to his left in the wing back chair who was hogging all the heat from the fire.

"Not a bloody thing," said Stinky (formally, Sir Stefan).

Harry (Sir) leaned forward. "I did hear something from the landlord over at the tavern today." He paused to sip his port and draw out the suspense.

All ears pricked up. "Don't keep us breathless, Harry. What was it?" Betty tried to keep the annoyance out of her voice.

"Something about a cloaked rider who rode in on a horse late last night. He stopped at the tavern for a bit of a nosh and seemed overly beardy to be wearing fine boots, if you know what I mean. Thanks to his hood, the landlord didn't get a very good look at his face, but the profile indicated a bloody long nose and too much whisker. Said his hands were pretty fuzzy, too."

"Well, that could mean nothing. You've seen the sorts that hang out at the tavern and you know our open-door policy. There usually are one or two wolves imbibing there amongst their cronies, not to mention the dwarves when they're not striking."

"True," Sir Harry agreed, "but our wolves don't pay their tabs with coins . . . from a purse. Or have opposable thumbs, for that matter."

"You intrigue me," Betty said.

"Basil, the landlord, told me the fellow got into an altercation with some seedy little wizard who approached him trying to off some magic tubers or some such. Chased the wizard right out the door, seething mad. That was when this rider's hood fell back and Basil got a bit better look, though just the back of his head. Said the bloke had either the world's worst barber or a bad rug. Thought he saw pointy ears, as well."

"And did this stranger return?" inquired the baroness.

"He did, in fact, dragging back the wizard, who oddly was covered in oil. Left a helluva slick on the floor, said Basil."

"What happened to the unfortunate wizard?"

"The landlord and this rider fellow locked him in the broom closet for safekeeping. Basil could tell that the magician was up to no good."

"They never are," muttered Stinky, darkly.

"Hear! Hear!" the rest agreed.

"Then the newcomer booked a room for the night and went up to bed."

"Well, for goodness' sake, didn't the landlord get a better look at his face at that point, Harry?"

"No, damn him. He said he was too busy cleaning up after the mangy magus and spraying him down with cleansers, Betty. And the rider had pulled the hood back over his face by then."

"Did the landlord have any idea why this cloaked person was there, at least?"

"He was just guessing, but thought it might have something to do with the wizard. The man seemed reasonable enough until the little bugger came in hawking his wares. Basil said one of the kitchen staff overheard the fellow seemingly talking to his horse outside, something about tracking the wizard. Sounded like he had a bone to pick with him."

"Curious. Still," said Betty, "it is just one man, or wolf as the case may be, not a gang. Naturally, we will wish to follow up on this visitor and find out why he's here. But this isolated incident doesn't seem the sort of thing to send Count D. into such a tizzy. You're quite sure he was traveling alone?"

"According to the landlord, he was. Well, except for his horse, at any rate," Harry replied.

"Ah, another talking horse. Must be this wizard's doing. I can see good cause for his ire in that case. It took us ages to reverse that nasty spell on our stallion, Billy."

"And what a ruddy great gas bag *he* turned out to be!" enjoined Heiny.

"Yes, it was quite dreadful. Billy would keep telling off-colour jokes to the staff. We thought we'd have to put him down. So, back to the matter at hand, has anyone else seen or heard anything at all?" Betty cast her glance around again at her guests.

"You know, I did actually pick up something a bit odd from the old *hoi polloi* but don't know if you can credit it much," Sir Friedrich offered.

"Do go on," urged the baroness.

"These two old bodies, crones that live down near the sties dontcha know, mentioned to your guard finding several whole sets of men's clothing, rather upmarket, along the path through the forest that leads into the village in the past couple of fortnights. And all the armholes of the jackets were burst."

"Oh, dear. That doesn't bode well," Betty muttered. "Did they ever come upon any of the former occupants of this clothing?"

"The older one, think her name is Doris, said not and that they were bloody glad they hadn't. They got it in their heads there must be some sort of depraved nudist cult scampering about amongst the hemlocks."

"Hmmmmm . . . I think it would be prudent if we encouraged them to keep thinking that for the moment. We don't want to startle the natives with an even scarier rumour. Well, gentlemen, I would be grateful if you would keep your ears pitched for any further news on the matter," the baroness concluded.

They polished off their nightcaps and donned their cloaks that Cedric had brought in. A small tray of breath mints was passed around. The baroness peeked out between the secured drapes at the sky. Luckily, the moon was hidden behind a thick cover of clouds and it was very dark. She turned to Cedric, who was opening a large, heavy chest. "I think we can do without the manacles and muzzles, Cedric. The moon's quite hidden. It appears we may get some rain."

"Well, I don't mind sayin' that's a relief!" ejaculated Sir Terry. "Didn't fancy tryin' to get into my Lamborghini with that lot on. Would probably set off the alarm." There were murmurs of general assent.

"Fabulous do, my dear. Damned grateful. Not much going on this time of year, and it greatly eases the tedium of dining on takeaway." Stinky donned his hat and turned to leave with the others.

"I do hope you'll all remember to report to me anything whatsoever that might shed light on this problem. I truly don't wish to take harsh measures if they can be avoided," Betty cautioned.

"Now you leave it to us, m'dear. We'll sort this out." Sir Harry tipped his trilby and they left trailing thanks, the baroness and Heinrich thanking them in return for their assistance.

"Well, thank gods that's over! Heiny, I honestly don't know how many more of these full moon dinners I can stand. Stinky completely forgot how to use his knife and fork and I was afraid I'd lose my dinner watching an entire hare's leg disappear down Friedrich's gullet. He will *not* remember to chew with his mouth closed! And Harry never once used his napkin. There must have been a pint of *au jus* drooling down his chin. I would have much preferred to wait a few days to invite them, but it seemed too urgent to put the meeting off."

"I know, my dear. It's dashed hard for 'em all this time of month. For me, too, come to that."

"Darling, you were the perfect gentleman. You always are." Betty petted his furry paw.

"That's because I keep telling myself, 'Use your thumbs, man, use your thumbs'!"

Betty yawned, "I'm flat off my feet and ready to hit the rack."

"Beddy-bye then. Sleep tight, dear,—"

" —and don't let the bats bite!" she answered coquettishly.

"Well, maybe just a nibble." Heiny waggled his brushy eyebrows, gazing down at her fondly, and led a giggling Betty upstairs.

CHAPTER 9

Out For a Bite

M*onday Morning.* Nigel was shouting orders to his crew, having set up his folding chair in the area behind the tavern's convention centre. Cameras and lights were being positioned for some test shots. Their star narrator, Sylvia LaMoânne, was due to emerge any moment from her trailer. Nigel always used Sylvia for films that needed that extra hook of sex: blonde hair (long) and tits (large). She even read lively and without stuttering. The only problem with Sylv was keeping track of her. Sylvia was more than a bit of a party girl. She liked to sample the local . . . fauna. The lads had nicknamed her "The Moan." Christ, last year he'd had to haul her back to a shoot in Zimbabwe from Budapest, after she went swanning off with their (non-)"African guide"! The comptroller hadn't liked that. So Nigel counted himself lucky that this time she really was staying local.

Gerry, one of the gaffers, was struggling with a boom pole. Derek and Ian were setting up steadycams and a jib crane, teetering on the cobbles.

"Ger, you seen Sylv?" Nigel shouted.

"Nope. Think she's still in her trailer."

"After you get that boom pole set, could you go over and ask her kindly to get a move on?"

"Sure thing."

Just at that moment an extremely dishevelled Sylvia emerged from her trailer, a bit staggery, in her white robe. Make-up had done its usual miracle of making her prettiness seem bookish and less sultry (this *was* a documentary). But there was something odd about her, besides her sullen expression and the clashing paisley scarf around her throat. A hush settled on the set. Then a crescendo of snorts and snickers. Sylvia's legs and arms were astonishingly hairy. Nigel couldn't remember when he'd seen that thick a pelt on a woman. At least they now knew she was a true blonde.

"Um, Sylv, darling. Could you come over here, please?" Nigel requested.

Sylvia slunk over in a pout.

"Did we forget our depilatory today, or are you taking steroids?"

"It's not my fault!" Sylvia whined. "Look, Nige, I did shave—my legs anyway—twice this morning. And I didn't know what to do about the hair on my arms 'cuz I've never had any, all right?"

"So what's with the plush look, then?"

"I don't bloody know, do I? It came on sudden." Sylvia looked abashed. Nigel figured she knew something she wasn't telling. Yet.

"Darling, you're not 'juicing', surely?" picturing to himself Sylv gone lady weightlifter.

"What? Like I'm some wrestling champion, or something?"

"Well . . ." Nigel let that rest. "Then some other kind of hormonal supplement? Come on, Sylv, you can tell Uncle Nigel."

Sylvia glanced around to see who all could be listening in, then satisfied they had some privacy, said, "There was this bloke I met."

"Well, of course there was. There always is."

Sylvia shot him a slitty look. "He was loads of fun, threw a heap of dosh about, kinda cute in a teddy bear sort of way. Said he was here on business, scouting the area, I can't remember for what. But I thought, 'Why not?' Sometimes a girl needs a boost, you know?"

"Of course, pretty girl like you. Hard to tie her down." Nigel thought that probably the opposite was true, but he did not want to go there. "So then what?"

"Well, you know—the usual." Nigel could certainly guess. "We did a bit of pub crawling, not easy in this area, mind you. Then we went up to his suite and the swanky champagne came out."

Nigel could see where this was leading. Sylvia was a sucker for any plonk that had a French name and cost more than her daily wage. He waited.

"After a couple of teensy little glasses," Sylvia continued, "I honestly don't remember much. He was a good kisser, that's for certain. Oh, and I vaguely remember going out to the garden to watch the full moon. After that, it's sort of a blank."

Oh boy, Nigel thought. "A couple of teensy little glasses" translated to probably the whole magnum. Sylvia fidgeted with the scarf around her neck.

"This a new fashion statement?" Nigel gestured to the scarf. "Rather Pavarotti, dontcha think? Not sure it will pass with Wardrobe." He figured it covered a hickey.

"I'm just a bit embarrassed to take it off, right now," Sylv murmured.

"Come on, darling, let Uncle have a look."

Casing the area again, Sylvia finally drew off the scarf. Nigel whistled. That was some hickey! He bent over and peered at the marks on her neck. *By gum, they were bite marks.* He looked closer. *And the man had some serious incisors.* The marks looked more like a dog bite from a really big dog. *Good job he'd missed the jugular.*

"Sylv, you want that looked at straight away! You say this happened this last full moon? Wasn't that was last night?"

"Yes," Sylvia replied. "He was really excited about how bright the moon was. Said it really turned him on."

Besides the area's history of werewolves Research had uncovered, rumours of recent werewolf activity had also reached Nigel. "Was he particularly hairy, this guy? You mentioned something about being 'cute in a teddy bear sort of way.' "

"Now that you mention it, it did seem that he was pretty woolly and got more so, but it could have been the champagne."

Nigel was quiet, thinking.

"Hey, you don't think he could actually have been one of those, you know, wolf-men, do you?" Sylvia asked. Her grey cells, what was left of them, were wobbling at the thought.

"I don't know what to think. But what I do know is that we've got to get that fur off you before we shoot and you need to see the doc." At his signal, Alice, his young gofer trotted up.

"Al, can you run round to a chemist, if there is one, and see if you can scare up some Nair? If you can't find a chemist, go up to the castle and see if any of the staff there know where to get some. This is urgent!"

Catching Winston's smirk of triumph, she saluted. "Right away, guv!" Alice jogged away, brunette ponytail bouncing.

If Sylvia's cuddle really had been a werewolf, Nigel thought they might need more than Nair. And he devoutly hoped he'd be the first to capture the story, if not the guy. Some clips of the real thing would send their ratings through the roof.

Alice soon learned that there wasn't a chemist in town and the nearest was miles away in the next village. Checking her watch, she saw with alarm how off-schedule they were. And, per usual, sodding Winston would make it all her fault. She opted for a run up to the castle.

Ern greeted her at the castle gates, pulling off his headphones. Things were looking up. Been a long time since a bird like this had come to the *Schloss* with enquiries. He doffed his helmet.

Out of breath, she called, "Hullo! I'm with the film crew down below. The one that's doing the documentary?"

"Only filum crew I know of," Ern said jocularly.

"Yes, right. Well, we're in a bit of a bind, seeing as there's no Boots in town. We urgently need some Nair or an on-call barber at the least."

"Ne're? That some kinda place that isn't—neither here or ne're?"

Alice chuckled. "No. It's a depilatory, you know—for removing hair."

Ern's expression changed to one of suspicion. "Whatcha want that for, then?"

"It's sort of a lady thing. I wouldn't like to elaborate."

"Only 'cuz recently there's been a rash of hairy folk, I been hearin'. Ones that didn't used to be. You're not the first one askin' after a clean shave."

"Really? Is it something that's going around?" Alice asked, wide-eyed.

Ern glanced about, turned down the sound on his UPad, and leaned over conspiratorially. "More like some *things* goin' around. If I was you, I'd stay clear of blokes yer don't know durin' the full moon, especially ones with whiskers and big teeth." He winked.

She felt relieved. He was just winding her up, playing the official werewolf card for PR's sake. The romance of predator (male) and prey (female). Nothing ever changed.

"You're certainly loyal to your employer's legends," she teased. "We're pursuing the werewolf angle, no worries. It does give the film an extra bit of excitement, naturally. The dark history and all."

"'Tain't just history, my flower. 'Tis recent, too, but no one we know. The baroness has asked us to keep our ears open and report anything new we hear, she's that upset."

Alice regarded him thoughtfully. "So . . . you're not just winding me up, then?"

"Nay. 'Tis all true, or at least wot I been told. You haven't been cavortin' with anything on four legs, have ye?"

"I prefer to stick strictly to two for my cavorting," Alice replied. "And anyway, it's not for me. It's some other . . . female."

"Women is who them guys prefer, right enough. They be quite the ladykillers. Something to do with fairy moans, they say. It's how they get away with it. Regular Joes like me don't stand a chance when they're about."

Alice stifled a giggle as she translated.

"This 'female,' she come over hairy all a' sudden like?" Ern pried.

"I believe so."

"She been out partyin' last night, mebbe? 'Twas a great big ol' full moon."

"It's possible. Well, with that one it's more than possible. Some corporate cur had been chatting her up lately, following her around like a puppy."

Ern nodded sagely.

"Look, I'm not really privy to the cause of this woman's condition."

Alice cursed herself for saying too much. "I just need the bloody Nair, okay? If you don't have any here, could you kindly let me know where I could get some?"

Ern pulled himself up. "I regret we have none on the premises. We don't have much call for that kinda thing. Judging by her husband, our baroness seems to prefer her menfolk on the hairy side, any road." As he saw Alice's slump, he added, "But I could probably get you a load of used candles."

"Candles?" Alice was stumped. "We have plenty of lighting gear. It was never a matter of bad light."

"Nay, my angel. Not fer lightin', fer meltin'. Drip enough of that tallow on, the hair should come off right well, though mebbe takin' some skin with it. 'Tain't for the faint-hearted, I'll allow. But 'twould solve yer problem."

Crikey! A Brazilian wax for the whole body! Daunting, but brilliant. Alice slowly grinned, recalling all the snipes she'd suffered from Sylvia. *Serve the witch right.* She smiled sweetly at Ernie. "That would be fab, if you could. Thanks ever so much!"

"I'll have to put in a request with the butler, but I doubt there'll be any problem. You just tell me where to send 'em, and I'll see that they gets sent down to yer toot sweet." Ern beamed at her.

Alice gave him the directions then went back down the hill as Ern trundled off inside.

Approaching the director back on the set, Alice braced herself for reprimand. "I'm really sorry, Nigel, but there's simply no Nair to be had. I did try, truly I did."

"That's all right, luv. I know you did." Nigel seemed oddly relaxed about it. Could he somehow be enjoying this? Defuzzing a hairy prima donna was probably good payback for some of Sylvia's unscheduled and pricey jaunts.

"But the guard at the castle did say they had a load of used candles they can send down to us, so I said okay . . . ," said Alice with straight face.

Nigel burst out laughing. He'd connected the dots rather faster.

"That's better than okay, my pet. I'd say that's just about perfect! We still have any of those handcuffs around or maybe some rope?"

Alice smirked. "I imagine I can scare something up. I'll grab a bottle of Jack, too, while we're about it. That should help with the sting."

"Go get 'em, Al!" Nigel chortled. This whole thing was getting better and better. He checked his watch and his clipboard. Sod it, the schedule was shot. Maybe they could still get some light values set.

They also needed to see where they were with non-union recruitment. And this might be a good time to run down more of the backstory to Sylvia's ravager.

Happily, the pub would be the best place to do both. His watch told him it was well past strong drink. He beseeched the cinema gods not to let it rain for a few more days.

In the tavern, Nigel and the lads were elbowing up to the bar, priming for a good session. Alice had reported that the gross of used candles had arrived from the castle and that she'd sent their masseuse and one-time shot-putter, Ursula, to do the honours. They'd left the set just as the shrieking commenced. Nigel's beer had never tasted so good. And even though only Monday lunch, the place was crowded as always. That would greatly help his chances for digging up information.

Spotting an empty table near the window next to a group of businessmen, he motioned to his crew. "Let's grab that before it's gone." As they sat down, he noticed that the conversation at the businessmen's table got suddenly quieter, then gradually louder. The subject had been abruptly changed, that much was obvious. Nigel swivelled his inner antennae in their direction. He'd give them five or ten minutes. That's usually all it took before people's guards hit the snooze button. In the meantime, he'd steer his crew's conversation around to topics that would be most likely to entice outside interest, say unusually hairy female legs. He'd see where that got him.

Without his nudging, Derek and Ian were already giving Gerry the gruesome details of Operation Hair Removal.

"Stop! Stop!" Gerry gasped. "I can't take it! What? She never! To

Sylvia? *Our* Sylvia? Oh, Christ, that's rich." Gerry was having trouble catching his breath. He mopped his streaming eyes with the sleeve of his jacket. Ian pounded him on the back and had him take a swallow from his pint.

"I expect you're referring to the unfortunate depilatory events of this morning," Nigel interjected somewhat loudly.

"That we are, Nige. Oh, God, you should have seen it. Priceless!" Derek sniggered.

"That must have been what all the hollering was about," Nigel observed. He felt the attention of the men at the next table swivel in their direction. "I don't recall ever having to send out for hair removal before, do you lads?" he asked innocently.

"Not for a female, that's for sure. You positive she's not on some sort of steroids, Nige?" asked Ian. "Maybe she has a secret hankering for barbells? I can see the headlines now: 'DOCUMENTARY STAR FOUND JUICING.' "

Nigel shook his head, smirking, "She said not. It was quite a sudden growth spurt. And then there was that 'love bite' on her neck."

"I've never seen anything like it, even on Ursula." Ian shuddered then added, "All that fur *would* keep ya nice and toasty in the winter. But what was that about a love bite? Was that why she was wearin' that poxy scarf?"

"Oh, Ian," said Derek, "you know how she's always draggin' herself back from one her escapades after a nip here and a tuck there." The lads burst out laughing again.

"It was rather more than a nip," Nigel said.

Gerry's interest perked up. "Worse than her last hickey? *That* was a doozy. Took Make-up an hour to cover it up, and then, with all that heat in Zimbabwe, the concealer kept running down her thigh. It was like the phantom bruise with drips on."

"And of course she insisted on wearing those silly khaki short-shorts. Said they were regulation safari gear," Derek put in. "Well, she was on a big game hunt, right enough."

The lads were off again. "I wonder what the bloke that bit her was like, if he's still alive. If I were he, I'd go in to the nearest vet and check for rabies!" Ian was in good form.

"I'm pretty sure Sylvia usually gives as good as she gets. But this looked more like a wild animal did it," Nigel replied.

"Ooh, Sylv really got lucky, then!" Ian hooted.

"Perhaps." Nigel felt a definite quiet come over the table next door.

"Is it hot in here?" asked one of the men at the next table, starting to loosen his tie.

"I wouldn't do that," said another, who eyed him meaningfully. "Short memory?"

A third said quietly, "Let's keep our voices down, shall we, Addison?" and motioned with his head at the next table. "It is a little hot. Let me just open this window a bit." Tyrone P. Upman, Chief Development Officer of Global Advanced Management, LLP, rose and cranked the mullioned casement open a few inches, letting in a breeze as well the noise of the traffic outside. He sat back down and took a sip from his glass, staring over his wire-rimmed glasses at his companions, Cyril B. Stonewall, VP Business Development, and Addison T. Brickheart, Chief Compliance Officer and nibbler of starlets. "I see you were both able to find good barbers and a decent haberdashery in the area. A shame about the mix-up with our luggage. Excellent suit, Addison. Italian?"

Addison was about to point out that his luggage had gotten there just fine, then thought better of it. Remembering exactly what had happened that night to his clothes, he turned red and became engrossed in his gin and tonic.

With the outside noise coming in the window, Nigel could now barely make out the next table's conversation. He had caught the remark, however, about barbers and new clothes. Might do to keep tabs on this lot. He turned in his seat searching, ostensibly, for the loos and catching a quick mental snapshot of each face. Nigel hadn't become a first-string documentary director without having a good eye and memory for details. Thin-lipped, thin man with wire-rims in the charcoal pin-stripe, long red tie: top guy. Balding, beefy blow-hard with beer gut in brown tweed and yellow tie: probably front man, business development or advertising. Aging playboy with brown, curly hair and deceitful dimples in navy gabardine and maroon-striped school tie: talent scout and strategic convincer. Might be Sylvia's Lothario.

Nigel got up and gestured at his lads with his glass, "'Nother round?"

"If it's on you, guv, definitely!" Gerry grinned at him. "Give you a hand?"

"Okay. I'm just off to the loo first. You order, and I'll be back in a tick to pay."

Nigel took his time walking through the crowd past the neighbouring table as Gerry went up to the bar to order. As he stopped to check his watch, Nigel overheard, "I really can't recommend your seeing this young woman again, Addison. Not under the circumstances. And you, Cyril, were deuced lucky not to be tracked down by those widows. The moon is still in the full phase, and you can't risk it." The speaker was the thin-lipped man in glasses.

Got it in one: t*hat guy* is *the big boss. And Addison is the teddy-bear playboy with the school tie.* Nigel turned and caught Tyrone's gaze and smiled blankly, careful not to show that he'd heard. "The men's is down this way, is it?"

Tyrone smoothed back his silver hair and tipped his head politely. "First door on your left, I believe."

"Thanks." Nigel wandered off in that direction, hoping Derek and Ian might pick up something from the men. But they were chatting up some young birds in tight bodices and dirndls at the far table. Oh, to have the keen ears of a beast.

As luck would have it, a beast with keen ears indeed was standing outside the open window, ruminating on his elevenses; the landlord had just replenished the water trough and hay mangers. With the film crew either absent or caught up in the giggly ploys of co-star hopefuls, the business titans resumed their previous discussion. Nobody noticed the horse or worried that he was listening in.

As Eduardo was getting an ear- and belly-full, Wolfgang and Rider, back in a suit underneath his cloak, came around the corner of the innyard to check on him.

"Have you heard any leads to where that wizard may have gotten to?" Rider asked quietly.

Not yet. But I've just been listening to a most illuminating conversation at the table opposite the window. It appears we weren't the only victims of Herald the Inept.

"How so?"

Two of these gentlemen also have suffered, apparently, from an unfortunate swipe of the wonky wand. They were quite surprised when they started busting out of their expensive suits and finding it hard to keep off the burgeoning pelt during the last two full moons. You'll notice Señor Beer Belly could do with a good dentist. And it seems last night one of them, at least, had an amorous liaison with the blonde, leggy film star, and things got very hairy indeed. On both sides. His boss just gave him a good talking to about it.

Rider crept up to the side of the building and peered in the crack between the casement and window frames at the businessmen talking at the table.

"The thin one in the pin-striped suit and wire rims is the boss?"

I would surmise. He has been insisting that Señor Don Juan in the striped tie leave the señorita alone. The rendezvous was noted by too many, and its outcome is endangering whatever business plans they had in the area.

"Sounds like damage control. They mention anything more about the wizard?"

Only that when they caught up with him, they would work him into their new development. Then there was much laughter.

"Did you hear what type of development they're working up in this area?"

It wasn't clear to me, but I heard some interesting key words here and there.

"Like?"

"Clearcutting," "logging permits," "payoffs"—that kind of thing. Eduardo tossed his head.

"I don't like the sound of that. I'll see what I can find out as well. Keep listening and let me know what else you learn. Good job, Eduardo!"

De nada. I'll be happy to lend an ear.

"Wolfgang!" Rider hissed across the yard to his friend. Wolfgang ambled over and Rider caught him up on things. "What say we grab a pint inside in the saloon bar?"

Wolfgang grinned. "That's that teeny lil' room that's jes' on the other side of where them suits is. As I recall, that ol' wall between mighty thin."

Rider grinned back. "I thought as much."

Luck was with them. As the small bar was still empty, they took the corner table next to the aforementioned wall. Rider hung his cloak on a nearby peg. "You have the better ear, so why don't you scoot over in the corner, Wolfgang?"

"All the better to hear them, my dear!" Wolfgang was enjoying himself.

"Exactly. What do you fancy? Pint of bitter?"

"Nah. I'm more of a cider man. You standin' the drinks?"

"Naturally," Rider said and fished for some coins. At least now he had pockets.

Maisie, the barmaid, came over and swung a saucy hip at them. Wolfgang thought Rider's eyes would pop out at the amount of cleavage heaving above the miniscule margin of white peasant blouse above the overstrung bodice. Rider found it hard to know where to look, other than where Maisie meant him to, so he focused on her luxurious auburn tresses below the pert mob cap. Too much excitement might stimulate other things and require an urgent visit to a barber. "What may I get you, luvs?" She batted mascaraed eyelashes shamelessly at them.

"Just a pint of bitter and pint of cider, if you please," said Rider.

"I can't interest you in anything else?" she asked provocatively. Rider wondered just how "full service" this joint was. "Only we do lovely bangers and mash. And as today's Monday, we have a special on—Woodsman's Lunch."

"What's in that?" Wolfgang asked.

"Oh, the usual: cheese, bread and pickle, and some rare slices of wolf flank."

Wolfgang's eyes got wider and he shrank back in his chair.

"I'm only windin' ya up." Maisie cackled as Wolfgang relaxed a bit. "It's really just pork, but we like to call it that. Sounds ever so exotic."

"Just the drinks, please," replied Rider.

"You're missin' out, but never mind. I won't be two ticks with your order." Maisie sashayed away.

For a second there, Wolfgang had felt a bit preyed upon. He just hoped that Maisie's tease wasn't indicative that his boastful tale had gotten back to Granny. Or worse, to her granddaughter, Red.

After the drinks came and they took approving sips, Wolfgang scooted up to the wall nonchalantly and swivelled one ear toward the occupants on the other side.

"They still there?" Rider asked.

"Yep. Can hear 'em loud 'n' clear. Smell 'em, too. Whew!"

"What are they saying?"

"Hush up. How can I hear with you jabberin'?"

"Fair point. I'll desist." Rider imbibed silently.

A young-ish blonde in dark glasses and a long-sleeved tracksuit entered the saloon bar and hesitated. It was obvious she had assumed she'd be on her own and was disappointed.

She sat down at last in the far corner and pulled the menu up over her face. Rider noticed the red paisley scarf around her neck that didn't really go with the slime green of the suit. Aha! This could be that film star who got bitten, if rumour was correct. It was warm inside and, without thinking, she pushed her sleeves up. Rider spied to see if she was overly hirsute. Nope. But her arms were exceedingly red and blistered. That was odd. *What could . . . ?* Wolfgang had to dodge out of the way to avoid the spume of beer erupting from Rider's nose as Rider figured out what type of cure must have been applied. He'd never look at a bikini wax the same way again.

She was joined by a comely, brown-haired lass in a baseball cap, her ponytail hanging out through the hole in the back. Her cap and navy blue windcheater both had a company logo on them with an acronym ending in "TV." Rider deduced she must be with the film crew, too.

A third, very large woman with a blonde crew cut came in and made to join them.

"Keep her away from me!" the star shrieked.

The large woman threw up her hands in apology. "Very sorry, Sylvia, but is my job. Must do what boss tells. Brought ointment, see?" She held out a somewhat oozing, unlabelled jar.

"I wouldn't put that stuff on me. God knows what's in it!"

"Look, Sylvia, Ursula's only trying to help," Alice coaxed.

"Is good for cows, so . . . ," Ursula began. Sylvia scowled at the woman, who just shrugged, stuffed the jar back in her pants pocket and stood at the bar. Patting her red curls, Maisie came over to the star's table and solicitously took their orders, then went back to the bar and got their drinks, before drawing a pint for the spurned Ursula.

Wolfgang seemed absorbed in the conversation in the adjacent room, so Rider thought he'd wander in the direction of the bar, closer to the women, and have a listen.

"I honestly didn't see it coming," whinged Sylvia to Alice. "He seemed so sweet and of course flatteringly attentive. Oh, you know how it is: the moon is full, the night is young, the blood starts racing and the chase is on."

"Yes, but from the state of you this morning, Sylv, I'd say he won the race."

Sylvia nodded her head in sad agreement. "Everything was going so well. We were drinking that lovely bubbly and, well, getting to know one another . . . and then the moon came out from behind a cloud, and suddenly he was a very different person. The moon *was* amazingly bright, quite romantic."

She reached again for her cocktail. "Oh. Gone." She gazed sadly at her empty glass, then caught Maisie's eye. The barmaid bustled over promptly with a refill.

"Tha's better. Come to Mummy," Sylvia cooed and took a long

swallow. "The whole ghastly thing is a bit hazy, but don't remember any ess'traordinary facial hair, leas' not until the moon came out. Then 'seemed like there was a bloody great searchlight in the sky and next thing, I was looking cross-eyed at a hairy face and some honking great teeth were latching onto my throat. Mind you," she hiccupped, "he was a rollicking good kisser! Knew just where to nibble." She nudged Alice. "But it got too violent, even for me, in the end. Had to whack 'im with my Gucci."

Alice murmured consolingly.

"Sssuch a waste," Sylvia pined. "He really has quite sexy eyes, a beautiful sort of moss green. Or were they brown? And lovely (*hic!*) dimples. An' he went to one of the best public schools. That always tells you a lot." She nodded sagely at her drink.

"Did he tell you anything about himself?" asked Alice.

"Well, lessee. Yes. He's some kind of executive for a big global cor...poration. Tha's what he said anyway. 'Said they're over here scoutin' out some new territories to set up business. Something to do with renewable . . . whatsits . . . um . . . resources. I think." Sylvia hooted. "And here I was hopin' to get my resources renewed!" She elbowed Alice, sharing her drollery.

"Oh! And they have their own ssstudio and make their own ad...verts and marketing thingies. Films." Sylvia burped, then giggled. "As we got . . . er . . . friendly, I think he was hintin' at offering me my own spot with his corpo, corpor . . . company." She tapped the side of her nose. "I'd be their ssole ssspokeswoman and be in every ad! I tell you, . . . wha's your name again?"

"Alice," said Alice. *After 11 films, the woman can't remember my name?*

"Right. Alice. I tell you, just between us girls, I was really tempted. I mean, no more swatting mosquitos in bloody Africa or climbing eight thousand ssstairs in some mouldy ttower. Jus' stayin' put in a nice, clean ssstudio with central air and takin' it all to the (*hic!*) bank. . . ." Sylvia fondly caressed her drink, shaking her head mournfully. "But then 't'all went pear-shaped. Oh, after I whacked 'im, he apologized profusely. Didn't know what came over 'im, 'ssaid. Kept 'is face in the shadow and sort of slunk off." Another gulp. "I was too shocked—" *and in the bag*, thought Alice—"to take in more (*hic!*) details." Arch was hard to pull off mid hiccup, but Sylvia was doing her best.

"When you got back to your trailer, did you notice anything odd, you know, on your body?"

"I was too wiped out, luv."

Oh, now I'm "luv"? That's rich, after all the snotty things you've called me. Aloud, Alice asked, "So you never noticed any extra hair last night, then?"

"I didn't even peep at the bite on my neck. I imagined it would be one whopper of a hickey but a little extra foundation would take care of it in the morning, so I just hit the sack."

Alice took a thoughtful sip of her pinot grigio as Sylvia slugged back her Rusty Nail and demanded another. Another appeared before her. She smiled blearily at the barmaid, took a genteel sip, and sighed.

Rider and Wolfgang weren't the only ones listening in. Ursula had been venting her woes to Maisie, who never lost any opportunity to gossip. Maisie was one of those rare individuals who can listen independently out of each ear, while taking orders and flirting with customers. And Maisie was great mates with Dinah up at the castle. A regular hotline. What Maisie's cerebral satellite dish was drawing in would keep the rumour mill grinding for decades, and could turn out to be worth someone's cold hard cash.

Maisie got Ursula another pint, then went to the other end of the bar and began polishing glasses, thinking furiously. She could still follow all the conversations, in that room anyway.

Wasn't there some talk last night about some other girl, besides the starlet, who went out with one of the foreign blokes and came back with a sore throat and a dreamy smile on her face? Seemed like there were a lot of new fellas in town these days, what with the film company, those suits in the other bar, and that odd fellow who came in Saturday night in a cloak and riding boots. Although, on the Saturday, she'd been mostly in the kitchen, Maisie had come out a couple of times to joke with her regulars and had seen him, though she couldn't remember much about him with that ruddy great hood and him sittin' on his own in the corner. He did look ever so dark and mysterious, make no mistake.

Something prodded her memory and she turned slowly to stare at the cloak and at Rider, who was intent in following the ladies' discussion. As she studied him, she reeled the tape back in her memory, then grasped at a snippet of a scene. *Could he be the one chasin' out some old codger in a pointy hat? Hadn't his hood fallen back a bit then? By heck, it had.* She was good with faces, even ones glimpsed briefly and swathed in hair, and could always pick out the right one after a shave.

Rider caught her eye and ordered another round. Maisie brought them fresh pints and a wink. *Not a bad-lookin' fella: nice green eyes, thick, dark brown hair with just a bit of wave in it.* Yet she could easily picture that clean-shaven face with lots of (reddish?) whiskers and . . . pointier teeth? Nay, couldn't be. She must be getting daft in the head. All this talk of werewolves over the years she'd always assumed was just the castle's idea of self-promotion. Total bunk. Right?

But it did fit with the stories she was hearing: the sudden furry face of a full moon, the lust for luscious throats, the howls she'd heard in the forest. And didn't Doris and Hazel mention something about finding men's clothing on the forest path? Could be the reason for the cloak. . . .

Well, if there was anything to this new werewolf story, that green-eyed fella in the corner certainly looked the most likely suspect. She couldn't wait to catch up with Dinah.

Wolfgang let Rider know that the men on the other side were leaving. Sylvia was now slumped over her fourth Rusty Nail. Alice was gazing vacantly at her original glass of wine, counting the minutes until she could shepherd the star back to her trailer. Ursula had galumphed back to the set. Nothing further would be learned from that corner.

Rider got up to pay their bill, then gestured Wolfgang to leave. "Any idea which way they went?"

"Hunh unh. They jes' mentioned goin' back to they hotel."

"They're not staying here at the convention centre?"

"Nope. It full up with TV honchos and groupies. Them execs probably down in Otternought."

"Maybe Eduardo can confirm. Let's find out what he heard." They headed for the courtyard.

On the other side of the wall in the main bar room, the three businessmen stood up, draining their glasses, and walked past Nigel and his crew, who were nattering to two girls who'd come in hoping to catch the director's notice. The three men piled into a sleek, steel-grey SUV limousine, Tyrone in the passenger's seat. Cyril, in the back with Addison, was on his mobile as the car glided away.

"Bugger! I had rather counted on their staying here and going about on foot," Rider groused. "We'll never tail them on horseback, Wolfgang."

"You think I'm gonna ride that ol' motor mouth?"

Hombre, who said I was going to let *you ride?* Eduardo whinnied through bared teeth.

"Relax, Hay Breath. I can run jes' as fast as you can trot."

"Guys. Knock it off. We're a team. I need both of you. Anyhow, people might wonder if they saw Wolfgang riding pillion behind me."

Es la verdad, Eduardo nickered. *I did hear, in case you're interested, that they're meeting up with some more of* their *"team" at the Otter and Hare in the next village.*

"Otternought?" Rider questioned.

On the contrary, I think we ought. Eduardo tossed his head. Rider did an eye-roll.

"Well, in that case, we oughter go soon," Wolfgang parried and slapped his thigh, wheezing at his joke.

Rider looked at the two comedians silently, then clambered back up in the saddle. "Wolfgang, why don't you catch me up on what you overheard on the way?"

"Oh, you gonna love this!" Wolfgang said, as they cantered away in tandem.

Inside the tavern, Gerry, Ian and Derek ordered another round for themselves and the girls, while Nigel went outside for a fag. He noted Rider, with the wolf he'd wanted to recruit, standing in the yard. It looked like they were talking to the horse. And the horse appeared to be responding. *Did* all *the animals talk here?* Up until now, it had appeared to be only a few of the wild creatures, and that took some getting used to. *We're definitely not in Kansas anymore, Dorothy.* He blew away the smoke, trying to clear his head. Either that was some strong brew, or there was a whole lot more going on in this odd little place than met the eye, or the camera. Werewolves might be just the tip of the weird iceberg. He wondered if he could talk headquarters into lengthening their stay. His nose for a scoop was itching with possibilities.

Back in the main bar, Derek grilled the girls. "So . . . you gals look like you're dressed for the 17th century. Or maybe a part in our film?"

"You could say that," said the plump one with the strawberry-blonde braids. The girls tittered.

"I guess it's obvious," the blonde's petite brunette chum, Barbara, said, smiling winsomely at the lads. "This embroidered bodice I'm wearing was my great-grandmother's."

"Yeah, and mine belonged to my great-great aunt Matilda," Sally chimed in. "She did all this needlework herself. Takes ever so long to put on. I usually need help with the laces. And I've got her original hoop and petticoats under." She made as if to prove it, reaching for her hems.

"That's okay! I believe you!" protested Derek, laughing. "Is all this old-fashioned gear on the folks around here the originals? You know, antiques?"

"Oh, I should think so, don't you, Sally?" the brunette asked her friend.

"Do you think we could afford to rent them with the wages we make up here in this . . . place?" Sally demanded. "'S'one reason we're hopin' to make some extra with your lot. But yeah, the whole village has got loads of vintage duds. 'Sides, they make us wear this stuff over at the convention centre, same as here."

"You girls work across the way, then?" asked Gerry.

"Yeah. Barbara's the concierge. I do room service."

Derek leaned on an elbow and smiled wickedly at Sally. "I'll bet." Sally winked back.

"The baroness does enjoy her traditional displays and parades." Barbara smiled enigmatically.

"You can say that again! All of us are constantly airin' out the ol' ruffled shirts, bustiers and such," explained Sally.

Barbara snorted into her stout. "And such," she murmured.

Ian grinned, enjoying where this was going. Leaning across toward Sally he said, "Tell me about the 'and such' part, lass."

"You cheeky boy!" Sally bumped pint glasses with Ian and swigged.

"So what was it you were startin' to tell us when those business twits went past?" Gerry had noticed that her tale stopped abruptly as the men came abreast of their group.

"Well, have you heard the recent talk about some women gettin' bit on the throat? From the way they tell it, the biters were all new to town and were throwin' around a lot of cash, hittin' on the womenfolk, even the widows! You can't really blame the girls, really, fallin' for the pitch. See, there's not a lot of choice up here, if you're after a good time with the fellas. A guy who doesn't smell like the midden, chats you up and buys you some pricey hooch, well, it makes a pleasant change, doesn't it? But then several of the ladies said these blokes did a quick change at the full moon. Scared the knickers back on 'em."

"What kind of change?"

"They all turned really scary hairy, like in a heartbeat, with big, slaverin' teeth as well. And then jumped 'em!"

"Sounds par for the course, if you ask me," Ian chortled.

"Oh, go on if you don't believe me. Anyhow, that's what we heard."

"Were any of the women hurt?" Gerry asked.

"Not so much. More frightened, really. And then when they got over the shock and were safely away, many looked a bit wistful, like they were still wonderin' what it might have come to."

Derek waggled his eyebrows. "Take note and learn, boys."

"Or not," warned Barbara.

"One of 'em told Dinah it was just like something out of one of those romantic novels, where the heroine is swooped away by a handsome ruffian."

"Every woman's dream," murmured Barbara. Gerry caught her sarcasm and smiled sympathetically at her.

"And did you notice that group of men havin' a powwow next to you? They're definitely not from here, not with those posh suits!" Sally vowed.

"How long has that lot been around here?" asked Ian.

"Month, month and a half, mebbe?"

"Anyone know what they do, why they're here?"

"It's all very hush-hush. They pretty much keep to themselves. But they do cosy up to the gals, from what I've seen. Did you notice the one with the striped school tie, flashing his dimples at us?"

"The one who thought he was God's gift to womankind?" grimaced Gerry.

"Didn't he just?" Sally agreed. "I heard people sayin' that they saw him and that snooty film star, the one with her own trailer, a few nights ago makin' goo-goo eyes at each other over a cracking great bottle of bubbly. It was that stuff that costs a week's pay per bottle, 'Dumb' something. It was French, anyhow."

"Dom Perignon?" Gerry repressed a smirk. "More like a month's salary, if that's the one."

"Sounds right. So any road, our mate Dinah, who works in the castle kitchen, was down in Otternought at the hotel bar on a night off and saw them go off together, gigglin' in the garden. She didn't take much notice until she heard screamin' comin' from the terrace and then the star comes sprintin' through the doorway and away to her car."

"What happened to School Tie?" Derek wondered.

"No one saw him leave," Barbara said. "I gather he went out the back. This is the first we've seen of him in days."

"But then," Barbara went on, "as Dinah didn't see what happened or where the biter went after the bitee retired, we don't really know who bit."

"I suppose that's true," allowed Sally.

"Don't forget, Sal, there's also that tall, dark and dishy fellow that came here Saturday evening in his mysterious cloak and riding boots," Barbara reminded her.

"Riding boots?" Gerry huffed. "Talk about stuff right out of a 'bodice ripper'!"

"Ooh, I never heard nothing about his rippin' any bodices!" Sally was dismayed at missing a juicy detail.

"It's just another term for romance novel, Sally," Barbara explained. "The reason he was wearing riding boots was, I imagine, because he arrived on horseback. Can't give you a reason for the cloak, though."

"Horseback! Probably trollin' for a part in our film. Method actors!" Gerry carped.

"Don't worry, old soul. I heard our talent spy turned him down flat." Derek patted Gerry's back.

"So, who knows?" Barbara continued. "He could be our biter as easily as anyone. He is travelling alone or was, anyway."

"Was?"

"He took up, of all things, with our local wolf celeb. You didn't see them going off just now with his horse?"

Gerry admitted he hadn't. His gaze had been occupied elsewhere.

"With a wolf, you say?" Ian asked. "Don't you think that's intriguing, given your village's history?"

"Oh, you mean the werewolves!" Barb snorted. "You don't take that seriously?"

"The baroness up on the hill apparently does."

"Well, she would wouldn't she?" Barbara got up and excused herself to the Ladies'.

Ian turned to Sally who was being unnaturally quiet. "But those werewolf stories are all just official P.R. bunkum, right? To rope in tourists?"

"If you say so." Sally shrugged and stuck her nose in her pint.

"Come on, Sally girl. Give us the dirt," they urged.

Sally glanced over at the still closed door to the Ladies'. "I wouldn't be so sure it's just PR blather. I've seen what I've seen and heard what I've heard all on my own. Believe me or not, there's been werewolves here for centuries. Stands to reason there'd still be some about. Hard to kill 'em unless you stumble across a whole load of silver bullets. No, I figure they just kept breedin' quietly. They may be wolves only a few nights out of the month, but those ol' hormones keep pumpin' for man or beast. Dinah tells us that there's some kind of blue-blooded order of werewolves up here and the baroness's own hubby's one. Comes from a long line of 'em, one of those distinguished families, they say."

"If that's true, imagine how they distinguished the local gene pool," clowned Derek.

"Hairy legs!" Ian cracked.

"Yeah, yeah." Sally blew out a sigh. "But suppose it *was* true?"

"Offhand then, I'd say this sudden activity doesn't make much sense," Derek replied. "I'm assuming things have been quiet and peaceable for some time, right?"

"That's true. Come to think on it, it only started up perhaps a month ago, at least the rumours did."

"Didn't you say, Sally, that's when those businessmen came around?"

"Yeah. That's right. But that rider showed up not long after the rumours started—just before that star got bit. He coulda been hidin' out like."

"There could be more than one, you know," Ian pointed out to Derek.

"The biters are in cahoots?"

"Or possibly recruiting new ones. Maybe there are rival gangs!" Derek whooped.

Ian sang, "Workin' on the wolf gang . . ."

"I'd like to be the one to scoop that story!" Nigel had just come in after finishing his cigarette and caught the tail end of the conversation. "Could be a wild spin on *West Side Story*." I could call it 'Beast Side Story.' He put his hands up, bracketing a headline: 'The Jets and Sharks . . .' No, make that 'The Fangs and Claws Rumble in . . . '

What do you call this place again?"

Embarrassed mumble from Sally: "Schlock-tongue-inna-bug."

"Say again?"

"*Schlachtungunterburg*," repeated Barbara, who had just returned from the loo. "It means 'slaughter under the castle.' "

Nigel's eyebrows went up. "Charming."

Barb shrugged. "We just call it 'Slaughter.' The other's too much of a mouthful."

"So . . . 'The Fangs and Claws Rumble in Slaughter'?" Nigel chortled. "That works."

"We certainly hope not!" Barbara finished her drink and thanked her hosts. "Sal, luv, we'd better get back to it." She turned to the film crew. "Let us know if you could use some extra wenches in your shoot." Barb lowered her eyelashes coquettishly at Gerry as Sally raised a bared shoulder at Nigel.

"Did I hear they work at the convention centre?" Nigel asked Gerry as they left.

"That's right." Gerry's gaze followed Barbara out the door, lingering a bit long on her pert little behind.

"Well, that should make things interesting for you lot," Nigel reflected.

"Yep, things are lookin' up," Derek commented.

"Maybe they can be our eyes and ears for what's going on in town. If we treat them well. What say I invite them around to our suite in a day or so for some refreshments and see if they've heard anything further?"

"Sounds fine to me!" said Ian. "But do you actually reckon there's anything in this werewolf rumour that's goin' around?"

Nigel stroked his chin. "I didn't at first, but now . . ." Talking to animals and *having them talk back* had seriously rearranged his world view. "I suppose anything's possible in *this* place. 'Where there's smoke there's fire.' And it seems like it's getting plenty smoky around here."

With smouldering thoughts of Barbara, Gerry sighed. "Hope so, mate."

“You just take care, my lad, *you* don’t get bitten!” Derek slapped Gerry on the back as everyone laughed, even Gerry.

“Time we’re getting back.” Nigel finished his drink and brought the empty glasses back to the bar, as the lads trooped out.

“Ooh, it’s all comin’ together!” Elmo rubbed his hands together. “I just love it when the plot thickens, don’t you?”

The three sprites had been sitting in the flowerbox under the tavern’s open window, watching the scenes unwind around them. Not even Eduardo had noticed them. Critics were always good at hiding.

“Yes, you can definitely feel the Hand of Fate stepping in,” said Dim.

Brain shook his head at the mixed metaphor. Elmo guffawed at the mental image.

“What?” Dim demanded.

“Nothing!” they said in stereo.

“Looks to me like the party is moving down to Otternought,” Elmo commented.

“Well then, what say we’re on Outa Here?” Brain punned. And they flowed off toward the next pub.

CHAPTER 10

News Agents

M*onday Night.* In her chamber, Betty was just emerging from her nap when there was a knock on her door. Quickly, she checked her refracted reflection. She liked being a kempt woman. A quick swipe to the coif. Good enough for servants. The baroness strode to her door, flicked off the inside latch, then gave the password to her staff on the other side to draw back the great oak bar.

Cedric entered bearing the customary tray. "Your 'tea,' my lady." He bowed and set the tray with goblet, vial and victuals on her tea table. "I've brought yer some nice ham and cress sandwiches to go with."

"Very thoughtful, Cedric."

"And I may have some news for yer." He waited for the raised eyebrow before proceeding. "Ernie, down at the gate was tellin' us that some lass from that film company came up askin' about gettin' some Nair, that stuff you banned on account of the rash your hubby got."

"Go on."

"Well, Ern questioned her and seems some woman in their bunch got suddenly hairier just since the full moon. Said it sounded to him like the woman mighta been carryin' on with one of them newcomers callin' themselves 'businessmen.' This gal at the gate was in a right panic to find somethin' to take off unwanted fuzz. Must be one of their stars, he reckoned."

"Indeed? I'm not persuaded of the connection between the so-called businessman and the poor woman's hair growth, however."

"Nor was I at first. But Ern, he vowed he's heard some peculiar rumours about this bunch of new fellas. Folks have been noticin' lately that one moment they're hanging about with their suits and briefcases, then come the full moon they've gone missin'. And soon after, women is showin' up with big grins on and bundled in mufflers round their throats like it were winter. The ladies all been claimin' it's some cold that's goin' round. Nobody's buyin' it, but the menfolk haven't been able to get more outa 'em. And they been hearin' a lotta howlin' in the forest and even the churchyard, followed by . . . er . . . other sounds.

"Besides that, I heard meself d'rectly from Doris and Hazel that they been findin' upmarket men's duds here and there on the forest path, just lyin' in heaps, with ripped armholes on the coats."

"Curious. They're the old women who live up by the sties, are they not?"

"That's right. Proper sober old bodies. Don't take to the drink and keep themselves to themselves, unlike their hubbies. They're not ones to gossip, them two."

"How did you come to speak with them, then?"

"As it happens, I was passin' by on me way to the market for His Highness's legs o' lamb and they stopped me. Said word had gotten round that you were interested in any odd goin's on in the neighborhood, 'specially involvin' strangers. Thought it was their duty to tell me."

"I'm glad to hear it. Please send them hampers of whatever you feel they would like to express our appreciation, but keep this information to yourself for now."

"Of course, Your Confidentiality."

Betty groaned inwardly. "Could you also find someone among the staff you feel would be discreet and send him or her out to check this story, please? I'd very much like to find out more about these businessmen and why they're here without delay! Even if there's no connection with the other matter, I feel we're overdue to know what they're up to."

"Dinah from the kitchen is quite chummy with the locals and good at gettin' them to open up. She'd be the best to suss out the situation.

With them dimples and that cute little figger, fellas fall all over themselves to get in tight with her."

Betty wondered if perhaps Cedric also was susceptible to Dinah's charms. "She sounds perfect. Just ensure she understands that no one is to know what she or we are up to. If they do, all will be lost."

"True enough. They'd clam up faster 'n a castanet. But you can rely on our Dinah."

"Wonderful. Would she be able to go out tomorrow?"

"Oh, I believe I can convince Cook to do without her. Shall I tell Cook we'll just do a cold supper for you?"

"If you must." Betty sagged. She'd been looking forward to something hot and tasty.

"What if Cook makes you a nice, hot rarebit?" Cedric had read her mind.

Betty beamed at him. "Just the thing."

Cedric bowed himself out.

Betty was finally sitting down to her tea when her phone rang. Taking a quick gulp of her restorative, she picked up the phone, doing her best to shrug off her annoyance.

"Oh, it's you, Ronny. I'm so dreadfully sorry I haven't been able to call you back, love. Things have been quite impossible here with this film crew in town. I think they're expecting me to throw a dinner party for them. Can you imagine? And now there's this new kerfuffle Count D. came to me about. Something about a bunch of new werewolves in the area who aren't minding their manners. I daresay he's just overreacting to some harmless slap-and-tickle, but one must follow through. What's that? No! In your village as well? This is getting positively gruesome. Do tell!"

The voice on the other end buzzed for a considerable time while Betty listened, agog.

"This sounds much like what Count D. told me, but I just put that down to his usual flair for the dramatic and need for attention. But you say you actually have some corroboration from witnesses?"

The emphatic buzzing continued with the occasional expletive percussion.

"And it's mostly women? Oh, only women. Sounds a bit misogynistic to me. Sure it's not some political prank? Mmmmhmmm. My thoughts exactly. Whoever they are, they're either amateurs or only shopping for hors d'oeuvres and select ones at that. After all, an old, wrinkled throat tastes pretty much the same as a young, pretty one."

The caller's voice buzzed in agreement.

"It's interesting that none of the victims died. And you say they all seemed rather giddy after it?"

Ronny guffawed and gave Betty the lurid details.

"Big grins, not screams? Really? Hmmmm. Quite. Not your usual werewolf, I'd say. This certainly confirms that our poxy predators are of the male persuasion. We really must put our heads together on this one. When are you free?"

Ronny checked her schedule. She could come to tea in a couple of days, if she moved her dental appointment.

"That should work. As long as it's before Prey Day. Shall we say 8-ish, then, this Wednesday? That should give you enough time to travel here after sunset, I think."

Ronny sounded doubtful, complaining about the recent increase in traffic, especially large lorries and excavation equipment.

"Then let's make it around 9 p.m., all right? Super! See you on Wednesday." Betty rang off and pulled the bell for the beleaguered Cedric.

CHAPTER 11

Truckin'

That Same Monday Night. Near midnight, a convoy of unmarked lorries, some with double trailers and some with flatbeds carrying bulldozers, cranes, chippers and other sinister-looking equipment, toiled up the winding pass through the mountains as the villages along its route slept. Few inhabitants would have noticed their progress at that time of night, despite the grumbling gear changes and occasional squeal of air brakes being applied as a turn tightened. Few of the *villages'* inhabitants, that is. High on a peak directly above the tightest turn in what was referred to as "Dead Man's Alley" was a white castle, ensconced in dark conifers. To those struggling to maintain momentum in heavy rigs on a twisty road in the dark of night, it was quite invisible. A single light might have otherwise been detected, high in a tower.

At the *Schloss der unsichtbaren Augen,*[*] Ronny stood at her window squinting through binoculars. "That's the fourth lot of those buggers this past month." Her pointy teeth champed in disapproval. She did not like this. Not at all. She rang for her manservant.

"*Sí, señora*?

"Manuelito, I'm going out. Would you fetch my motorbike, please?"

"*Pero*, at this hour, *señora? Es muy tarde* . . . er . . . late."

"I know how *tarde* it is, but it's important. I'll need you to ride in

---

* Castle of Invisible Eyes

the sidecar. And bring the shotgun."

Manuel's eyebrows shot up. "*Sí, sí,* right away." And he ran downstairs.

Faithful Manuel. No matter what they said about cheap Spanish labour, she could always rely on him. All five feet of him. Still, it wasn't size that mattered, it was aim. And Manuelito had excellent aim.

A few moments later, in helmets and goggles, Ronny and her manservant were hurtling full throttle down the narrow drive from the castle to the highway, Manuel crossing himself fervently. Sitting lower in the sidecar, he was mostly able to duck the pine boughs that hung over the drive. There was just the occasional thwack. As they rounded the last bend, they saw that the last of the lorries was just about out of sight. Ronny adjusted the setting on her goggles to infrared.

"Where are we going, *señora*?" Manuel readied himself for the worst.

"After them!" The Countess of *Badüberwachung*[*] and dependable Manuel sped off in pursuit.

Back in Slaughter's End after their reconnoitre, Wolfgang returned to his flat with Rider, leaving Eduardo in the paddock with fresh water and hay. Rider flopped on the couch, harrowing his hair in frustration. "Is there any beer on hand, or paw?" he asked Wolfgang.

"'Course. I get it delivered by the keg. Got a special spigot that don't need no thumbs. It's not bad. Wanna try some? It's stout."

"Thought you were a cider man."

"Usually. But the vendor don't deliver no cider on account of he pissed off the baroness by pinching her apples without special dispensing something or other."

"Dispensation?"

"Yeah. Like the pope. In these parts she as good as. Here you go." Wolfgang brought over a large mug by fitting both paws through its two oversized handles.

---

[*] Literally, "Bath Monitoring"; origin obscure. Possible mistranslation of "bad oversight.

Rider took a long pull. “Thanks. Just what the doctor ordered.” Still depressed, he moaned, “I just don’t understand how we managed to miss that wizard again. And there was no sign of the businessmen either.”

“Ah, don’t beat youself up. Who knows where them corporate twits has got to? And that wizard, he a slippery customer, that’s for sure. Part of bein’ a wizard, I ’spose. But you jes’ wait. We’ll snag him.”

“I wish I had your faith or at best your nose. That’s what vexes me. With your excellent sense of smell and Eduardo’s excellent hearing and handy talent for surveillance, you’d think we’d have run him to earth by now. Perhaps he’s really left the area?”

“Maybe. But my gut feelin’ is he ain’t gone. I been hearin’ that a fella answerin’ his description has been scoopin’ up the dough at all the local bingo games. Got me to thinkin’: a wand and a knack of vamoosin’ fast would come in mighty handy with bingo. Know what I’m sayin’?”

“I believe I do. Do you ever go these bingo games?”

“No sir! I seen what it done to mates of mine back home.”

“Oh, come on. It’s only bingo. I’d go with you, but the rotter would recognize me.”

“Unh uh! I know where this goin’. I ain’t sittin’ in a room of ol’ blue hairs. No way, man!”

“I get it. You can’t read. Can you?”

“’Course I can. Granny taught me. I jes’ dyslexic.”

“Mmm*hmm*. Well, we need to come up with some plan.”

“Plan? Well why didn’t you say so?” Wolfgang grinned.

“I’m listening.”

“How you get turned into a werewolf?”

“I told you the story.”

“Yeah, but according to the wizard, he wasn’t meanin’ to turn nobody into a wolf, jes’ rearrange they teeth, right?”

“That’s what he said.”

“And didn’t he tell you there was somethin’ messed up with his wand?”

“Well, yes. I do recall its end looked a bit bent.”

"So what would a wizard need to do about a funky wand?"

"Get it repaired? But where could one do that in this back of beyond?"

"Ah ha! Yours truly happens to know jes' the place. Surprised you didn't notice it while we snoopin' around Otternought. Got a big ol' pink neon sign."

"Seriously?"

"Yep. Called 'Wands R Us'. Strange dude named Rumpbuckle owns it. Been in his family a long time. Got his granddaughter running the front. She fixed it up all trendy so it look more like a mobile phone shop. But it the real thing, all right."

"This place is a constant astonishment. Not only a mall and cinema, but a wand repair shop."

"They do got them hidden depths." Wolfgang grinned.

"So you do, my friend." Rider finished his stout. *Why is it people insist on thinking animals are stupid? Once we have this latest environmental fiasco under control, I'll ask Dad if we can't take on some animal rights cases. With the help of Eduardo's multi-species communication skills, I'm sure we're in for some big adjustments.*

"Let's just hope those businessmen haven't thought of that shop before we did."

"It weird we couldn't locate them either, seeing as how they have bidness with the wizard, too. But they obviously have other fish to fry. Too bad it ain't the other way around," Wolfgang growled, rooting for the fish.

"Indeed. At least they haven't checked out of their hotel, so we know they're still there. What time you think this wand place opens?

"Probably nine o'clock. Feel like headin' over there tomorrow?"

"I do. Let's get a good night's sleep and check there first thing, shall we?"

"Fine by me. You go first." Wolfgang pointed to the bathroom. "I need to get out the hardware."

"Blast. I keep forgetting the 'cycle,' " Rider said, using air quotes. "Wish this thing only happened a single night out of the month." *Or none.* "I'll just go outside a minute to check on Eduardo."

"Um, why dontcha let me do that?" Wolfgang asked, carefully closing the curtains.

"Ah. Right. Just be nice, okay? And leave a window ajar at least so in case anything's up, Eduardo can give us fair warning."

Eduardo was snoring softly outside in the paddock but woke instantly at the wolf's approach and whinnied.

"No sneakin' up on you, no sir!" said Wolfgang.

I should hope not. It is my job, after all, to protect my master, Eduardo huffed.

"Tha's good, tha's good. 'Cause, see there some badass dudes around here that don't mind usin' they teeth and claws on somethin' looks appetizin'. I hear horseflesh real sweet."

Señor, I am aware of the dangers. But I also possess a secret weapon. He lifted his tail.

Wolfgang almost made it back inside before detonation. Back upstairs, Rider was sorely wishing he hadn't asked Wolfgang to leave the window open.

Rider sat patiently while Wolfgang, wrapped in a fuzzy yellow robe and blue bunny slippers, manacled him to the bed.

"Nighty night. Sleep tight." Wolfgang shut off the light.

"Thanks, my friend." *This is about as tight as it gets.* Rider didn't have much room to move, but that was probably a good thing.

At the Motel 9 down by the rotary, a light was left on for Herald, who was just then coming through the lobby to his room, humming a bawdy song and jingling a largish purse of coins in one of his pockets. This bingo gig was turning out to be better than winning the Lotto! And in a day or too, he could pay off Rumpbuckle, get his old wand back, and be on his way before anyone put two and three together.

The wizard kicked off his scuffed, pointy-toed shoes and flopped on the bed, punching the remote for Paid-Purview. He scrolled down to "Raise Your Sorcery Acumen" and clicked. It had been a while since he'd been able to continue his night classes. Sadly, like most students, he was soon sound asleep. Except most students don't sleep with their pointy hats on.

CHAPTER 12

Slippery Customers

W*ednesday Morning.* After two blessedly uneventful nights (and another day of fruitless search), Rider had Wolfgang unchain him once again from the bed and made an abrupt dash to the loo. That last pint of bitter probably hadn't been a good idea. He took a long shower, steaming his chafed wrists and ankles in the hot water, then towelled off and peered in the mirror. He could see only slight remnants of his wolf-man shadow. Incongruously, his facial hair had a reddish cast. Combined with the dark hair on his head, when he was in full wolf form it made him look a bit like an Alsatian. He was heartily glad that phase was wearing off!

Rider could hear Wolfgang moving about the kitchen making coffee. It was wonderful how his friend had adapted conveniences engineered for the handicapped. Wolfgang may have been a homeboy from Brooklyn, but he had the makings of an inventor. He also knew how to make a mean cup of Joe. It smelled heavenly, with just the right metallic edge in its European grind to satisfy Rider's recently thwarted cravings. A couple of strong cups would also help take away the sting of the past two days' unrewarding wizard hunt.

Rider dressed and walked into the kitchen, took a mug from the cupboard and helped himself to coffee. The mug had baby ducks on it.

"Got any Equal?"

"Don't you know by now they ain't *nobody* my equal?" Wolfgang's teeth gleamed broadly. He got an eye roll from Rider. "Hey, I know what you mean, but I don't touch that rat poison. I got the real stuff—in that bowl over there with the daisies on it."

"Sugar?" Rider wanted to make sure what substance he'd be putting in his java.

"What is it, darling?" Wolfgang's eyelashes batted.

Rider smiled and spooned the sugar into his mug.

Wolfgang was sitting on a stool, poking with two digits at a laptop. *No different from humans*, thought Rider, *well, males anyway*. He'd never yet seen a male *Homo sapiens* able to touch-type.

"Thought you were dyslexic." Rider raised an amused eyebrow. He stirred his coffee.

"Tha's right. Only it not all the time."

Rider nodded and sipped.

"Jes' when I'm stressed."

Rider nodded again. "And bingo stresses you?"

"Hell, no. Bein' in a whole room full a blue-hairs does! It all that coochy-cooin'. Gets my hackles up. They all nearsighted and wants to drag you ass home, be they little 'Rover.' "

"Ah. So what are you looking up?"

Wolfgang pointed to the Ogle Map he was enlarging. Rider sipped his coffee and peered over Wolfgang's shoulder.

"Remember what I was tellin' you about what them men was discussin' at the pub yest'day, when they didn't think nobody could hear 'em?"

"I do indeed." Rider's expression was black.

"See that marker there? That the baroness's castle. Here's the hill opposite it with that forest path you came in on. And that the village of Slaughter under it, with them silly little one-way streets. That main street comes out there, where you join onto the big highway. Goes all the way west to the next county where it finally turns into a motorway. Couldn't make it no bigger up here on account of the terrain."

"Terrain, huh? That your new word?"

"Tha's right. Mountains and waterfalls and such. Lots of twisty terrain up here. Steep, too. Land mostly owned by the aristocracy so can't jes' go in and dynamite it to straighten the road out. No way the rulin' class would let that happen. Tourism might dry up. Them tourists love all that oldie-world, quaint stuff, including they pointy mountains and bendy roads."

"Okay. . . . Where's this going?"

"Ever tried to drive one of them big double-trailer rigs up a road like that?"

"Can't say I have. Have you?"

"No, but I rode in one. Driver was cussin' up a storm negotiatin' them turns and keepin' all wheels on the road without jack-knifin'. It hard work. Have to use jes' the right combination of air brakes and down-shiftin', then go like hell when you see a straightaway before the next rise. You should see that road in snow. Whooee! Asphalt that jes' plannin' for a accident."

"I noticed a large cross on the top of one of the hills."

"That's where them truck drivers cross theyselves, hopin' they make it."

"If it's so bad, why don't they go another way?"

"They do. The big rigs go 'round. All the provisions that come into these towns is brought in by your smaller trucks. Except lately, there's a whole bunch a big equipment comin' up the pass and always at dead of night."

Rider rubbed his stubble, reminding himself to shave before they left. "If they always travel late at night, how do you know they're coming through?"

"Them air brakes. Make a heck of a racket, but you humans rarely hear it, cause you so used to it, 'specially if you asleep. But it painfully loud to us critters, like a elephant bellowin' through a bullhorn. We can pick that up miles away."

"When did you last hear it?"

"Who said I did? I good but not that good. Check out how far away that is."

Rider did. "I guess you'd need to be a bionic wolf in that case. What is it—about 20 miles?"

"More like 15, but they's lots of stuff in between. But see that dot there?"

Rider nodded.

"That Countess What's-Her-Face's castle. Veronica something. Big pal of the baroness. Her castle is right above that tight bend down there, only you can't really see it much from the road. It surrounded by forest with jes' the highest towers peekin' out from the top. You sure wouldn't notice 'em if you wrestlin' a steerin' wheel around that turn. But Ronny, she got ears like a bat. Likes to stay up late, too.

"What's worryin' me is I ain't sure these rigs is going *through.* Nobody's seen or heard 'em come out the other end of the pass. And why go through all that hassle of bringin' big rigs *through,* when you could go around . . . unless you wasn't doin' either?

"Now, see them roads windin' up away from the highway into the forests between them castles? That practically virgin forest, huge ol' trees, some big around as tanks and more 'n 300 feet tall. Lotta companies would love to get they hands on that. But it supposed to be protected.

"And see that river going down in between? Long time ago, locals noticed some kinda sparkly rocks tumblin' around in there."

"Gold?"

"Nope. Gotta silvery kinda sparkle. I'm bettin' somethin' rare and most likely marketable. All this enchantment here, talkin' critters, wizards, and such, they put down to something in that river, 'cause ever since folks way back started pickin' it up or wadin' in the water, magic stuff been happenin'. My guess is these bidnessmen found out about it and that's what they after. And them big ol' trees is jes' the icin' on the cake. Anyhow, that river makes a handy dandy sluiceway if you needed it. Jes' sayin'."

"You have been doing your reading, haven't you?"

"I always tryin' to better myself.

"Now see, they a bridge higher up linkin' the lil' road on the west, which is the countess's land, to the track on the baroness's land on the east side."

"But look here, Wolfgang, I know these places have galloping grapevines, but are you trying to tell me that this countess heard something last night and you've already gotten the message by, what is it, 7:00 a.m.? Are you some sort of midnight messenger or something?"

"Don't have to be. I heard it from the boys in the 'hood."

"The hood?"

"Sure. Same as back home, only the boys hang out in the woods instead of slums. You think I the only wolf around here?"

Rider was beginning to get the picture. "There *was* some howling last night late, wasn't there?"

"Tha's right. You gettin' it."

"I thought I was dreaming or getting . . . frisky."

"Don't worry. We can tell the difference between wolf-men and real wolves. You guys jes' ain't got the chops or the rhythm."

"And apparently can't make coffee as good, either. Got any more?"

"Sure. Hep youself. And get me a fill-up. They's some croissants and elderberry jam somewhere, too. Check the fridge."

Rider came back with their mugs and a plate of pastry and jam and sat back down. "If this stuff in the water is so precious, why haven't the locals mined it long ago?"

"On account of the baroness and countess. Crown, too. They'd have folks' hides if they did. 'Sides, people kinda suspicious about it and feel it jes' best to leave that glitterin' rock alone.

"Now see this little dot here, between them two castles?"

Rider nodded. "Looks like it's on some unpaved path right in the middle of that woods there."

"Yep. That's Granny's house. It off by itself in a dell, but only about a half mile from the highway. She know all the boys, too. She make a point of befriendin' the beasts and birdies. They say she a witch. Makes no never mind to me 'cause that woman can cook!"

Either talent would come in handy, Rider thought, as his stomach rumbled. "Being that close to the road she'd be likely to hear the traffic, too, if it was loud."

"I 'spect she would." Wolfgang crossed his arms, smugly. "And today's Wednesday."

"That's the day you go over to her house for mid-day dinner, right?" Wolfgang nodded. "Think she'd mind a half-wolf as a guest?"

"I'm sure she be glad to have you. Why don't we go sample her cuisine and see what we can find out?"

"Don't forget, we need to go to that wand place, though."

"No problemo. We hit the wand place first and have plenty of time to get over there by lunch. Oh, and bring Eduardo. She jes' might have a cure for that ill wind he's blowin'."

"What a relief that would be! I just hope the wand shop pans out, searching for the wizard. If we're lucky and pick up the wizard's trail, I don't want to lose it, even for a home-cooked dinner."

"Now see, tha's you negative thinkin'. But I feelin' lucky. We'll track him down one way or another. That's where Granny will come in handy."

"Oh? Do moronic wizards visit her, too?"

"Nah. She play bingo."

Rider and Wolfgang were creeping stealthily down the street toward Wands R Us, peering into walk-through passages between the old buildings on the way. Eduardo had gone ahead, stepping daintily, doing his best to muffle his hoofbeats on the cobbles.

A new pub-to-pub canvassing for the wizard had come up a loss so far in Otternought. Eduardo had also stuck his head in at every stable he came across inquiring of the residents within. Several folks had seen the wizard, just not recently.

As they were coming up to the wand store's entrance, they heard a sudden commotion. It sounded like firecrackers going off inside a troll's iron lingerie. A short, bearded figure burst out of the store's door, ducking amid showers of whistling sprials, bangs and starbursts in pink, purple and acid green exploding violently about his head. He was wearing a singed, starry robe and a pointy hat.

"That's the wizard! Eduardo, go round the other way and see if you can head him off!" Rider panted, running after the fleeing figure. Wolfgang passed Rider easily, but even with a wolf's agile cornering and speed, he lost him. "Damn! Bugger! Son of a—" Rider broke off. Waste of breath.

Eduardo cantered back to them, having failed to locate the wizard from the other direction. He snorted in annoyance. *Merde.*

When it came to *merde*-ish moments, Eduardo preferred the pithy French as opposed to his native Spanish, unless, of course, the circumstance was on the squeamier side. Then he found *mierda* did quite nicely.

"My sentiment exactly, Eduardo." Rider collapsed against a wall in defeat.

"Well that jes' beats all," fumed Wolfgang. "Thought for sure we'd catch 'im. Damn, that old guy fast! 'Course it help to have some magic."

Eduardo nuzzled Rider, who put an arm absently around his neck.

Just before you got to the store, peeping through the window I witnessed a rather heated altercation between the wizard and the proprietor.

"Yes, it's obvious something went wrong there," Rider said, rubbing his brow wearily. "I want to go back and talk to the owner. That okay with you guys?"

Eduardo nodded his head. Wolfgang was quiet.

"What's your thought, Wolfgang? Or are you pining for pork roast?"

"Nah. It ain't that. But I think we gonna need Granny's help for sure. That wizard, he long gone now. Anyhow, we still in time to eat. But it wouldn't hurt to talk to ol' Rumpbuckle before we hit Granny's."

Rider and the dispirited Eduardo agreed and they turned back toward the storefront.

The bell tinkled when they entered the store. Eduardo shied a bit at the sound. Through the open door he commented, *I hope the percussion has concluded. My nerves are a bit frayed. I'll just wait a few doors down, if it's all the same to you.*

Rider turned back and patted Eduardo's withers. "Don't blame you. I'm feeling a bit thrashed, myself. We shouldn't be long."

At first, they couldn't see anyone about. Only the disarray amongst the fluorescent-lit displays indicated that an unwelcome visitor had been there. Then a small head with blonde pigtails and fuchsia fringe poked cautiously above a counter on the side wall.

"'Cor! I thought it might be that wizard come back!" Standing up, she looked about her, a bit dazed. Then she forced a dutiful smile and said, "Sorry about the mess. I'll tidy up straight away. May I help you gentlemen with anything?"

"Yes, in fact," said Rider. "Can you tell us anything about that wizard who burst out a moment ago in a display of fireworks?"

"Er . . . ," the girl dithered nervously, sliding her eyes toward the back room. The curtains parted.

"I believe I can help you in that regard. Rumpbuckle's the name. Dr. Rumpbuckle." The proprietor bowed and extended a hand to Rider and nodded cordially to Wolfgang. "Shall we go back? It's more private and not quite so . . . bright," he finished with tact.

They went through to Rumpbuckle's cosy back room.

"This real nice," Wolfgang remarked approvingly. "No offense, but I prefer the old style. Real homey."

"I agree with you heartily, my friend," said Rumpbuckle. "But my granddaughter out there insisted the business needed a 'fresh face,' as she called it. She's all for the glittery and modern. And after all, one day this will be hers. Dorie's all that's left of our family."

"That okay. Family's important."

"So . . . you were inquiring about the wizard who just left?"

"Yes. Do you know where we might find him?" Rider asked.

"And your business with him is . . . ?"

Rider made introductions and filled him in on the sorry saga, Rumpbuckle nodding at intervals. "So you see, Doctor, my acquaintance with your customer has been rather life changing, and not in a good way. I'd very much like to reverse that process."

Rumpbuckle stroked his chin in thought. "I deduced as much. I've been hearing of various other nefarious dealings and misdeeds concerning that wizard."

"Boy, that some display when the dude left! You hire that stuff out?"

Rumpbuckle chuckled. "Not usually. But I am sure you can appreciate the, er, karmic humour of it."

"That we do!" Rider chortled. "I just wish we could have nabbed him. He keeps slipping away from us. But why all the fireworks?"

"That, my good fellows, is just a little insurance I install in my products. When a customer tries to pull a fast one, he gets a rather spectacular surprise. It's a fairly simple spell, but they never seem to see it coming. Astonishing, really, being that my serious clientele are well schooled in magic. Still, they always say a scoundrel never expects detection."

"He tried to get outa payin'?"

"Partly. He came to me to have his defective wand repaired and I'd given him a temporary wand to use in the meantime. What customers don't know is that it keeps a secret log that tracks any unethical dealings the user employs. The results are then reported to me. We wandmakers are not permitted, by our fellowship, to interfere unless bodily harm is imminent. I also installed an anti-theft spell. If *that* alarm had gone off, you would have heard it in the next valley!" Rumpbuckle was enjoying himself.

"So what happened?" Rider asked.

"Well, he came in to pick up his old wand, which I had just repaired. It turned out beautifully, too, better than new. I gave him my bill and asked for return of my wand. He counted out the correct *looking* coins and I pretended not to notice they'd been enchanted. My wand had reported that to me previously. They were actually toll tokens. Naturally, I don't enjoy being cheated, and I *had* warned him from the start that payment would have to be legal tender. But I bided my time, as I was interested to see just how stupid the man was. My suspicious were soon confirmed. As Dorie turned her back to wrap his wand, he tried to pocket mine."

"That musta been when Eduardo saw you all hollerin' at each other."

"I admit I allowed myself to get a bit riled. Still, I shook him down for the gold and you gentlemen got the entertainment of seeing justice served."

"Granddad's the best at that!" Dorie said, entering the parlour. "I'm so sorry, Granddad. I let that old duffer get the best of me."

"Don't distress yourself, Dorie. I myself have had a few get off with the goods, or nearly so. You're young still. You'll learn. I have great faith in you." Rumpbuckle put a fond arm around her. "And that's what insurance is for."

"Thanks, Granddad." She gave him a grateful smile and a hug.

"I've been hearing things, Doctor," Rider pursued, smiling, "that make me think that my horse and I aren't the only victims of this interfering wizard around here."

"Yes, Mr. Rippon, I've been hearing much the same. My sources have mentioned some male visitors in the area who are suspected of shape-shifting and attempted ravage during the past full moon or so. I've made inquiries about the attacks, and everything seems to confirm that they were done by werewolves." He studied Rider with interest.

"Well, I didn't do it!" Rider replied hotly. "I've been trying to find that bastard who changed me and make him turn me back to normal so I can return to my old life. Wolfgang here has been a true friend, binding me to the bed at night to keep me from . . . being a monster. I was damned lucky to have met him."

"Ah, thanks, dude."

"Now, now. I didn't really believe you were to blame, Mr. Rippon."

"You may as well call me Esmond," said Rider, pacified.

Rumpbuckle bowed his head. "In that case, you may call me Lucius."

"Wolfgang, tell Lucius what you heard at the pub about those businessmen."

"Oh! Right. Well, it like this . . ."

As Wolfgang concluded his report, Rumpbuckle steepled his fingers under his chin. "Well, this certainly puts a different spin on things. As I'd put a spell on his old wand to discourage any further silliness, I was willing to let the idiot go. But now it seems imperative we find him and that we also learn more about these corporate visitors and what they're planning. From what you've told me, it seems more than possible that there is a connection to these new werewolves I've been hearing about. Of course, there has always been werewolf activity in this region, going back centuries."

"You say 'of course.' So that really isn't just colourful propaganda to entice tourists or another of Wolfgang's stories?" Rider ignored the look Wolfgang shot him.

"Oh, dear me, no. But the baroness, with my help naturally, has helped the native den see the error of their ways and keep their habits under civilized control. Her own husband is one, you know."

Wolfgang whacked Rider's arm. "See?" Turning back to Rumpbuckle, he added, "But that gotta bite!" His intentional pun went noticed.

Rumpbuckle actually guffawed. "Yes, indeed. What wonderful vernacular you young folk use! Oh, my!" He wiped his eyes. "But you know, the bite goes both ways," he chuckled anew.

"What you mean?"

"The baroness, as you probably know, Wolfgang, is a vampire."

"Crikey!" Rider exclaimed. "It's really true, then?"

Wolfgang harrumphed, arms crossed.

"Indeed," Rumpbuckle wheezed. "It's quite a good story. But we must put our heads together on this. I have some excellent brandy. Shall I get some glasses? I could do with a drop of something myself."

"Thanks for your kind offer," Rider said. "I very much want to hear your story, but I'm afraid we have a luncheon appointment and must go."

"Ah, well. Another time, perhaps."

"I wanna hear it, too. Hey, y'all gonna be around this evening? When we get back from our appointment, we'll catch up with you, if that okay."

"I would be honoured. Just ring the bell, even if it's after hours. Dorie will fetch me. We live just above."

"Thanks, Lucius. I'm very glad to have made your acquaintance." Rider shook his hand. "We'll be back as soon as we can. I can tell I need a good filling in!"

Eduardo trotted up as he heard the store's bell tinkle again. Rider climbed on and set off with Wolfgang to Grandmother's house.

CHAPTER 13

Summit Meeting

W*ednesday Night.* Just as a flamboyant orange sun ceased its fandango and plunged petulantly offstage, like a rebuffed contestant, behind the dark conifers surrounding the baroness's castle, there was a crunch of wheels on the gravel of the circular drive before the baroness's main entrance. Swathed in gold lamé under her black cape and feather boa, a voluptuous redhead descended from a shiny red carriage, resplendent with gilt embellishment and heraldic crest. With her height, the black sombrero she was sporting barely cleared the door of the carriage. Her manservant scurried around and banged the ponderous knocker. On the door. The sloppy slap of slippers was audible from within and, after some muttered oaths accompanying the grinding of keys in rusty locks, the huge oak door was pulled open slowly, with foreboding screech. Cedric peered myopically at the countess.

"Oh, it's you, Your Countless. We was expectin' you. Walk this way." Cedric limped on his bunions down the flags of the hall, with Ronny and Manuel following behind.

"*Lo siento, señora, pero* I no sure I can walk that way." Manuel whispered.

Ronny stifled a guffaw mid guff and replied with a straight face, "Why Manuelito! *Es muy facile.* First you put your right foot so, and then . . ." She demonstrated—hop, stagger, stagger—mimicking Cedric's bizarre gate, Manuel giggling behind.

"Ronny, pet! It's too good of you to come!" Betty bussed her friend's cheeks, taking care not to smudge her lipstick. "Come in, come in! I've got a little treat for us." She ushered her friend into her private parlour. A chuckling fire lit the room charmingly from beneath the marble mantel.

Not troubling to see if it was occupied, Ronny tossed her large chapeau onto the settee next to the hearth, thereby bonking Durrell, the cat who'd been napping there. A dangling peacock feather swiped his nose. With a startled yowl, he jumped down and stalked off in high dudgeon, sneezing violently. *Immortals! (Pfft!) You just can't (Pfft!) train them to be (Pfft!) civilized.*

"Oops. Sorry. Didn't see the poor fellow." Ronny was more of a dog person: she much preferred her pets to be sycophants. She shrugged, gave her red bob a fluff and threw herself down next to the hat, her long legs propped up on the far arm of the settee, toasting her tootsies by the fire. The cat hunkered in the shadows, glaring at them through yellow eyes slit in speculation.

"So what's the great treat, darling?"

Betty brought her over a crystal goblet of crimson liquid, holding a goblet of her own in her hand. "It's *Château de l'Égouttoir*, 1949. Take a sip. Scrumptious!"

Ronny was pleased. "That *is* a lovely treat! Your own?"

"Of course. All local," Betty replied.

"Chin-chin!" They clinked glasses and Ronny sipped appreciatively. She held her glass up to the light, twirling it. "Nice legs."

"The veins were even better," Betty giggled and swallowed, savouring the complex flavours of iron and tobacco, with just a hint of diabetes for sweetness.

Ronny patted the red plush chair next to her. "Here old soul, take a load off, for heaven's sake. No need to play hostess with me."

Betty drew the chair over and sat down with her stockinged feet up on the Sheraton coffee table. Her staff would be aghast. "So tell me your big news, darling. I've been dying to hear! Well, not literally, obviously. I've plenty to tell you as well, and I'd rather speak here. We have a little time before dinner."

Ronny set her glass down carefully on a side table and sighed heavily. "It's worse than I thought," she began.

Ronny told Betty about the night she and Manuel had followed the convoy down the highway, adding the details Ronny's solicitor had later filled in.

What happened was . . .

Ronny and Manuel had seen the lorries turning up the small logging road that wound up the mountain, instead of continuing down the highway out of the valley. She had quietly pulled her motorbike under the cover of overhanging brush about a quarter mile up the logging road, switched off the engine and dismounted. Manuel took the rifle from the sidecar's bracket, and the two of them followed the lorries quietly at a distance as the rigs toiled up the old, dirt road. Ronny tracked them easily, using the infrared sight on her binoculars. The road twisted and turned through the trees along the left side of the river, mirroring its turns. Another mile or so up the road around a left-hand bend, the rigs came to a stop in a clearing. *That clearing wasn't there before!* She could see that someone had recently felled some young trees to make a space wide enough to park large equipment. On her land!

Ronny was revving up to accost the men and give them a thorough dressing down. *What in blazes did they mean by this trespass!* She felt a tug at her sleeve. Finger against his lips, Manuel pantomimed, "Wait! Better first to see what they're up to." Ronny nodded and they crept closer.

It was obvious that the foreman supervising the off-loading was already familiar with the layout of the terrain. He directed the men unerringly where to put what, including two alarming bulldozers and something with a folded up crane and man-sized bucket aloft. Ronny's heart was beating wildly, but she calmed herself. Logically, they couldn't set to work for some time, and certainly not in the dark. *But how soon before they* did *start?* she worried. *And start doing what, exactly?* Time was definitely of the essence—to her and to the forest and all its creatures. It might also be to these villains.

With her binoculars, she scanned the sides of the lorries for a logo or some other indication of whose company they belonged to. They were all unmarked.

"*Muy* sneaky," Manuel whispered.

"*¡Verdad! Muy, muy* sneaky," Ronny whispered back.

They waited a while for further enlightenment, but the crew merely finished unloading and climbed back in the lorries, turning with difficulty in the small space to go back to the highway.

Not wanting to get caught in their headlights, Ronny and Manuel retreated hastily, creeping under cover back to her bike. They just managed to duck out of sight as the convoy lumbered past. She clamped on her helmet and goggles, fired up her bike and charged off to follow them, at a distance, to the highway. Manuel had to use the muzzle of the rifle to vault into the sidecar to avoid being left behind. Just as she expected, they went back the way they came.

"Why aren't you wearing your helmet, Manuel!"

"I did not have the time, *señora*." He dragged on his helmet obediently, then felt surreptitiously under the cowling for any damage to his man parts, which had taken the brunt of the vault. *Bueno. Los dos muchachos están intactos. The little wife will be glad.*

Ronny was steaming mad when she returned to her castle. Without considering the time, she rang up her solicitor. He wasn't too pleased to be wakened at that hour, but when he heard about what she and Manuel had witnessed, he sat up at complete attention and grabbed his spectacles, pen and notebook off his nightstand.

"My dear Countess. This is intolerable! I can see why you're in such a state. I will make inquiries first thing in the morning. That land is under protection of the Crown, as well as yours and the baroness's, and has been for centuries. It's quite clear in all the documents. Whatever is going on cannot be above board. I'll get to the bottom of this, you may be sure!

"You say there were even trees that were felled?" Ronny heard scribbling accompanied by a growl from the other end. "When I find out who's behind this, I'll make sure they're prosecuted and fined cripplingly. We'll stop them in their tracks, damn 'em!"

"Thank you, Sidney. I knew I could rely on you. Will you ring me tomorrow to let me know whatever you've learned, even if it's not much?"

"That I will, Your Ladyship." Sidney Van der Chase rang off, and sat pondering in his bed.

He too was furious. Those woods were sacred to everyone in the valley, not just to the gentry. The owners of the tracts under concern had been gracious, right down the years: locals had always been allowed to walk the land and even fish in the river, as long as they didn't litter or sell the fish. The forest was in their blood.

Sidney had fond memories, as a boy, of tramping up the little trails by the river and even catching his first trout. The way the light had streamed down in shafts through the ancient high canopy . . . A true sanctuary. By God, they weren't going to get away with this, even over his dead body! (The countess could help with that obstacle, if it came down to it.)

By 7:09 a.m., he'd gotten on the horn to various parties he knew to be reliable and discreet, including a private detective. This last party was normally called only when a trail of blame went dead, but Sidney wasn't taking chances.

The countess owned the western side of the river and the baroness the east, with a stone bridge crossing the river connecting their lands. Sidney, of course, had also interviewed the baroness, just to tie up any loose ends.

Betty'd said she'd not been approached by anyone, since possibly some time around 1840, concerning the river and its mineral store. And no one would dare ask permission to cut any of their trees! And it had been decades since the Crown had scared off those blackguards in the hafnium caper over on Mt. Otter. Although . . . the baroness did recall that a while back, Count D. had made some attempts to purchase the tracts on both sides of the river from Ronny and her. They had both made it clear that they were not interested. What could he want with their land anyway? Count D. owned the whole top of the mountain above it. His castle had a better view than either of theirs, for heaven's sake. And the river flowed straight from his estate.

Sidney called Ronny back, relating what Betty had said about Count D.'s estate.

"That's right! I'd quite forgotten that," Ronny said.

"As had I, Countess. His estate is so far back and so much higher, I was concentrating on the land to the immediate sides of the river, up to where the logging road continues onto his land. How does one get to his place?"

"Oh, he has his own road on other side of the mountains, not from our side. It's a lovely drive, though a tad long."

"But one wouldn't have to go that way to gain access to the river, I take it?"

"Not at all, Sidney. There's always been a track of sorts all the way up from Betty's side. It continues from where the logging trail crosses that old bridge. Gets a bit narrower just there due to new growth. The village kiddies are constantly trooping up and down it through the woods."

"Interesting. But why is there a logging road, if the trees are protected?"

"The trees on the baroness's side are protected, as are mine. That's mostly virgin, old-growth timber in there, positively primeval. But the count hasn't placed any protection on his lot. You know how he is. What the locals call the 'logging road' came into being to gain access to his woods above to hunt. We also allow our villagers to cull any fallen timber for firewood. That track continues up over the rise into the backcountry a bit, more or less to the base of the next biggish hill, which is the one that goes up to Count D.'s. He said the reason he wanted to buy those specific bits, or at minimum obtain an easement giving him access to both sides of the river, is that he wanted to widen and pave the old road and continue it up to his castle, so that he could come down our way more easily.

"But doing that would have meant taking out some of the largest and loveliest trees. I must say, we're truly blessed that the people here, as ill-educated as they are, love our old forests and would gladly lynch anyone who harmed them, including ourselves."

"I feel exactly the same, Veronica," Sidney replied fervently. "Er, excepting yourselves, of course. To you I would merely serve papers."

"Thanks. And anyway," continued Ronny, "what does he care about how long his bloody drive is, when he can fly whenever he chooses?"

"Perhaps to lower the cost of the delivery of goods?" Sidney speculated.

Ronny snorted. "The only 'goods' he's interested in these days are the jugulars of young maidens. And even for that, he usually 'dines out.' "

Sidney withheld a humorous rejoinder. "But someone still has do the washing and such, and staff must find it difficult to go that far."

"What staff he has now live in, although they all have cars. There's a large garage for them. The occasional carpenter or whoever comes by van, and Count D.'s road is quite good. Even if there were a road put in from our side, his castle would be much easier to reach from the flat plain on his side. No one in our valley would work for him."

"Could he be interested in gaining the water rights to the river?"

"I don't see why. I've always heard that the source is right on his land."

"Yes, the baroness said as much."

"I know he diverts some of it for his household needs," Ronny continued. "And isn't there some law that prohibits a private citizen's owning the water itself?"

"There is indeed. Permits of use one may be obtained, as Count D. has evidently done. But the river itself is owned solely by the Crown for the general use of its citizens, up to the high-water mark."

"Well, there you are! Barring the odd seasonal flood, there's bloody little variation in the water height of a river."

Sidney removed his glasses and ran his fingers through his thinning grey hair, thinking hard. If the high-water mark were to be expanded several feet and kept there, what could be gained? "What if the river were dammed?"

Ronny tittered, "You're talking to one of the damned, Sidney. Or so those preachers constantly tell us. But the river can't be damned. The vicar draws his holy water from it."

"No, no. I must rephrase: What if someone put a dam on the river?"

"Oh, I see! But why on earth would they do that?" Ronny demanded. "And anyway, they'd need our permission, which we wouldn't allow."

"But what if someone wangled a variance to divert the river, where it crosses beneath the highway, for some concocted reasons?"

"Surely, they'd have to notify us!"

"Unless they were planning to place blame on bureaucratic torpor," he murmured. "I'm just thinking. If the high-water mark were higher, say by at least 20 feet on either side, what would happen?"

Now Ronny was truly alarmed. "Well, for one, the trees on either side would sicken and die from the flooding and would have to be felled as potential hazards. That tract straddling the river has become a sort of unofficial national park. We've even put in picnic tables for the residents, which means we owners have a duty to maintain safety. And some of the biggest and handsomest trees are found right along that trail."

"Would those trees fetch a good price, if they were felled?"

"Good God, you're not suggesting . . ."

"I'm not sure what I'm suggesting. But it seems there's at least one lucrative resource up there that has caught the interest of persons, as yet unknown, and I wouldn't say it was due to a philanthropic bent of mind."

"And if one were on the up and up, why the dead-of-night foolishness and unmarked vehicles?"

"Why indeed?" The phone line went quiet for a spell. Gears were mentally turning. "Well," Sidney resumed, "I have my best gumshoe out sleuthing the matter. And I think I'll have a chat with the count. I suppose I'll have to wait until after sunset, as usual?"

"Not necessarily. Old Count D. likes to dabble in all sorts of new technology. I've heard he had an entryway and a whole suite on the ground floor made light-proof. That must have cost a bundle! He has that new light-proof carriage, as well. He might even be amenable to coming to your office."

"Has he? That puts things in a very different light," Sidney reflected.

"I'd always assumed that, like you and the baroness, his movements were limited according to the hours of daylight. With such a vehicle, he might be able to go almost anywhere at any time. And without the need of petrol, any distance, as long as the horses held out."

"Hmmm. Maybe Betty and I need to reconsider this progress stuff. He does love to goad us with tales of his travels. Count D.'s very fond of outings. Says he gets lonely up there. I suppose it is a bit remote. I don't know what I'd do without the telephone. How did we manage without it all those centuries?"

"I'm sure I wouldn't know," Sidney smiled to himself. "I think, my dear Countess, it wouldn't hurt to send someone up that track in daylight. When's the last time you went up?"

"Gosh, I couldn't say. But what a cracking good idea. I'll send Manuel. He blends in beautifully. Those small, dark Spaniards tend to, don't they? And he walks as quiet as an Indian. I've seen him scare the living daylights out of some wolves he sneaked up on."

"How did you manage that, I mean to see him? Without getting . . . burnt?"

"Infrared binocs, naturally," Ronny smirked. "And it was twilight."

"Not much gets by you, my dear."

She sighed. "Sadly, it appears that it has."

Sidney clucked in sympathy. "But not for long, dear Countess. Not for long."

"So that's the scoop," Ronny finished. "I'm hoping to hear more shortly, but Sidney says they've encountered quite a number of blind alleys."

Betty wilted in her chair, her aperitif forgotten. "I had no idea. This is quite dreadful. Here I was wrapped up in this niggling 'wolf' problem. This activity you've uncovered appears far worse."

"True. The potential for disaster on a catastrophic scale is much deadlier."

Betty got up and paced the floor. "Destruction of natural beauty aside, do you realize what would happen to this valley if that old growth on those steep hills were cleared? The mudslides from the erosion! Why, the valley would be buried in a heartbeat with the first spring torrent."

"And all the woodland folk! They'd die, too, or lose their homes." Ronny reminded her.

Betty couldn't bear that. Both Ronny and she had wandered the mountains in the happy days of their youth, before "the change." They knew all the birds and beasts living there, and their children, and, thanks to their off-beat heritage, could converse with them as well as they could with each other. These creatures were *family*, not sentimental projections. The two of them had made a blood-sister vow that when they came of age and took over running their respective castles, they'd take just as good care of the creatures as their tenants. (Possibly better.) They considered it a sacred trust, as had their forebears. It wasn't simply a matter of protecting supply.

Betty flopped back down on her chair and stared at the fire.

Ronny patted her hand. "Don't stress yourself, lovey. All will be well. I know it will. And don't forget," she grinned evilly, "if it appears to be getting out of hand, 've haff vays'!"

Betty sat back, mollified. Ronny always could get her out of a funk.

"Yes, damn 'em, we do, don't we?" Betty grinned back. "Although we've worked so long and hard to get past all that and be proper stewards. I'd hate to erode the trust we've gained from our people by resorting to those old tactics, even if it is with enemy outsiders."

"I understand, truly. But I'd do it all the same, if that was the only way to keep these parvenus from destroying our little Eden."

"So would I, Ronny. So would I. Let's just hope it doesn't come to that."

Ronny picked up her glass again, taking a healthy swallow. "Well, that's my news. Wish it were better. So tell me yours. Last I heard you were up to your elbows in hairy claws and fangs, figuratively speaking."

Betty chuckled at Ronny's turn of speech. "Honestly, I still don't have much more to tell you, but before you say it, we can definitely state that whoever these half-wolves are who are causing problems, they're not our bunch. Heinrich made sure of that. Yes, I know ours get up to some high-jinks now and then, but they stick to the rules nonetheless. All consenting adults and no mortal injuries. Just playful nips."

Ronny was about to ask, impishly, where said nips occurred when they heard the sonorous clang of the front door knocker echo up the stairs.

"Whoever could that be?" Betty looked at Ronny.

"What a bonehead I am! I completely forgot to mention that I'd taken the liberty to invite Sidney Van der Chase over tonight. I hope you don't mind?"

"Not at all. Glad of it. I'd like to hear his recommendations."

"Oh, goody."

"Let me just tell Cook there will be another at dinner. Don't worry. We have plenty." She rang for Cedric. They both jumped at the immediate answering knock. *'Struth! Was the old codger sleeping out there? Or listening, damn him?*

"Yes, Your Anxiety?"

"Cedric! Were you were eavesdropping?" Betty accused.

"No, madam. 'S'no need to drop from them eaves. I ken hear just as easily outside the door."

Ronny chortled. "I'd forgotten what a dear clown Cedric is!"

Cedric sneaked her a sly smile.

" 'Clown' is the operative word, here." Betty turned steely eyes to Cedric. "I'm referring to your unrepentant listening in on our conversations, as you well know."

"It's me job, in't it? Gotta keep up with what's going on so's I can anticipate what's going to go on, if you get my drift."

"And you think that's good excuse, do you?"

"Good enough for me, assumin' you want me to go on screenin' your calls, friskin' callers, monitorin' for nefarious activities, and so on. And don't forget them background checks on the donors," he added, aggrieved.

She knew when she was beat. "Yes, well, please remember that one needs one's privacy at times."

"I wouldn't have bothered tonight, Grand Inquisitor, only you'd asked me to send out our Dinah, see what she found out about your new wolf problem. Figured you'd want to know. I'm missin' me show on the telly."

"I'd quite forgotten about Dinah. But I believe Ronny's solicitor has just arrived. Please tell Cook there will be another at dinner. And when we're through with dinner, send Dinah to us."

"She's 'ere now, with yer new guest."

Cedric opened the door and Dinah came in, curtseying, a bemused Sidney in tow.

"Very efficient staff you have here, Baroness." Sidney's eyes swivelled uncontrollably toward the withdrawing Dinah.

Gad! Those dimples are *quite lethal! Cedric, the old dog, was spot-on regarding their allure. We appear to have more weapons at our disposal than previously supposed.* Betty smiled.

After Dinah deposited Sidney, Betty stood and held out her hand to him. "Mr. Van der Chase, how good to see you again. Veronica and I are both so fortunate to have such a tireless warrior in our court."

Ronny nodded. "And canny."

"Thank you for the compliments." Sidney bowed over Betty's hand. "I hope I continue to deserve your respect, although these days I'm not sure about the 'tireless' aspect. But I'll fight the good fight as long as there's breath in my body, you may both be assured. And please, it's just Sidney, amongst us."

"Pull that chair over to the fire, Sidney, and get comfortable. Dinner should be ready momentarily. Would you like a glass of something?" Betty gestured to the set-up on the sideboard. Sidney eyed the bottles dubiously.

Ronny noticed and chuckled, "Don't fret, old bean. We won't try to make a convert of you, not unwillingly anyhow. If you prefer white, I'm sure Betty can rustle up a nice Pouilly-Fuissé or something."

"I prefer red, actually, as long as it's vinous, not, er, veinous."

Betty tittered, "My dear Sidney, never fear. In that case, I had this lovely 1940 bottle of Louis Cadeau beaujolais brought up. It's quite drinkable, even to us." She poured him a glass and brought it over.

Sidney thanked her and took a sip. "Very nice. I'll have to remember the vintner."

"Oh, we've given up on *that*, haven't we, darling? The veinous ones, I mean." Betty and Ronny exchanged amused glances and burst out in snickers. The sonorous echo of a metal bin lid's being struck sounded below. "There's the gong!" Betty hopped up. "We'd better leg it to the dining room or Cook will have a tizzy."

Sidney appeared only mildly discomfited at Betty's previous remark. He was reasonably certain that he was safe from their predatory interests and thus unlikely to become a donor. After years of service, he knew where their skeletons were and, more to the point, when.

After dinner, the castle staff cleared away the remains (of the meal) while Betty and her guests returned to her parlour, taking their glasses with them. Cedric came in and replenished the logs and their beverages as they settled themselves around the fire, then withdrew. In a moment, there was a respectful tap on the door. Dinah, in starched apron and cap, entered demurely, stopping just inside the threshold. Betty glanced sideways at Sidney to see if his gaze was where she figured it would be. It was.

"You asked for me, my lady?" Dinah enquired.

"Yes. Thank you for coming so soon after dinner. I've heard good reviews from Cedric of your success with surveillance."

Dinah curtsied her thanks.

"We've been discussing tonight some other business that concerns us, which may require your help as well, but for now I'd be grateful to hear what you found out yesterday concerning this rumour of new wolfish pestilence."

"Yes, madam. I'm happy to help."

"Here, take this chair, Dinah. You may as well be comfortable."

Durell hadn't wanted to miss anything so had slunk closer. "Very kind of you, madam." Dinah sat gingerly in the proffered chair, one foot just missing his tail. Post-haste, he scooted back to his corner, harrumphing cattily.

"Well, I went first to see my friends, Sally and Barbara. They work over at the convention centre."

Betty nodded. "I think I remember them. Go on."

"The girls told me a few of the local womenfolk have been mauled by a man or maybe men new to this area. Each time, so the women said, it seemed like a sudden change came over the gentleman when the full moon came out and what started out to be a bit of canoodling turned into something a lot more violent."

"Can you be more specific?" Betty asked.

"Yes, madam. I only hope you won't take offense."

Betty knew Dinah was referring to Heinrich. "One should not take offense at the truth, however personally close it may be. My husband joins me in that sentiment." She smiled graciously at Dinah.

Dinah filled them all in on what Sally and Barbara had earlier related, including the chewed film star and what she learned from various indignant husbands.

"I wonder if these corporation men here on business might have any connection to this rash of ravishing."

Dinah looked a bit dubious. "Possibly. But Maisie, she's the barmaid at the tavern, didn't credit it. She's always kept up with what's going on in the area. I mean, she's in a perfect position to do so, isn't she?"

Betty nodded at Dinah's logic. "And she has her doubts?"

"Yes. I went to see her after talking to Sally and Barbara. You see, there's another gentleman who's also come into the region just recently, on horseback. He came into the pub wearing a cloak, with a hood covering his face, and was making inquiries."

"What sort of inquiries?" Ronny asked.

"Well, Maisie wasn't positive, as she wasn't waiting on him the night he came in. Basil was. But I heard there was some kind of ruckus involving a wizard. Folks who were in the pub that night saw this mystery man chase an old fellow in a pointy hat with stars on out the door and into the stables. Basil said it was some wizard the rider was after. When he came back inside a while later, he was dragging the wizard by the collar, and he was oozing oil."

"The rider was oozing oil?" Betty pictured a tinker turned auto repairman.

"No, the wizard was. They have a grease pit in the old stables. Richie, their mechanic, makes a bit of money on the side, working on customers' cars."

"Sounds like this wizard fellow took an unintended swim." Ronny crowed.

"It was more likely sinking than swimming," Dinah said. "Someone had left Richie's creeper in the way and the old guy hit it and got launched into the pit. Richie said he's not taking the blame. He puts all his tools up neat and regular." She'd been sweet on Richie at one time.

"Could have been a setup to nab the wizard, planting the creeper like that. Perhaps this equestrian had an accomplice," Sidney considered.

"I don't know anything about an accomplice, but he's been hanging around with Wolfgang. He's one of our local grey wolves—frequents the tavern," Dinah explained to Ronny and Sidney. "Oh, and someone said they thought they saw the stranger talking to his horse."

"A mere eccentricity, probably."

"It's possible, sir, but Maisie said it seemed like the horse was answering back. That film director thought so, as well."

"Did they indeed?" With all the magic that oozed out of the region's very stones, Sidney had never before heard talk of a horse's being able to speak. Nor cows, pigs and sheep, come to that. With goats, it was never a certainty, but goats were wily that way.

"Yes, and then she told me she overheard the businessmen on Monday also complaining about some wizard *they* were trying to locate. They weren't at all happy with him, from the sound of it. It was one of those businessmen I was telling you about who was out with that starlet the other night."

"Did you happen to get a look at him, this businessman?"

"Yes, sir."

"And did he look at all peculiar?"

"Not really, not when I saw him. When she started hollering that night, no one I know saw who did it. Could have been almost anyone. Excepting your husband and his friends, I'm sure," she added hastily. "But Maisie says her money's on this mysterious rider, especially as he's chums with Wolfgang."

"Well, your report has been very enlightening, my dear. I'm sure my patronesses here are grateful, as I know I am." Sidney beamed at Dinah.

"We are indeed exceedingly grateful, Dinah," Betty assured her. "It sounds to me as though we should find Wolfgang's new acquaintance and have him brought here for . . . examination." She hesitated and looked at Sidney. "As the moon is past full I think it would be safe." He nodded and Betty turned back to Dinah. "Would you be available to do some more sleuthing for us, when time permits?

"Of course, madam. It makes a nice change. I've already asked the girls to keep their eyes and ears peeled. Not a lot gets by them, especially Maisie."

"I would imagine the four of you can be mighty persuasive with the male gender."

Dinah lowered her eyelashes at Sidney. "I imagine so if we choose to."

"Remember, this must remain strictly on the QT," Sidney cautioned her.

"Yes, absolutely hush-hush," Ronny put in.

"Of course," said Dinah. "So shall I see if I can find this rider for you, then?"

"That was exactly our hope," Sidney replied. "And if he makes a stink about coming here, I'm sure the baroness can send some of the men here to assist."

"Oh, sir, I doubt that will be necessary. For one, he won't be hard to find. Several of the lads told me he's stopping over in town in Wolfgang's guest room. I'm sure I can persuade the gentleman to come for a visit."

"Yes. I am quite sure you can." Sidney tilted his head gallantly.

Ye gods, is old Sid flirting? Who'd have thought it? "Wonderful," said Betty. "And the sooner the better, Dinah. I'm sure you appreciate there is some urgency to this matter."

"I do, madam, and I'll do my best. I'll send word through Cedric as soon as I've located the man." Dinah rose, curtseyed and left.

Just before the door closed, a ginger-striped tail disappeared through the gap.

CHAPTER 14

Watching the Watchers

W*ednesday Night.* Far above the baroness's castle, at the top of the highest mountain, a steel-grey SUV limo purred quietly in the dark outside the ornate gates of the *Schloss Sturm und Fang*, the car's tinted windows concealing the three occupants within. Another meeting, of a very different sort, was to take place.

A light came on in the gatehouse and the gatekeeper ambled to the gates, struggling into a mac against the constant drizzle. The driver's electric window descended in response to the man's query. Satisfied with the reply, the gatekeeper opened the gates and motioned the car inside. In immaculate black suit and tie with striped vest, Ivan, the butler, opened the huge Baroque doors and bowed the three gentlemen in.

"You made good time, gentlemen. I hope the drive was not too tedious. The count has arrangements for you in the drawing room."

A few eyeballs shuddered open at that, but none detected any wit to his words. They therefore presumed they were safe from some deadly double entendre. The butler led them through to where the count sat in expectation.

Count D. rose from his chair by the roaring fire and extended his hand to Tyrone Upman and then to the others, who were eyeing the ox-sized spit in the fireplace somewhat nervously. Besides the spit (apparently still functional), Tyrone noted the lack of mirrors and the low lamp light, which helped disguise the frayed bloom on the once-grand furnishings. At least there were no implements of torture *visible.*

Those were in the basement, he presumed. The count's reputation had succeeded him through several centuries of vivid history.

"Velcome to my humble abode!" the count twinkled, bowing creakily. "Vill you have zome refreshment?" His hand swept toward the sideboard set with decanters and glasses.

"Some scotch and water would be welcome," Cyril ventured. He was avoiding the red stuff in the tall Waterford decanter. The others likewise assented.

"Of course. How remiss of me! I haff alzo a vonderful 200 year old zingle malt, if that vould do?"

They were reminded of the otherness of their host: the extra nought in the age of the scotch wasn't accidental. The count poured out three generous portions into Viennese snifters etched with his crest. "Help yourselves to zome water. Or I haff zoda, if you prefer," indicating an antique syphon.

Their drinks set up and in hand, the three men sat down around the fire, sipping discerningly. One would expect scotch that old to be beyond peaty, more of an archaeological sampling, really. But this was incredibly smooth, with a slight honey undertaste. The count himself sipped from a tall wine glass. Something red, naturally.

"Did you bring ze papers?" he asked.

"Of course." Tyrone set down his scotch on the inlaid, mother-of-pearl top of an occasional table, pulled over his attaché case and opened it with alacrity.

"Shall I go over the terms?" Tyrone's eyebrows arched over his glasses.

"Please. Ve must go carefully. Ferry, ferry carefully."

Outside, two figures crouched to the side of the gates, waiting for the gatekeeper's light to extinguish. Rider held his finger to his lips. Wolfgang rolled his eyes, but reminded himself the dude was a newbie at stalking prey. Above them, three lights hovered, offering some illumination, before floating through the wrought iron palings into the castle park.

Several of the others padded softly up to the gate and sat on their haunches. The muffled sound of hooves across the spongy forest mast was barely audible. Swooping to a pine bough above them, a snowy owl rotated its head in surveillance. He'd removed his boots to reduce drag.

At last, the light inside the gatehouse went out. *Okay, boys, you know what to do*, Wolfgang telepathed. There was a nodding of heads. Rider pulled his hood over his own as Eduardo approached the gates. As he was about to mount his horse and clamber over the fence, he saw the viciously pointed finials along the fence top and remembered the long skirts of his cloak.

With amusement, Wolfgang noticed his reluctance. "Here, you better let me do that. You'll get that tent you wearin' in a twist, and then what we do, you snagged up there all night? 'Member, we ain't got them opposable thumbs, which might come in handy later."

"Eduardo, would you mind this once?" Rider addressed his horse.

As long as he doesn't drag his gigantic toenails across my back, I suppose I must consent.

"I be as delicate as fluffy lil' ol' lap dog."

Just get on with it.

Wolfgang bounded up on Eduardo's back, taking care to alight only on the saddle and blanket beneath, then sprang over the top of the fence. Rider had to admit Wolfgang did that much more agilely than he could have.

"Nice. But now how are *you* going to open the gates, without thumbs?"

"This ain't my first rodeo, you know. Plus, I been here before. See this big ol' handle here? It jaw-sized. And lookee that. Big ol' key left jes' lyin' in the lock." Wolfgang clicked his tongue.

"Security's not too tight."

"Not too many folks in a hurry to go for miles up a mountain to meet a bloodsucker. 'Specially this bloodsucker. He fond of them pointy sticks."

"Good point. Or . . . not."

A brother wolf, sent by Granny, came forward with a small

saddlebag strapped to his back. Digging in the bag, Rider drew out an oil can and squirted all the hinges and the lock liberally. Several held breaths were slowly expelled as the gates swung open silently. The troupe filed in and carefully shut the gates, leaving all as it was before. Eduardo remained outside, retreating to the cover of the forest. He was the getaway conveyance.

The three sprites swarmed back toward them as the group slunk into the shadows of massive shrubberies surrounding the castle.

"They're in the drawin' room, on the ground floor to the right rear of the *Schloss*." Brain informed them.

"And they're drinkin' some pretty stiff booze. We made sure of that," Dim added.

"Yeah, the count thinks it's his precious 200-year-old scotch, but we switched it with what we like to call 'Tell-You-More-Do.' " Elmo chuckled.

"What's that do?" Rider asked.

"Well, besides givin' you one helluva headache the next mornin', it makes yer babble like a baby," Elmo told them. "Lawyers hate the stuff."

"Some of them might," Rider huffed.

"Present company excepted, of course," Elmo amended.

"So, sort of a truth serum, then?" Rider contemplated its usefulness in the witness box.

"In a manner of speakin', yes. Very entertainin' stuff," Brain said, smirking. "This should be good. Let's have a listen."

The group moved soundlessly to the back of the castle outside the stone-mullioned windows of the drawing room. The owl floated on ahead and perched on an overhanging gutter, swivelling his gaze across the gloom.

Luckily, the count preferred not to draw his drapes at night, mostly because the moth holes would be more evident. They peered in on an astounding scene. Wound-tight Tyrone was slapping his thigh. His glasses were off and he was guffawing at some amusing story the count had told. Rider was gob-smacked to find that the CDO possessed a single humorous gene in his slippery DNA. The others in the room were likewise disabled, wheezing in laughter and slugging back more "scotch." The count alone seemed under control, having preferred his usual nightcap. His mouth was smiling. His eyes were not. They were asquint at the change in his guests.

"Oops," said Elmo. "We forgot to doctor the count's drink."

"That might not be a bad thing," Rider whispered. "At least one of them will be able to speak coherently, so we might finally get to the bottom of this, or at minimum be better able to follow the gist." He strained his hearing toward the window. The wolves had no problem following the conversation, nor did the sprites. Or the owl. It was good to have allies with enhanced senses.

Finally, it seemed the meeting was winding down. The count's guests drooped in their chairs, insensibly sawing sequoias. Twiddling with his goblet and drumming his fingers on the arm of his chair, Count D. looked on in grave surmise. He pondered the ramifications of what the gentlemen had told him. To be sure, there was much to his advantage. His house was in sore need of repair and his bank accounts were beginning to appear as wasted as he, upon arising from his coffin. But there were legal consequences, possibly dire, to consider and avoid, as well as the damage to his reputation among his peers if it were discovered he was behind this venture. The locals wouldn't like it either, that was certain. Seeing their precious woodlands laid waste bit by bit was sure to cause trouble and gain the notice of the Crown. They must be careful to illustrate how the mining of tantalum would more than compensate the Crown's coffers (as well as his own) for the loss of merely a few thousand trees. Since the closing of Global's mine in Widgeton, the price of tantalum had sky-rocketed. It was only a narrow swath of trees in any case. And in his lifetime, which was going on 600 years now, 420 just in this country, he'd seen similar devastation over and over owing to warfare. He was confident it would all grow back in quick order, at least from his vantage point.

Count D. took a thoughtful sip from his goblet and made a face. One of his guests had poured his last glass and must have substituted the pinot noir for his usual beverage. Wine was such an acquired taste. Still, the mild buzz was pleasant. He took another pull. And another. And nodded asleep in his chair.

The owl swooped off in the direction of Granny's house and the wolf pack followed on foot.

"Well, that worked out a treat, din't it?" Dim slapped Brain on the back.

"Yeah, except he ain't talkin'. He's sleepin'," Brain pointed out. "That ol' count loves talkin' to himself. Gives him a bit of company, see. Coulda been entertainin'."

"Well, I think we've heard all we need to in any case, and I'm very grateful for your help." Rider unbent from his crouch and rotated his stiff shoulders.

Brain and Dim floated off back toward the entrance to the estate.

"Glad to help," said Elmo. "Any friend of Granny's and all that." Elmo set off after his mates.

As Rider and Wolfgang stole back to the gates, Eduardo stepped quietly out from his cover. This time, they let themselves out quietly, relocking them from the outside. Rider just managed to replace the key in the lock on the gate's inner side without completely dislocating his shoulder.

Well done, sir. I am grateful you didn't find it necessary to vault onto my back from a height. Your aim was not the best on the last attempt.

"Nor would yours be if you had to aim for a moving target," Rider hissed. "Would you please hold still?"

As Rider rose up in Eduardo's stirrups, he commented *sotto voce* on the day's proceedings: "Well, I have to say our luncheon with Granny turned out to be well worthwhile, not only for her cuisine."

Eduardo nodded his agreement. He had never had such a delicious repast. And the herbal seasoning seemed to be helping with his gas problem. There was, as well, the crucial heads-up regarding the count's meeting.

"She seems to be the area's Central Intelligence. A remarkable woman!"

Indeed. She was most kind and canny.

"That the truth! I told you Granny would have the skinny on things. That ol' owl with them boots and my buddies probably 'bout at her house now givin' her an earful."

"It's clear we have to work fast, though. Tomorrow, I need to put in a call or two to my office to let them know what's going on here. With luck, within the week Father will be able to liaise with the Crown's ambassador, if not the Crown itself."

"Plus, we oughta go back and talk to Rumpbuckle, let him know what's goin' on."

Are you sure that's wise? What if he's secretly an ally of the count and tips him off? Eduardo had a point.

"Even if he is, if he tipped off ol' Count D. it would prob'ly put the kybosh on the whole thing, and that kinda the point."

"It might, but these scoundrels can be pretty tenacious when it comes to a deal as lucrative as I'm sure they see this one. They might just come back and try it another way." Rider spoke from good experience (or bad, as was usually the case).

"Yeah, but then we know who they is."

Unless they wait and make the attempt through another of their corporate entities.

"I see what you sayin'. You damned smart for a horse. But in any case, I pretty sure Rumpbuckle's no friend of ol' Count D."

"Why's that then?"

"On account of the last time somebody tried somethin' like this. Wanted to blow the top of Mount Otter off. That time, they was after hafnium. Said it was the richest deposit ever found. They supposed to be all sorts of rare minerals around here."

"Hmmmmm. That's used in filaments and electrodes. Something to do with semiconductor fabrication, I believe. Big business! What happened?"

"Well see, that mountain top was the home of Olivier's kinfolk way back. That the name of that owl who came with us. He a good buddy with all the bros now. Them owls is some kinda rare species that's under specific protection of the Crown. Even got 'em on queenie's family crest. Some ancestor noted that them spots on they wings resemble them French *floordeelees*. Only place they can be found is either up that ravine or on Mount Otter. Folks said Olivier was hopping mad when he heard about it."

So I take it the Crown didn't go for the scheme?

Wolfgang chuckled. "You got that right. Olivier, he barely outa the nest, but he flew over and told queenie what was what. He don't like to brag, but you could say he their royal messenger. That was when Otternought got its name. One of them inside jokes."

Rider laughed. "A warning to others, I take it. That's very encouraging."

I like their sense of humour, Eduardo whinnied.

"You would have liked Rumpbuckle's sense of humour, too!"

"Oh?" they asked.

"He may jes' look like an ol' wand salesman, but I hear the dude is one serious sorcerer."

"I was reaching that conclusion."

As was I!

"Granny told me that Rumpbuckle and Olivier got every single bird in the area in on the scheme. Rustled up a spell that turned their guano into cement when it landed. Didn't hurt the birds or plants none and them birds thought it was hilarious, as they would of course. See, humans don't realize jes' how good a bird's aim is. The crows and gulls kept competin', showin' off who made the best splat. Even the little bittiest birds got into it and did theyselves proud. Them birds just shat up a storm—all over that company's cars and trucks, big equipment and small, even they shiny black limos. And they didn't jes' stay in the valley. No sir, they followed them right back to where them company fellows came from. Wish I'd a seen it, but that was before I got here."

"I would have enjoyed seeing that, as well!" Rider snickered.

"But the best part was every time somebody in one of the vehicles stopped to try to wipe the stuff off from the windscreen before it hardened, he got bombed so fast he was nearly petrified on the spot.

"When the baddies finally made it back to headquarters, those three sprites were ready with they tiny rocket launchers. Talk about gettin' a firecracker up you butt!"

Rider and Eduardo had a hard time stifling their snorts. "We'd better get out of here before we wake the gatekeeper!"

As they cleared the forest cover, Rider continued, "I trust the blackguards learned the error of their ways?"

"I think it safe to say they learned about all kindsa slings and errors of they outrageous fortune."

"You never cease to amaze me, Wolfgang!"

Wolfgang ducked his head, "Oh, it jes' the public library. Granny got me a card once she taught me to read."

Rider slapped him on the back and they set off toward Otternought.

CHAPTER 15

The Summons

T*hursday Night.* Business at the Bat and Whistle was bustling when Rider and Wolfgang walked in. Rider struggled up the queue to order their drinks as Wolfgang went over to his usual corner table and joined Olivier and the others of their scouting party. Waiting for their order to arrive, Rider turned and rested his elbows on the bar, scanning the crowd. He noted an increase in females tonight. In particular, there was one pert brunette in animated conversation with a couple of other girls. Rider thought he recognized two of them, placing the girls at the convention centre. But the bright-eyed little brunette was unfamiliar to him. As he was gazing admiringly at her, she chanced to look up and caught his eye, smiling. The beer arrived and he raised his in salute before joining the pack in the corner.

With a collective scraping of stools, the posse pulled up to their pints. Olivier had launched into his report to Granny and what ensued. They were in such deep discussion, none of them noticed the presence of an intruder until they sniffed her scent: a delicious mix of soap and jasmine. They all found themselves smiling inexplicably as they lost track of their subject and looked up at the pretty, dark-haired girl dimpling down at them. Who said aromatherapy doesn't work?

As their conversation stuttered to a nervous halt, the girl caught their reaction. "Hello. I'm so sorry to interrupt. But don't worry, I didn't hear a word. It would be hard to in this din!" She extended a dainty hand.

Rising, Rider extended his own hand and took hers. "That's certainly true. I haven't seen the place this busy before. Is there something we can do for you, miss?"

"My name's Dinah. I'm looking for someone, actually."

"Who you be lookin' for, babycakes?" Wolfgang asked.

"*You're* not from here, are you?" Dinah teased Wolfgang.

"Now how could y'all tell that?" They all howled.

"Please, sit down." Rider drew over an additional stool. "Our discussion can be put on hold for a bit."

"Okay, thanks, but just for a bit. I'm out with my mates over there," Dinah explained, tipping her head in the girls' direction. "I wouldn't want to leave them on their own for too long. There's no telling what they'd get up to."

"So, whassup?" Wolfgang inquired.

"I work up at the castle in the kitchen and am trying to locate a certain gentleman."

"You boyfriend run out on you? Shame on him if so, pretty thing like you."

Several heart rates accelerated as Dinah lowered her long lashes winsomely.

"No, nothing like that. I don't actually know his name. I only have a description."

She gazed a little overlong at Rider. He found himself trying to decide if her irises were more gentian or periwinkle. "I'm told he's rather tall, with brown hair, and often wears a hooded cloak and expensive riding boots. They say he's a newcomer and arrived on horseback. The locals have taken to calling him 'Rider.' "

Silence and a sudden shuffling of feet and shifting of bottoms greeted her pronouncement.

Olivier spoke up, "Why are you looking for zees man?"

"I'm on an errand for the baroness, if you must know. She would be grateful if the gentleman would call on her at the earliest opportunity to discuss some recent developments that have come to her attention."

Rider resisted the urge to draw his hood over his head again. Much too late for that.

"I believe you must be looking for me," he said. "Am I under suspicion of some dastardly deed?" He donned his most charming smile.

Dinah played coy. "I'm sure it's nothing of that sort, sir. At least, the baroness never said so in so many words. I understand she's only hoping you can help clear up rumours of some activity that has caused her some concern."

"And how could I possibly help with that?"

"Of course I'm not privy to all that goes on upstairs, but I believe the baroness is hoping that you have made the acquaintance of other newcomers and so perhaps can provide her with better information than what she currently has."

"Why would she think I would have information?" Rider asked, his brows knit.

"Word has come to her that you've been making enquiries, sir."

Rider's hackles would have risen a few nights previous. "Is there some law against that?"

"None that I know of, sir, but I'm under the understanding that the type of enquiries you have been making are similar to those she herself and her husband have also been making."

"Are they indeed? And what are these enquiries?"

"It wasn't my place to ask."

"Well, at the moment, I'm afraid I will have to decline her invitation. The business we are involved in has urgent deadlines that must be met. But please give the baroness my regards. Perhaps another time . . ."

Dinah looked very uncomfortable. Was she losing her touch? Olivier swivelled his head, his excellent hearing having picked up the stealthy approach of three largish individuals who now loomed in doublets, tights and helmets. At present, their swords were still sheathed but menace implied itself loud and clear. The baroness was never one to chance things to leave.

"Uh oh," Wolfgang said. His observation stirred growls and hoots of derision among his friends.

"Um, the baroness was really most insistent. She said it was quite urgent. I wouldn't like to disappoint her. . . ."

Dinah demonstrated her ability to multitask by wringing her hands and dimpling simultaneously.

Rider, threw back his ale and stood. "Does the baroness always send three goons to summon her guests to call upon her?"

The others at the table rose also. Rider waved them back down. "Lads, you don't need to be involved in this. You've got better things to do." He stared at them meaningfully.

"*Vraisment*," replied Olivier. "*Dans tout case*, I am often in communication with the baroness, and am sure she will treat you fairly. And *well*." Olivier stretched his wings, ruffling his quills at the guards. "I will be sure to let ze others know what has transpired and contact you *demain* if we do not hear from you." Even the goons got his threat.

The rumble of growls subsided somewhat.

Rider yanked his cloak about him. "Gentlemen, shall we go? Or should I stop by my room and fetch my pyjamas?"

The guards didn't hold with sarcasm not their own. "I am sure her ladyship will provide all that will be necessary," countered Bert, the head guard. Refraining from a leer, he jangled the large ring of keys on his belt. It had been ages since they'd gotten to lock anyone up, so he enjoyed every opportunity to use his favourite line. It was a guard humour thing.

"Oh, goody." Rider gave Dinah a hostile grin. "You know as bait, you're not bad. I suppose permitting a refusal to pop in for a visit would be 'more than your job's worth,' " he sneered, miming finger quotes.

Dinah couldn't remember the last time someone had made her blush but here she was, reddening rapidly. Rider seemed a decent sort, not the villain she'd been expecting. And he was certainly nice looking. Even smelled nice—a distinct improvement upon the local males. She suddenly found herself feeling sorry for the part she'd played if it went badly for him. Still, she reminded herself, people always said serial killers could be real charmers. If he really was the one who'd been mauling the women, she'd be proud to be the one to bring him down. Clinging to her righteousness, she flounced away.

"For a human, she got a nice behind," Wolfgang commented.

"There is that," Rider concurred. The rat and crow just shrugged.

Damn! Two blushes in a single night! Dinah fled to the loo.

From inside the tavern's inglenook, three lights swarmed in agitation. "Looks like our boy's headed for a spot o' trouble," Brain said, as patrons were jostled aside by the guards.

"Oh, I dunno. If I was Rider, I wouldn't mind a little bit of *that* trouble. I'll bet you she has quite a followin'," Elmo remarked, ogling the retreating *derriere* of Dinah, who'd made a break from the Ladies' just after Rider was hauled off. Elmo considered himself quite a connoisseur of swaying female backsides. "I wouldn't mind followin' it meself."

"That makes two of us," said Dim dreamily.

"You louts! I'm talkin' about Rider bein' summoned to the castle!"

Elmo and Dim snapped to, reluctantly.

"You're right, Brain," Elmo nodded his head sagely. "This doesn't bode well."

"And it looks right dodgy, if you ask me," Dim added.

Elmo and Brain turned on him and gave him a clout around the ears. "Same thing, you nitwit!"

"Is it? Oh. Sorry," said Dim, abashed.

"We'd better let Granny know what's happened." Brain threw back the remains from his thimble-sized flagon and stood, the others following suit.

"That was quite a nice scene, though, wasn't it?" ventured Elmo.

Brain refused to be placated: "A bit trite, I thought, especially that 'more than your job's worth' part. Our man's been watching too many period dramas, if you ask me."

"Aye," agreed Dim.

The other two just looked at Dim, bleakly.

"What?"

"Well, I'm off!" Elmo downed his drink, too, and left Dim to pay.

"Hey! It was your turn this time!" Dim complained.

"Was not," came the doubled reply.

"Was . . . too!" Dim's retort faded in the absence of audience. He grumbled and fished out some rubble from his pocket, separating some coins from the acorns, lint balls and fuzz-covered jelly beans. "It's always me payin'." He slapped the money on the table and floated off after the others.

Wolfgang caught up with the sprites. "I'm coming with you. We gotta help Rider."

"*Moi aussi.*" Olivier fluttered to the coat rack by the door, then glided out with them into the night. They were joined in the innyard by two more wolves from their scouting party. Eduardo, who'd been listening in, offered a ride to Wolfgang.

"Well, that's right neighbourly of you!" Wolfgang grinned at Eduardo.

Needs must, et cetera.

"Ah, I knew all along you jes' a big ol' softie."

Yes, well, don't let the observation get abroad.

"Dude. You on you own in that department!"

Eduardo whickered, smiling inwardly. Wolfgang wasn't such a bad chap. Except (ouch!) those claws. *Careful there!*

"Sorry!"

The other two wolves said they'd prefer to lope on ahead and reconnoitre with Olivier, who was bound to get there first.

The rat with the tartan scarf and the pipe-smoking crow scurried up, awaiting their instructions. Ross's ratty talents were best used infiltrating buildings and creating mayhem where necessary. Conrad could make himself quite invisible when he chose, and could even pick locks. Crows were clever that way. Wolfgang decided to send them to scope out the situation at the castle. With a squeak and a caw, they set off up the hill.

The rest trudged off to Granny's. It was late, but she always kept a light on. Even without a full moon, they could see their way easily: the three sprites lit the path as they wound through the forest. Handy, when one hasn't a torch.

Outside the castle's kitchen door, a ginger cat sat waiting in the dark. He heard a flutter of wings and looked up as a crow alighted on a branch of the mulberry tree in the kitchen garden opposite. The cat's night sight picked up the glossy black feathers as they settled. He also picked up the strong scent of apple-wood cured tobacco and sneezed violently.

"Honestly, Conrad, you really need to cut back on the smoking!" he complained.

"I know, I know. At least it's not that menthol rubbish." Conrad coughed quietly.

"Yes, thank the gods for that!" A quick tattoo of tiny nails brought Ross into view, winding his scarf more closely around his throat. "You know how us rodents hate anything minty-fresh!"

"Any news?" Conrad asked the cat.

Durell answered, "They just took the man called 'Rider' up to see old Bitey."

"Do you know where in the castle?" squeaked Ross.

"I heard Bert say the drawing room."

Ross and Conrad exchanged glances. "That doesn't sound good," Conrad croaked.

Durell licked his left shoulder. "Might not be that bad. Sometimes Betty simply fancies the instant fright technique when she wants information fast. And anyhow, she's topped up for the night. I saw her drinking her nightcap an hour or more ago."

"How long ago did they take Rider up?" Ross was trying to figure out how quickly he could run up to the next floor.

"Not more than 10, 15 minutes, I would say."

"Is that cat minutes or human minutes?" Ross loved winding Durell up.

"Oh, very funny. I checked the kitchen clock, of course."

"Okay. I'll use the kitchen stairs, then. If someone happens to see me, they'll simply figure I'm one of the residents."

"Really? With a tartan scarf on?" Durell hissed sarcastically.

"Oh. Perhaps not. It's just this cold I've been trying to fight off."

"Well, chuck the scarf if you don't want to be flattened by a broom.

You'd never make it past the pantry with that on."

"Durell's right, Ross. Save the sartorial splendour for the pub." Conrad pulled Ross's scarf off him, folded it respectfully, then bunged it under a yew.

"Hey!" Ross objected.

"'Sallright. Them needles will keep it clean. 'Sides, think where all that thing's been."

Durell chuckled. "Off you go, then." Ross plunged through the cat flap and headed upstairs.

"Which window is it?" Conrad asked.

"Other side, to the left of the entrance. There's a bank of three windows, but the curtains are drawn."

"Damn! How am I going to see anything?"

Durell smirked. "Ye of little faith. I made sure one of the windows was left ajar by pulling its curtain closed before the others were shut. Silly humans never think to check, do they?"

"Good man!"

Durell bowed. "Oh, one thing."

"What's that then?"

"Your pipe."

"Drat. Right again." Conrad deposited his pipe with the scarf under the yew, dipped a wing at Durell and flew off. There was just room for him to wriggle through the gap of the drawing room's open casement. Giving the window the tiniest extra shove to ensure a quick exit, he settled down behind the heavy curtain and cocked his head. Presently, he heard the skittering noise he was expecting. Ross scampered up to him and they hunkered down to listen in.

Conrad mouthed, well, beaked, to Ross, "Be ready!" If anything like bodily harm to Rider appeared imminent, their orders were to cause a frenzy and bite where necessary. Durell had previously assured them there were no brooms kept in the room.

"Come," Betty addressed the knock on the door. Bert and his guards ushered in Rider with a prod. The baroness gestured from her porta-throne to a chair at the other side of the fireplace. "Please. Do sit down.

We are civilized here, after all."

"How curiously societies judge their own 'civilization,' as you call it." Seething, Rider took a seat, dipping his head to her in mock obsequience. He hadn't missed the room's unusual furnishings. And she hadn't missed his riposte.

"Please forgive us if we did not have time to clear the most . . . industrial . . . of our furnishings before your arrival. But I hope you will be encouraged to see we have quite modern technology, at least. And one has to make a living."

"A sanitary death is a better one?"

"You misjudge me, sir. All that is a thing of the past. This is a 'living room' in the truest sense, not a 'dying room'. We only take a small contribution. Let's call it a tithe."

"And who are your donors, may I ask, beyond anyone who might annoy you?"

"I had understood that my colleague, Dr. Rumpbuckle, gave you an idea of our activities here."

"He gave me the gist, yes. But I'm still curious as to your answer, my lady."

"My 'donors,' as you describe them, are my people—the villagers you have met below. The donor pool seldom goes beyond the confines of my lands. I pride myself in avoiding turf wars with my neighbors."

"And your people donate willingly, do they?"

"Oh, yes. They much prefer it to the onerous taxation of previous generations."

"An enlightened tyrant, then." Rider smiled with only his mouth.

"If you prefer. An improvement, I hope, over what has beset them for so long. I do regard my stewardship of this area quite seriously, despite the drawback of my . . . condition. We do not take only, we give back. You see that large cabinet next to the table? It contains medicines that help our people. Naturally, the drawing process requires testing the donor first, which often reveals various maladies for which we provide medical care. So, actually, this room also functions as a clinic and dispensary."

"Impressive, Baroness, all things considered."

"I'll take that as a compliment." Betty smiled back in kind.

Rider remained silent. The fire crackled. An indistinct rustle behind a curtain went unnoticed by his hostess. He sat back in his chair.

Deciding on a different tack, the baroness gestured to a make-shift setup of decanters and glasses. "Would you care for some refreshment?"

"I'm not sure I'm up to sampling just now," Rider demurred.

"It's strictly organic, I assure you."

"Aren't we all?"

Betty laughed obligingly. "By that I meant extracted from vines, not veins."

Askant, Rider tapped his foot while he considered. "Perhaps in that case . . . I've heard good things about the local vintages."

The baroness arose, poured a glass and handed it to him. "We've won several awards, here at the castle."

Rider took a tentative sip, smelling first for any odours of bitter almond or other deleterious chemicals. So far so good. Olivier and Wolfgang had told him that the baroness had strict rules against poisoning. Much easier to simply drain one's enemy; the problem of removing opposition was solved and one's daily dose was provided at the same time.

Enough of bush beating. Rider set the glass down hard on a metal cabinet next to an IV stand. "So . . . what can I do for you, Baroness?"

She turned to her guards. "Bert, you and the others may go. I shall be quite safe without your assistance."

"If you're sure, my lady. We'll be right outside, so if yer get inter trouble, just give us a shout."

Betty smiled icily at his liberties. "I'll do that. Thank you."

The guards withdrew.

"I apologize for what must seem to you a rather heavy-handed summons."

"A simple note might have accomplished the same result, Baroness."

"Possibly, but I couldn't take the risk. And Dinah did say you at first declined my invitation."

"Your hulking guards changed my mind for me."

"I am still learning. Old family habits die hard, I'm afraid. Had you pressing business to attend to?"

"I did, in fact, and do. A most serious business."

"Yet you seem far from home."

"As indeed I am." Rider wouldn't be drawn.

Betty repressed a sigh. It wasn't easy, always having to play the heavy. "It's come to me that you've been making inquiries in the region."

"Don't most tourists? You know—'Where's the closest pub?' 'Where can I find a room?' 'Where's the loo?' "

"Quite. But I've heard your inquiries have gone beyond the necessities of acclimation. Can you enlighten me on your interest in my realm?"

"My interests are my own and quite legal, last time I checked. Further, I'm not aware of any statute that permits you to hold me without just cause, made evident by a warrant from the Crown."

"You have studied our little country's laws then?" Betty raised an imperial eyebrow in disdain.

"One must, in my profession."

"And what is that?"

"I'm a barrister."

"Are you indeed?" Both eyebrows now rose.

"You're surprised. Is it the cloak?"

"Perhaps." She let her gaze slide down to his riding boots. "I had assumed you had hopes of being cast in this documentary being filmed here."

Rider allowed himself a thin smile. "It is rather fancy dress for me. But I felt it necessary for the search I was conducting."

"And the horse was also necessary?"

"Quite necessary, as it turns out. My horse has proved to be an invaluable asset. But I see you are well informed."

"I make it my business to know what's going on here. I know you arrived on horseback just before the last full moon, for instance, and took a room at the inn. I know that during that time you kept your face hidden under a hood, accosted a wizard, and later revealed a visage that was suspiciously hirsute. I'm told you then befriended one of our local wolves. I know that soon after, you appeared clean shaven, forearms as well as beard, and were seen in company with this wolf in various locations, asking about the whereabouts of the wizard who had managed to escape your grasp.

"At the same time, it came to me that a number of our local women were being accosted by a male or males quite new to the area, who, during amorous arousal and under a full moon, became suddenly both toothy and hairy and demonstrated a fetish for the female throat, biting the same."

Rider shifted in his chair and considered his best strategy.

"Can you account for your movements, sir?"

He decided attack might be the best opening defence. "I can. Can you also account for the movements of your husband, Your Ladyship?"

"Ah. Rumpbuckle has told you of my husband, I presume."

Rider nodded.

"You must have won his confidence, then. He is not usually so . . . divulgent. As to my husband, like myself, Heinrich has a genetic dependency upon the blood of others. However, he is bound to a code of honour of both his family and mine to follow strict, humanitarian guidelines in controlling the urge and manner of getting his needs met. We have even made this code law. We both take seriously the effect that our unavoidable conditions impose upon others. I can assure you it was not my husband, Heinrich, who was to blame. He is, in fact, an officer of The Order of Lupo, a local support group, you might call it, for his kind."

"Could it not have been one of the other members? Every support group has its backsliders."

"Not here. I, or we that is, won't allow it. There are dire consequences imposed upon any who do not follow the edicts we have set down."

Rider could imagine what those consequences might be. The baroness appeared quite capable of carrying out punishment, whatever her protests of right thinking. He'd have to be satisfied, for now, with her defence of her husband.

"In that case, dear Baroness, do you have any ideas about who might be the perpetrator or perpetrators?"

"You have not yet given me any reason not to consider you a suspect, sir," Betty reminded him.

"Very well. I came here looking for this wizard, as my sources told me this was the most likely area in which to search."

"And what was your business with this wizard, may I ask?"

"I think you've discovered my condition, which is the same as your husband's."

The baroness nodded in triumph. *Aha! Now we're getting somewhere.*

"But, unlike your husband, my condition is quite recent and much resented. In my case, it is *not* hereditary."

The baroness waited.

Rider submitted, "I was on my way to court a couple of months ago when a short, bearded fellow in a pointy hat bumped into me, waving a stick. I didn't pay much attention to him, my thoughts being on the case. Then there was a commotion, and I ended up getting knocked down in the melee.

"When I came to, the air seemed odd, shimmery, and I heard some men shouting. As I stood up to gather my documents, to my amazement they were doing their best to run away from me, seemingly unaided. When I'd managed to get them all back, the chap in the hat was scampering away, glancing over his shoulder at me and two others in alarm. I tried to run after him but there were too many people in the way. So I gave up and sprinted the rest of the way to court."

"How long was it before you realized you were not . . . as you had been?" Betty asked.

"My life continued as usual for perhaps a week, then I began having increasing urges for juicy steaks, the rarer the better. *Boeuf tartare* began to look tempting." Rider made a face. "I've always preferred my meat well-done. I found myself, when no one was watching, drinking the *jus* from the butcher's carton when I brought home a choice cut."

Betty nodded in commiseration.

"One night, I began to have hideous aches all over my body. I couldn't sleep and finally got up to get a drink of water, passing by my bedroom window as I did. Something made me pull aside my curtain. It was a full moon. I can't describe what I felt. It was both terrible and exhilarating. In the wee hours, when I got out of bed I glanced in the mirror and nearly passed out. I couldn't recognize my face. Or my arms or legs."

"And you put your sudden condition down to this wizard's bumping into you?"

"I didn't at first. As a rule, the City doesn't tolerate magic, excepting the odd witch or wizard passing through. But about the same time I began changing, I noticed a change in my horse, Eduardo. I was suddenly able to understand him!"

Reminded of her once-enchanted Billy, Betty bit back a smile. "And was he able to relate anything . . . intelligible?"

"Actually, ma'am, he's quite articulate and annoyingly erudite. Who knew?"

"Who indeed?"

"With his help, we were able to trace back to when our separate changes began, symptom by symptom. Horses, probably all animals saving the human sort, catch a lot of sensory nuances that evade us. He could actually smell the magic on me and remembered when he started smelling it. So I told him about getting knocked out by the wizard. His memory is so exceptional, he was able to pinpoint the start of my change. Rather like carbon dating. Incredible.

"The two of us then began making inquiries in our different ways. Eventually, between his connections and mine, we got information leading us here."

"But why on horseback?"

Rider gazed at her under his eyebrows for a beat.

"Oh, how silly of me. He wouldn't have fit in your automobile, of course."

Reluctantly, Rider chuckled. "True, but apart from that, the wizard figured out straight away he'd do best by dodging through the woods rather than sticking to the open roads. Even my compact all-wheel-drive wouldn't have fit between the trees. Besides, Eduardo turned out to be an excellent spy."

“And what had you planned once you ran your wizard to ground, pray?”

“Besides a good box about the ears, you mean?”

“And perhaps more?” Betty suggested.

“No, I’m a stick-to-the-law sort of man. But I did hope to persuade him to turn me back. And I’ve been known to be exceedingly persuasive when needed.”

“I don’t doubt it. So what happened to your plan?”

“The bounder got away.”

“Ah, that must have been the scene in the tavern.”

“Alas, yes. However, I retrieved the fellow, with some help, and the landlord and I locked him up in the broom closet for questioning the next morning. But he escaped again, blast him.”

“Oh, bad luck. But surely you didn’t expect him to stay put, possessing a wand.”

“That’s just the thing—he’d lost it!”

“Lost it! Not much of a wizard, I’d say.”

“My thoughts as well, which made my outlook even bleaker. During my interrogation of the wizard, he claimed it was an accident—something the matter with his wand. Said he’d been aiming for someone else entirely. Eduardo’s change was, according to the wizard, the fallout of a failed experiment in genetic engineering. Unknowingly, my horse had browsed among the results in the wizard’s rubbish.

The baroness toyed with her goblet, thinking. “What did this wizard look like?”

“Oh, the usual: pointy hat with and robe with stars on, blue I think although it was hard to tell through the grime. He was rather scruffy, especially that matted beard. Rather short. Spoke more like a yokel than a proper wizard who had gone to university. And I recall there was a distinct bend in the tip of his wand.”

“Is that all you can recall?”

“Pretty much. No, wait. He had odd eyes: one green and the other golden, like a lion’s of mixed parentage.”

Pensively, the baroness searched her memory for where she’d seen eyes like that. Rider resumed, filling her in with the rest of the story, including the rascal's being chased off by Rumpbuckle for bad behaviour.

The baroness could well imagine the explosive departure and smothered a laugh. "How frustrating for you. You didn't consider it time to return home and carry on with your life?"

"I don't see how I *can* continue my profession, having to make excuses for myself every month. Judges are not inclined to accommodate disabilities beyond the sanctioned types. More importantly, I couldn't face myself if I ever gave in to the urge and . . . harmed someone."

"What if the 'someone' were a villain?" Betty ventured.

"That's what the law is for, ma'am. It's not up to us as individuals. Or shouldn't be."

"My heavens. In a moment you'll convince me you're actually an ethical barrister!"

"Is that such a bad thing? If so, my family missed the memo."

The baroness was intrigued. "What type of law do you practice?"

"Environmental, my lady."

"Hmmmm . . . Well, there are two sides to every suit, of course. Whom do you represent?"

"We have quite a cadre of clientele, but client confidentiality prohibits me from divulging their names. I can assure you, however, that we represent the good guys: the opponents and victims of all the crooks who think they can use their corporate clout to rip off landowners, pollute the waters, kill off species, and decimate forests for the sake of their own greedy gain."

"You sound quite a crusader."

"I wouldn't be the first in my family to be called that, or in my firm for that matter. I'm happy to say even those without a voice know they can rely on us. We've rid the world of quite a number of scoundrels and built a reputation on it. Our enemies have discovered that we can't simply be swatted away with a healthy bribe or a tempting settlement."

"It seems we have more in common than I had first believed. But you still haven't given a good alibi for your activities during the full moon."

"I was upstairs in my room at the inn."

"The entire night?"

Rider smiled genuinely this time. "Yes, thanks to Wolfgang, your resident grey wolf raconteur. He's turned out to be quite a good friend. Wolfgang figured out the very first night that I'd been changed and that it was an unwilling alteration. Thank God he came to my aid and chained me to the bed so I couldn't hurt anyone. I'm forever in his debt."

She was becoming convinced. He didn't appear to be her rogue werewolf. "Wolfgang is one of our favourite colourful characters." She smiled back.

"He's remarkably intelligent, too, besides being capable of getting me to lighten up."

"A canny canid, in fact?"

Good lord, the baroness is bantering with me! Perhaps I can relax. As if reading his thoughts, the baroness rang for Cedric. Presently, there was a shuffle at the door and a knock.

"Come in, Cedric."

"Yes, Your Inquisitor?"

Betty tried not to show her irritation in front of her guest. "Could you bring us several more logs for the fire? It's gotten quite chilly."

"Thought yer wanted it that way."

"Yes, well I've changed my mind. Our guest shouldn't be forced to keep his cloak on in my home, especially in the drawing room." She aimed a piercing look at Cedric.

"Certainly, Your Contrariness. I'll be right back with yer wood."

Rider coughed lightly, to cover his smile. He decided to take advantage of the baroness's warming regard and leaned forward in his chair. "You haven't told me anything of the events that are concerning you, Baroness. May I enquire what they are? I've also heard the rumours about these alleged new werewolves."

"Have you? Well, I suppose by now it's been broadcast through the village. What have you heard?"

Rider proceeded to tell her about some of the conversations he, Wolfgang and Eduardo had heard at the tavern. For now, he left out the part about the visitors' corporate designs on her barony.

"So you see," he finished, "I'm not the only one on the trail of that wizard. My guess is that there have been some more 'accidents' the wizard has caused."

There were a couple of woody thunks outside and another knock at the door. "Come *in*, Cedric, and next time, please use the wood scuttle."

Cedric was struggling with an armload of logs that seemed determined to slip out of his grasp like oiled ziti. He pulled aside the screen and dumped them with a grumpy clatter, sending showers of sparks onto the rug. Luckily, the hearth rug was asbestos. Betty liked to be prepared for his worst.

"Will there be anything further, madam? Shall I stoke the fire?"

"That *would* be helpful."

He grabbed the poker and stirred the fire vigorously without much result.

"On second thought, leave it to me."

"As you wish, madam." He bowed with a victorious smirk and left.

Rider rose and went over to the hearth. "Shall I, Baroness?" he asked over his shoulder.

Betty debated only a moment about the prudence of allowing her former suspect use of a potential weapon. Ah, well—hardly a match for fangs with syphons.

"Thank you, yes."

"Your man has been with you some while?"

"I think *that* must be obvious! He used to be our gardener, as was his father, but staff is hard to come by up here. I'm sure he'd rather be rummaging in the rhubarb. Still, he and his family have been loyal and very useful to my own. One has to choose one's battles. Like this new werewolf business. I do not intend to treat it as a trivial concern, despite other pressing matters."

"I guessed that they were not your only cause for alarm, my lady."

Betty gestured toward the wine decanter to buy herself time. "More wine?" She was still not sure if she could completely trust this man.

"No, but thanks. I prefer to keep my wits about me. I was not inventing excuses when I said I had urgent business to attend to." He set his emptied glass down on the phlebotomist's tray.

There was a tapping at the window, followed by a scuffle of claws and a muffled squeak behind the curtain. "You're on my tail!" Ross mimed to Conrad. A quick hop to the side took care of the matter, but the two cringed, afraid the baroness had heard them. Luck was with them—the fire sparked a couple of loud pops just then which covered their skirmish. They were well out of the way when the baroness drew aside a curtain. *Funny,* she thought, *I don't remember leaving any windows open. No wonder it has become chilly.*

"Ah, it's you, Olivier. Please come in." She drew the curtain aside farther, Ross and Conrad shrinking into the folds, so that the owl could fly to his perch. Betty had foreseen that he might pay her a visit tonight, so moved his post to the drawing room. She was counting on his counsel.

He settled his white feathers, swivelled his head and, taking care to face away from Betty, gave Rider a slow wink. Betty closed the window and resumed her seat.

"Bugger! Now I'll have to go out the long way," Conrad groused.

"Welcome to my world," Ross returned.

"I hope you have news for me, Olivier. By the way, may I introduce to you . . ." Betty just realized she'd never actually learned Rider's real name. "I do beg your pardon, what is your name, sir?" she asked Rider.

Rider arose and handed her an embossed business card.

"Rippon, Rippon and Magnus." She looked up in surprise. "I know it well, through my own solicitor. Tell me, what is your father's name?"

Rider smiled. "The same as mine, only one fewer Roman numeral. I'm Esmond Rippon, III. But please feel free to check my credentials. The number is on the card."

"I will do so, of course, but please don't take any offense. One hasn't lived as long as I without learning not to be gullible."

"No offense taken. Good fact-finding is essential in any worthwhile endeavour, especially when preparing one's defence."

"*Madame*, if I may interject . . . ," Olivier interjected.

"Please do."

"I can vouch for zees gentleman, as can *mes amis,* whom you know well."

"Indeed? I think you'd better give me your report, then."

"*Volontier, madame.* I think much of what I am about to tell you can be corroborated by your guest." Olivier told Betty about what he and the others had learned about the alleged new shape-changers and their business in the area. "So you see, whether or not zese businessmen have anything to do with your wolf problem, they have revealed themselves to be more dangerous still."

The baroness turned toward Rider. "Is this what your more recent inquiries disclosed?"

"I confess it is, Baroness. As much as I am anxious to locate the wizard, as are, apparently, at least two of these businessmen, when I learned of their plan to clear-cut the old-growth forest around the stream on your land so they could get to the minerals, I knew I had to do all in my power to stop them."

"But surely this is my fight, not yours. It is my land, after all. Mine and the countess's."

"Forgive me, but the time is long past for thinking in terms of 'my land' versus 'your land.' What affects your own land will eventually, and, it seems, sooner and sooner these days, affect the rest of the world. Think also of the creatures who live in those woods who will lose their homes and probably their lives. Among them will be many friends, like Olivier here and his family, as well as all of Wolfgang's friends. Granny's house, as well, is at the bottom of those woods."

"It is true, *ma chère* Baroness. My own family has survived *tout semplement* because of your kindness and ze *environnement particulier* of ze forest upon which we depend."

"Believe me, Olivier, I have no intention whatsoever to let anyone drive you out or do damage to any of my lands and its peoples. I am only surprised to find a foreigner so willing to join us in battle." She gazed at Rider. "I do see a resemblance to your father. You are much like him. He was a crusader, as well."

"You know my father?"

"Knew him. Long ago. He was quite young then, just out of university. He also loved hiking my woods. Came here on a post-graduation trek." She smiled, remembering. "But all young people are full of ideals at first. Sadly, life soon erodes most of them. I would have thought success would have gotten the better of his sensibilities."

"I suppose in a way it has, though not his sense. He no longer wears his outrage on his sleeve. My father has quite a reputation in the courts for keeping an unassuming poker face. Opposing counsel never sees the pounce coming. He's never lost his ideals, he's just found a better way to fight for them."

"I am so glad to hear it and happy, too, that you are proud of him."

"More than I can say. I doubt I'll ever be able to equal him, especially now. . . ."

"I would not lose heart, Mr. Rippon. I have a very good feeling we will both be successful in our endeavours."

"Meeow!" There was a plaintive cry from behind a closet door.

The baroness got up and opened it and Durell trotted out.

"Gracious. How did you allow yourself to get trapped in there, cat?"

Sixteen years with the woman and she still calls me "cat."

Betty was about to open the door to the hall for him, but Durell dove instead behind the curtain and emerged with a struggling rat in his mouth.

"Good fellow! You nabbed the nasty rascal, did you? Well, take him downstairs to Cook, then."

Rider's eyes popped open at that remark but he was determined to believe the best. Durell gave Rider a flick of his tail as he went past. "Trust you to a get a lift out!" Conrad muttered. Ross merely squeaked in mock distress.

"I imagine you'll be anxious to get back to your family, Olivier. Give them my regards." She opened the window wide. While she turned toward Olivier on his perch she missed a second set of wings zipping out the opening.

"Whew! That worked out well, then!" Conrad was relieved he didn't have to hop and skid down several flights of stairs and then grapple with the cat flap.

"I understand you're staying with Wolfgang."

"I am, yes."

"In that case, I know where you can be reached. You may as well go and get what sleep you can tonight. I have no further reason to detain you . . . for now."

"Thank you, Baroness. Though I'm not sure how much rest I may expect for a while."

"We will be in touch, one way or another. I hope I can rely upon you to let me know if you learn anything further in these matters." She offered him her hand.

"I will," he replied, bending over it. "I have sent the information to my firm as well. They will be researching this corporation and its connections to the area. I may even hear from my father by as early as tomorrow. Shall I give him your regards?"

"I would be most grateful if you would. We are glad to have you as an ally. Bert will see you out."

Rider gathered his cloak and bowed himself out. This time, he was able to ambulate unhindered. Bert sauntered behind, keeping close tabs on him as far as the gates.

CHAPTER 16

The Game Is Afoot

Friday Morning, Barely. It was well past midnight when Rider dragged himself back into Wolfgang's flat. He found his host hunched over the laptop with a steaming cup of coffee next to him on the kitchen table. "Any more of that left?" he gestured at Wolfgang's cup.

"You bet. Grab a cup."

Rider poured himself a mug and pulled up another stool, resting his elbows on the table and inhaling the aroma gratefully. "You waited up for me?"

Wolfgang swivelled around, grinning. "'Course! What's a friend for?"

Rider smiled and took a grateful swig. "Did you get to talk to Granny again?"

"Yep. She wait up for us. More of them trees down, and some new trucks arrived today."

"Damn!"

"I hear ya, man. The boys found new tracks from a small 'dozer, blazin' a trail even higher up, definitely headed up to ol' Count D's place."

"How big were the trees?"

"So far, just little 'uns, mostly still along the riverbed. That ol' growth not yet touched, but it just a matter of time, at least in they minds."

Rider gazed out the window at the night sky. "Perhaps they won't bother with more clearing once they get a good spot to mine."

"Dude. You really believe that?"

"No, not really."

"They always start with 'We jes' need to cut a few.' Next thing you know, the whole place is cleared right down to bedrock, and it's 'Oh, sorry! There jes' wasn't room for our rigs to get in and turn around,' blah, blah, blah. Next thing, it sawmill time."

"You're right."

"Same ol', same ol'. But anyhow, ain't no way Granny and boys, nor Betty and Ronny neither, gonna let 'em get that far." Wolfgang switched off his laptop. "How'd your evening go? That baroness treat you okay?"

"Surprisingly, yes. I guess I had rather stereotyped her."

"Easy to do, she bein' a part-time bat and all."

"But, unless she was doing a superb job of winding me up, she seems genuinely concerned about the land and the people around her."

Wolfgang smirked. "Yet she still bleedin' 'em."

"Yes, but not dry or dead. She thinks of what she does as a combined blood bank, admittedly mostly for her, and clinic. Not perfect maybe but a long way from what it used to be."

"And since she swapped that ol' taxation for 'donation,' bidness sure improved. She a regular Renaissance vampire."

"She is, indeed. And I am encouraged to think we're on the same side. That will greatly help."

"She know about Count D. yet?"

"I don't think so. I didn't bring it up. Didn't seem the time to do so."

"Yeah, woulda looked like you pointin' the blame in another direction just to save you ass."

"Precisely. Plus, we don't know how deep their friendship, or at least their association, goes. Once she knows, they might still close ranks on us, being the nobility here."

"Yeah, that possible. But I still don't think she'll condone takin' them trees and minerals. That would be completely outa character from what I always heard."

"I admire your positive attitude. I guess I'm just tired and feeling a bit depressed."

"Long day. But with all the stuff we found out, we a lot more ahead of the game than I thought we'd be. Tha's good, right?"

"Right. Well, we need to get some sleep. I'll check in with my office tomorrow. And we should go back and talk to Rumpbuckle. I'm sure he'd appreciate being kept up to date, and I feel somehow he's going to be very useful in the near future."

"I can imagine some ways he be that, all right. And it would sure be worth watchin'!"

"See you in the morning. I'll just go down to speak to Eduardo."

"Oh, forgot to tell you. He stayin' over at Granny's tonight. I think she sweet on him, and he gettin' the jones for them herbs she put in his food. Said it reminded him of home—kept goin' on about some kinda meadow flowers in the pasture when he was just a colt."

"Lord. So now he's an epicurean equine?"

"Seems so. Said he pick you up in the morning. Well, nighty night."

Next morning, Rider awoke to a tapping against the bedroom window. Struggling to focus, he pulled aside the curtain. Conrad was perched outside, his black head cocked and an unlit pipe jutting out as usual from the corner of his beak. "You going to let me in?"

"Uh, yeah. What time is it?" Rider opened the casement a crack and Conrad hopped in. "You can't smoke that in here, by the way. Wolfgang doesn't like it."

"I know that. But it's not like I have pockets."

"So what's up?"

"Eduardo sent me to tell you he's taking Granny into Broke-on-Spent. She's got a lead on that wizard. Said he's been making the circuit of all the pubs that do bingo sessions. Word's getting around that the wizard's been making a killing, and folks are pretty sure he's cheating. Only stays one day in each village, then moves on after he rakes in the winnings."

"And Eduardo left me behind?!"

"He was going to come get you, but Granny said better not."

"Hunh. I doubt the idiot wizard is dangerous. He's too inept."

"It's not that. She knows he's not ept. I think she's counting on figuring out a way to trap and expose him. Would save you a lot of bother that way, not having to chase him around anymore."

"He's certainly given us enough of the run-around. Granny did impress me as being very good at summing up character and getting the better of it when needed."

Conrad nodded. "She's a regular Miss Marple, Granny is. Doddering old ladies can be right good at pulling a fast one, when you don't expect it."

"Well, thanks for bringing me the message. I have some other matters to attend to anyway which can be easily handled on foot. And thanks for your help last night."

"We didn't do much, as it happens. Turned out you didn't need us."

"Which was a fortunate turn of events, but you were at the ready."

"That's us, all right. Anyhow, glad to oblige." Conrad flew off.

It was Friday lunchtime at the Line and Tackle. Not the nicest pub. A bit of a pick-up joint and rather grotty, truth be told. Greasy brown panelling with cheap vinyl trim, smeary windows and way too many tellies and fruit machines. What décor there was tended toward brewery adverts, displaying beer maids in mini-dirndls and armoured bras, and charts for the football pools. The loos were smelly (as was much of the clientele). But it did a bang-up trade every Friday lunch with bingo. Thirty tables or more were set up in the barn-sized back hall, and the landlord made sure the drink kept flowing.

An elderly woman with lavender braided hair and a virulent, tie-dyed T-shirt topping long, black skirts was sitting sedately at a small table at the back to the left of the door with a dry sherry next to her knitting bag. The first game started at half past twelve. By a quarter past, the place was almost full and rowdy with the cross-banter of the regulars. From where she sat Granny could see everyone who came in. So far, no wizard. Maybe their hunch was faulty? She was surprised, if so—her boys seldom got it wrong. Conrad, Ross and the wolves were at another table at the back on the right side. They were excellent back-up. But she had on her high-top trainers, just in case.

At twenty-five past, the door behind her opened and she heard a phlegmy cough and the singular sound of curly-toed running shoes, still tacky from motor oil, hitting the hem of a heavy robe. She smiled to herself and, watching over her spectacles, saw the wizard paying in and getting his game card. The only table left was next to the boys. They'd made sure of that.

The bingo caller at the head of the room caught her eye and she nodded very slightly. He nodded back, smiling. For a sorcerer of Rumpbuckle's class, it grew tiresome to stay chained to the store. It was agreeable, on occasion, to get out and about and he did enjoy a good bingo session, not so much for the dull game as the thrill of the chase. Thwarting a cheater was such fun. He felt sure Herald would pull his usual shenanigans and, thanks to his tracking spells, it would be child's play (for a precocious child) catching him at it. It also helped to get a tip-off from a good friend like Granny. When the landlord called needing a fill-in bingo caller, Rumpbuckle was happy to offer his services.

Being rather short and sitting at the very back, Herald hadn't gotten a good look at the bingo caller. Even if he had, Granny was positive he wouldn't have recognized Rumpbuckle. Few would. It was a modest trick of donning a nondescript, tan golf shirt and doing a little magic with his hair, now a burnt umber. For a comb-over, Rumpbuckle's was one of the more spectacular ones. It swirled round his head until it emerged as a pompadour, like the top of a Mr. Whippy cone.

They were into their third game. The crowd was feeling good with cheap beer and beginner's luck. The wizard was obviously holding back, saving himself for the biggest winnings later on.

At an intermission before the next game, one of the wolves got up to get a fresh pint and stumbled into the wizard. Herald's hat had been lying on the table, its brim hanging over the edge, obscuring the sight line to his right-hand pocket. The hat tumbled to the floor and the wolf retrieved it, apologizing. As he did so, he placed a small acorn inside. Being common currency among non-humans, acorns would never be questioned, if dropped from a paw. This one, however, was special. Unseen under the hat, it began to glow, transmitting its magical signal to Rumpbuckle at the front. The wolf nodded at Rumpbuckle and strolled away. The wizard was too busy studying his next card to notice.

Herald felt he was in great form. He was chuffed he had his own wand back and was well pleased with its new, turbo-charged performance. This should be a walk in the park. Beat the hell out of flogging GMO'd rutabagas.

Another of the wolves had manoeuvred his chair away from the table and slightly to the rear of the wizard, with a clear view of the right pocket of the wizard's robe. No one noticed a rat under the table quietly gnawing a hole at the bottom of the pocket. (Prudently, Ross had again left his scarf behind.) Conrad perched nearby, ready for action.

As a new game commenced, Rumpbuckle called "G9." His pencil on the table lit up from the signal the acorn was sending. He knew the numbers on the wizard's card were shuffling. "B2." The signal was getting stronger. "I4." His pencil started softly strobing. Sure enough . . .

"Bingo!" shouted Herald.

"Bring your card forward, please," Rumpbuckle instructed. In his rush from his seat, Herald didn't feel the wand slipping out a hole in his pocket nor hear the clatter on the tiles. But he was alone in that.

As Herald reached the podium with his card, an affronted bellow was heard from Barney in the back, "'Ere, wot's that then?" An animated discussion broke out.

"Yeah, wot's that blinkin' thing there on the floor wot fell outa that fella's pocket?" demanded Steve.

"Why it's a bloody wand, that's wot it is!" said Big Willem, eyeing the wand close up.

"And look, Jake, 'is pointy hat's right there on the table," added Toby.

"Well that's all right. Wizards is allowed in, same as beasties and birdies." Jake believed in being fair.

"Mebbe so, but they're not allowed to use their bloody wands."

"Well, p'raps 'e didn't actually use it," offered Fergus.

Heads were bent down studying the refurbished wand, now strobing like a disco ball in day-glo purple.

"Go on, Fergus, pull the other one," growled Barney.

Suddenly he room went completely silent. The back door swung closed. Then the hall was filled with the din of chairs forcefully scraped back and thunder of determined boots to the front. Unseen by the gamblers, a ball of yarn was rolled across the back exit, unspooling a resilient, red strand that became tightened from both ends.

Conrad hopped up on the bingo caller's table with the wand in his beak. "Drop this, mister?" As the mob awaited the wizard's response, there resonated an audible gulp. A star-spangled pointy hat was passed forward.

"Oh, and 'ere's yer 'at." Big Willem thrust a meaty hand bearing the hat at the wizard who was cringing several feet beneath Willem's glower. Herald grabbed his hat and wand and made a dash for the door. The meaty hand simply snatched him up by the collar. Willem wasn't just big. He was fast. And not happy.

"You know wot we do 'ere with cheaters?" Big Willem snarled.

Herald didn't and didn't want to. "Terribly sorry. Seems I've made a mistake. Must have misheard—not a bingo after all. Oh, is that the time? Been lovely, but must be going. Train to catch."

Herald ducked suddenly under the big man's legs and sped to the door. What with the crowd and mayhem, no one could pursue.

"Oi! 'E's gettin' away!"

Twaaaaaaaang! Thunk! "Oof!"

"Gotcher!" Herald was flailing miserably between two sets of furry, canid arms. The wolves had nabbed him.

"Good work, boys." Granny rose from her table, reeling in the red yarn. Barney sauntered forward.

"I'll take 'im from here, Granny. And thanks." Barney went to grasp the wizard, but as he stepped forward his boot set down on a hard, round acorn. Barney slid and went down with a reverberating thud.

Pop! A puff of purple smoke was all there was in the place where Herald had been. Big Willem wasn't the only one who was fast.

"Drat. Should've seen that one coming," Rumpbuckle muttered, vowing to make better use of his scrying orb in future.

Back at Wolfgang's, Rider had a productive morning after getting through to his firm, including a most illuminating conversation with his father. They'd made good progress and had discovered the name of the corporation behind the illicit logging and mining operation on the baroness's and her friend's land. They even had the names of the corporation's top brass staying in the valley.

"Brilliant, Dad! Quick work. But I'm still not clear on how this bunch thinks they can get around the legal stipulations. The laws seem fairly ironclad to me."

Viewing a situation less heatedly than Rider, his father was always better able to envision what wiggle room there might be for the opposition. He spelled out the anticipated loopholes to his son.

"But, Dad, even if no one technically owns the waterways, how do they expect to get around gaining access to the river across ground that *is* owned and staunchly protected? And what about the trees they've illegally felled?"

Rider had, in fact, predicted many of the wormy methods they would attempt to excuse, justify or explain, and the hush money behind it all. It wasn't that he was a rookie, he just needed to vent. A pang of nostalgia hit Rider, picturing his father leaning back in his leather chair, tie loosened and raking his dark hair in thought, his hazel eyes missing nothing. Dad was so good at breaking things down into bits you could tackle. Rider fervently hoped he could catch the wizard and be able somehow to return to his old life. He'd missed sorting things out with his dad.

There was a tap on the glass. "Hold on a sec, Dad." Putting the phone down on Wolfgang's kitchen table, he crossed to the window. Conrad was back. He hopped in as Rider opened it, swivelling his pipe past the casement.

"I'm on a call right now. Where's Eduardo, Conrad?"

Conrad croaked in embarrassment. "He'll be coming back shortly. But Granny sent you a message. Thought you'd want to know soon like."

"Is Eduardo okay?"

"He's fine. Everyone's okay. But I've got some good news and some bad news."

Oh, flipping perfect. Why must news always come in sodding opposite pairs? Rider could have used the good part. The bad part, not so much. He looked expectantly at Conrad.

"Well, the good news, you see, is Granny found the wizard and the boys nabbed him."

"Fan-flipping-tastic! So . . . ?"

There was a long pause. "Ah. Yes. So . . . er, you want to hear the bad news?" Conrad stepped back a bit and set his pipe down on the sill.

This couldn't be good. Conrad was normally chatty. Rider drummed his fingers on the counter. "Do I have to guess?"

"No, but I bet you can."

Rider's shoulders sagged. "You lost him again, didn't you?"

"Not so much lost, you see." Conrad ruffled his feathers. "It's complicated."

Rider raised a palm to Conrad, signalling to hold that thought. He picked up his phone again. "Dad, something's come up. Let me ring you later. What's the best time?"

His father gave him a short run-down of his schedule. "Okay. I'll try then. Bye. Oh, and thanks, Dad."

Damn that wizard! It looked like he wouldn't be resuming his old life any time soon.

CHAPTER 17

Blow-Ups by Amateurs

Meanwhile... The Bat and Whistle that Friday resembled the cast lunchroom at Ubiquitous Studios. It was crammed wall-to-wall with costumed actors and crew groupies, taking a break from the shoot. Basil was pleased to have this much custom without even a bingo game to entice. Maisie was dashing about with fists full of tankards.

Nigel et al. were ensconced at their usual table by the window. Maisie'd saved it for them. They'd had a successful shoot that morning and were making good progress with the film. Amid hoots over a blooper they'd had to delete, a young man in dress shirt and tie and carrying a satchel approached them diffidently. Nigel smiled at him and reached for his pen.

"That's all right, sir. I'm not troublin' you for your autograph," said the young man, rubbing his red buzz cut in embarrassment.

"Oh. Right. Then what can we do for you?"

"I'm sure you've got your crew all set for your filum, but I've been doing a spot of filming on me own for some time here. I've got some pretty good stills I thought you might like to see. Maybe use 'em for the credits . . . or something." His voice dwindled.

"Have you? I very much want to see them! We were just saying that it would be nice to locate some archived photos of the area, maybe even some shots taken by the villagers, to give it more verisimilitude."

"Really? That's great! I have them here with me."

"Here, pull up a chair. What would you like?"

"Oh, I don't want to be a nuisance. I can buy me own."

"No, I insist." Nigel motioned to Maisie.

"Well . . . I am fond of the bitter here, if you really don't mind."

Nigel gave Maisie the order. "What's your name, lad?

"It's Clive, sir."

Nigel introduced himself and his crew. "Good to meet you. These photos, they're of the village, or the area at least, are they?"

"Oh, yes. I grew up here and I've been taking pics since I was little. Got loads. But not to worry, I only brought a few of the ones I thought might interest you concerning this filum."

"Well, let's see them, then." Nigel wiped down the pint prints on the table with a sleeve to made a clear area.

"Okay, then." Clive laid out several glossies in a mosaic pattern.

Ian whistled. "Nice work, man. You do the processing yourself?"

Clive beamed. "I do, yes. Learned a bit at school and been continuing with it ever since."

Maisie placed a brimming pint on the table for Clive. He took a timid sip and thanked his host, moving the beer onto a coaster. Derek leaned over Nigel's shoulder and looked at the photos. "Good lighting, that. Got a nice mood and the resolution's excellent."

Nigel's eyebrows arose. "I agree!"

"This one's of the castle gates." Clive pointed at the next picture. "Got a nice pic of the baroness's carriage going past. And this one's of the inn, the night she had her anniversary bash. Invited the whole village. She can be a good ol' egg when she wants to. Didn't half stagger, gettin' meself home that night."

Derek chuckled. "What's this dark, moody one? I really like that one."

"Thanks. I took this at the last full moon. Liked the way it came out behind that cloud and all those trees framing it."

"I don't recognize the location." Ian was peering at the photo. There were some baroque stone balustrades and some large, showy plants in urns. Seemed to be some kind of terrace.

"I was down in Otternought that night. I took that from the garden terrace behind that big hotel. Liked the combination of the moonlight and those two lovebirds sitting on that stone bench there."

Derek and Nigel leaned forward, suddenly alert. "You don't happen to have a photographer's loupe with you or anything?" Derek asked.

"'Course I do." Clive reached into his satchel and pulled out his loupe.

"Good man!" Derek took it from him and placed it over the faces of the couple.

"Is that who I think it is?" asked Ian.

Derek turned to Ian and Nigel. "Yep. Our Sylvia. The one and only."

"Give it here," Nigel demanded and took the loupe and photo. "Well, I'll be. Clive, you say you took that during the last full moon?"

"That's right. It was Sunday last."

The guys looked at each other.

"Something wrong?" Clive's shoulders climbed toward his ears. "'Cos, I have plenty others of the village and the castle, if you don't want one from the village down the road."

"No, no. It's a great shot, a lucky one you might say."

Clive's shoulders descended again. "Thanks."

"Any idea who the fellow with her is?" Nigel asked. The face of the man was in partial shadow.

"Never saw him before a couple of weeks ago. Think he might be one of the businessmen that's doing some deal up here. He's not a local, that's for sure."

Derek turned to Nigel. "Maybe we should check on this bloke. Bet you anything he's got a suite at that hotel."

"Yeah, and a bloody great expense account," said Ian.

Just then Gerry walked in and joined them. Nigel introduced Clive and filled Gerry in. Gerry dragged the photo over and studied it. "Yep, that's Sylvia. And doesn't that look like one of those corporate blokes who was here with his mates last Monday? They were sittin' at the next table, remember?"

Nigel examined the photo again. "It's pretty dark but, yes, it does rather look like him."

"You think he's Sylvia's 'teddy bear'?" Ian suggested.

"Could be. Sort of an old boy thing about him, all that curly brown hair, full of *bonhomie*." Nigel turned to Clive. "Any chance we can keep this one or get a copy?"

" 'Course you can. I've got the originals, so no problem."

Nigel put the enlargement into a folder in his coat. "Would you also be able to get it blown up any larger?"

"I'd be happy to!" Clive grinned.

"And I quite like several of the other shots. I think we could use them. Why don't you give me your card, or your number if you don't have one, and we can arrange a time to go over what you have under proper lighting," Nigel suggested. "We can discuss terms then, if that's okay."

"That would be great!" Clive scribbled his number for Nigel and gathered his other shots. "Thanks so much. I'll be glad to help however I can, sir."

"Good job we met you." Derek smiled at Clive.

Clive blushed and swallowed the rest of his beer. "For me, as well. Thanks very much. Be seeing you soon?"

"That we will," Nigel assured him.

The crew regarded Clive thoughtfully as he left the tavern.

"Well, that was a bit of luck." Nigel sat back with his arms crossed.

"Too right, Nige. Best lead we've got so far. 'Spose Teddy Bear's still in the area?"

Nigel looked at Derek. "One way to find out."

"I'll just get my gear, shall I?" enquired Gerry.

"I think that would be good. Bring all the tackle you can. Derek, why don't you grab a couple of cameras. Ian can bring some lights, just minimal stuff. We don't want to frighten him or them off."

"Right you are, guv." Ian stood up, putting some money on the table. Derek did the same.

"No, no. My treat. Not often we get a clue like that to chase."

"Thanks, Nige! Decent of you. Shall I ask Alice to get the car?"

"Yes, please. Oh, and Ian, make sure it's got plenty of petrol."

"What time shall I tell her?"

Nigel consulted his watch. "We've got the next scene to shoot at

1:00 p.m. Say five-ish?"

"Okay, then. We're off. See you on the . . . sets." Ian bounced his eyebrows and gave Nigel a snarky grin.

While the crew were talking inside, Rider rode into the innyard on Eduardo, dusty and tired from another foiled chase. The wizard's trail was stone cold and Rumpbuckle was still out when they called at his shop. Rider dismounted and tethered Eduardo by the drinking trough.

Thanks, jefe. I thought my tongue was going to roll up like a parchment scroll.

He slurped noisily, then pricked up his ears. Eduardo's excellent hearing tuned in to the crew's conversation. He motioned Rider to shush with a toss of his head. Rider crept over to the open window and listened. After a moment, they heard the chairs pushing back. They both turned away innocently as the men exited. Eduardo nudged Rider with his muzzle. Rider got the idea.

As Nigel stepped outside, Rider approached him.

"I understand you're the director of the film that's being shot here."

"That's right." Nigel cocked his head quizzically.

"Might I have a word with you? In private?"

"I've only got a moment. We're due to shoot in ten."

"That should be plenty of time. I'll walk with you back to the set, if that's all right."

Nigel shrugged as they set off. "I'm afraid we've already chosen our extras."

"Thank God for that!" Rider laughed. "I've no hankering for stardom."

"Okay. Then what?"

"I think we may have a common interest."

Rider filled Nigel in with what they were learning about the businessmen and the rumours he'd heard about the assault on Nigel's starlet. Naturally, he left out the part about his own recent shape-changing.

Nigel stopped and studied Rider. "It's interesting that you should show up just now. We've just got a lead on this fellow."

Rider looked down with a shrug. "I admit it was a happy accident that I arrived when I did, but not an accident that I, well, overheard your conversation. In my defence, a friend alerted me to it first."

"It's all right. I'm used to it. I get a lot of eavesdroppers in my business."

"In mine, it becomes a necessary evil, I'm afraid."

"And what is that?"

"I'm a barrister. Environmental law, actually. For the good guys." Rider gave Nigel his card.

"Rippon, Rippon and Magnus, eh? I think I've heard of your firm. Very good things, in fact. So your interest isn't just to see if this fellow is the alleged werewolf who's going around nipping at the natives?"

"It's that, of course. I came into the area recently myself, and I want to make damned sure I'm not considered a suspect. But what we've discovered about this corporation and the men who are visiting here presents a much bigger menace. One that's within my purview. I'd be grateful for your help. And I feel certain the baroness would be, too. Might even get you an audience with her," Rider suggested.

"That *would* be helpful. She's turned down our previous requests. And I may have something in the way of evidence to present to her."

"The photo that photographer gave you?"

"The very one. Say, after this afternoon's shoot, we're going to see if we can run this guy down. Oh, of course you know that." Nigel smirked.

Rider winced. "I do, or at least I gathered that."

"Fancy joining us?"

"I was rather hoping for an invitation."

"I wouldn't have thought you were the sort to wait for one."

"You're right. I'm not. But the chase is so much easier when one joins forces."

Nigel slapped Rider on the shoulder. "Here's my card. See you outside the set around five?"

"I'll be there. Thanks." Rider turned and went into the tavern. The desert in his mouth reminded him it was time to end the drought.

This storyline is fleshing out amazingly well, mused Nigel. There was a good chance this wouldn't be any mere documentary, at least not the travelogue he'd pitched. He made a note to ring Clive and see if he could get the blow-up *tout de suite*.

Inside the tavern, the window over Rider's shoulder opened wider as he sat inhaling his well-earned pint. A breeze of horse breath rippled the foam on top. Rider's head dropped. "What's up, Eduardo?"

I just saw Rumpbuckle go by. We could probably meet up with him back at his store, I'm thinking.

"Do you *think* I could at least finish my beer? Maybe get a sandwich?"

Quizás.

"Thanks. Big of you."

Just trying to be helpful. I could use some hay out here, too. Oh, and here comes Conrad. Shall I ask him to follow Rumpbuckle? Save time locating him later.

"Excellent thought. Please do."

Rider summoned Maisie and ordered food for himself and hay for Eduardo. As he was diving into his lunch, he could hear Eduardo giving Conrad his instructions. Granny and Wolfgang surely had useful friends.

Some moments later, Conrad flew in the door and hopped up on the table while Rider was finishing his chop and chips. "You gointer finish those?" Conrad pointed his beak at the chips.

"Help yourself. I'm stuffed."

Conrad held a soggy chip in one claw and gulped it down bit by bit rather like an engorged worm. "Needs more salt," he commented.

Rider pushed the salt shaker over. "Shall I?"

"I can handle it, but thanks, mate." Conrad grabbed the shaker with his beak, turned his head sideways and gave it some hearty shakes over the last of the chips. Rider was impressed. Crows really were clever.

"You know, Con, that's bad for your health, all that salt."

"So's smoking."

"Where is your pipe, by the way?"

"I'm cutting back. Can't get the blend I like anymore."

"And salt's your trade-off?"

"Might as well be. I use it on everything, 'cept snails. Makes 'em fizz." Conrad gulped down the rest of the chips. "Thanks! That was a treat. Beats eating bugs."

"So did Rumpbuckle go back to the shop?"

"Yep, to his flat above it. Granny, too. I took the liberty of telling the doctor you're looking for him. All right?"

"That's fine. Any idea how long they'll be there?"

"Most of the evening, I'd say. Granny was going to cook him supper for helping out at bingo."

"Great! So we should be able to hook up with him. I'm anxious to give them both the latest news."

Conrad cocked his head. "Since lunchtime?"

"If you want to come with us, I can fill you in."

"Ready when you are."

Rider paid his bill and Conrad hopped on his shoulder as they left to get Eduardo.

"Eduardo, Rumpbuckle's gone back to his shop with Granny. Let's pick up Wolfgang and head over there, shall we?"

Sí. Claro. Sounds like a plan.

Rumpbuckle leaned back in his wing-back chair by his fire, tenting his fingers, considering what Rider and the others had told him. "It seems quite clear, then, that at least two of the new lycanthropes are with this corporation, Global Advanced Management, LLP. I myself have heard rumours about what appears to be another of those gentlemen chasing some women down here with nearly dire results. My granddaughter knows one of them. Woman had to be treated by the local doctor for bite marks to the throat. Canid bite marks, in fact."

"Do you have any description of the second fellow?"

"Balding, middle-aged, on the beefy side. Looks like he loves his comestibles, from the paunch on him. Wears those confounded yellow 'power ties.' "

Rider consulted his notes. "The first man, or at any rate Sylvia LaMoânne's assailant, we think is one Addison T. Brickheart, the corporation's Chief Compliance Officer. Your description of the second man matches what I have on their VP of Business Development. Cyril B. Stonewall is his name."

"Apt surname, considering what they're trying to pull over on us."

"Boy, that for sure!" Wolfgang growled.

"And what about the third?" Granny asked. She came in with a tray of beef-and-onion pasties hot from the oven. Rumpbuckle heaved aside some books from the tea table and made room for the tray.

"Those smell delicious, my dear! Rider, would you do the honours and fetch the glasses, please? There's a rare old bottle of port there on the sideboard. And I have some excellent Stilton, too, that I'll fetch in a moment."

"Your granddaughter didn't want to join us?" Rider asked him.

"Alas, she doesn't care for port. She's at the cinema, with friends," Rumpbuckle replied. "But what can you tell us about the third man?"

"Well, from what our sources dug up, he's the company's CDO. Name's Tyrone P. Upman."

"That the slick fellow with them wire-rims and silver hair?" Wolfgang peered over Rider's shoulder at the notes.

"That's right."

"See, that show you right there this must be some super-secret deal they tryin' to pull off, sendin' they top brass like that. Don't trust they minions not to botch it."

Granny twinkled at Wolfgang. "Such a bright one you are, dear." A happy tongue bannered at the praise. "I'll just go fetch that Stilton. You stay there, Rumpy."

Rumpy? Rider subdued a snort. Rumpbuckle had told them he and Granny went way back. Way back where was the question.

After a thoroughly satisfying tea, Rider declared at last, "That was wonderful port, Dr. Rumpbuckle. A perfect accompaniment to the Stilton and Granny's delicious pasties." Rider wiped his mouth with a linen napkin and placed it on his side table, then checked his watch. "It's time we headed back. It's nearly five and I don't want to miss my appointment with the director."

"No indeed. Like you, I hold no doubt that the man in that photograph is one of the new werewolves, but an enlargement would make a better presentation of evidence."

"They still no evidence, though, to link the dude to what's going on up that ravine," Wolfgang pointed out.

"Unfortunately not. I'm hoping, Doctor, with the film crew's help, we'll be able to gather considerably more. Then we can present what we have to the baroness." Rider arose. "Thanks once again for your hospitality."

"The pleasure has been entirely mine." Rumpbuckle stood and walked them to the front door.

"Not entirely yours," Granny corrected, putting her arm through Rumpbuckle's. "I always enjoy feeding up my boys."

"Granny's just plain magic with food, that for sure!" Wolfgang licked his lips.

"I certainly have no complaints, dear lady! Your scrumptious efforts are much appreciated." Rider was becoming quite fond of Granny.

They heard a whinny of agreement from Eduardo outside.

"Well, we won't delay you further," Rumpbuckle replied. "Let us know what you find out as soon as you can."

"Rumpy, do you think it might be good to send my friends, Olivier, Conrad and Ross, on ahead to scout things out?" Granny suggested.

"Maybe the boys, too? They come in real useful," Wolfgang added.

"Oh, why not?" Rumpbuckle smiled at her.

"I'll let them know, then." Granny smiled back at them. "Safe journey."

Rider thanked his hosts again and said his goodbyes. He turned to Wolfgang after the door closed, "It might be best if Ross left that tartan scarf behind again. Bit of a red flag."

"Oh, I don't know. That his lucky scarf. He real partial to it."

"And why is that?"

"On account of it differentiatin' him from the rest of the rats so he don't wind up somebody's dinner. Gets him some respect, see. Kinda like you in you ridin' boots when you ain't always ridin'."

Rider scowled. "I packed light. At any rate, I hope what respect I garner is based on more than that."

"Maybe. But them damn fine boots."

Outside, Eduardo clopped up with a posy drooping from his mouth.

"For me? You shouldn't have!" Rider pressed a hand to his heart.

My apologies. I was just finishing my dinner. If had known you were fond of Matricaria chamomilla, *I would have brought you more than a mouthful.*

Fists on hips, Rider shook his head. "Eduardo, how in hell do you know the botanical name for German chamomile?"

Señor, there is much you do not know about me. Our dear Granny, she has also given me the library card.

Rider threw up his hands and saddled up. Wolfgang patted Eduardo's withers. "Good one, man!"

Eduardo tipped his head. *Gracias.*

They proceeded back to Slaughter's End at a stately trot.

CHAPTER 18

Gangin' Up

F*riday Après Tea.* "All right, you can come out now," Rumpbuckle addressed an aspidistra in the corner of his lounge from which sounds of a scuffle were issuing.

"Oi, get yer bloody great boots off me back!"

"I can't help it I fell off that dead leaf, can I? Needs waterin'!"

"If I have to tell you two one more time to watch where you're goin', there's gonna be one less of us."

"Ow! Get yer elbow outa me eye."

Rumpbuckle crossed his arms and waited. Eventually three lights disentangled themselves from the foliage and floated over to the settee. Granny came back from the kitchen, setting three thimbles of tea down on the table in front of the three sprites.

"Ta, Granny. We was fair parched." Brain reached out for his thimble.

"What, no pasties?" asked Dim.

He got a whack on the back of the head from Brain and Elmo. "Watch yer cheek," warned Elmo.

Granny clucked her tongue. "As if I would forget to feed you. I'll be right back."

She returned with a Dresden saucer, holding six tiny pasties, and a small pot of brown sauce.

Dim rubbed his hands. "Fab! You're the best, Granny."

"So whash the plan?" asked Brain, mouth full of pasty.

"Rumpy offered to walk me home. Isn't that sweet?" Granny replied.

"After taking advantage of her considerable culinary skills, I felt it was the least I could do," Rumpbuckle professed. "And as it's such a fine evening, a detour on the way through the woods might be a pleasant and informative diversion, might it not?"

"And you want us to come with?" asked Elmo. Rumpbuckle nodded.

"Would this detour take us up along that stream with that funny stuff in it, by any chance?" Brain caught on fast.

"Quite so. I saw no harm in our doing our own reconnaissance," Rumpbuckle replied.

Dim was doubtful. "Ooh, I dunno. That stuff scrambles my brain."

"Everything scrambles your brain, what little there is of it," Brain snapped.

"Now, Brain, there's no call to be like that," Elmo chided.

"It's true, though," Dim insisted. "Somethin' in that water does a number on my synopsis."

"That's 'synapses,' yer twit," said Brain.

"Those, too."

"Gentlemen, I am aware of the effect of tantalum on magical powers, so we will take precautions. But you three are much abler at remaining unseen than are we.

"Told yer size mattered!" Elmo crowed.

"In this case, it certainly does. As long as you remain a prudent distance from the river, we should be all right. And your presence will eliminate the need for torches."

"Okay, I suppose, long as you bring yer wand."

"I am never without it."

Granny tilted her head, regarding Rumpy. "Never?"

Rumpbuckle coloured. "Well, almost never."

Rider, Wolfgang and Eduardo got to the film site just as Nigel and his crew put the set to bed. Nigel walked over to Rider as he climbed down and shook hands. "Perfect timing. We just finished."

Rider introduced him to Wolfgang. "I remember you," Nigel said.

"My scout hoped to recruit you. Forgive me, but is that really your name?"

"It is now." Wolfgang crossed his arms.

"Only it's so perfect for the role we were filling. We get a lot of hopefuls changing their names so they'll sound like celebrities. But of course people change their names for other reasons."

"That they do." Wolfgang wouldn't be drawn.

Eduardo nudged Rider. "Oh, forgive me. And this is my friend, Eduardo."

Eduardo nodded his head at Nigel.

"He really can understand us, then?"

"Oh, he understands quite a lot, sometimes more than is in his best interests." Rider shot Eduardo a look. Eduardo merely tossed his head. Lowering his voice, Rider added, "But I wouldn't mention the talking horse on TV to him. He gets upset at the comparison."

"I'll keep that in mind." Nigel shouted to his crew, "Gerry, you guys about ready with the gear?"

"Just loading the car now. How many are we?"

Nigel did a head count. "Looks like six." He turned to Rider. "By the by, we got intel that the bigwigs have left the hotel and are headed up to the ravine. The two of you okay riding up on your own?"

"Sure. Eduardo qualifies as an ATV and might come in handy if we find ourselves in tight spaces, like between trees. Plus, it gives me justification for wearing my fancy riding boots." Rider daggered eyes toward Wolfgang, who just chortled.

"Oh, sorry, Nige. I forgot Alice. She's comin', too." Gerry amended. "Alice is a crack driver," he told Rider.

"Okay, then. Let's head up," Nigel said.

The crew and Wolfgang climbed into a large, unassuming, maroon 4WD van. Alice walked over and got in the driver's seat, introducing herself. Her ponytail was tucked up under a hunting cap. She quickly stowed her infrared binoculars in the glove box and put the van in gear, then turned the car in the direction of the ravine. They needed to make good time if they were to get there before sundown.

Rider remounted Eduardo and motioned to Alice to hold up. "You go on ahead, Nigel. We'll be a bit slower, but not by much, I shouldn't think. Granny showed us a short-cut. I'll watch for your van on the trail, but depending on what we find, I may take a different approach. Let's try to meet up by the first group of picnic tables."

"Sounds like a plan," Nigel said. "If we don't see you there by nightfall, we'll carry on on foot. Okay, Al. Tally ho!" The tyres spun on the gravel and they were off.

Up the ravine, a steel-grey, cross-over SUV limo wallowed its way over the stones and ruts to its assigned meeting place. The chauffeur wasn't too happy thinking about the wear and tear to the suspension. They barely had 3,000 miles on this one. Inside, Cyril Stonewall cursed as half of his whiskey and water splashed onto his suit trousers. Addison reached into the car's mini-bar and handed Cyril another miniature of Doers scotch, then poured himself one. Struggling for patience, Tyrone turned away and leaned forward to the chauffeur. "How much farther, Randall?"

"According to the GPS, only about a mile, sir."

"Good. Everything's on schedule." Tyrone sat back and tapped on his laptop.

"How's the count getting here?" Addison asked.

"Flying in, I presume."

Cyril sprayed out a mouthful of whiskey.

"Good God, Cyril. Are you going to drink that or wear it?" Tyrone passed Cyril some cocktail napkins.

Cyril mopped his lap while Addison stirred his drink in silence.

The grey limo rounded a bend and came to the appointed clearing. In the dusk, they could make out the foreman's trailer. Its metal door slammed and an electric torch was coming their way. Through the chauffeur's window, a large belly in a blue shirt appeared, the buttons straining to contain its occupant. A small, semi-automatic handgun was tucked into the belly's belt and the name tag on the shirt read "Bill." Randall lowered the window for Tyrone. "Everyone here, Bill?"

Bill leaned down to ID his visitors. Good. No unexpected ones. He straightened up and consulted his clipboard. “Yep. They’re all ’ere, Mr. Upman. Ready when you are.”

“Excellent.” The three men exited the limo, leaving Randall to park it off to one side of the clearing. “I see you’ve made progress.” Tyrone glanced around approvingly. The clearing was considerably larger than two days ago. It made it much easier to park their vehicles and equipment.

“Too bad they didn’t make better progress on the bloody road!” muttered Cyril.

“Oh, cheer up, Cyril. I feel sure there are more bottles in the mini bar.” Tyrone couldn’t resist. He admitted the two had been through a lot, especially “the change.” *That* was something he’d never anticipated. Still, sorting it out would have to wait until they had concluded this current deal. In the meantime, it seemed reasonable to demand some decorum. As Tyrone unwound his long frame from the limo and stepped into the torch’s circle of light, he made a mental note to reassess their job descriptions when they returned to home base.

“’Struth! What’s that?” Bill stepped back smartly as what appeared to be an extremely large raptor settled in their midst, swirling a black cape.

“Ah, Count. Prompt as ever.” Tyrone reached into the limo’s rear compartment for his briefcase. The count nodded to Bill and the other crew as Tyrone made his introduction.

Reggie and Martin, the other two crewmen there, goggled. *Well, that’s something you don’t see every day.* Reggie couldn’t wait to tell the wife. Martin just crossed his chest, hung back, then pulled up his collar.

“I zee you have brought ze papers.”

“Of course. They’re certified copies of those I left with you at your castle. I trust you have had a chance to read them?”

“I haff. Everyzink appears to be in good order, Mr. Upman.”

“Good, good. Then shall we move to the trailer where you can sign more comfortably?”

Cyril and Addison joined them. In the evening quiet, a twig snapped. Bill’s head swung around with his torch beam.

"Do we have company, Bill?" Tyrone's gaze followed Bill's torch.

A pine cone crashed down to the forest floor, its fall assisted by Ross and Conrad, invisible in the dark canopy. "Just a pine cone," Bill decided. The men turned and entered the trailer.

The frantic whispering on the banks of the stream was covered by the burble of water. Ditto the stealthy clop of hooves. When the door to the trailer was closed, the spies joined up, staying at a distance and undercover.

"Is that you, Nigel?" Rider whispered.

"Yeah, we're here. We missed you at the picnic tables. Thought we'd better keep going while there was light."

"Good choice. We came another way, that short-cut I was telling you about. I hadn't remembered that it bisected the trail higher up."

Wolfgang padded up and sat down, sniffing the air. Two other wolves skulked forward and sat next to him.

"Where's Alice?" Rider asked.

"We left her down the hill with the van to play look-out," Nigel explained, "in case any unexpected guests arrived."

"Will she be all right, if anything rough occurs?"

"Oh, our Alice can handle pretty much anything," Derek vouched. "Has to with this one." He jerked his head toward the director. Nigel had the grace to smile.

"To clarify," Nigel put in, "Alice is not only a crack driver but a crack shot. We began keeping a rifle in the car ever since that near-disastrous African film."

"Speaking of shots, have you been able to get anything here yet?" Rider asked Derek.

"A few, but it was tough to set up a tri-pod on this uneven ground. Didn't want to risk a flash, so I'm shooting wide-open and slower than I'd like. Ian got a few off with his infrared lens, but the acuity isn't as good and infrared shots are notoriously ambiguous to read."

"I believe I may be of some service in that area, gentlemen." A familiar baritone was now just audible next to Rider, making Rider and the others jump.

"My apologies for the alarm."

"Rumpbuckle!" Rider whispered. "I thought you were in front of your fire, enjoying your port."

"The port has waited 70 years to be consumed. It can wait longer. It was a nice night for a stroll."

"And it wasn't much out of our way." In the shadows, a lavender-grey head with a red bandana appeared above a patched denim jacket adorned with runes and peace signs.

"Granny?" Rider croaked. "How did you keep from breaking your necks? Eduardo and I barely made it without doing so, but we had the advantage of light."

"We did, too." On her cue, three tiny golden lights swarmed out from under the trees. Three small brown faces grinned out at them above some fern fronds.

"See. Good things come in small packages," beamed Elmo.

"Wouldn't miss this for worlds. We love a good farce," Brain said.

"They have been a great aid. Perhaps they can also give you the lighting you require for your photography?" Rumpbuckle motioned for the sprites to do a demonstration.

"Neat. Seems like you can regulate the brightness, too, right?" Derek was considering his lens settings.

"Sure can, man," said Dim. He was fond of American films.

"And they just look like a bunch of fireflies so the baddies won't know they're bein' shot in glorious Technicolor." Ian grinned at Nigel.

Nigel pointed to the trailer door. "Derek, you set up over there, catch them coming out. Do your best to grab face shots." Derek crept over with his tri-pod, Elmo following.

"Ian, you go wide, so we can get shots of the set-up here. Get as much of the trailer and the equipment in as you can. I'm thinking you can probably stay low behind that holly under the big oak." Ian nodded, crouched and tiptoed behind the bush with his camera bag. He switched his lens to a fast, non-infrared wide-angle with a zoom feature, then screwed his camera onto a tripod and adjusted its legs. Brain hovered above.

"Gerry, do you think you could rig up something to record their conversation?"

"Already done, Nige. Bug's by the window." Gerry crept behind the trailer and put his headphones back on. Nigel nodded.

"Where do you want me, boss?" Dim asked.

"You can run interference," Nigel decided. "Keep 'em distracted. Nothing worse than an insect buzzing in your face." Dim swelled with pride and saluted, then sailed off to the window of the trailer to keep watch.

Rider grimly surveyed the clearing. "I see they've been cutting more trees, curse them. And that looks like some kind of mining dredge next to the bucket loader," he whispered to Rumpbuckle.

"Sssshhh! They're about to come out," Dim announced.

Everyone ducked for cover and got ready to roll.

The door to the trailer opened and the men inside emerged, Bill shining his torch on the ground in front of them. Count D. and Tyrone shook hands. "It has been a pleasure dealing viz you, Mr. Upman. Und viz you, alzo." Count D. bowed to the others, and stuffed his copy of the signed documents into a large pocket in the red lining of his cape. "Zo how long do you zink it vill take to get ze ore out?"

Eh?! Derek and Gerry looked at each other. They hadn't seen any 'ore go in. Then Gerry stifled a snort.

"You're referring to the tantalum, I presume?" asked Tyrone.

"*Ja, ja,* ze tantalizing sparkly goodies."

"Working at night . . . I shouldn't think more than a month or two. We brought the most advanced equipment we could fit in such a restricted location. In any case, I will give you a report on our progress here within a fortnight," Tyrone told him.

"Und I get to keep ze biggest timber, *ja*? I haff a lot of repairs to make to *mein Schloss*."

"That's right. It's all in the contract."

"Vunderful! Zo . . . I look forward to your report. Vell, I must fly!" With a tremendous flap of his cape the count took off. Martin crossed himself again.

Bill panned his torch around the site. "What is it, Bill? More pine cones?" Tyrone asked.

Bill scratched his chin. “Funny, I don’t remember seeing those fireflies before, do you?”

“I really couldn’t say, I’m afraid. Aren’t there normally fireflies up here?”

“I reckon. Just seems a bit late in the season for them.” Bill started walking toward the end of the trailer behind which Gerry crouched with his headphones. Diving maniacally, one of the fireflies did loops in front of Bill’s face.

“Get away, you!” Bill dropped his torch as he slapped frantically at the determined insect. “Can you believe that bug?!” Gerry froze.

Martin handed Bill’s torch back to him. “Christ, Bill, the way you’re going on, you’d think it was a swarm of wasps!” Tyrone and the others sniggered.

“Sorry. It’s just I was bitten bad by a bee when I was a tyke. Swelled up like a zeppelin and had to go to the doc. Let me walk you to your car, sir.”

Gerry’s shoulders sagged. The armpits of his shirt were soaked. Among his colleagues, the moisture content had likewise increased in various articles of clothing.

The grey limo pulled up, more hands were shaken and the car’s doors slammed. The limo circled around then lumbered back down the pot-holed ravine, the mining crew going back inside the trailer. Outside, several breaths were slowly expelled. It’s incredible how long you can hold your breath when you really apply yourself.

“Phew! That seemed close there for a bit.” Gerry had crept back with his gear to the group in the shadows.

“The look on your face when Bat Man asked about the ‘ore.’ ” Derek grinned at him, joining them behind the oak.

“What about your own?” Gerry retorted.

“Psssssst! Lads, I think we’d better keep quiet until we get well away,” Nigel cautioned. The three sprites swarmed up as everyone packed their gear. “Lead the way, fellows!” Nigel whispered. The path was instantly bathed in gentle golden light, making it easy for the crew to avoid ruts and roots. Wolfgang, Olivier and the boys, of course, had no problem seeing stuff in the dark. It made scents. Or in Olivier’s case, squeaks. He sailed silently into the night in search of supper. Ross was glad he'd kept his tartan scarf on.

Rider climbed back onto Eduardo, who did a neat dressage turn, bringing up the rear. Conrad and Ross hopped on for a free lift. Every now and then a spotlight brightened on a lurking hazard.

"Now that's just showin' off, Dim," Elmo complained.

"Guess I'm not so dim after all, eh?" he smirked.

When the group got back down the ravine to Alice in the van, they made their way over the river and through the woods to Granny's house for a nightcap and a recap.

"What a delightful place!" Nigel and his crew took in her half-timbered home crouched under its eyebrowed thatch. With lamps inside shining through the lead-paned windows, the pink geraniums cascading from the window boxes almost glowed. It was practically a Kincaid moment. The twee threat was alleviated, however, by the front door: the curly wrought iron hinges had a motif of poison ivy. Between them was a faded, hand-written cardboard sign that read, "Go   away."

Nigel raised his eyebrows in bemusement.

Granny opened the door and saw his expression. "It used to read 'Gone away' but the 'n' and the 'e' got rained on one too many times. I couldn't be fussed to make a new one. Either way, it suits my purposes." She shrugged.

"Ah, she ain't foolin' us." Wolfgang murmured to Nigel. "Anybody who's welcome here knows it. That sign's for everybody else."

Rider patted Eduardo on the rump, relieved to have made it back without their stumbling on unseen roots. "Good footwork!" Eduardo did a little razzmatazz flick of his tail and trotted over to his trough. They left him noshing on wildflowers and trooped inside.

"Take your coats off and make yourselves at home." Granny motioned to the coat tree in the corner, a living evergreen with its roots digging right through the floor. They draped their jackets over its branches, still with lights on.

"I never could stand taking down a Christmas tree," Granny said. "And it really spruces up the place. I'll put the kettle on."

Rumpbuckle stoked the logs in the hearth, sat in the best chair beside the fire, and picked up his pipe. He was clearly at home here. Wolfgang and the boys curled up in their doggie beds. On a stand next to the kitchen door stood a bird cage with its door open. Conrad flew to his usual perch and, from habit, located his pipe. Granny'd gotten his favourite tobacco so how could he disappoint her? Fishing a wad from one of the food cups, he packed the pipe. Rumpbuckle got up and lit it for him.

"Thanks, mate." Conrad took a long puff and sighed contentedly.

"I'll second that," said Rumpbuckle as he retrieved his own pipe.

Ross climbed up to the back of Granny's chair, and tucked his scarf around him. The rest pulled up chairs and stools and got warm. Alice and Derek were sharing a large hassock and looking cosy.

In a moment, Granny returned with trays of tea, hot scones and ham sandwiches for everyone. She then put out small dishes of dried corn for Conrad and Ross and miniature tidbits for the sprites. Alice began passing plates around. Derek took the first one.

Rider pulled a steaming mug and a sandwich toward him. "Thanks, Granny! I was famished."

"This just the ticket!" Wolfgang mumbled around of mouthful of ham. "Mmmm, *mmmm*!"

Derek and Ian pulled out their cameras. Between sips of tea and sandwich bites, they began viewing the footage. Gerry plugged his headphones in again and rewound the tape. The others were quiet, wolfing down the grub.

Granny sat in her chair with her own mug. *Nice to have company, as long as it's good company.*

"Good work, everyone!" Nigel lifted his mug in a toast. They joined him.

"I was listenin' to some of the tape and I think I got some good stuff, all right. How about you lot?" Gerry asked Derek and Ian.

"First rate! A sight better than I feared, thanks to you three," Derek said, nodding toward the three sprites.

"Super lighting technique!" Ian agreed. "Nigel, what say we put them on the payroll?"

"It's a distinct possibility," said Nigel.

Brain, Elmo and Dim grinned back at them. "We always did want to get into show biz."

At last, Rider set aside his empty mug and leaned toward Rumpbuckle. "So, what now?"

"I think it's time we spoke to the baroness. Do you still have that photo of the man who attacked Ms. LaMoânne?"

"Yes. The first print is in one of my saddlebags. And I believe Nigel was getting that photographer to enlarge it."

"Got it right here." Nigel handed Rumpbuckle the blow-up of Addison. "The kid was most accommodating. He had it ready for us before our afternoon shoot was done."

When Rider came back with the smaller print, Rumpbuckle studied the two copies. Derek scooted his stool over and panned through the shots he'd taken at the worksite for Rumpbuckle and Rider. Nigel and the others looked over their shoulders.

"Yep. Definitely the same bloke. No doubt about it," Ian confirmed. "Derek got some good close-ups of him and the rest, too, as they were leaving the trailer. Take a gander at these."

"Great shots, Derek! The lighting is even full face." Nigel was astonished. He turned to Elmo. "How'd you know to do that?"

Elmo kicked his feet against the mantle he was sitting on. "Dunno, really. Just seemed better than lighting from above." He ducked his head and took a sip from his tea thimble.

"And the brightness is perfect, as well. Very natural." Ian said.

"If you keep on like that, 'e's gonna get a big head." Brain cautioned. "Any road, all of us been around the cinema since it began. I reckon we've seen us enough filums to know what's what. It's in our genes, you might say."

"Well, thanks to all your talents," Rider included the rest of the room, "I don't think we'll have any trouble convincing the baroness who the bad guys are."

Rumpbuckle leaned forward. "I realize it's late but, judging by what we overheard at the site, I really think we ought to go to her right away."

"You don't think she'll be annoyed by the late hour?" Rider consulted his watch and Wolfgang.

"Nah. Betty just be gettin' up from her nap and havin' her own 'tea' 'bout now."

"You are correct, Wolfgang," Rumpbuckle confirmed. "Except in an emergency, the baroness doesn't entertain until nightfall. In which case, I think it prudent if we proceed to the castle as soon as we've finished here."

"I don't think we all need to come. Just Nigel and his crew and I. The rest of you can enjoy yourselves and get some sleep. I know Eduardo will be grateful for a break." Rider looked at Nigel for endorsement.

"I agree." Nigel wiped his mouth with his napkin. "Alice, how are you bearing up?"

"All right. I had the easy part, just loitering about waiting for you lot."

"Gerry? Ian? Derek?"

Derek patted his stomach. "After that scrumptious feed, I could go several more hours. Thanks again, Granny!"

"Same goes for me."

"And me." Ian and Gerry were both on board. "Ta, Granny!"

"Yeah, great nosh-up," everyone chorused.

Granny's face shone. "You're always welcome here."

Nigel stood and extended his thanks to Granny. Rumpbuckle left his chair and shook Nigel's hand. "I'm very grateful that you joined us in this endeavour. Let me know how I may be of service."

"I will, sir. And thank you, as well." Nigel turned to leave but was stopped by Ian.

"Actually, there is one thing, sir."

"Yes?" Rumpbuckle turned to Ian.

"We'll be a tight squeeze with seven of us. Any way that you could temporarily shrink some of our gear so we can all fit in the van?"

"I'd be happy to."

Derek spoke up quickly. “Oh, no need. Alice can sit on my lap. Gerry can drive.”

Wolfgang and Rider exchanged looks.

“That works.” Nigel motioned for the rest to leave. “We’ll get back to you tomorrow morning with an update.”

CHAPTER 19

Cedric Gets Knocked Up

F*riday Night.* Cedric heard the door knocker bang on the front door. "Bollocks!" Switching off the telly, he grumbled his feet into slippers and shuffled out of his room, then grabbed one of the flaming torches from its sconce in the hall and trudged to the door. "This better be good!"

His visitors heard the heavy scraping of the bar being dragged back and the piercing squeal of rustified hinges.

What a terrific sound effect! Gerry wished he'd recorded that. Maybe he could later.

The basket-sized braziers to either side of the door flamed on.

Neat trick! How did they do that? Gerry wondered.

Cedric poked his nose through the crack of the opened door. "What is it?" Cedric recognized Rider. "It's you again. Couldn't chase yer away, I see."

"How could I resist your gracious hospitality?" Rider replied. "And I've brought a party with me." Cedric stepped out farther, waving his torch over the small crowd, in case there were pitchforks.

"Oh. You're that film bunch, the one that the baroness sent on its way last time you came callin'. She told yer she was busy." Cedric was quite put out. He was missing his favourite show.

"Please." Nigel stepped forward. "It's not about the film. It's important that we see the baroness right away. We have some information on those new shape-changers. I know she'll want to see what we have."

"Oh, all right. Wait here. I'll go up and tell 'er." The big door screeched closed. They waited. In the dark, Nigel thought he heard the click of nails on the cobblestones. He felt panting breath on his back and nearly jumped out of his Reeboks.

"Surprise!" said Wolfgang. "Didn't want to miss the fun."

"Well, that got my heart rate up!" Nigel bent over, inhaling deeply. "It's all this talk of werewolves, I guess."

"Oh, you don't need to worry about that. You in good company."

"Wolfgang! Glad you're here." Rider pounded him on the back. "If she or her husband need further convincing, I think it will help to have your wolf's viewpoint."

"Yeah, I figured. See, y'all just can't do without me."

They held their ears as the door screamed open again.

"That door could use some oil," Ian observed.

"The baroness likes it this way. More atmospheric . . . or somethin'." Cedric turned and beckoned them in.

"Whoa! Will you look at all those heads!" They gaped at all the mounted trophies on the wall. "Usually, it's just animals. . . ." Gerry's voice trailed off and he glanced back at the door. Which was firmly shut.

An imperious voice declaimed from above, "We are all 'just animals,' are we not?" Its owner was descending the curved staircase toward them wearing a vampy, black evening dress with a sequined train. One bangled arm swept toward the grisly display. "Meet my ancestors, the ones who met untimely ends at any rate. My grandfather was too cheap to hire a portrait painter and it saved on framing costs."

Cedric was smiling now. Seeing the expressions on their faces was worth giving up *Monsters Got Talent.*

"Please don't concern yourselves," Betty purred. "We are no longer in the practice of mounting our dead." Several pairs of peepers swept sideways like crossing searchlights. "I understand you have some important information for me?" Her patrician nose tilted.

"Yes, Your Ladyship, we do. Better than information, in fact. Hard evidence." Rider withdrew a glassine sleeve of negatives from a manila envelope marked "Photographic Materials. Do Not Bend."

"Then perhaps you would care to visit my darkroom?"

"Very much, dear madam," Nigel said.

"Very well. Please follow me." They followed her up the staircase, Cedric lighting the way. Cedric opened the door to the darkroom and bowed them in. They noticed this one didn't screech. "Different atmosphere in *here*," Gerry whispered to Derek.

"You can say that again!" Their heads swivelled as they took in the photos in the developing pans and on the drying pegs.

"These recent?" Gerry gulped, holding a grainy black and white of a victim taken mid-suck.

"Goodness, no. Reprints. We're going through the all the castle's photos, archiving them for historical purposes. Those were mostly taken during my papá's reign."

"Mostly?"

"Perhaps all. I'm not sure. Now, what is it you have to show me? And, do please make yourselves comfortable."

Rider and the others scraped forward metal lab chairs, while Betty sat on the cushy one with gilded legs. He handed her the two photos of Addison taken by Clive. The baroness took out a magnifying glass to make sure the enlargement was identical to the original, then looked up. "Certainly identifiable. And this is the man you believe to be one of the outsider werewolves?"

"All the evidence points to it, yes," Rumpbuckle replied.

Gerry leaned forward. "I was able to tape a discussion among the three big-wigs, as well. The CDO was giving two of 'em a proper dressing-down for their wolfish rampages."

"Well, done!" Betty handed back the photos.

"There's more, Your Ladyship. A lot more." Nigel said.

"I would quite like to see them."

"And we have access to the negatives, as well."

"Do you? Excellent. If you're cramped for space at your site, you could do further prints here."

"That might come in handy," Nigel admitted.

"Well, we may as well have some refreshment." Betty smiled as Gerry shrank back. "Just ringing for Cedric." She reached for the bell cord but the door opened before she pulled.

"I had a feelin' you might be needin' somethin' to buck you up." He creaked in with a huge tray laden with drink and some finger food. Gerry didn't spy any actual fingers, but decided he didn't need further bucking after Granny's nosh.

"Cedric, you're becoming astonishingly good at reading my mind," the baroness said with threatening squint.

"Dinah had the kettle on already," Cedric murmured unctuously.

That hardly accounted for this spread or the speed, but never mind.

Cedric set the tray upon the counter, next to a shrouded enlarger, then stoked the fire before asking, "Will that be all, Your Grateness?" *Gotcher on that one!* thought Cedric. *She can't hear the spelling.*

A voice entered his mind: *Oh, yes I can.*

Oops. "Well, er, let us know if you need anything else." Cedric beat a retreat.

There was a soft tap on the door before it was opened by an apologetic Heinrich. "Oh, sorry, love. Didn't know you had guests. Saw the light and thought you might want some company. Don't mean to intrude." He turned to go.

"No, please stay, darling." Betty turned to the others. "This is my husband, Heinrich." Heiny bowed to them. She introduced them, adding, "I'm sure you remember Wolfgang."

"Yes indeed! How are you, old boy?"

"I just fine as frog hair," said Wolfgang.

"Glad to hear it!" Heiny indecorously hopped up and sat on the counter's edge. Betty gazed fondly at him. She always loved the way he could mingle. "So what's the occasion?"

The men filled them both in. It didn't take Heiny long to come to the conclusion that this would not be a mere one-bottle session. His backside was sore from perching on the counter. "Betty, dash it, why don't we vacate to the library, what? There's a cracking good blaze in there and these high-tech thingies are deuced uncomfortable to sit on!"

Noticing some half-smiles sliding off her guests' faces at the use of her pet name, Betty passed him her firmest "not-in-front-of-the-guests" look. "I think that's a splendid idea, *Heinrich,*" she said, taking control.

"The *baron* and I will send for additional provisions to be sent to the library," she addressed the others and arose from her gold-leaf facsimile.

"Oh, let's not disturb old Cedric, my dear. If you fellows can bring the tray down, while you're following the *baroness* to the library, I'll just nip down to the cellar and grab some more grog. See you in a jiff!" And off he trotted.

As they all settled in the roomy library, the baroness urged them to help themselves to her husband's stash of single malt, in the event they were too parched to wait for more wine. Seldom had any of them seen a larger private collection of books. The towering mahogany shelves and galleries filled with hand-bound tomes published as far back as the fifteenth century, the various papyrus scrolls protected in their hermetically sealed glass cases, the astrolabes and celestial globes were ample advertisement of their owners' wealth . . . and longevity. At the end of the long, main room was the requisite large desk in front of a set of French doors. The desk was clear of paperwork, Rider saw, and gleamed with polish.

On one side of a long wall was a Gothic-arched stone fireplace. The fire threw a warm light over the room and its bemused inhabitants. Above the mantel was an enormous gilt-framed oil of a 19th century woman with brown bouffant, beribboned party dress and merry golden eyes. She bore a distinct resemblance to Heinrich. His side of the family, it seemed, preferred to commemorate their ancestors in a more traditional manner.

While the rest seated themselves around the fire, waiting for their host to return, Rumpbuckle wandered off into one of the stacks and returned with a first edition of *Hormones, the Moon and You.* It would be a wonderful way to pass the wee hours when sheep were unaccountable. He was sure his host would be glad to loan it. *Eine kleine Nachtlese.*

Presently, Heiny elbowed the door open with an armful of ancient, dusty bottles. He set them down lovingly on the sideboard. "There! That's better. What's your poison?"

Gerry's eyes slid over to Nigel and the lads at the epithet.

Nigel nodded a "You first" at Gerry. Gerry shrugged and got up to pour himself a glass. Probably safe. Heiny did seem a nice old sport. Long as the moon wasn't full.

After several hours of show-and-tell and enough scotch and *vin rouge* to refloat the *Titanic*, Rider rose and stretched. He was sure his eyes were bloodshot. Everyone's else's were. And it was past four a.m.

"Forgive me, dear Baron and Baroness. I hate to leave a good party, but I'm fading fast. And I promised Father I'd check in with him first thing, which is only hours from now. I'll need to go over my notes beforehand and be as clear-headed as possible. Thank you both for hearing us out. And thanks, awfully, for letting us sample some splendid vintages!"

"It is *we* who should thank you. Without all of your good sleuthing, we would have still been stumbling about for clues for absolute ages, which would have given the opposition further opportunity to wreak their hav(*hic!*)-oc and destruct(*hic!*)-tion!" To keep up with the men, Betty had had to switch to an alcoholic blood substitute. Struggling to maintain propriety, she breathed deeply. "Heinrich, dearest, I think we should ring Ronny right away and tell her the news, don't you?"

"No time like the present, my dear. She'll be cross with us if we don't give her the juicy, and ASAP, you know. She'll want to get on the horn to Sid."

"Yes, but we'd better remind her not to ring Sidney until he breakfasts. You know how she is. Sidney will want to have all his wits about him and that usually requires caffeine. In any event, he won't be able to put in a call to the queen until at least 8:00 a.m., assuming she's in residence."

Rider hadn't thought of that. Another thing his dad would have factored in. "Is she often away?"

"Yes, certainly. She likes to keep her hand in with all her concerns and fiefdoms. But she always leaves someone quite capable to administer while she's away. I wouldn't worry. They'll see us. Of that you can be sure. Are you still staying with Wolfgang?"

"Yep. He with me." Wolfgang got up with a huge yawn and show of purple-stained tongue. "We can send that crow over to you for a message tomorrow, if you like."

"You're not on the telephone?"

"Sure, but it sorta a party-line. I can give ya the number, just need to be crafty what you say is all."

Betty arched an eyebrow, smiling. "I don't think that will be a problem."

"Perhaps it will be simpler if you just call my mobile," Rider said.

"That will be easier, I think." He read her the number as she wrote it down. "So," she resumed, "I shall ring you tomorrow after sunset, then, and let you know what arrangements we have made for an audience with the queen."

"Okey dokey." Wolfgang pawed open the door.

"We will take our leave, then, dearest Baron, Baroness. My thanks for the loan." Rumpbuckle waved the volume at them. "I'll return it to you promptly."

"Oh, no hurry, old boy. Glad to oblige," said Heiny. "Know that book inside out by now."

With a bow, Rumpbuckle took his coat from the obsequious arm suddenly appearing through the gap in the door. Betty was glad to see Cedric was still on his toes, instead of his bark-a-lounger, and had remembered their coats.

One by one, they bowed and renewed their thanks, grabbed their coats, and backed out of the room—not an easy thing when running on fumes. Cedric led the way to the front door with a torch that had been dialled down to "guttering" so that it would throw the maximum shadows.

The last to leave, Ian stumbled blearily against a chased bronze canister just outside the door. An umbrella stand?! His mind boggled and he suddenly felt quite sober.

CHAPTER 20

An Audience Is Granted

Saturday Evening. The next evening Rider's mobile rang as he was walking in Wolfgang's door, just after sunset. He checked the number. It was unidentified but from the local area code. Hoping it was the baroness, he snatched it up. "This is Esmond."

Silence, with a question mark. "Er, Rider speaking," he amended.

"Ah, yes. I had forgotten your *Christian* name, but I tend to do that. . . ." The weighty meaning in the baroness's comment stomped off, trailing big footprints. She herself was not a follower, having an allergy to crucifixes, but she assumed most Western mortals were.

"So happy you called, Baroness. Were you and the countess able to reach the Crown and book us an audience?"

"We were and we did." Rider couldn't miss the smuggery. Over 400 years of being the baroness in these parts had to be worth something.

"That's wonderful news, Baroness. Can she see us tomorrow?"

"I'm afraid that's the *bad* news."

Here we go again! thought Rider.

"The queen is in fact away, but her daughter, Princess Verisimila, will see us. However, the earliest opening is Monday morning."

Blast! Another day lost. Meanwhile, what in hell would be going on up that mountain?

Rider had to be careful here. "Thank you for arranging that, Baroness. Forgive me, but I must ask—are they aware of the seriousness of the matter and the urgency?"

"Naturally. I was most insistent they be put in the picture, else how would we have obtained an audience on such short notice?"

"Yes, of course. And I am grateful, truly. It's just that yesterday we heard from Granny's friends that the crew has become quite daring and more trees have been cut, ahead of what we believed to be their schedule."

He heard a quiet groan from the other end. The baroness really did care.

Summoning strength, she asked, "Do we know where the trees were cut?"

"Some lower down on the countess's side, where they seem to have set up a base. But more at the very top on your side by the river, perhaps a mile or so past the stone bridge and just below the count's land."

"Not my grandfather's 600-year-old chestnut!" Betty cried, abandoning decorum for the moment.

"No, thankfully. None of the largest trees have been touched." *Yet.* He could hear the expulsion of relief into the mouthpiece. His heart went out to her. A 400-year-old yew that he played under as a child had been later hacked down by new owners: a silly man whose nagging wife wanted to put their daughter's pony pen there. On 80 acres of parkland, 50 of them cleared, nowhere else would do for their darling.

"From what they saw, only a few of the smaller trees and saplings closest to the river were taken. But several queenfishers were . . . displaced."

The poor things! How in hell will the daft king*fishers get plucked out of the drink now?* It was the larger queenfishers who hauled their menfolk's tail feathers out of the water when they took on a fish a little too large. And wasn't that always the way? The queens weren't as flashy, but they got the job done.

"Can something be done?" she asked. She heard a dry chuckle.

"Something *is* being done."

Betty's shoulders descended a notch.

Rider told her that the mining crew had been beset by marauding wolves and several species of angry birds. "And I recall that there was some unusual and annoying 'firefly' activity. It appears the gentlemen didn't know fireflies could bite."

"What would we do without our Granny Loveanger?" the baroness mused.

"I really don't know, my lady. We could greatly use her services at home." Rider paused as he recognized the surname he'd just heard. "Did you say 'Loveanger'?"

"That's right."

"Not the Loveangers of—"

"The same. But, thankfully, she left all that behind when young. I do not think she would ever care to leave these mountains."

"Then you are fortunate indeed." On both ends of the line there was a fond silence, as they remembered all they owed to Granny.

Considering the contrary implications of the surname, it was nonetheless apt, at least to Granny. Her male forebears had lived up to the name in a very different way. They *liked* 'going away mad,' and made sure everyone else went that way, too. But with Granny it was the combination that applied: love *and* anger. And lots of both. But always the love first, hence the anger toward anyone threatening what was beloved.

He remembered his lunch with Granny. Wolfgang and he had arrived just as she was storming in the back door with a look of thunder, carrying a small rabbit whose right hind leg seemed halfway torn from its torso by the cruel teeth of a trap. The boys were waiting on the back stoop, one with the sprung trap in its jaws. They weren't waiting for lunch. They'd brought the rabbit to Granny to mend. They might be wolves, but using traps wasn't playing fair. In the game of Flee-or-Feed, fair was keeping your wits about you, with no outside aid or hindrance, and the odds more-or-less even. And natural. Natural was big in Granny's books, as it was in all the creatures'. Even those without libraries.

Granny had laid clean towels on the kitchen table and tenderly placed the trembling rabbit upon it. Rider expected the rabbit to try to bolt on its three good legs, but instead it just gazed up trustingly at Granny. She smiled at it and crooned something in its ears. The rabbit closed its eyes and rested its head on the table. It was still alive, just letting Granny get on with her mending.

"Wolfgang, you know where everything is. Could you show our guest the 'necessary'? Washed hands and paws, the both of you. Then perhaps you two could set the table? Shouldn't take me long to set the food out, but the wee one needs me now. Perhaps you should also turn the oven down a bit in the meantime."

When Rider came back from the necessary, which was amazingly spotless and spider-free, he saw Granny applying a curious-smelling salve to the neatly sutured leg and stroking the rabbit's head, muttering something he couldn't make out. She laid a fresh blanket on Wolfgang's bed. "I hope you don't mind, Wolfie."

Wolfgang shook his head. "Gotta do whatcha gotta do."

Granny laid the rabbit carefully in the basket and pulled a corner of the blanket over it. She placed bunches of mugwort around the blanket. "For the fleas." In a few moments, the rabbit opened its eyes, which were bright and seemingly pain-free. "That's better, then." She reached down and tucked in a small bunch of parsley and broccoli stems for a snack later. The rabbit snuggled under the blanket, safe.

After Wolfgang and Rider returned to Slaughter's End, word got back to them what happened to the fellow who'd set that trap. That was one dirty deed that wouldn't be repeated. You might say it bit him on the arse.

The baroness had her own memories of Granny's benevolence. There was a time when the baroness, like most of her own family, seemed incapable of love, her woods excepted, of course, but she had taken those for granted. She'd never considered that they mightn't always be there.

Then Granny had come along, and next, Betty's sweet Heinrich. And they changed everything. There was so much she learned from them. Betty understood at last that unless you loved something or someone a *lot*, you'd never trouble yourself working up a righteous anger when they were messed about. But now she *did* love, and by gods she was seethingly angry.

Anxiously, Betty focused on the business at hand. "The violators have suspended work then for the moment?" she asked.

"Yes, but I'm sure they will start again as soon as possible. Ross saw new markings on some of the bigger trees up the hill." Rider detected another groan.

"Please, Esmond, urge our spies to stay vigilant and *safe* and . . . tell them 'keep up the good work,' and so forth. . . ." Her voice dwindled as her mind mentally wrung its hands. "I'll let Ronny know, too. If anyone can get a dander up and scare the devils off, it is she."

Rider thought to himself, *There's another these devils should fear more if they had any wits: a fury in grandmother's clothing.* Aloud, he said, "We still must go carefully and not tip our hands, dear madam. If they know you and the countess are aware of their enterprise, they will be much more careful, which will make it harder to catch or even to observe them. As it is, they work mostly at night."

"How fortunate then that she and I are night owls, as it were."

Rider smiled at the phone. "And you have many other friends who are, as well. In two days' time we will be able to put the case before the Crown. From what you've told me they won't drag their heels in taking action."

"The queen and her daughter are every bit the arboristas that the countess and I are. What is it you call them? 'Bark cuddlers'?"

"Er, I believe the term is 'tree huggers,' my lady."

"Is it? Seems a bit . . . mild."

'Bark cuddlers,' eh? It appeared the nobility here had closer relations with their woodlands. Or, considering her husband, perhaps it was a Freudian slip. "So what time shall we meet and where?"

"Ronny is fetching us in her carriage. It has all the mod cons—light proofing and so on—so she and I can travel comfortably and arrive . . . refreshed. Most accommodating inside. It can hold quite a mob. But let's hope it doesn't come to that. So why don't we swing by and pick you all up?"

"Thank you very much, Baroness. I'm sure we'd be glad to accept your offer. Who shall I say will be coming with?"

"You, of course, and that director fellow. Nigel, I think he said was his name. And Wolfgang, naturally, and Dr. Rumpbuckle. Then there'll be Ronny and I and our solicitor, Sidney."

Rider's eyebrows rose. "That must be some carriage to hold so many!"

"It *is* a stretch carriage, when needs arise. Dwarf engineering. Clever, those folk."

"All right, then. What time shall we be ready?"

The baroness checked her digital sundial, which doubled as a moondial at night. (Another clever dwarf invention.) *It's really too bad they keep on striking.*

"Let's see. Our audience Monday is at 10:00 a.m. Sharp." The Crown considered sloth-like attendance to be pointless. "It should take us four hours give or take, depending on traffic, to get there."

The local shepherds and cowherds took advantage of the quiet early hours to cross the roads and highways. They found it was easier to get the beasts all going in the same direction when they were half asleep. But it could create some maddening and smelly delays.

"And there will undoubtedly be a lot of royal folderol to go through before our audience. That might mean another hour. Bring snacks. So I think if we leave no later than 4:30 a.m. we should be all right." *At least I won't be looking like death warmed up at that hour*, thought the baroness.

"We will be ready, Baroness. I'll be happy to contact the others."

"I'd be grateful if you would handle that. If anything important transpires between now and then, please be sure to telephone me."

Rider checked his mobile to make sure he had the baroness's number now stored in his phone. "I will, Baroness. Monday, then."

CHAPTER 21

Wild Goosed Chase

Rider rang off and checked his other messages: one from a paralegal at his firm and one from his father. He dialled the paralegal first. As she was giving him the latest data, Wolfgang came in. His fur was muddy and matted. And he was bent over as if he were in pain. Wolfgang dragged himself to the fridge and got himself a brew as Rider finished his call. Dad would have to wait.

"What the hell happened to you?"

Wolfgang grumped, "You don't want to know."

Rider had never seen anyone so down. Maybe after Wolfgang had a couple of good swallows Rider could coax the story out of his buddy. He sat down next to Wolfgang on a stool at the kitchen counter and put a brotherly arm across his shoulder, attempting a happier note.

"I heard from the baroness just now and it's all fixed for Monday."

"Monday, hunh? Means we lose another day. But I 'spose them gentry never deign to entertain visitors on weekends. 'Least *I* wouldn't bother if I was in they shoes."

"Well, we're lucky they agreed to see us as soon as they did, don't you think?"

"Yeah. You right, you right. What time we meet?"

Rider told him the details.

"Eduardo won't like that. He not a morning person."

"He's not one of the invited, so he can sleep in."

"Hunh! They can't use some more horsepower for that ol' carriage?"

"I hadn't thought of that. I could ask, I suppose. Why do you think

Eduardo needs to be there?"

"I guess he don't, but his feelin's will be hurt." There was a guilty pause. "Okay, okay. I 'spose I'll have to tell you. See, Eduardo just saved my butt."

"That was kind of him."

"Yeah. He a cool dude. Guess I kinda misjudged him at first."

"So . . . ?"

"Yeah, well. So Conrad spotted your ol' wizard. He down in Fester-on-Fen at the Grab and Tickle. It that marshy place at the bottom of the pass."

"Bingo again?"

"Bingo, all right." Wolfgang nodded bleakly and took a lengthy swig. Rider waited.

"So there we is, sorta tippy-toein' through all these lil' twisty alleys, followin' that wizard after he leave the pub. Didn't know a horse could tippy-toe so quiet, but Eduardo, he real good. So he go one way and I go the other, and I see this blur of blue with them stars on it. I send up a high-pitched howl to Eduardo. He catch on right away and try headin' him off from the other direction. We can tell pretty soon he spotted us. So we playin' hide-and-seek with the wizard. He dart into one of them dark doorways and wait for us to pass. Only we figured that's jes' what he'd do and Eduardo, he already hidin' hisself in a cross-alley ready to pounce, right?

I sit myself down, casual-like, lookin' in one of them shop windows, where I can see the wizard's reflection, jes' a scratchin' my ear with a hind leg, like you do." Rider remembered doing just that.

Wolfgang took another long pull. "So when that ol' wizard finally darts out, we jump his ass."

Hard Experience told Rider it wasn't the end of the story. It also proposed that he put his fingers in his ears.

"But see, Eduardo hadn't figured on his height versus all them hangin' signs. Hadn't figured on the sandwich board neither. Or them laundry lines with they unmentionables hangin' out from the windows." Wolfgang sighed. "It really coulda worked if it hadn't been wash day.

"So he launches into the air to apprehend the wizard, but the chemist's sign knocks him cold, right on the nose. Musta saw stars for sure. Still gotta imprint on his forehead, says, 'Just Say Yes to Drugs.'

"But he up again, bless him, scramblin' after that wizard. I'm racin' like a maniac past Eduardo with my eyeballs glued to the wizard and run smack into a sandwich board outside the tea room. Which collapses."

Wolfgang's rump still had remnants of pink chalk. Up close and backwards it read, "Special Today: Cockles, Buck-a-Shuck."

"Well, *that* was bad. See, that lane's got one helluva slope. Goes quite a ways, too. Before you hit a bend. Lots of time to build up momentum. Eduardo canters past me and says, 'Don't worry, my friend. I'll catch the *pendejo!*' or somethin' like that.

"Only now I'm on my butt on that sandwich board ridin' it down the street like a toboggan and pickin' up speed. That wizard, he jes' poppin' in and out of every doorway, around carts fulla onions, big-ass melons, and them granny drawers big enough to fit a elephant, and he throwin' them all back in our direction. We skiddin' around on that board tryin' to follow him. Them things don't turn too good."

"Both of you?" Rider asked weakly.

"Yep. See, I caught up to Eduardo. He now sittin' on my lap, more or less. But hey, he ain't heavy, he's my bro.

"So it gettin' a little hard to see how to steer. I'm countin' on Eduardo to do that, him so tall and in front. Next thing, some little white poodle with them dumb-ass pink bows on its ears has got its leash wrapped around a leg of that sandwich board, and he jes' a surfin' and boppin' up and down behind, yappin' up a storm. Some fat lady in a pink apron is screechin' after us but she can't keep up. We goin' too fast. And that wizard, he just peltin' us with produce and panties."

Rider saw Wolfgang's bottle was empty and wordlessly got him another from the fridge, twisting off the cap.

"At that point, we comin' up to this big jog in the lane at the Bank of Fester. Got them big columns in front. Lotta stone, too. It don't give much. And them shiny windows with fancy little panes. We did *not* want to hit that! That ol' wizard now playin' hide-and-seek behind them columns, hopin' we'd follow. Well, we not *that* dumb, and anyhow can't steer that quick, so we just zoom past intendin' to wait for him at the corner of the buildin', Eduardo usin' his right-hand hooves to sorta fend us off. But that blasted poodle, he still hitched. As we skid around the corner that ol' doggy, still lassoed to us and yippin' ki-yi-yay, somehow wrapped hisself up around that last column with his leash.

"Gotta say, that stopped us short. That leash musta been a deluxe model. Yanked us right up against them ol' granite blocks. Man, that smarted. But we better off than that lil' doggy. Leash finally snapped and he went whizzin' away through them fancy windows into the Loan Department. Don't think it did him any good. Doubt he was good for much collateral after that.

"So, now that we stopped, Eduardo get off that sandwich board and gallop after the wizard down the next street. 'Bout then some man with a giant barrel of used oil shows up rollin' it outa the chip shop to his van. Ain't no way Eduardo can slow down in time. He send that fella flyin' and now Eduardo on top of that barrel, like a hamster in a wheel, only on *top* of the wheel instead of *in*, see what I'm sayin'? He got fast foot-work, I'll say that! He jes' a tap-dancin' his way on top like some variety act, fast as can be, still after the wizard. Whoooee! Eduardo one determined horse.

"I yell to him, 'Dude, get off!' But he too afraid. Can't get no purchase to spring and anyhow, he jump off that barrel at that speed, it hit him in the hind legs and he be on his ass, maybe with a coupla busted legs. But he doin' pretty good, so I keepin' my fingers crossed, runnin' after.

"Then that barrel starts splittin' open and oil be oozin' out everywhere and attractin' stuff. We musta passed a poulterer's cuz now that barrel and Eduardo covered in goose feathers. He runnin' peculiar, too. Next, I hit that slick and go down. Now we both tarred and feathered. At least that oil gets Eduardo off the damn barrel. He jes' slide off the back side. The barrel though, it go bouncin' off down the hill findin' all sortsa things to hit. Holy crap! And damned if they ain't a goose now stuck on top of that thing, scramblin' and honkin'.

'Bout this time jes' about everybody in town be peepin' out they doors, offerin' advice or worse. Some be draggin' out they chairs to watch and takin' bets.

"We about to lose the wizard so Eduardo jump up over that barrel. It a perfect leap, like a ballerina or somethin'. Must be that Lippity-zany blood. Jes' beautiful. I'd call it a 5.8 at least."

There was a prolonged pause while Wolfgang took another long swallow. Rider was taking slow, careful breaths to dampen his emotions, torn somewhere between commiseration and guffaw.

"That when old Mrs. Knickertwister decide to lower her washin' line." A big gulp. Wolfgang shook his head in sorrow.

"Maybe she tryin' to help, thinkin' she could snag that wizard about to run by. But all it caught was the top of that pointy hat, on account of he so short.

"Eduardo so busy lookin' this way and that for the wizard he gettin' whiplash, so he don't see that clothesline in time. I try to shout out, but I'm too late. Probably cuz I'm too busy bustin' my ass laughin' at that wizard runnin' down the street with the biggest ol' brassiere you ever saw, streamin' from the point of his hat.

"Eduardo, he lucky. The line hit him mid-chest. Otherwise he be the 'Headless Horse.' But they big ol' drawers and y-fronts is flappin' around him like flags, the ends trailin' nappies and socks. And he covered in feathers, can't hardly see. So I come up and grab hold the two ends of the clothes line, help him steer. 'Cept the barrel's still leavin' a helluva smear and he come down on his butt with me swervin' behind like I'm water-skiin'. Lucky for us that street ended at the village pond. Kinda ruined a few ducks' day, though. Not to mention leavin' a feather-covered oil slick to clean up. Don't think we be welcome back in that town any time soon."

"So . . . ," Rider gulped and stifled a snort, "the wizard got away. Again." He regretted it as soon as he said it. It wasn't really a question, just the inevitable rhetorical conclusion.

Wolfgang glared at Rider. "What you think?"

"I'm so sorry." Rider took another careful breath, biting his lip. "But how did Eduardo save your life?"

"I can't swim." Wolfgang downed the rest of his scrumpy.

CHAPTER 22

On the Road Again

M*onday Morning.* Two days later, the alarm on Rider's mobile beeped way too early. He pried open an eyelid and peered at the time.

From the other bedroom he heard a moan and then, "What the hell time is it?"

"The crack of God Awful." Rider hated to wake Wolfgang after the painful ordeal he and Eduardo had had with the wizard, but it was Monday and, helpfully, his friends had gotten a day's rest in between. Meantime, he had been busy on calls to his dad and the firm. Rider felt encouraged. With his dad's and their staff's help, and the help also of Sidney, they'd have an excellent case to present. His notes were in great order and it was showtime. "Sorry, brother, but time to rise and shine."

Another moan and a creak that might not have been bedsprings. "Okay if I have firsties in the john?" Wolfgang mumbled.

"No problem. I'll put the coffee on." It might take Wolfgang a bit longer to rise, let alone shine.

Rider looked out the window. Rain. *Just great. Days and days of sun and now this.* It would make the roads slick. And poor Eduardo was outside getting dripped on. He grabbed a mac, tarp and a blanket and brought Eduardo his breakfast. "How are you feeling, buddy?"

Como mierda.

"Brought you some cover."

Gracias.

Rider stroked Eduardo's back gently, put down new hay and filled the water trough.

"You hanging in there?"

Sí.

Rider's spirits sank. It was hard to see friends hurt and feel so helpless about it. "You're sticking around here, right? Getting some rest?"

Quizas. Maybe I should go see Granny later.

"That's a grand idea! I'll bet she'll fix you up good as new."

Espero que sí. But I am more worried about Granny. It would be good to be on hand if she needs me.

"Did you hear anything last night?"

Sí. The boys and birds came to tell me she is most upset about something. Something new . . . in the woods.

"Did they say what it was?"

They were chattering so fast I did not catch all of it. My brain is perhaps not working so well at the moment. Eduardo stopped, turned his head sideways and shook it violently. Some water poured out of his left ear. A couple of sodden white feathers flittered down. Rider gave him another careful pat.

I think the bad men have accelerated the schedule and they are now going after the old trees toward the top. Our amigos said something about hearing saws there.

Rider's heart rate amped up. *God damnit!* He ran both hands through his hair. His instinct was to run up there and beat the crap out of those bastards. He actually considered it for a moment, but knew it wouldn't do to go off half-cocked. Moreover, his friends would need all the legal expertise they could muster, both his and Sidney's, to advance their case. *Mierda* and double *mierda*.

Looking up at the mountains, Rider saw that a big cloud was hanging over the top, enveloping part of the ravine. Maybe a downpour would slow the sods down. And maybe it was just as well Eduardo was staying behind. He said as much to Eduardo.

Sí, that is what I was thinking. I want to be there if she needs me.

"Okay. Just be careful, both of you. You won't grow back."

Eduardo nuzzled Rider. *I will be careful. Hasta luego y buena suerte.*

The rain was coming down hard now, so Rider bolted back into the kitchen. After hanging up his dripping mac, he got out mugs and started the coffee. Rider could hear the shower blasting. When the coffee was brewed, Wolfgang, wrapped in a towel, crawled into the kitchen and reached up a paw.

"Coffee!" he croaked. Then he dragged himself up on a stool.

Rider handed him a mug and started to reach into a cupboard. "Doughnut?"

"Maybe a big one for my butt," Wolfgang grumbled, rubbing said anatomy. The kitchen stools were feeling pretty hard this morning.

"Eduardo said he's going to go up to Granny's later, in case she needs him. Maybe you should stay and go with him? Looks like you could use some of her medicine."

"Nah, I'm okay. This coffee'll fix me up."

"Well, I'll jump in the shower then. It's already a quarter to 4:00."

"Get you best duds on."

"I intend to. What are you wearing?"

"You jokin', right?"

"Right."

When Rider emerged from his bedroom, freshly showered, shaved and dressed, his roomie made a long, well, wolf whistle. "Dude, you lookin' pretty snazzy!"

"All the better to eat me?" Rider swivelled in his sartorial splendour.

"Um, well, you not exactly to my taste, no offense. But you do clean up good!"

"I thought I'd better pull out the big guns with my wardrobe. The wrinkles steamed out nicely."

"Unh *hunh*. And you pack all that stuff in you saddlebags?"

"One needs to be prepared, socially."

"Dude!" At last Wolfgang was his old grinning self again.

Rider was wearing old-fashioned, blue breeches, with gold braid at the knee, and white hose, below a matching high-collared, blue velvet jacket with more gold braid and gold-leaf embroidery down the front. And a sash. "Actually, Dad sent them by courier two days ago, along with decent running shoes. Is the sash too much?"

"Hmmmm. Maybe. Better bring it along. The baroness'll let you know. She understands all that stuff. But you might lose them sneakers."

Rider looked down at his black Nikes. *What* was *I thinking?* "All I have are these or the boots." He looked up in mild panic.

"I'd go for the boots, if I was you."

Rider left to change. There was a knock at the front door.

"That be Rumpbuckle and the film crew, I expect," Wolfgang called out. "You mind gettin' it?" Clutching his towel, he limped as fast as he could to his bedroom.

Rider went to the door and let in Dr. Rumpbuckle, Nigel and his lads.

"Blimey! Do *we* feel underdressed!" said Ian, looking at Rider and the doctor.

Rumpbuckle coughed. "I'm afraid I neglected to inform them of the usual protocol in the haberdashery line. But I don't think we need fear being tossed out. These are modern times, after all."

Rider saw that Rumpbuckle, like himself, was old school. He looked splendid in a bottle green Jacobean coat, complete with lace *jabot* and ruffles at the wrists. The gold frogging across the placket matched the gold piping on the deep, turned-up cuffs. These were complemented by wine-coloured breeches, the obligatory white hose, and brass-buckled shoes, much like the ones Rider had forgotten to ask his dad to send. They were shined to perfection.

"Very smart," said Rider. Rumpbuckle bowed. Rider made a note to spiff up his boots.

"It is not often I am called to Court." Rumpbuckle was preening just a bit.

"I know the feeling," Rider mumbled. He then noticed a single, small diamond in Rumpbuckle's left earlobe. The influence of Granny, no doubt. Rider rummaged under the sink for a rag and polish, hiding his smirk.

As Rider pulled on his polished boots, Wolfgang came out from his room. They stared.

"What?"

"Nothing," they chorused. "Let's go."

Wolfgang had decided he needed to hold his end up with the wardrobe thing. To this end, there was a beautiful red satin bow around his neck (velcro fastened) with a round medal hanging from it beneath his chin—a gift from Granny. It read, "To Wolfie. What a good boy!"

Wolfgang caught Rider reading it. "Damn straight!" and marched out, swishing a well-brushed tail.

The drive to the queen's castle was tedious but safe. Thanks to Rumpbuckle's skill with his wand, the slick roads were completely dry under their horses and wheels. The rest of the poor slobs on the highway were mostly in controlled skids. And the baroness was right—Ronny's carriage did have all the "mod cons." After decades of suffering Count D.'s flaunting his spiffed-up carriage and tired of being outdone, Ronny had sprung for the current upgrade. It was a pity the dwarves had not yet developed the same technology for automobiles. The ride would have been so much faster and smoother in her Daimler. But the new carriage was cushy enough. It had its own mini-bar, customized to her taste and Betty's. For mortals, there were other adult beverages, including hot coffee.

Fidgeting a bit, Rider was tempted to help himself to one of the miniature brandies, but thought better of it. Sidney seemed immune to nerves. He reclined calmly, dressed in a beautifully tailored grey suit, his briefcase on his knees.

The countess leaned forward and checked the side mirror. She smiled to herself at the long queue of vehicles creeping behind her carriage. The drivers were fuming, but seeing the white rectangular plate on the back with an "N" denoting nobility, they kept their fumes mostly to themselves out of respect or fear of reprisal.

Stuck behind them were Doug and Marjory Simms, on their way to the Sprout Growers' convention, a well-earned day trip to celebrate their 50th wedding anniversary. Marjory was thrilled to be so close to the gentry. "Ooh, look Doug! I think that's the countess's carriage, Ronny whossername! Why's the N red? I thought it was usually black."

He reminded her that red meant she was a vampire.

"Oh. Still, it is nice to see the lovely old carriages out these days, isn't it?"

Doug grit his teeth as the windscreen wipers lashed back and forth. They were going to be late for the reception. Just his luck—their first holiday since Tom went off to uni and here he was, stuck behind a bloodsucking nob.

Wolfgang was having a little problem with travel sickness, so begged permission to crack a window to hang his head out. Frowning, the baroness checked her wrist sun/moondial. "It's not daylight yet, so I suppose it would be all right. But the second we see a ray of light, we must batten down the hatches!" Wolfgang nodded and pointed his nose into the wind.

After they reached the bottom of the pass and pulled through Fester-on-Fen, Rumpbuckle's wand began to hum. "Curious. I'm picking up something from my tracking spell, but I have no idea why. I don't recall selling wands this far out of range. And I have a strict, anti-resale clause built into them." He demonstrated by tapping his wand and flourishing clockwise, incanting "*Luminos T et C!*" In the air a scroll unrolled from the wand with interminable headings in capital letters and stretched across the width of the compartment, bearing the title, "Terms and Conditions."

Rider peered over his arm at the verbiage. It was quite thorough. "Neat! But how does one access it?"

"Quite simple: a sharp flick of the wand to the right." Rumpbuckle demonstrated.

"And if the user doesn't do so?"

"Then the user doesn't get to use the wand."

"Clever."

Nigel, Ian and Derek were going over the photos they intended to present. Sidney counselled them concerning their order and importance. Rider went over his own notes again, trying not to fret.

It was getting light. Wolfgang dragged his head back in. Ronny placed a red-varnished nail on some buttons in the side of the carriage door. The windows went up and became translucent black. One could still see out but no light at all could get in. Rider thought he'd try to convince his father to help on the dwarf integration issue.

They were in the plains now with rows upon rows of turnips, sprouts and onions growing on each side. In the distance on an escarpment they could see glimpses of Castle Crossmenot, where the queen lived. It was impressive: in what was easily 50 acres of wooded parkland and gardens, the massive hulk of the castle itself loomed. Its pointy, stone arches, crenelated towers and pennants advertised the pomp and power within. Encircling the base of the escarpment was the tidy, tile-roofed village of Festminster, its cobbled streets spiralling up toward the castle gates, through which a great deal of cart-laden commerce was entering. Gasoline-powered vehicles used a separate entrance in back, away from the coin-fed binoculars of the highway's Scenic Underlook lay-bys. The baroness checked the time again.

"Are we there yet?" Ronny asked with a nudge at Betty.

Betty's shoulders descended a bit and she smiled back. "Another hour I think. We're on schedule at any rate."

Ronny massaged her friend's shoulder. "It'll be all right, you know."

"Of course it will." Betty turned to gaze out the window at the odiferous crops, even more glad for the raised windows.

CHAPTER 23

Ta, Very Much

On the Plains of Fetidston, it was full daylight now. As the sky finally cleared and a smug ray of sun lit the main tower like a spotlight, the countess's carriage reached the main gates of the castle of the queen. (In case you're wondering, the king had died a few years back of a lethal sinus infection.)

They were halted by two guards in plumed helmets and blousy, blue-and-yellow striped jackets with matching knee breeches, and carrying large, pointed sticks. These were the queen's honour guards, the Guards of Swizzle. Well, they weren't hers in actual fact. They were just on permanent loan from Swizzle, the country next door. (And a Mai Tai force they were.) Rider noticed that the sharp points at the top of their sticks oddly resembled colourful, folded umbrellas.

"'Alt! 'Oo issa going dere?" enquired Enrico, tucking a faultlessly curled, dark lock back under the rim of his helmet.

The countess took in the dreamy dark eyes with long eyelashes and the curly locks, which drew their gorgeousity solely from genetics. "Hmph! Bet he's got a cute bum, too, only who can tell with those puffy pants on? It's not fair all those good genes going to a little country like that and the bad ones coming here. And anyway, I should think it's bloody obvious 'oo issa going here with my crest on the bleedin' door!" Ronny believed in advertising, as big and flashy as possible. But the guard had to stick to the script.

Enrico, as well as Mario next to him, had been sent by their families at the age of 13 to be raised in the Guards, for the honour of it.

Certainly not for the eye-watering stench rising from the plains. Their nonnas had been sure they'd fit right in, coming from Flatuenza, their village in neighbouring Swizzle.

Inside the carriage, a light-proof partition glided up smoothly between the passenger compartment and the driver. Then the driver's window slid down. He showed their papers to the guards.

"Ah, *sí, sí! La Contessa di* (mumble, mumble)." The countess forgave him—her full name *was* a bit of a mouthful. "*Vengono lì, per piacere.* Over there, please." Enrico pointed them toward the Vampire Gate to the left. "*Sí, sí, a la sinistra.*" He then spoke into his official walkie-talkie, alerting the guards at that gate of their imminent arrival.

Their driver turned the countess's carriage so that the passenger doors on the right side were opposite the gate. As they waited, the two guards unfastened a long, accordioned, light-proof sleeve built large enough to form a seal around even the biggest carriage doors.

Oh ho! You wondered how that was going to work, didn't you? So did I.

To continue . . .

Passing through the tube, the party proceeded with due pomp into the castle proper. Normally, light would have been streaming in through the embrasures, but these were now covered by rubber-backed tapestries in deference to the queen's guests. A new and strikingly buff guard ushered them upstairs into the groin-vaulted throne room. Ronny and Betty did admire nice groins.

They were instructed to wait. The dais and its throne were as yet unoccupied. Wolfgang lifted a hind leg. In stereo, he heard the countess and baroness hiss, "Wolfgang!"

"What? Just havin' a scratch."

The baroness wilted. "Best not here, if you can avoid it."

The leg went back down. Rider gave him a commiserating scratch behind the bow.

"Thanks, dude. Not used to wearin' this thing."

Nigel and his lads wished they'd been allowed to bring their cameras inside. Their necks craned at all the gorgeous art and architectural features. Rider, Sidney and Rumpbuckle were filling in the time, counting heraldic flags. At last, the resounding tap of shoes was heard coming down the long hall. Approaching them was a girl in her late teens wearing a long gown of virulent and battling hues, beneath which protruded the toes of what appeared to be fashionably hob-nailed slippers. A crown of inter-locking Goth dragons adorned her long red hair, which had a vivid fuchsia stripe running the length of the left side. Her page was running frantically after her, duty-bound to announce her arrival, if after the fact. "The Princess Verisimila!" he quavered.

The party separated into two rows, so that she could proceed between, and bowed.

Stepping up onto the dais the girl turned toward them, fiddling with her tie-dyed sash.

"Sorry, Mummy couldn't come. Another dwarf strike, I'm afraid. So it's just me."

She sat and waved her page away. Informality was more her style. Her guards pulled up chairs for her audience. The princess didn't see any reason for people to be uncomfortable. Until there *was* a reason.

"Well. Hullo! And welcome to the castle and all that. I'm Verisimila." She made a face. "I know, it's a pretty dreadful name. Most royal names seem to be. Verisimila Millicent, actually. Bit of a tongue twister."

Rider agreed: he'd never get that out unmangled after a pint or two.

"Call me Millie, if you like. Or even 'Red,' as I know at least one of you already does."

Here, her gaze drilled Wolfgang, who thought *Uh, oh.* A kernel of recognition was growing between his synapses, which were complaining about the pinch. He was pretty sure he wouldn't like what it grew up to be. The red hair, the purple streak, the tie-dye, the hob-nails. *Dang! Me and my big mouth!* He had a sudden need to know just how many flags there were in here, too.

"Please, sit."

They sat.

"So!" Millie smiled brightly. "Who wants to go first?"

A pause while several elbows indecorously nudged.

"I already know Ronny and Betty. Oh, sorry! Would you prefer 'Countess' and 'Baroness'?"

"Whatever *you* prefer, Princess," the baroness responded with what she hoped was a gracious nod. *Really, young royals these days!*

The princess would have preferred to be playing with the dragon pups in the castle kennel. *Their* attitude about protocol was simply to incinerate it. "Sorry, our announcer chap's indisposed. Would you introduce me to your entourage, Baroness?" Millie had not missed Betty's patronizing nod.

"Of course, Princess. May I present our colleague and good friend, Dr. Rumpbuckle?"

Rumpbuckle stepped forward and bowed. Millie nodded, trying to remember what she knew about him. *Wasn't it something to do with wands?* He stepped back.

Sidney stepped forward next and bowed, holding his briefcase. He knew his place in the scheme of things.

Betty fluttered a well-manicured hand in his direction. "My solicitor, Sidney Van der Chase. *Our* solicitor, actually, the countess's and mine, that is."

He stepped back.

Next, Nigel, Derek, Ian and Gerry were presented. The princess didn't appear impressed. There were always film crews prowling about these days, scrounging for a free shoot.

The baroness motioned to Rider, who next stepped forward. "Esmond Rippon the Third." He bowed. "An environmental barrister, Your Highness." Here the princess perked up.

"Ooh! I've heard of your lot, er, firm! Granny's said wonderful things about it for years. Said you're carrying on the good fight and whatnot."

The baroness turned to the princess in surprise. It appeared there *were* some things she didn't know, even after all these years. . . . "And may I enquire who this 'granny' is, Princess?"

"Gosh. Thought you knew! It's Granny Loveanger, of course. Mum's her daughter, so of course . . . She lives quite near you."

Damn. I knew it! Wolfgang ducked his head, checking the exits.

"You *are* referring to Boadicea Gertrude Loveanger, are you not?" Betty wanted to make very sure.

"Of course, but she prefers to go by 'Gerty' or 'Granny.' But you know that, surely?"

"I do indeed. But I was not aware of her relation to you and your mother. How very interesting." *How very convenient!* There should be no further fear of opposition.

"I suppose that's because the castle PR men thought it wisest to keep Mummy's maiden name a bit hushed. Although Mum's the very *best* kind of Loveanger, like Granny." The baroness's judgement of the young sovereign began to unfreeze. Betty chastised herself for being out of circulation for so long. She should have known the connection.

"And we are already acquainted with your wolf friend," continued Millie (a.k.a. "Red"). To Wolfgang, Millie's smile seemed more of a smirk. He also noted her switch to first-person plural. And got it. He ran a paw under his red bow.

Sidney stepped forward again and addressed the princess. "Knowing now your relation to our beloved Granny Loveanger, I feel we are in the best possible company to consider the case we wish to present before you."

Millie nodded to him to proceed.

"Are you aware, Princess, that there is an outsider corporation setting up illegal logging operations on the countess's and baroness's lands that span the river below Count D.'s estate?"

There was a sharp gasp from Millie. "Not that lovely, old-growth forest we used to tramp through as kids? With the enormous chestnut, several hundreds of years old?"

"The very same, Princess," Betty replied, bitterly.

"And we have confirmation that they have already begun work, Your Highness," Sidney added.

"Over my dead body!" Millie stamped a hob-nailed slipper. "Mummy's as well!" If she were one of the kennel drakes, the carpet before her would have been ash. The resemblance to Granny was now obvious.

"Have you a table, Princess, where we could spread out our notes and photographs?" Sidney inquired. "Perhaps something close by?"

A footman stepped forward and Millie delivered her request, twisting her sash in her hands. In a moment, a gilt-edged trestle table was drug in and stationed between the throne and their chairs.

"Thank you, Ted." The footman bowed and returned to his station against the arras. "Mummy did say she'd heard something about some foreign big-wigs up your way." The royal brow was furrowed.

"Indeed, Your Highness. And they also intend to help themselves to the ore that flows down the river, just there." Sidney pointed at a map.

"Wait! Wasn't there another bunch who tried the same thing years ago? What was it Mummy was telling me about that?" Now it came back to her who Rumpbuckle was. She sat up. "Dr. Rumpbuckle," she said excitedly, "it was you, wasn't it, who chased the buggers away!"

Honestly, the language! Betty thought.

Oh, knock it off, old stick. I like her spunk, Ronny thought back.

Rumpbuckle smiled and nodded his head. "You are too kind. I had excellent help, you might recall."

Rider had let Sydney take the lead; it was his turf, after all. Now Rider stepped up with his notes. "My firm is most anxious that this corporation be restrained from proceeding. It would be disaster if they were to go forward, and set a dangerous precedent, as well. And you can be sure they would find any excuse, however flimsy, to remove any old-growth timber in the way, preparatory to extracting the ore."

"Well, they're not going to get it!" The slipper stamped again. "The trees or the ore!"

"They will want to convince you, Your Highness, that the financial compensation for such a valuable mineral will offset the destruction, of course. No doubt, they'll make you and your mother a very handsome offer to share the profits."

"Oh, pooh! Since poor daddy made that exclusive trade agreement with Fresco and Swizzle, we've been rolling in it."

Considering the surrounding agriculture, inquiring minds wondered: in what?

"Who knew," the princess continued, "sprouts would be so in demand? But thank gods for that. Has to be some justification to put up with the stink. But remind me again—what's the name of the mineral they're after?"

"Tantalum, Your Highness," supplied Sidney.

"Ta."

"Er . . . you're welcome."

"What? Oh. No, 'Ta' as in big 'T' little 'a.' Just our little school joke. Ta's the periodical table's symbol for tantalum. If I remember my A levels right, it's got an atomic number of 73. It's that shiny, silver-grey metal, am I right?"

"You are quite correct, Your Highness." *So* . . . not *just another vapid royal face, then*, Sidney reflected.

"Very stable stuff, until you get it around certain types of acids, then where are you? It would be all right if manufacturers had just stuck to surgical equipment. But nooo. They have to go and use it in all those appalling '*personal* devices'—mobile phones, DVD players, and, and . . . video games. Do you know those bings and boinks carry right through stone walls?"

She wouldn't admit that it was *her* video game's bings and boinks that carried through the stone. She quite enjoyed a go at *Mirror's Edge.* Mummy disapproved, complaining it kept her up at night, so Millie loyally stuck to the official line.

"And it seems every week we lose someone under the wheels of a cart. Too busy peering and poking at poor Alexa. Can't even carry on a decent conversation.

"Well, that's right out! I know Mummy would agree. She and Daddy, before he died, put in place an edict restricting use of tantalum to purposes that benefitted only science and medicine. Well, use by the commoners, that is. All ore deposits belong to the Crown anyway, in this country. That's us," she added, unnecessarily. "Besides that, handling it directly seems to make creatures go peculiar. So how does this lot propose to get away with it?" she demanded.

"They believe there is a loophole that may be defensible."

Millie drew herself up to her full five-foot height and scooted forward on her throne so her feet didn't dangle. "And what is that, pray?"

"They believe that because the ore, in this case, is found in the waters of the river, and because technically, no one owns the water *on paper—*"

"Except us, in the general sense, for the use of our people!" the princess interrupted. "But I see your point."

Rider continued, ". . . they should therefore be able to extract it with impunity. Moreover, they have a signed purchase of sale, Your Highness."

"Signed? By whom?" Millie looked piercingly at Ronny and Betty.

Betty threw up her hands in supplication. "I assure you, Your Highness, neither the countess nor I would ever sell the land on either side. Your dear mother, at least, will remember quite well how viciously we fought back last time such a thing was tried."

"And if one can't own the water, then what in gods' names is being sold?" she demanded, pacing back and forth.

"There is a third party, you may recall, on the mountain above who has been most eager to take advantage of the river's profitability," Ronny reminded the princess. "And the timber on either side," she muttered darkly.

"Count D., you mean."

Several heads nodded in united disgust.

"I suppose I shouldn't be surprised. He is *such* a persistent old b—er, blighter." Millie twitched one foot. "But I'm still confused about something."

"What would that be, Princess?" Rumpbuckle asked.

"If you can't own something, how can you possibly sell it?"

Rumpbuckle nodded to Rider an 'over-to-you.'

"That is a conundrum that has bugg—, um, badgered litigators for eons," Rider complained. "But it's never kept people from trying. It's precisely because it's *not* owned by anyone that they think they can sell it, as long as they get to the negotiating table first. Take empires, for example. If you get right down to it, no one owned anything back at the beginning, but they still tried to flog it to someone else."

Rider stopped his tirade, his face turning cerise. "I beg your pardon, Your Highness."

"Let's return to the evidence, shall we?" suggested Sidney.

The princess was still struggling with the logic or lack of same. Finally, she gave it up as a bad job. "Yes, show me what you have, if you please."

One by one, glossy blow-ups were slid her way as Rider and Sidney went over their notes, taking care each point was well attended.

When everything had been gone over, Millie looked up, perturbed. "Thank you, gentlemen and ladies. The evidence you have presented really is conclusive. Mr. Rippon, your firm has been exceedingly thorough and helpful. Mr. Van der Chase, you have demonstrated once again your vigilance in preserving what is dear to our hearts. So now we know exactly whom we have to go after. And I assure you all, the Crown *will* pursue them, instantly and relentlessly. Mummy's due home this evening. May I keep the photos, at least for now, to show her?"

"Of course, Your Highness. Mr. Rippon and I have also provided you with our briefs on the matter," said Sidney.

Rider kicked Wolfgang on the sly as he heard the beginnings of a snicker. "Not *those* kinds of briefs!" he hissed.

The princess, whose imagination tended to run along the same alleys, stifled a snort, glad the old solicitor was referring to the legal kind. What if his had hearts on? "Yes, well, that will be most appreciated. But tell me," she addressed Rider, "how did you become involved with this? I am grateful, of course, that you have."

Rider hesitated. He didn't want to alarm an ally. On the other hand, dealing as she did with three vampires and at least one werewolf surely built up one's tolerance. *Okay. Here goes.*

He cleared his throat and told her about the wizard. They'd left that part out of the narrative, not wanting to cloud the issue.

The princess leaned forward again over the enlargements of Messrs. Brickheart and Stonewall, squinting.

"These are the two other werewolves who have also been hunting this wizard, you say?"

"Yes, Princess, without a doubt," Nigel chipped in.

"And they are also higher-ups in the corporation behind this plot?"

"Indeed, they are," Rider assured her. She sat back.

"Tell me, Mr. Rippon, what would you like me, er, the Crown to do about that, the bite-and-go bit?"

"For my part, Your Highness, I would dearly love to find the wizard and force him to change me back." Rider refrained from mentioning throttling. "The rest of it I leave to the excellent judgement of the baroness and countess et al."

"And how did you describe him again?"

They repeated the description.

"Ah. Well, I think I may be able to help you with that.

"Ted," she addressed the footman, "please inform my cousin his presence is required." *Golly, sometimes it* was *fun doing this snooty royal thing.*

"Immediately, my lady." Ted bowed and hurried away.

Millie's gaze was distant while she waited. A slow smile spread across her face.

Presently, there was a cough, then a short, grey-bearded man in a shopworn, blue, celestially patterned robe was prodded into the room by Ted. His head was bowed and he was clutching a pointy hat.

"May I present to you my cousin Herald. Cousin, I believe you already know some of these persons."

Herald looked desperately toward the door. Which was shut firmly by Ted.

Momentarily forgetting in whose company he was, Rider leapt to his feet, pointing. "You!" Then he turned to the princess. "This . . . man . . . is your cousin?" Stunned, he stared again at Herald. "Princess Verisimila and you are related?"

Herald nodded, wishing he'd spent more time perfecting vanishing spells.

"Cousin Herald is Mummy's first cousin once removed, from the Fetidston branch of the family," Millie explained, rather wishing he'd been removed farther. "Cousin Herald, these gentlemen have been just telling me about some considerable trouble brought on by a short grey-beard in a pointed hat who couldn't keep control of his wand. From the description, he sounds remarkably like you."

They waited. From Wolfgang's throat, a growl was growing.

"I owe you gentlemen an apology," Herald mumbled.

"What was that? Speak up, Cousin."

He did.

"So it *was* you, then?" she pressed.

"Yes, and I'm very sorry. It's the university loans, you see."

"Oh, honestly! You dropped out of wizard school some 40-odd years ago, didn't you Cousin?"

"Yes. But that doesn't stop the interest on the loans from piling up. It's why I turned to bingo. With that wand Dr. Rumpbuckle fixed up for me, didn't see how I could lose. I didn't know about the tracking spell then, of course."

"Or the alarm that goes off when one is using it unethically, I presume?" Rumpbuckle raised an unamused eyebrow.

"Is that what it was? I did wonder."

"Cousin Herald, as my mother and yours, rest her soul, told you many a time, if you'd only *applied* yourself at school, you could have made those loans disappear."

An embarrassed rumble was Herald's only reply.

"Well, speaking of wands, now that we finally have caught up with you, would you mind too much changing me back?" Rider asked.

Silence. Shuffle. Cough.

Drumming of fingers on arm of throne.

"Can't."

The drumming stopped. "What do you mean, you can't, Cousin?"

"Lost it."

Rider slapped his forehead. "What? Not again!" He turned in circles trying to calm himself. Wolfgang could feel a vicious itch coming on. Nigel and his crew stayed still, not wanting to spoil the scene.

"*Where* did you lose it this time?" Rider steamed.

"Down in the Grab and Tickle. A bit literal with their name," he grumbled. "After I, er, tickled the numbers, they grabbed my wand."

"Hunh! That explain why he didn't go 'poof!' when Eduardo and I was chasin' him," Wolfgang observed. "Hadn't got that wand no more."

Rumpbuckle put a comforting hand on Rider's shoulder. "But you *could* undo the spell if you had the wand back?" he asked Herald.

"Oh, yes. Or, er, I *think* I can, if I can remember the words. . . ."

"There is a light at the end of the tunnel, then." Rumpbuckle explained to the carriage party, "That signal I was getting when we were passing through Fester-on-Fen must have been from the wand I repaired for Herald. In which case, we should be able to retrieve it on the return journey. And, if Your Highness will permit, we will bring our . . . friend . . . Herald with us."

"I'm sure Cousin Herald will be most pleased to accompany you," Millie twinkled, shooting Herald a look that said, *And don't even* think *of clearing off.*

Business concluded, the princess stood. "I am grateful to you all for coming and for being such champions of our concerns. You have our permission to take any steps necessary to bring a halt to their enterprise and bring Global Advanced Management, LLP to justice. So long as it doesn't put the woods and our people at risk, naturally. Expect a summons from my mother, the queen, of the count and corporate VIPs by tomorrow. She won't wish to waste another day."

They bowed and backed out.

As they were nearly to the hall's doors, Millie called out, "Wolfgang, remember me to Granny, would you? Please tell her I'm so sorry I haven't been able to visit often. It's all those 'business managers and potential entrepreneurs.' I do miss her. Oh, and tell her 'Cheese Girl' sends her regards."

Yep. Busted. Wolfgang slunk out.

A chastened Herald was waiting for them when the baroness's party returned to the carriage outside the castle, holding a flat, square box inexpertly wrapped in brown paper and string. When they were all seated, he joined them in the back seat.

"You shouldn't have!" teased Wolfgang, a paw to his chest.

Herald turned bright red and mumbled, "It's just something that needs returning."

As Herald tried to slide over, he stumbled over Wolfgang's tail. The package rapidly unwrapped itself and Mrs. Knickertwister's size triple-E brassiere tumbled out.

Wolfgang whistled. "Dude! Hope that look better on her than the top of you pointy hat."

Herald slunk down in his seat. It would be a long ride to the Grab and Tickle.

As they left the castle, it began to rain again. Their carriage wound down the streets from Crossmenot Castle and joined the traffic back toward Otternought. A few cars made a desperate dash to pass them before the countess's carriage was fully onto the highway. The rest remained behind, grim and checking their watches.

"I don't bloody believe it!" said Doug, pounding his palm on the steering wheel.

"What's that, luv?" asked Marjory, sleepily. They'd had a very nice luncheon and she'd drunk rather more champagne than she ought.

"Look!" he demanded, shaking a forefinger at the vehicle in front of them.

"That can't be the same carriage we was followin' up, can it, Doug?"

"The one and only."

"Fancy that, bein' behind 'er up and back. What are the chances, eh?"

Doug glowered at the lowering skies and wondered which rotten little god he could blame this on. *And they tell you lightning can't strike twice in the same place. Fat lot they know!* He turned the wipers up to high and violently punched on the radio. Maybe at least he could get the football score.

It was late afternoon by the time the countess's party regained Fester-on-Fen. By the time they'd retrieved Herald's wand and anonymously left the brown paper parcel at Mrs. Knickertwister's, they were parched and hungry.

"Hey, Rumpy, how much further to Slaughter?" Wolfgang asked. "My stomach's rumblin'."

Gerry slid across the seat to the door.

Ian whispered to him, "Relax, Ger. That's the name of the baroness's village, where we're staying, remember?" Derek was chuckling.

Rumpbuckle consulted his pocket watch. "Only another hour or so, I should think."

"Well, I'm famished, aren't you?" Ronny asked Betty.

"I must admit I am feeling a bit peckish," Betty agreed. "Is there somewhere we could stop in Fester?"

"You see," Ronny explained to the others, "Betty and I aren't used to staying up this late."

"If I recall, there's quite a nice place in the centre," said Sidney. "They do a very nice stork and gallbladder pie."

Hunh. The things humans eat, Wolfgang thought. *Poor ol' stork musta pissed off somebody. Probably took the baby to the wrong house.*

"But wouldn't we need to 'order in,' as it were?" Rumpbuckle gestured to his two hostesses. "You know, lunch boxes or something?"

"They have, in fact, a special entrance for patrons traveling incognito or with, let us say, special needs. It's quite safe," Sidney assured them.

"I admit I was hoping for a sit down. Is this the place that has a dining room in the old wine cellar?"

"It is."

"Then I know it, Sidney!" Ronny exclaimed. "I got them to fix up one of those accordioned thingies the queen has on her back door has so I don't fry. They have terrific dance bands on the weekends. A girl likes to get out now and then. Oh, do let's go there!"

Ronny was twirling her pearls, lost in the memory of a good beat. It had been a long time since she had dined in the Bishop's Arms.

CHAPTER 24

Granny Goes Airborne

Back up the mountain in the baroness's valley, while the delegation were on their way to see the queen, a war was about to break out.

In the early morning light, Olivier had flown through the storm to Granny's with the latest awful news. Soon after, several of the boys came loping along with more, shaking the rain from their pelts. The mining crew had crossed over onto Betty's land and started up their big saws and chippers. Olivier was terrified—one of the marked trees was his family home, the baroness's beloved 600-year-old-chestnut.

This couldn't wait for a royal ruling. Her forest and family were under attack. Granny wasted no time. Breathing fire, she stomped up the stairs and dragged her pointy hat out of her closet and slapped it on her head. Then she crammed her feet into her dependable hob-nailed boots. Back down to her scullery, she pried her old broom from its bracket. It had been a long while since she'd had need of it, but she remembered how it went. Wrapping her cloak about her and straddling the broom, she launched into the sky. It really *was* just like riding a bike, only without wheels. Or handlebars.

Conrad flapped up parallel to her. "Hop on, if you're comin'!" Conrad perched behind her. "Just don't light that dratted thing!" she pointed at Conrad's pipe. "Bristles are dry." Or *were.* With the rain beginning to pelt down around them, she very much doubted he'd get a flame. Except Granny knew how to pelt right back. Large rain drops dodged away around them.

Below, Ross hitched a ride on one of the wolves. With his tartan scarf flying like a banner, he brandished a tiny claymore. Granny swooped up toward the ravine, following Olivier and the wolves. "Show me the way, boys, show me the way!" she shouted.

In less than an hour she was above the cloud hanging over the ravine. *Hah! That's why they're sawin' in the rain. Thought that cloud would hide 'em. They thought wrong.* As Granny's pack got closer to the worksite, they could hear the roar and grind of the chippers. Granny kicked her broom into turbo-charge. If ever there was a sound that made a right-minded person's heart and stomach do back-flips, it was the sound of chainsaws and chippers.

She circled above the new clearing, sickened by the carnage below. Several lovely young aspens lay on the forest floor. They were done quaking. A handsome fir, too big to be anyone's Christmas tree, then joined them. She could hear the screams of alarm from her people as they scampered and flew to what safety they could find. The cries of anguish from the trees reached her mind as clearly as the creatures' voices.

"Don't you cry, Gerty!" she scolded herself. "Don't you cry! You need your wits about you and all the power you can summon."

A large, hairy man with an evil grin was eyeing the massive chestnut. The grandfatherly monarch stood in its own natural clearing, encircled by its court of smaller sisters. Its branches spread out twenty feet or more from the hoary trunk, which was easily as wide around as a school bus. Despite the rain, shafts of light slanted down through the boughs, spot-lighting the forest floor and the droplets glistening on its leaves. The sovereign's sisterhood had already curtseyed their skirts to the ground, but the king still retained his leaves, now autumnal bronze, and held them out in burnished glory. Wendell's neck cracked as he looked up, up and still further up to the chestnut's gilded crown, soaring above its subjects.

"That thing should make a lot of timber." *And mebbe some of it could wind up on me new extension on the house.*

The other workman's brow furrowed with worry. "Wendell, that one's not marked for cuttin'! See? The tape's yellow, not red. Din'tcher see the latest memo?"

"Yer mean that bit o' paper slipped under the door this mornin'? Had yesterday's date. Thought it was trash, so wiped me bum on it. We was runnin' low on TP."

Despite his bravado, a flash of a memory popped up from Wendell's grey matter. He was six years old, back on the farm, and weeping after coming home from school and finding the glorious, big oak in back cut down to the ground. It had been a sheltering friend. He'd climbed it and played under it his whole life.

"You stop that blubberin', my lad!" his dad threatened. "It's just a bloody tree!"

When he couldn't stop hiccupping, his dad sneered, "Don't you be such a bleedin' sissy. Time you learned to be a man. That's just timber is all that is. Will go a ways to repairin' the barn." With that he snatched up Charlotte, Wendell's pet hen, and wrung her neck, tossing her corpse up on the back step. "And *that's* just dinner."

Oh, he'd learned, all right. After that, his dad made a point to take him hunting, and Wendell got right good at bringing down the creatures, supplying food for their table. Even got to liking it—that power over life and death.

He quashed the shameful memory and, smiling to himself, started up the saw. *This would make Dad proud.* It would be a challenge that should also put him one up on the others, if he managed to fell it by himself. *What was the big deal anyhow? As his old dad always said,* "You seen one tree, you seen 'em all."

"Wendell! I'm tellin' yer, we're gonna get in trouble if you cut that one down!"

"What's that, Rollo?" Wendell shouted over the roar of the saw. "Can't hear yer." Grinning, he advanced toward the tree.

Swooping back and forth, Olivier signalled their location, hooting in panic. The brutes had started driving their equipment toward Betty's grandfather's chestnut. Granny yelled down to her posse, "You lot don't need me to tell you what to do. Get to it! Conrad, peck their eyeballs out if you have to!"

As squirrels and smaller birds were bombarding the men with conkers, Conrad flapped his wings and sprang off the broomstick, diving for the big man operating the chainsaw. The man flung his hands up to fend off the crow, sending the chainsaw spiralling upward and nearly shredding his hands on its downward arc.

When he reached again for the saw, the light went suddenly slanty and silver. All the leaves and bark of the forest were limned in light, as if electrified. Wendell's hearing went weird, too. He knew that Rollo was shouting something at him, but it was merely guttural gibberish, like an LP recorded at 78 rpm played at 33. He felt his heartbeat slowing down, too, and got the shock of his life looking down at his hands as they turned into branches, twigs and leaves and his feet and legs into a woody trunk. He tried to scream. But, of course, he couldn't. He no longer had a mouth. Or eyes. Yet he could "see" everything around him. Wendell was aware that Rollo had likewise been transformed and was rooted several feet away. What's more, he could sense Rollo's panic as clearly as his own. Somehow, he could also "hear" the wails of anguish and fright from the neighbouring trees, as well as those of the creatures around him. A feeling of helpless sorrow welled up in and around him, mourning the forest's kin he'd butchered, now dying in agony on the ground.

The chainsaw stuttered to silence and quiet descended upon the forest. While he and Rollo listened in wonder, a communal sigh went up from the trees like a benediction. Mixed with grief, they could almost taste the relief about them. Like a calming elixir, a surge of goodness coursed up Wendell's roots from the nurturing earth. The rain abated and a shaft of sunlight pierced the canopy, illuminating their limbs. Amazed, he could feel the cellular tingle of joy and blessing in his leaves and marvelled at the delicate touch of a bird's feet alighting on one of his branches. A squirrel raced up Rollo, chattering, and he sensed giggles wriggling up them both, amid the benevolence of their neighbours. For an ageless, sweet moment, the two of them were struck with the sense of one caring community, not limited to place or the pride of a protector. The good company of trees.

Then Wendell perceived the chainsaw's starting up again. He could even recognize who was holding it. There was no doubt that the woman with the saw meant business. At last, he knew the terror and hopelessness of those without a voice.

Granny stalked toward him with the roaring saw and a determined set to her jaw. This was worse, oh, much, much worse, than those nightmares where you're trying to outrun a monster on feet feeling stuck in glue. Wendell couldn't run. He couldn't even hide.

"Well, how does it feel, my boy?" Granny raised the saw. "Could use a bit of firewood and I doubt very much anyone would miss *you*." Wendell quaked. "But maybe I'll just give you a bit of trim."

Granny flew up into the air on her broom, brandishing the saw toward his top-most branches. "Short back and sides, I think." As the twigs flew, she hummed.

The pain from losing even a few twig-ends came as a big surprise. Everything in his being screamed at her, "Stop! I'm sorry!"

If a tree can be said to sob, Rollo's was doing it. Granny heard him. She heard the thoughts of all the trees and creatures. It was merely a matter of matching the speed of their thinking with your own.

When it appeared the men were sufficiently terrorized and repentant, she descended. Folding her arms and cocking her head, she listened to their thoughts, keeping the saw running. "Right," she said to no one in particular. Then she made an odd encircling gesture, sparks streaming from her hands. The light changed again. The men were restored to their human shapes.

Wendell saw he still had all his fingers and limbs, then felt his head, finding only some tufts of hair missing.

"Not much of a barber, I admit," said Granny.

Rollo got down on his knees, blubbering and thanking Granny for her mercy, promising he'd never, ever cut down another tree.

Wendell's own relief was profound. But coupled with that was a renewed feeling of loss, being robbed once more of the trees' companionship. In the blink of a vengeful eye, those feelings vanished, replaced by anger equally profound. His father's poisons were too strong. *Why should some entitled toff's favourite tree be spared, while Wendell's beloved oak had been sacrificed to the ax?* Chortling wickedly, he snatched at the saw, still buzzing its menace.

But the rain had resumed. In the downpour, Wendell slipped in the mud and lost purchase of the chainsaw, which flipped back on him, tumbled and sputtered off, then rolled into the river, carrying some bloody digits with it. Enraged and in pain, Wendell chased it, slipped again, banging his head on one of his newly-made tree stumps, then plunged unconscious into the river himself. Rollo tried to save him but it happened too fast. Only his head could be seen, bobbing up and down in the rapids. The wicked smile was gone.

"One down!" crowed Conrad.

In case Rollo also had a similar change of heart, Ross ran up his leg. And you know how that goes. Holding himself, Rollo ran screaming into the forest, branches gleefully thwacking him the whole way.

"I think my work is done here." Dislodged, Ross got a high-five from the boys. He squeaked up at Granny that he wanted to check in at the main site, and scampered down the hill.

Granny circled above the chipper and pointed her right hand at it. *Karma incineratus!* Cerulean flames shot from her fingers and instantly engulfed the huge machine. "Hunh. Didn't lose my touch with that either!"

The foreman, Bill, having heard the commotion, was bumping fast up the trail in the small bulldozer. "Oi! Wot's goin' on 'ere?" he demanded when he got to the new clearing. He heaved himself out of the bucket seat and looked around, bewildered. "Now, where in hell did the lads go?" The forest was now strangely quiet. You could have heard an owl poop. If you'd had the sense to expect it.

Suddenly, he was showered in *la merde des hiboux*. Olivier's family had all chipped in, and being French didn't make the *merde* any less . . . *merde*-y. Olivier's wife and daughters were also hawking up pellets and aiming, with astonishing accuracy, at Bill's head. In his haste, he'd forgotten his hard hat. "Bombs away!" they hooted.

Bill sprinted back to the bulldozer, seeking shelter . . . but the 'dozer was seeking him. It was in gear and driving toward him at a speed he didn't think possible. And there was a . . . wolf?! . . . behind the wheel, with . . . a rat??! . . . running back and forth, squeaking directions. He dove out of the way just in time, then took off down the trail as fast as his lolloping belly would let him. The 'dozer made an adroit spin and was following him, weaving expertly between the trees.

Granny had taken over the controls from above, after she saw that Ross and her wolf had dived clear of the machine. It was a simple trick of harnessing anger—true, righteous, burning anger—and a well-directed index finger. Child's play . . . if that child had grown up as a witch. She was one with her broom and the magic. And it felt good.

Around a bend, three yellow lights flew through the trees, swarming around Bill. The rain didn't seem to affect them. They were in "the zone." Swatting at them, he stumbled on a root and went down. Above his heaving breaths, he could hear the throaty rev of an engine. The dozer's headlights brightened, finding their prey. He scrabbled upright and tried to run, but a shoelace of his work boots had gotten wedged under the root and he was yanked back into the cross-hairs. Bill's sweaty fingers fumbled frantically at the laces. Useless. He couldn't see a bloody thing with those headlights blinding him.

Sobbing, he called out, "Wot is it you want? I'll do anything, *anything* you want. Just *please* don't kill me! I'm sorry . . . for whatever it is."

He heard the engine switch to neutral, idling. Bill was panting and praying. The three lights still circled his head. From his prone position, he looked up at the toes of some stout black boots which had just descended from the air. Above them were two sturdy legs in day-glo striped socks and the skirts of a large, black cloak. When he looked all the way up, he saw a mouth set like a trap and two steely grey eyes boring into him from underneath a black, pointy hat. The mouth and eyes and everything in between were beyond wrathful. More like wrath^2. The voice from the mouth was deceptively calm and quiet.

"Did I hear you correctly? You said you'd do 'anything' if I spared your life, did you not?"

Bill nodded vigorously.

"Hmmmmm." Granny drummed her fingers on her broomstick, milking the suspense. "You see, I was interested more in what you *wouldn't* do, if I let you live."

"That too, that too! What *is* it you want?"

"Oh, my lad. It's not so much what *I* want. It's what this forest wants. It's what this earth wants, and wants badly. You might even say it's what that fella up there those hypocrites pray to wants. Oh, yes."

Granny could feel the man's excuses cranking up in his thoughts.

"And don't you go justifying one damned thing, my lad. It's greed, pure and simple. Just bloody, selfish greed that's hurting this world. Make no mistake!" Her voice was now like thunder. It echoed up the ravine.

With Granny's stare boring down on him, Bill felt like a possum in the headlights though he didn't much feel like playing dead. Trying to shield himself from the mesmerizing effect of those eyes, he rolled over on his right . . . and felt the gun that was still in his waist band. The courage that a .38 bore can give a man came back to him, and he slowly moved his gun hand.

But Granny had seen his look turn sly. *He just doesn't get it, does he?*

"I wouldn't touch that. Not if you want to keep that hand."

Bill shrieked. The gun had become searingly hot. A hole was burned right through his thick work overalls. Also the palm of his hand.

"Oh, hang on," she cackled. "Knew there was something I forgot." At this, Granny whirled around and pointed a finger at the sky. A colossal fork of lightning shot down from the heavens. The bulldozer vaporized in an explosion of yellow flame.

Bill's eyes bugged out. *Now maybe he's gettin' it!*

"Oh, go on," she said to the man flapping his hand in agony. "You fellas were intendin' to sneak off with that sparkly ore, weren't you? There it is, then, in the river. That should put your fire out." She waved a hand and his shoelace mysteriously untangled. Bill lumbered to the river and lunged in. In curiosity, one of the yellow lights followed him.

"Too close! *TOO CLOSE!*" Brain and Elmo shouted at Dim.

Too late.

As Dim did uncontrolled loop-de-loops over the water, a white-hot current of energy arced up to him then back down to the river's surface. An interesting sizzle was heard: kind of a cross between frying bacon and an oscillating hum in the key of "EEEEEEEEEEEEEEEE!" In the river, Bill was lit up like a pulsing, neon billboard. Mouth stuck open in a silent scream, he flopped like a hooked fish.

Then Dim broke away and the connection was cut.

"You all right, Dim?" Brain and Elmo sped over to him in dismay as he crash-landed on a nearby branch.

"Wow! What a ride!" Dim seemed dazed but there was a grin on his face. Brain and Elmo just snorted.

"Tsk, tsk." Granny shook her head at the man smouldering in the water. "Come on boys, haul him out." Two wolves came forward, each taking a singed arm in its mouth.

"Tantalizing, that ore." She leered nastily at Bill when he'd been hauled to shore. "Put the fire out, didn't it?"

Bill lay gasping on the ground. Granny tutted, then rooted through the pockets of her cloak until she found the jar of salve. It wasn't that the men didn't know what they were doing. They knew all right. They just didn't care. But either way, ignorance and meanness were no excuse for torture. She opened the jar, muttered over it, and took out a clean handkerchief.

"This may sting a bit."

Bill groaned and shrank back. But after the initial sting (to improve the patient's memory), he felt the pain retreating up his limbs as Granny applied the salve. She only had to do the right hand. Seemingly on its own, the medicine kept on spreading. That was what the spell was for. She had no intention of laying hands all over a man she didn't like.

He sat up, testing his hands, feet and limbs, then regarded Granny with amazement and respect. "Who are you?"

"Someone I don't think you want to cross again."

He nodded.

"Now about that agreement . . ."

"All right, I'm listenin'."

"Good. And you'd do well to write it down, too." Granny fished out a pen and pad from another pocket and thrust it at Bill. He stared at them, embarrassed.

"I never was one for book-learning," he mumbled.

"Is that right? But you think you know what's what even so, do you?"

"*Thought* I did."

"Well, I guess you were just plum wrong, weren't you? Haven't you ever heard the saying, 'Ignorance is no excuse'?" He nodded.

"Well, it's true. But damn me if I can reckon how folks think ignorance still gives them license to do whatever they want, never mind what it does to anybody or anything else."

Bill felt like he was back in Mrs. Hodgkin's class after throwing a spit-wad. He nodded again, head bowed.

"Oh, give it here. I can do it faster." She waved her hand over the paper, and it filled out with alacrity, in perfect copperplate. Like Rumpbuckle's magic terms and conditions, hers were just as thorough but more succinct. There'd be no mistaking them.

The three sprites hovered overhead so he could read it. "Need more light?" she asked.

The smoking bulldozer belched out new flame.

No, no!" said, Bill, wildly waving off the offer. "This is fine."

"Right." Granny waited, arms crossed, while he read. When he had finished, she handed the pen back to him. "You can write your name, at least, can't you?"

"Yes."

"Good. Then sign there."

He scribbled.

"And there." Scribble scribble.

"And there." Scribble scribble dot.

She extracted the document from his grip, folded it carefully and placed it in the dry-pocket in her cloak. The salve was returned to the first-aid pocket.

"All clear, then?"

"Yes. Quite." He looked up. "But how am I to work now?" Bill complained.

"May I remind you that you still have a *body* to work *with*?"

There ensued a penitent silence.

"Hmmph. You can retrain, if you put your mind to it. I hear there's a good future in biofuels. And papyrus is getting a re-think. Any road, that's *your* problem. *My* problem is keeping people like you *out*."

The rain had suddenly stopped and the cloud lifted. Just like magic. Bill stood up, steam rising from his work clothes. He was shaking his head, still staring at his hand that was now completely healed.

A fist shot out again from the cloak holding several copies of the agreement, with more signature lines to fill in. "And here are some more copies. Mind you get *all* your men to sign. Trust me, I'll know if you don't. When you've finished, you can either leave them with my friend, Dr. Rumpbuckle, in Otternought, or send them to me by way of owl." Bill jumped as Olivier swooped down, talons extended, and landed just next to him.

"What did you say your name was again?"

"I didn't. People in these parts call me 'Granny.' "

"Well, there's lots o' grannies. Could you be more specific? I mean, who do I say gave this to me?"

"Tell them Boadicea Gertrude Loveanger, then."

"Not the Loveangers of—"

"The very same."

Granny watched with satisfaction as Bill paled. Where magic couldn't persuade, fear and clout could.

She whistled for her broomstick and hopped on.

"Wait! How am I gointer get down this mountain?"

"Oh, I'm sure you can see yourself out. And don't forget your gun."

She whizzed away. Bill picked up the molten lump, then tossed it back down. A sunbeam broke through the clouds and flooded him in bright scrutiny. He was beginning to see the light.

While the battle was raging above, a round-up was about to take place below. Kevin, the rabbit Granny had fixed up, sprang through the cat flap at the baroness's castle.

"Psssssst! *Psssssst!* Durell! Where are you?"

The castle tabby bounded down the stairs into the kitchen. "What's up?"

"All hell's breaking loose up the mountain," Kevin said. "You gotta come quick!"

Durell jumped through the flap, his heart pounding. "Is Granny okay?"

"I reckon so. She flew up there with Olivier, following the boys. Those bad men were starting to cut down more trees, one of them Olivier's home!"

"You mean she's on her broom?"

"Yep. She is."

"Blimey! It's been decades since she's taken that out. Thought she'd never ride again."

"Seems to have recovered the knack. She was riding just fine."

"So what do we do? Think she needs more help?"

"The twitter I got said not, she had it under control. But there's more of those men at the main site, and more equipment, too. I sent one of the jays down to alert Eduardo. He's on his way up now. Come on!"

Kevin loped away, with Durell at his heels.

At the main site, Martin, Bill's second-in-command, was on his walkie-talkie inside the trailer. "I'm not sure, sir. Haven't heard back from anyone yet. Over.

"Yes, sir, they went up early, just as you asked, with the saws and a chipper. It's raining like a bastard, so maybe they had some malfunction with the equipment? Over."

Cringing, Martin pulled the unit away from the forceful harangue on the other end, then attempted reassurance. "I shouldn't worry. They'll likely be back soon, maybe after it clears up. Over.

"What's that? Over."

Martin's shoulders slumped. He really, truly did not want to go outside in that downpour. "Yes, sir. I'll fire up the ATV and go up and check and get back to you. Over and out."

He signed off and grabbed his anorak. As he stepped out of the trailer he looked for Reggie who could usually be found inside the cab of the big bucket loader with headphones on, listening to Motorhead. Reggie was there, all right, but he was a little tied up at the moment. His wrists were bound with vines of bittersweet and lashed with the cord of his headphones to the steering wheel. His mouth was gagged by a tartan scarf. As Martin took a step toward Reggie's bucket loader, he heard a whinny.

Going somewhere, señor?

A large chestnut horse was now standing in his path. An exceedingly large horse. It appeared to be smiling, and not in a nice way. And Martin could *hear* it.

If you will just step into my . . . tackle.

Eduardo held some lengths of rope and leather thongs in his mouth. Martin backed away, and started to reach for his gun. Before he could do so, a rat ran up his leg and nipped his Saturday Night Special. As the man was dancing and shaking his legs, several wolves ran up, grabbed the ends of the ropes and ran in opposite directions, pinning Martin's arms to his sides. Not having opposable thumbs, they couldn't tie a knot, so Eduardo simply rolled over a 70-gallon drum and secured the ends underneath. The drum read, "Danger! Flammable!"

Anyone got a match? Eduardo queried.

Martin passed out when he heard the explosion. But the sound had come from up the mountain. When he came to, his trousers were rat-less but damp.

Conrad came flying in. "That was Granny blowin' up the bulldozer! Lads, you should have seen it! Everything cool down here?"

Sí. Mucho cool.

Eduardo trotted over to Martin and raised a large, menacing hoof over the approximate area where the Saturday Night Special had been. Congenially he inquired, *How many are there in your party, señor?*

It took Martin a moment to translate. His brain cells weren't speaking to each other at the moment. "Um, you mean how many of us are there here?" he squeaked.

Sí.

"There's just me and Reggie down here, then Bill, Rollo and Wendell up at the top site."

Only five of you, then? What happened to the others, the ones who drove all this equipment up here?

"The rest went back to headquarters after they made the delivery."

Bueno. And the three men in the suits? Where are they now? I heard you speaking on the talkie-walkie just now with someone.

Martin thought he'd better keep mum about that. If they found out the brass were still lounging about at the hotel, who knew what these crazy animals would do?

"Er. I'm not positive, but Tyrone, he's the head boss, said somethin' about headin' this way soon. They could be here any moment!" he added desperately.

Eduardo could smell the man was lying. So could the others. The wolves grinned.

As they were considering their options, Kevin and Durell ran into the clearing, panting.

All is well, my little friends, Eduardo told them, *but thank you for coming.*

"Sod it! Missed the fun again," complained Durell. "Sometimes I really hate being a house cat."

Do not worry, little ones. I think there is still something you can do. Eduardo did not like a loose end, until perhaps one was necessary.

"Great!" said Kevin. "What do you need?"

Eduardo led them out of earshot from the men and bent down in a huddle with the cat and rabbit. Durell and Kevin nodded eagerly. "We're on it!" They bounded down the path toward the road.

A moment later, the sky cleared, and they heard the memorable sound of broom bristles breaking the sound barrier. Presently, a grandmotherly woman in a pointy hat and *merde*-kicking boots descended from the forest canopy and alighted. Reggie's and Martin's mouths froze mid-shriek. The animals looked anxiously at Granny.

"It's okay, my lovelies. We were in time. Mostly. Any road, took care of those three up there. It'll be a while before they make it all the way back down here. And they won't be walloping the wilderness any time soon, I'm thinking any time *ever*."

A cheer went up, of various sorts. More wolves loped into view then sat on their haunches, yipping their congratulations.

Granny set her broom aside and walked over to Martin. "Now I'm here, I may as well tie those ropes properly." She hung onto the ends while Eduardo rolled the drum away. Relieved to be unhitched from that thing, Martin stopped holding his breath. His relief was short-lived.

"There. That should do it. Now, if you'll hand me that tackle, I'll just run it through these ropes and through that handle on the drum. Just in case he gets a mind to run away."

Granny stood back admiring her handiwork. "Pretty good knots, if I do say so. Used to do a lot of macramé back in the day. Amazing what comes back to you after all the years."

She leered at the miserable Martin. "Wouldn't smoke around that drum you're wearing if I were you."

Referring to things that go 'Bang!', Granny, this pendejo had a gun.

On Eduardo's cue, Conrad hopped over with Martin's handgun held gingerly by the grip. He and the gun were right next to the drum.

"For Crissakes, don't let that thing go off!" Martin implored.

"What, this little thing?" Granny took the gun from Conrad and studied it. "Hmmmm. Wonder if it's loaded."

Martin's drawers got damper. Granny fired off a couple of shots into the back tyres of the bucket loader. It sagged to the ground. Now it was Reggie's turn for damp drawers.

"Yep. Loaded."

Shall we search the trailer for more?

"Might as well."

The wolves came back with three more guns and a large box of ammo.

"Aha! You have room in your saddlebags for those, Eduardo?"

¡Cómo no! he nickered.

Granny made sure the guns were unloaded. Eduardo trotted over so she could stash them and the ammo in the saddlebags and secure them.

"Anything else useful inside?"

"Just some clothes and cigarettes. And food—mostly staples," replied Ross.

"Like sugar, perhaps?" She turned toward the trailer, a very wide smile spreading across her face. This wouldn't even need magic.

She returned with three economy-sized bags of sugar. "My, you fellas must have one helluva sweet tooth!" Granny hummed as she set to work, opening the caps of all the gas tanks and filling them up. "Just a tank fulla sugar makes the engines go down, the engines go down, the engines go down," she crooned tunefully.

What shall we do with these men, Granny?

"Oh, I don't reckon they'll be going anywhere soon. And, look. Sky's cleared up."

"You're not going to kill us?" Martin couldn't believe their luck.

"Not unless you do something to really tick me off. And anyhow, Bill's bringing down a document for your signatures. The terms are quite binding, a concept you must be familiar with by now."

She removed the gag from Reggie's mouth and handed it to Ross. "I'd wash that first before wearing it, if I were you."

"What if we don't feel like signing?" Reggie demanded. He always did have a mouth on him and now that it was free it was getting exercise.

"I'm quite sure you'll feel like it. It *is* an offer you can't refuse, assuming you do wish to keep all *your* limbs on." She snapped her fingers and the broom whisked up and waited for her, hovering. She got on and waved her hand at the bucket loader. Its engine started up, Reggie still trussed to the wheel. As her finger traced a circle, it turned slowly so that it was facing Martin . . . and the drum.

"I can put it in gear, if you like. Should still take a few minutes for the sugar to cook the engine, and you're only, what, 20 feet away?"

Martin was shaking his head sideways very fast. Reggie was nodding his head up and down even faster.

Granny looked back and forth at the contradictory head language. "Well, which is it, 'yes' or 'no'?"

"Yes!!" came the unanimous answer. "We'll sign! Just turn the damned thing off. *Please!*"

Three golden lights flew over the bucket loader, then circled down toward Granny, catching her attention. Granny hailed them, her wave incidentally kicking Reggie's bucket loader into gear and heading it toward Martin's drum, with Martin in between. Five feet away, it chugged to a coughing stop. "Hmmm?" Granny glanced around from her conference with the three sprites. "Oh, beg your pardon." She saw the bucket loader which was now considerably closer to the drum. "Humph. Only made it 15 feet. Sugar must be top-shelf. I shall have to be more careful with my hand gestures."

There were now discernible ammonic puddles beneath both men. Getting a taste of their own medicine had been distressful. A giant crack of thunder rolled down the mountains and it began to pour again.

"Oops. Spoke too soon. Well, that should freshen you lads up," she said.

Granny got onto her broom, and Conrad hopped on front.

"Where to now, Granny?" he cawed.

"I think we'd better check on Durell and Kevin down by the road. Picked up a high-pitched signal," she said, shaking her head and smacking one side of it with her hand. "Bloody GPS!" (Gormless Positing System.)

CHAPTER 25

Doorway to Heaven

Earlier that Monday Afternoon. As the countess's party was leaving the Bishop's Arms, Rumpbuckle's wand began vibrating, then emitting a four-note whistle repeatedly.

"My apologies, all. I need to take this." While the others re-entered the carriage, Rumpbuckle stood aside and flicked his wand. A new scroll flickered in the air. It was a text from his granddaughter: "GAM blokes driving past in grey stretch SUV. Headed toward ravine."

He'd asked her to keep a watch for them and report any suspicious activity. Now he flicked his wand in a counter direction: "Check scrying ball. See what they're up to."

After a minute or two, a reply text appeared: "Done. Granny up mountain on broom. More trees cut. Going after big chestnut now. Looks like war zone. Boys fighting them off. Come quick!"

Rumpbuckle flicked off and sprang into the carriage, telling the others what he'd just learned.

"Oh gods! Not Grandfather's chestnut!" The baroness bit her fist. "They'll pay for this, so help me!" Ronny noticed Betty's dog teeth were elongating rapidly. "Where's my damned cape?" she demanded, searching the carriage seats.

Ronny put out an arm to stop her. "Wait, love. You can't possibly fly right now. It's still light."

"Damnation!" The baroness's mouth was trembling. "Rumpbuckle, can't you do anything? It'll be another two hours before we can reach the ravine, going by carriage. We'll be too late!"

Rumpbuckle was thinking hard but coming up skunked. He could possibly get another 10 mph from the horses with that hastening spell he knew. But that wouldn't be enough. Heartsick, thinking of Granny and the others, as well as their beautiful forest, he shook his head. "Maybe we won't be too late, dear Baroness. And Granny can be quite a fierce opponent, you know."

Ronny called up to her driver, "Morris, get this thing up to the ravine as fast as you possibly can! It's urgent, man!"

Morris snapped the reins and flicked his whip. Thankfully, their horses had been fed and watered and were somewhat rested. They surged forward, doing their best. Even so, the scenery seemed to be lollygagging past. A polite rumble of a cough was heard from the farthest seat back.

"There is one thing," the voice said, "er, Baroness."

Betty's squint skewered Herald. "If you have an idea, speak up, man! This is no time to mumble!"

"It's not a way to go faster, *per se*, just a way to get there faster."

"*And . . . ?*"

"It's called Shirk's Portal. It's actually quite easy. One of the few things that stuck from my schooling. I use it all the time, myself."

Rumpbuckle nodded. "I seem to recall something about that. Is that what you use when you disappear?"

"It's, um, come in handy from time to time. . . ."

"Well, it would come in handy right about bloody now, if you could get it to work," the baroness barked.

"Yes, well. I could show you, if I had a wand." Herald lowered his gaze.

Betty eyed Rumpbuckle beadily.

"Oh, all right. You'll get your wand back," Rumpbuckle said to Herald. "But tell us how it works, first. No surprises, understand?"

"It's very simple. You just draw a door on a wall, say the spell, and walk through. Oh, and you've got to name the place you're going *to*, naturally."

"Well that sounds simple enough. Except for one small item." Betty's arms were crossed. "We are out in the country surrounded only by ruddy fields and trees. Where are you going to find a wall, then?"

Herald pointed out the window to a large, stone bridge they were approaching.

"Well spotted! Would that work?" Rumpbuckle asked.

"I've been in tighter places," Herald admitted.

"How many of us can go through before the door shuts?"

"Depends on how big you draw the door. It's just your basic molecular displacement. Obviously."

"Obviously." Rumpbuckle repeated dourly, then instructed the driver to pull over at the bridge.

Herald started to get out. Rumpbuckle told him, "You wait here. I want to check the site," and clambered out. In a moment, he returned. "Assuming this will work, we're in luck. There are stairs going down the far side, so access to the bridge's base will be easy and hidden.

"And you remember the words correctly to this one?" he asked Herald.

"Oh, yes. Wouldn't do me to forget, would it?"

"How long will the door remain open?"

"A minute at least. Five max, I should think."

"All right." Rumpbuckle turned to the others. "Who wants to come?"

Derek and Ian were keen, as were Rider and Wolfgang. Nigel and Gerry felt it prudent to approach the problem from another angle.

"Okay to take our cameras and such?" Derek asked Herald.

"Anything you like, long as it doesn't get caught in the door."

"Brilliant! Can't wait to see this." Derek grabbed their film kits.

"Perhaps, under cover of the shadows from the bridge . . . ?" Betty began wistfully.

"Darling, I really wouldn't risk it," Ronny said. "If you turned crispy, who'd be our Champion of the Forest?"

"What remains of it," Betty muttered.

"Look, the second it turns dark, we'll both fly up there and see what's to be done," Ronny assured her. "I could do with a good old-fashioned feed, if it comes to it."

Vengeance wouldn't replace the forest. But it would make them both feel better.

Ronny pushed the button that slid the light-blocking partitions up around the two of them.

"Maybe I'll come after all," Gerry volunteered. He grabbed his recording gear.

"If you lot don't come back, it's me who will have to explain it to corporate and your families," cavilled Nigel.

"But if we do, think of the footage!" Derek countered, with a dig of the elbow.

After the explorers had piled out and descended the stairs by the bridge with their paraphernalia, Ronny urged the driver to continue with due haste to the mountain. Betty checked her watch and fumed, wishing she could telephone Heiny. Nigel dialled Alice on his mobile and asked her to bring their van around to the bottom of the ravine. Craning a look, Betty studied his mobile.

"Might I borrow your telephone when you've finished?" she asked.

Nigel held up a finger, signalling 'hang on.'

"Right, luv. See you there." He ended the call and handed his mobile to the baroness.

"Glad to." *Now see, there* was *a good reason you stayed behind*, Nigel told himself.

With Nigel's instruction, Betty dialled her husband, making a mental note: *Perhaps it is time to embrace the new technology.*

When the group got to the bottom of the stairs, they went under the bridge and faced the broad abutment. Herald locked hairy eyeballs with Rumpbuckle, who handed the wand back to him. "This had better be good, Fetidston!" Rumpbuckle barked.

In low dudgeon, Herald took the wand, spoke some words, and pointed the wand at the wall, outlining a very large door. He then drew in a doorknob, a keyhole, and long and elaborate curly hinges. He was just adding the gargoyle door knocker when Rumpbuckle lost his patience. "Stop showing off, man, and get on with it!"

"Sorry. It's just that it's the only way I know to draw the big ones. I was afraid if I drew my usual cat flap, some of us might get stuck. Wouldn't want that—half in, half out."

"Fine. Can we go in, now?"

Herald pushed at the door. Nothing. He scratched his head.

"I knew it! Why should this be any different?" Rider ranted.

"Hang on, hang on!" Herald protested. "The doctor here broke my concentration. Forgot the hinge pins."

Herald drew them in carefully, said some more words and—

Derek thought his eyes would Slinky out of their sockets. He lifted his camera and began shooting, glad for the shade of the bridge and a high ISO. The entire parameter of the door lit up in bright chartreuse. A low thrumming was heard. Herald tried the knob and it twisted. One moment the knob and key plate were just a two-dimensional, rather childish drawing on stone, and the next they were solid hardware. With a click of a released lock, the door swung inward. No grinding of stone, just a smooth glide.

"Wow," said Derek.

"I'll second that," Ian said.

Herald turned with a relieved smile and bowed. "This way, gentlemen."

I didn't think the little fellow had it in him, thought Rumpbuckle.

That was close! thought Herald.

One by one they all walked through the portal, Wolfgang bringing up the rear.

"Would y'all get a move on? I'm the one with the tail. Don't want that door to put a crimp in it!"

They all got through safely, but it was pitch dark. "Wolfgang, you're the one with good night vision," Rider said. "You want to take the lead?"

"Okay, I guess. Just don't hang onto my tail."

As Wolfgang started forward, Herald called from behind, "Shouldn't need to go far. Rumpbuckle, what was that spell again for lighting?" Rumpbuckle was about to tell him when two lights came on at once. Ian sniggered, holding up his flash, "Minolta, maybe?"

"Thought it was Nikon," chortled Derek, holding his.

"Clever. Now, let's see where we are." Rumpbuckle turned and stopped. It was Herald's turn to chortle.

"Fast, isn't it? It's all in the wrist, of course."

They were staring at the point, far up the pass, where the highway was intersected by the unpaved road going up along the west side of the ravine . . . a two-hour carriage drive away from the bridge. Behind them, the portal closed slowly but distinctly and faded from sight.

CHAPTER 26

Beating About the Ambush

Rumpbuckle started forward to cross the highway. Hearing the approach sooner than the rest, Wolfgang abruptly restrained him with a paw. GAM's grey SUV limo was driving at speed toward the entrance to the ravine. The group shrank back into cover as the big car slowed, preparing for the turn. Suddenly, all hell broke lose. A rabbit dashed across the slick road, just missing getting squashed. As the chauffeur slammed on the brakes, the limo fishtailed, hydroplaning across the road and, making an unscheduled stop on the far side in the ditch, fetched up against the mountainside. They heard some oaths as the chauffeur tried to unwedge his door and extricate himself to assess the damage, and in so doing, activated the moonroof. At the same moment, there was a blur of orange as a cat flung itself from an overhanging branch through the open moonroof. Howls of rage and pain erupted, with a frantic batting of hands. The howls had not come from Durell.

"Get it off me! Get it off me!" Addison Brickheart hollered. His seat belt had locked, and he was bleeding.

With aggravating calm Tyrone responded, "Simply open the door and it will leave. It's only a little pussycat, Addison."

"Only a little pussycat, is it?" Durell was slicing and dicing like a demented Veg-O-Matic. With a jab of his uninjured elbow, Addison managed to knock Durell toward Tyrone, who simply ducked, thereby making the VP Business Development the new goalie, as Durrell ricocheted off the saloon's partition. Cyril screamed like a six-year-old.

"Christ! Thing's a demon. Open the door, damnit, open the door!" Cyril punted the cat back. Durell's claws ripped through Tyrone's £60 scissor cut. Streaks of blood ran down Tyrone's scalp, staining his red Turnbull & Asser tie. Tyrone scrambled over Cyril's paunch and frantically tried the back side door. Jammed. His claws still whirring, Durell had puffed himself up to maximum threat. Bloodied arms flailed at him in vain. Then he jumped up on the pass-through window and turned round, lifting his tail. Cyril sprang forward to turn the cat around, but Randall wasn't having any of that. Durell fired. Several manicured hands tried to work the electric windows. Alas, the limo had stalled.

Durell vaulted back out through the moonroof and ran across the highway to the others, a wide grin beneath his whiskers.

"Well done, Durell!" Kevin hopped up.

"Well done, yourself," said Durell.

"Randall, for Chrissake, turn on the bloody engine and roll down the windows!" Tyrone demanded.

The limo started up and windows blurred downward.

"See if you can get the passenger door opened, man!" Cyril had gotten the brunt of the barrage and urgently needed to air out. Randall scooted over to the right side and got the front door open, then walked back to their passenger door. He yanked on the door several times.

"Put some muscle into it, Randall!" Tyrone ordered. The chauffeur kneaded his sore left shoulder, musing on his denied pay rise. Serve 'em right if they were stuck in there all day. He shook his head. "No good. Crash musta cooked the electrics."

"What do you mean? The windows rolled down, didn't they?"

"Yeah, but they're on a different circuit from the locks, see. This fancy car has a default of locking the back doors while her engine's runnin'. When she crashed, musta short-circuited somethin'. I already tried unlocking everything from the driver's seat, but it's knackered."

Addison and Cyril were mopping wounds, fanning themselves and holding their reeking shirts away from their chests. "Well, you must do *something*. We can't stay in here forever."

"You could always climb out the windows," Randall suggested, carefully deadpan.

Tyrone slithered through his passenger window as effortlessly as an eel, a shirt sleeve snagging only a moment on a gold cufflink.

It's all right for some, thought Cyril bitterly, wishing now he'd cut back on the Bakewell tarts. *Trust Tyrone, the skinny weasel, to get away.* For a corporate couch potato, the moonroof was also a no-go.

Addison wriggled through with a little more effort, but eventually made it to the ground, then righted himself. "Coming, Cyril?"

Cyril glared back. "As if I'd fit through that." *Why was it manufacturers never designed the back windows to roll all the way down? Had to be some kind of slimming conspiracy.*

"Oh. Right, then. Er. We'll send someone down from the site with a crowbar . . . or something," Addison said encouragingly. "You just wait with the car."

"Do I have a bloody choice?" *You prat.*

"I'm staying with the car, as well," Randall told them. *Only outside it.* "I'll put in a call to AA for a tow."

"I suppose there's nothing for it, then, but to go on foot," said Tyrone, master of the bloody obvious. "Do you recall how far it is to the main site, Randall?" he asked.

"I should say no more than three miles, give or take a couple."

That had better not have been a smirk I saw. The chauffeur almost seemed to be enjoying himself, Tyrone reflected. "Keep your mobile and walkie-talkie on so we can communicate."

"Will do. Sir."

Now that *was decidedly a smirk.* Perhaps he shouldn't have passed Randall over for a rise last year.

Reaching in the window of the dented driver's door, Tyrone pulled the lever to unlock the boot, then went round and opened it. He took out the emergency kit he always stowed, unsnapped the two clasps and opened the lid. Everything accounted for: 1000-lumen torch, bug spray, first aid kit, high-powered rifle with infra-red sight and silencer, extra ammo. He snapped the lid shut, picked up the case and closed the boot.

Tyrone set off up the hill, tossing back to Addison, "Do keep up."

Addison trotted obediently after him, devoutly wishing for a hot bath and a martini.

When the two men were out of earshot, Rider whistled a three-note call, hoping Eduardo was near and in earshot.

Wolfgang's ears pricked up. "He comin', Rider."

Bless Eduardo's heart. Rider felt a horsey nudge to his shoulder. *He does indeed "tippy-toe" quietly.* "Wolfgang," Rider whispered, "what say you run across and convince those two men with the limo to stay put?"

"Sho 'nough, Boss!" As Rider rolled his eyes, Wolfgang dashed across to Randall, baring his teeth and growling in his scariest predatory manner.

"Crikey!" The mobile dropped from Randall's hand to the ground as he bound up onto the high bonnet, retracting his legs as Wolfgang made repeated jumps at him, his claws raking the limo's glossy body. Randall rolled, sheering off a wiper, pulled himself up to the roof and dove indecorously through the moonroof. A buffed black loafer tumbled down the windscreen. Randall started the engine and stabbed at the moonroof 's controls. He collapsed with relief as it slid shut. But only for a moment. The stink was palpable—full-bodied and muscular. It had taken on a distinct and pugilistic personality. Wolfgang bounded up to the moonroof and looked in, with a wide doggy grin.

"Y'all comfortable in there?" He sat down on the bonnet, relishing the view inside.

"Blimey! Talking wolves. What the blasted hell next?" Randall said aloud.

He was about to find out.

Around the bend a nondescript maroon van came hurtling toward the disabled limo. The scream of brakes was heard and a rending crunch of metal, followed by the scream of the limo's occupants. Alice hopped out and ran over to the other car. Nigel had told her what vehicle to look for when he'd called her. And what to do about it.

"Oh, gosh! Didn't see you there, with the rain and all. Are you all right?"

The boot of the limo was shoved enough inward so that Cyril was sitting with his knees pinned against the door of the mini-bar. The limo's front left corner had been forced into the rocky outcropping above the ditch. There was a growing stream of greenish liquid making its way across the macadam.

"Just peachy. Everything tip-top. Couldn't be better." Cyril struggled to manoeuvre himself onto one side so that he was no longer pleated.

The film crew's van had only a small scuff on its front bumper.

"Oh, you're bleeding! I'm so sorry! Let me call an ambulance for you." Alice reached for her mobile.

Getting the police involved would not do. Cyril waved her off. "We're fine, really. The blood is not a result of the accident, not yours anyway. We slid off the road, you see. Hit an oil slick then ended up in the ditch. But it's only minor damage."

Randall noticed the wolf was gone. *Funny, that.*

"Well then, an ambulance, surely?" Alice persisted. "And I'll be happy to exchange license numbers, insurance cards, etc."

"No, no. It's all right. Really. We're just waiting for AA to arrive. They should be along any minute. Appreciate the offer but don't trouble yourself."

"Well, . . . if you're sure. I am so awfully sorry." Alice backed away. *What* was *that smell?*

She returned to her van and slowly drove off. Nigel had instructed her to leave all the doors unlocked so Rumpbuckle's group could sneak from across the road into the van while she was talking to the men. They were now inside, crouching beneath the van's window line. As she pulled away, her left-side tyres crunched over Randall's mobile, flattening it into a bookmark.

"Hey! Where are you going?" Cyril shouted at her as she turned up the road into the ravine.

"Meeting some mates of mine up at the picnic tables. It *is* a public preservation, you know."

In the rain? he fumed. *Kids these days!*

She toodle-oo'ed and, switching to four-wheel-drive, drove away up the hill. On the blind side of Alice's van, a fleet-footed quadruped and its rider tippy-toed past.

Cyril squirmed in his seat, trying to reach his mobile, but he was unable to wriggle his hand into his pocket, due to the cramped angle he was stuck in. It was crucial that they contact Tyrone and the crew to let them know the maroon van was heading up the ravine. The picnic tables were too close. *Damn.* No use. "Here, Randall, lend me your mobile. We need to warn the others that they're about to have company."

Randall searched the front seats and under them. "I don't see it. Oh, wait." *Shite.* "I think I dropped it when that wolf pounced on us." He crawled back over to the passenger's side and cautiously opened the door. A hairy paw with long claws slid, puppet-like, into view at the door's opening and waved.

"Y'all lookin' for somethin'?"

Randall jumped back inside the car and slammed the door. The paw rose to the window, holding a dripping, flattened phone, with tread marks across it.

A wolfish grin appeared next. "Why, Randall. What big eyes you have!"

The wolf showed no inclination of shifting. *Bollocks!* "How long will it be before AA arrive?" Cyril asked Randall.

"Well, actually . . ."

Cyril massaged his sinuses. "You didn't call them."

"Er, no. Was about to, but then the wolf . . ."

"Terrific. What about the walkie-talkie?"

"Yep, still got that." Randall removed the walkie-talkie from the glove compartment. "Only, it's not secure." The dark expression on Cyril's face was clearly legible. "So, then . . . you want me to call or you?"

"Oh, why don't you call? I'm not particularly in the mood for dislocating my shoulder just now, if it's all the same to you."

Randall nodded and punched the talk button. "GAM1, this is GAM2, come in. Over." Randall waited, listening to static. "GAM1, this is GAM2. Urgent. GAM1, this is GAM2. Come in. Over."

Nothing.

"Mayday! Mayday! This is GAM2. GAM1, come in! GAM1, come in! Over."

More nothing.

Weird, Randall thought. *I've never known Marty to be without his ruddy walkie-talkie. The man takes it with him into the toilets! He's like a bleedin' Boy Scout.* "Maybe he's out of range, sir," he said to Cyril. "The boss did ask him to check out what was going on up at the new site."

"We're screwed," moaned Cyril. "I can't even open the mini-bar. And I need to take a wee."

Randall scrounged up an empty 20 oz. Happy Chef drink cup and handed it to Cyril through the pass-through window. "Will that do?"

"Just. Except . . . um . . . I can't reach."

Randall poked his head through the pass-through to see what the difficulty was. Cyril's arms were pinned so that he couldn't quite reach his zipper. *Bloody hell! These tossers do* not *pay me enough!* Randall gritted his teeth and reached out and did the necessary. And not a moment too soon. Getting the brimming cup back out through the pass-through without sloshing on himself was a feat worthy of Houdini. Now, how to get rid of it? Randall looked up through the moonroof at Wolfgang who was reclining on the bonnet, whistling and waving the broken wiper like a baton. The rain didn't seem to faze him at all.

Pressing the window control with his left hand, he tossed the contents outside as soon as there was room for his hand and the cup, then quickly brought the window back up. Only now the emptied cup added its bouquet to that of *eau du chat.* He hit the window controls again and inched them all down just a crack. Being on the same knackered circuit as the doors, the pass-through window was stuck open. It was going to be a long wait.

Cyril's arms were starting to go to sleep. He prayed for another vehicle to come along. Surely they'd get some help then.

Be careful what you pray for.

Tyrone and Addison struggled up the path in the downpour, slipping in rivulets of mud and water. Tyrone's hair was plastered to his skull and his glasses were fogged. His £1200 suit was history. Pity. He'd particularly liked this one. It was also a pity he hadn't thought to include an anorak in the emergency case.

Addison was plodding stoically behind, brushing the sopping locks out of his eyes and holding his jacket over his head, keeping off the worst. He really couldn't see why Tyrone had to know right this minute and in person what was going on up the hill. That's the whole point of mobiles, for Chrissake. It wasn't as though this was their only PV (Plunder Venture, as the office lads joked). So what if this one didn't work out? Plenty of other dupes to diddle. He really could do with a bath, a warm towel, and a lie down. Maybe even a warm body next to him and a large bottle of bubbly. He pictured the body he had in mind. She was a tasty morsel, that Sylvia. If it hadn't been for rotten timing, he felt sure he would have found out just how tasty she was. At least he wasn't stuck in the stink back there in the limo, like poor Cyril. Sometimes you had to be philosophical.

After a mile and a half, the two came upon the picnic tables. Tyrone set the case down to give his arm a rest, shaking it. He checked the sky. It was getting a bit lighter.

"The storm seems to be slackening. Let's take a break." Tyrone slipped off his Ferragamos and poured a pint out of each. Not the best choice for hiking. He made a mental note of another thing to add to the emergency kit: shoes with tread.

"Fine by me." Addison was doing a bit better. With his bad arches, he preferred trainers, unless he was making a sales pitch or attending a meeting. Or going out on the town. Tyrone had always despised the incongruous get-up of a man in a good suit wearing Nikes. But now he envied Addison.

Still holding his jacket over his head, Addison sat down on the wet bench and gazed about him. "This is a pretty place, you know. I can see why they don't want our bunch ruining it."

"And you can keep *those* sentiments to yourself at the next Board meeting," Tyrone warned.

"As you like." *Still*, Addison thought, *seems a shame to destroy something so lovely*. Mind you, greed had served him well. But it was one thing to read on paper about a project hundreds of miles away and think to yourself, "Oh well, what's a few more trees gone?" and quite another to go there and actually see the trees that were slated to be slaughtered and the spectacular country they lived in.

Looking at the fantastical limbs, boles and knobby branches, they seemed to have actual personalities. He could almost feel them talking to him, but of course that was just naff. They *were* alive, though. They were beings. In which case, it was a good job they weren't also *doings*. If you believed the new research, trees were even sentient. They had *feelings*. Best not to think about that. He, for one, knew he would not like someone coming after him with a chainsaw and not even be able to shout out or leap out of the way.

I would have really liked to have brought Hilda with me to see this before it's gone, if she weren't so busy with her "personal trainer," Sergio. At least they had an understanding: his wife had her "projects" and he had his. But he missed the old days before the kids were grown and gone to university. They all used to enjoy long walks through the woods and countryside.

He was glad his children didn't know about this venture. They would never forgive him for being part of it. Just another three years and he could retire, collect his pension and a very nice severance package, thank you very much, and be shed of all this. Especially *that* one.

That one was opening his case and fitting together the scope and the silencer onto the rifle.

Addison knew about the rifle, but never considered it was more than just corporate readiness overkill. Now he was alarmed. "Expecting trouble, are we?"

"One can never be too prepared." Tyrone's mouth stretched in a nasty smile.

Says he who's wearing no mac and bloody designer loafers. Addison fished around in his inner coat pocket, brought out a Kit-Kat and, after some struggle, unwrapped it. *Perishin' plastic*. Dissolving in the rain, chocolate was soon running down his sleeve so he shoved the rest of it in his mouth at one go.

"If you're quite ready?" Tyrone had no patience with bodily needs. He stood now, carrying the rifle, but leaving the case behind. "Here. Make yourself useful." He handed Addison the electric torch to carry.

Addison grunted. *I'll bet Hilda never thought I'd be carrying a torch for "The Fuhrer,"* he wisecracked mentally. They resumed their upward march.

With the roar of the water cascading down the swollen river and the constant pounding of rain, they never heard the creeping approach of the maroon van. It idled quietly at the picnic tables as its passengers decided on the best strategy. Unnoticed as well, a horse and its rider came out of the forest and stepped noiselessly up to the waiting van.

"Let's give them some distance. Keep the element of surprise," Rider counselled.

"I agree. We should go on foot from here, I think," Sidney said. He peered hopefully at Rumpbuckle. "I don't suppose you can do anything about the rain, as you did before?"

"It would be my pleasure." Rumpbuckle waved his wand, and each of them proceeded in a dry bubble.

Except for Herald. He supposed he had that coming, after all the trouble he'd caused. But still, he'd gotten them all up the ruddy mountain in a trice with no limbs missing. *There's gratitude for you.* Herald waved his restored wand and a moment later stood wearing a blue mac and a plastic, pointed cover over his hat. Not as flash, maybe, but it did the trick.

Derek and Ian were hauling their lightest cameras out of the van and fitting lens hoods and rain canopies over them, in case Rumpbuckle's bubbles popped. Gerry grabbed his recording gear. He figured he could just shove it under his anorak if need arose. He did a sound check to ensure the level was high enough to record over the tumult of water. Now to make certain the batteries were good and everything was operating well. Thumbs up. Gerry and Derek nodded at Rider that they were ready.

"Alice. You coming or staying?" Derek whispered.

She shrugged. “Staying, I guess. Someone needs to mind the rental. And you might need it in a hurry. Ring me if you need back-up, okay? I should be able to get this pig up the hill if I have to.”

“There’s no doubt in my mind about that,” he said, smiling.

As they set off, she turned the van around across the path to block any get-away by the baddies above. She checked her mobile to make sure it was on and held enough charge. So far so good. She checked her watch. It had been an hour since Nigel had called her. In another, it would be getting dark, possibly sooner if the rain didn’t let up. By then, she supposed Nigel and the vampire ladies would have caught up. From what little she knew about the women, she reckoned the slimy weasels up top were in for a world of hurt. Hell hath no fury like an old bat with a severe overbite. Settling down in the driver’s seat, she prepared for the wait, keeping the keys in the ignition and the doors locked.

CHAPTER 27

Payback Is a Bitch (or Two)

Tyrone and Addison were almost to the main worksite. Apart from the gurgle of the stream, it was uncharacteristically quiet. "Looks like the men—" Addison began. Tyrone waved him silent. He raised the rifle to his shoulder and squinted through the infrared scope. Motioning to Addison to keep back, he stepped into the clearing and swung the rifle in an arc. The scope was picking up a heat signature near a 70-gallon drum in the clearing ahead. He stepped forward, lowering the gun sights in the vicinity of the drum. A tattoo of feet scuffling on the ground was coming from its direction. A hoarse voice reached his ears in time.

"Don't shoot! For God's sake, Tyrone, don't shoot!"

Tyrone lowered the rifle cautiously. "Is that you, Martin?" He came closer, noting the labelling on the drum. He supposed it was a good thing he hadn't fired, seeing that it most likely would have taken some important equipment with it, assuming it was still full. In his pique, Tyrone didn't much think he would have regretted the loss of Martin. But it would have meant masses of paperwork, possibly an inquest.

"How the hell have you managed to get tied up?" Tyrone demanded.

Oh, like it's my *bloody fault*, thought Martin. "Yer wouldn't believe me if I told yer." They heard a banging from the direction of the bucket loader.

Tyrone whirled around.

"That'll be Reggie, I expect," Martin commented dryly.

"What? Both of you tied up?" Tyrone set the rifle down on a folding table set up in front of the trailer, removing and pocketing the magazine. "Unbelievable." He next pulled out a folding knife, presumably to set the men free. Addison gaped at the size of the thing. It was long and shaped like a hunting knife; its wicked blade refracted what light there was with a fearsome gleam.

What in blazes was a CDO doing with a knife like that *in his briefcase? Most of them just carried a dinky little pocketknife with a folding nail file.* From the comfortable way Tyrone carried this thing, he and the big blade were old friends.

Tyrone walked first over to Reggie in the bucket loader. Martin was the second in command, under Bill, so it was fair game to pin this cock-up on him. Might as well make him suffer a bit longer. "Addison, could you lend me a hand with the ropes? If you aren't busy."

"It was you who told me to stay back," he reminded Tyrone.

"Yes, well. It's safe now, isn't it?"

With Reggie banging on the sides of the loader, they didn't hear the soft hoof-steps approaching the table, nor the tchick of a spare magazine being clicked into place.

"In answer to your question," a new voice rejoined, "I suppose it would depend on how you would define 'safe.' In this situation."

Tyrone spun and crouched instinctively, knife ready. He was looking at the stamping legs of a horse, then up past riding boots to a man with a rifle. *His* rifle. His reloaded rifle, to be exact. Tyrone cursed himself for setting his gun down. However, he hadn't gotten to be Head Weasel without having the instincts of one. Being below the long sights of the rifle, he calculated that he was close enough to the man on the horse to close the gap before the cross-hairs could track him. Ferret-like, Tyrone sprang and lunged for the rider, thrusting upward, like nipping up someone's pant leg. Except this pant leg nipped back. He only saw a flash of tartan before a set of sharp teeth pierced his knife hand. The knife fell to the ground from his skewered, bleeding hand and was kicked under the trailer by a powerful hoof, just before another hoof biffed him upside the head.

Tyrone rolled away from the striking hooves, lumbered upright and staggered behind a tree. Addison was still frozen in place next to the bucket loader.

"Bloody typical," commented the rider. "You're only now finding the protection of trees to be useful?" Rider had the sights of the rifle accurately pinpointing his target. Taking careful aim at the pin-striped tail of a jacket peeking from behind the trunk, Rider smiled. *Wanker should have chosen a bigger tree.* With apologies to the tree, he squeezed the trigger. *Pfffffffftewt!* A small divot of flying bark was followed by a yelp.

"The game, as they say, is up, Mr. Upman. Now be sensible and come out with your hands in the air. You also, Mr. . . . Brickheart," Rider added, his plosive intentionally soft on the 'B.' The rifle now veered in Addison's direction, then down. Addison was cowering in front of the bucket loader.

"Like hell I will!" Tyrone spat at Rider and scuttled away, limping fast from tree to tree, taking cover.

"Derek, Ian! Secure Mr. Brickheart, then hand me that big torch he was carrying," Rider shouted. "Gerry, grab any walkie-talkies you find from the trailer. There's probably one on the guy tied to the drum, too."

"Yep. Here." Gerry tossed Rider Martin's walkie-talkie, then entered the trailer and returned with a couple more.

"Switch to frequency 13, the baroness's private channel, in case there are any more GAM-types listening. I'm going after the bastard."

"Right."

Rider grabbed Tyrone's torch. Eduardo swung around and galloped away in the direction of the sounds of bushwhacking.

The rain had decreased to a drizzle. It was becoming full dark. With all the brush beneath the canopy, a horse and rider would soon find it difficult to follow, even with a torch and infrared scope.

But there were some who had excellent senses in the dark.

About a quarter mile into the forest, Tyrone reached a dell and rested, catching his breath. His left hip felt on fire but it was only badly bruised. His wallet had taken the brunt of the bullet, the advantage of traveling with a fat wad of cash and plastic. The dell was a near-perfect circular clearing, above which shone a waning gibbous moon. As his vision adjusted to the gloom, he saw a large hollow at the base of an immense oak on its periphery. He crawled over to it and powered on his mobile, shining it into the recess. A man his size could just fit, if he curled up tight-ish. He crawled forward and saw small tunnels leading off in several directions inside . . . with carpet runners on the ground.

"'Ere, you! Wot you mean tresspassin' like this?" Three dazzling lights shone back out at Tyrone. A second later they were swarming and diving at him. Each of the lights carried a miniature *sgian-dubh,* which were playing havoc with the hosiery. Tyrone backed out abruptly, his bloodied socks slashed to ribbons. The three sprites whirled like dervishes about his head, raining curses and jabs. Then, just as suddenly, they darted away and began flying in a circle around him. By their light, he noticed he was in the middle of a circle of toadstools. Make that a concentric set of circles. *Weren't they called "faerie rings" or something?* The lights were now strobing steadily. Tyrone realized he was sitting in the exact centre. *Unusual configuration . . . like a bull's eye. Or a heli-pad.* He felt more than heard the steady whoosh of wings overhead. What moon there had been was blacked out by two large airborne shapes. No, not helicopters.

There was a moment of stunned horror before the black capes enveloped him. A piercing scream reverberated through the forest.

Coming up the hill, Rider reined Eduardo to a halt. Checking the time and then the darkened sky, he nodded to himself.

Dinner time?

"Oh yes. And I imagine CDO is on the specials."

"Well . . . that was . . . interesting, though a bit too *nouvelle* for *moi.* Not as tasty as I'd anticipated." Betty issued a small burp. "Oh! Pardon."

"Yes. A bit sour, I thought. But, consider the source." Ronny lounged back, revelling. "Still, he made a nice deviation from the new diet." She smacked her lips.

"Perhaps just a bit more. I'm trying to get a handle on that odd base-note. Not quite copper. Sulphur?" Betty leaned over for a re-fill.

"Oh, darling. Don't drain the wretch. Not that he doesn't deserve it, mind you. But you want to leave some for later. And we don't want to 'turn' him!"

"You're right, of course." Betty shuddered. "We certainly don't want any more of *that* sort!"

"Or his living forever, barring the possible jab with a stake."

Ronny felt Tyrone's pulse. "Plenty left to be going on with. At least a couple of pints."

"For the morning?" Betty giggled at Ronny.

"Exactly. Either way you spell it." They both howled.

They felt a rush of air above them and a whistle of bristles. "Incoming!"

The sprites flew up in formation to guide Granny in. Her boots thumped on the ground, and she swung a leg over.

"Ah. See you've dined, then."

"Just a tasting. We were peeved," Ronny told her.

"And feeling peckish," Betty added.

"Ergo, the man was punctured." Ronny nodded owlishly.

"Peeved, peckish and punctured," Betty crooned. "What was that song—'Bewitched, Bothered and—'?"

" 'Bewildered'!" Ronny shouted. "That's more in your line, Granny!" Betty and Ronny fell over, snorting.

"When you're quite finished," Granny harrumphed. "we'll need to do something about this one. I take it the bleeder's still breathing?"

"Oh yes. Although he is looking a teensy bit drained." And they were off again.

Granny saw the fallen mobile on the ground. Though she didn't hold with the contraptions, she'd seen enough of them she knew which buttons to push, which she now did. "Hmmph. At least that's useful." She shone the light around the clearing. "This'll do for us. Elmo, would you, Brain and Dim fly down to Rider and Eduardo and give them some light so they can find the circle, please?"

"On it, Granny!"

"You bet!"

"Make way for the Charge of the Light Brigade!" Dim zoomed off.

Brain shook his head. "It's all them filums. Gone to his brain," he declared to no one in particular, then flew after him.

"Now then. Do we need to find something to bind the blighter?" Granny asked the two women.

"Shouldn't think so. He's nearly running on empty." Another snicker from Ronny.

"Didn't know you two were such clowns."

"We apologize. A bit. It's been a long, dreary time since we had any fun, legally. But to answer your question," Betty continued more soberly, "he won't have the reserves to make a run for it for some time. Let's see, it takes the body roughly 24 hours to replenish a pint. Doing the maths, two maybe three days?"

"Crikey! You *were* peckish."

"And peeved."

"Don't you two start again." Betty and Ronny tried, unsuccessfully, to appear contrite.

"Anyway, I can always smack him with my broom, if it comes to that."

"Righteously peeved, Granny," Betty reminded her. Then, somberly she asked, "Is my grandfather's tree—" She couldn't finish her question.

Granny saw Betty's tears starting up, and gave her a fond pat. "Don't you worry, luv. We sorted them out good and proper. That ol' tree will be around for a few more centuries yet."

Betty made a sound that was a cross between a hiccup and sniffle, followed by a belch. "I'm so glad, so very glad. And so very much in your debt." She wiped a corner of her cape across her nose.

"I know you are. We all are glad, 'cept for this one and his band of hoods. As far as debts go, there isn't one, not to me at any rate."

"But there is still a debt," Betty persisted.

"You're right there, but one we all share."

"A debt to the forest, to the wild," declared Ronny. "Who was it said, 'In wildness is the preservation of the world'?"

"Some smart bugger, I'll allow." Granny lay back, making a pillow of her cloak.

Betty nodded. "Quite so."

The forest around them resumed the murmurs of its nighttime business. A scurry here, a hop there, the soft drop of a cone, the sleepy call of a nesting bird.

"It's been worth it, hasn't it? The abstinence and deprivation. Teaching ourselves to be kinder, gentler . . . well, bloodsuckers," Ronny asked her friend.

"Yes, darling, it has. *This* is what's worth fighting for. Much the best trade-off."

Betty's hand reached out for Ronny's and clasped it. They all gazed up at the night sky, now crowded with stars.

CHAPTER 28

Rousting Weasels

Heinrich was the first to find them in the dell. His night vision was nearly as good as Wolfgang's. Even without it, the four sets of snores would have alerted him to their location if his vision had not. When he'd gotten the call from Betty earlier, he was alarmed but knew exactly where they'd end up. They could always rely on the magic of the forest to guide all the parties in the right direction, according to need. He grabbed his revolver, his London Fog and a torch, and headed over to the ravine. But not before making a couple of quick calls of his own.

Now he bent over Betty and tenderly brushed a lock out of her eyes, then wiped off a dribble of blood before the others saw it. She hated appearing untidy. Rider came up behind on Eduardo. The trail had been well lit by the sprites. He vaulted off the saddle and came over.

"Is she—?"

"All right, yes. Just sleeping it off." Heiny beamed fondly at his wife.

Hearing their whispers, Ronny roused herself blearily and squinted up at Rider, then at Heiny.

"All right, Ronny?"

"All right, Heiny."

"Granny okay, too?"

"Of course."

"Well that's good, then." He saw the dimming mobile on the ground. "Ronny! You had a mobile here and you never called back? I was worried sick!"

"Not ours, so it wouldn't have you as a contact. And I never could remember your number."

"Never mind, then. How's the suckee?" With a toe, he jostled Tyrone, still prone, pale and snoring.

"He'll recover. Unfortunately."

"It's for the best, you know. Let the Crown and courts sort it all out, what?"

"What if the Crown and courts make a hash of it? It's happened before," Ronny reminded him bitterly.

At this, Rider intervened. "I'll make sure, and so will my dad, that that doesn't happen. For one, we'll insist on the trial's taking place in this country. I'm quite impressed with *your* Crown's zero tolerance toward environmental sabotage."

"Good-oh!" Heiny rubbed his hands with glee. "If I know Eleanor (that's Queenie, you know), she'll go for maximum sentencing, not to mention payback!"

Betty roused herself. "What's 'good-oh'?"

Granny was still snoozing. She'd had a long and tiring day with her legs wrapped round a bristly bit of wood.

Heiny helped Betty up and dusted her cape off, picking twigs out of her hair. "We were just discussing the justice that's coming to this bunch of marauders."

"Too right." She snuggled against his shoulder. "Which reminds me—where is Sidney, and has anyone put through a call to Eleanor or Millie?"

"Yes, dear," Heiny replied. "I put in a call to Crossmenot Castle straight away before coming. Also to Sidney's mobile. He's rung up his office and asked them to start drafting an injunction to fax to the queen. I believe he's also alerting the police. A van should be on its way. Sidney should be here any minute too, come to that."

Shortly thereafter, Sidney and Rumpbuckle arrived at the circle. Rumpbuckle went over to Granny and took her hand, waking her gently. She sat up, rubbing her back. "Not quite the spring chicken, eh?" Riding about on a broom had reacquainted her with bones she'd forgotten she had.

"Nevertheless, you're my chick." Rumpbuckle twinkled at her.

Granny hmphed, but let him help her up. "Just as well. Who else would have me? A bit long in the tooth."

"Oh, I think there are some here with longer." Ronny never could avoid a pun.

They all burst out laughing at that, except for Tyrone, who came to for a bit, spied the vampires and muttered, "WTF?!" (or acronyms to that effect).

"I alerted the police," Sidney confirmed, "and they're *en route*. But I'm uncertain how far their van can make it up this track. They aren't normally all-wheel drive with high chassis."

"But Nigel's van is. Ring up Alice. I'll bet she can make it most of the way. We can make a crude litter and drag him over to the trail."

"There shouldn't be any need for all that." Betty stepped forward with Ronny. "We shall go as we came, except for some additional baggage."

"Are you certain you're up to it?" Heiny asked her.

"Fed and fit!" She patted her midsection. "Perhaps Granny would care to come, too, just to whack him if he gets funny?"

"And me!" Ross ran up to Granny and hopped on her now hovering broom.

"Me, too!" Conrad hated to be outdone. Plus, he was the better navigator.

"Well, if you're sure," Heiny said. "I'll give Cedric a shout and tell him to leave a light on in the dungeon then, shall I?"

"That would be splendid." Betty gave him a peck on the cheek. "Ladies? Shall we?"

Tyrone fainted as the black capes surrounded him once more. They tsked at his lack of fortitude. Still, it made him all the easier to manage.

"And we have lift-off!" Ronny cried. The three women and their deputies rose in a swirl of black satin and hazel twigs, then shot off into the night toward ze *Schloss* with their quarry.

'And a hearty Hi-Yo, Silver!' Eduardo whinnied.

"Well," Rider said, "at least the rain's stopped. Let's get back to the main site and see if any more of the men have turned up."

Right on cue, Tyrone's mobile tweeted to life again. Rider picked it up and checked the caller. It was Rollo, one of the three up at the top site, trying to warn Tyrone. He scanned the text quickly, then took out the walkie-talkie from his saddlebag, switching to frequency 13 to call the film crew. "Easy Rider here, calling for Fellini. Fellini, come in. Over."

The film crew responded, "Fellini here. State your position. Over."

"At the launch site and returning your way. Over."

"Copy. ETA?"

"20, give or take. Back-up? Over."

"On the way. Al's already here. Over."

"Good. You have company coming. Over."

"Already arrived. Over."

"AOK? Over."

"Roger. Signed, sealed and delivered. Over."

"Repeat—delivered? Over." To whom, Rider wondered.

"Correct. And signed and sealed. Back of the van. Big D with them. Big guns to meet us at the bottom. Over."

Rider recognized Ian's voice. The captives must be in Alice's van then and 'Big D' had to be Derek. He was the tallest and quite handy with knots. So that was under control.

But Rider puzzled over the "signed and sealed part." Then it came to him. Granny had said something about some sort of treaty she'd forced on the men, threatening them on pain of dismemberment for their signatures. Another recommendation to make to Dad. A law firm always had room for a good persuader.

"Nicely done, Fellini. On our way. Over and out."

Alice was waiting for them at the main site with Gerry and Ian in the front seat. Derek, as expected, was sitting in the back with a gun trained on Bill and Rollo, who were trussed up and looking wretched. "Don't know if you'll all fit," she said. The two prisoners in back were squeezed as it was without four additional passengers: Sidney, Rumpbuckle, and the two other workmen, Martin and Reggie. They'd need someone to mind the last two prisoners. Rider would remain on Eduardo.

"I can stay here with these two gentlemen," Rumpbuckle offered. "I believe I can make them stay put."

"I'll be happy to wait with you, Doctor," said Sidney.

"At any rate," Alice said, "they're still tied up, so I suppose it's safe to make a second trip and pick you lot up next. This rental handles the terrain far better than I would have thought."

"We'll go down with you," Rider said. "Maybe the police have an ATV of their own to send up and see to proper security. Would save you another trip. In the meantime, I don't think they'll object to our taking any necessary precautions." He patted Eduardo and they set off behind Alice. If anything went wrong, he still had Tyrone's rifle.

When they reached the bottom of the road, blue lights from several police vans and an ambulance were flashing, and capped men in fluorescent green vests were milling about. Bill and Rollo were handed off to the coppers. Wendell had been collected from the bottom of the river, stuck half-way inside a culvert. DOA, he was zipped into a bag and trundled away. Slaps on the back and 'well dones' were paid to Alice's party.

While a sergeant was talking to dispatch, a large tow truck hooked up the bashed grey limo. They'd managed to extricate Cyril. He and Randall had come quietly and were sitting in the back of a cruiser, the sliding panel between firmly shut and the vent fan turned up high.

A large police ATV set off up the ravine road to fetch the other two suspects, along with the rest of the group. The countess's carriage was parked behind the line of police vehicles, Nigel standing outside. Her exhausted horses had their noses buried in feed bags and the driver was wiping them down.

Rider craned his neck, searching. "Where's Herald?"

In the excitement, they'd all forgotten him. "Aaaaaaargh!" Rider banged his forehead with his fist. "The bugger's scarpered *again*?"

Some bings and boinks emanated from inside the carriage.

Coloured lights could be seen flashing intermittently. Dismounting Eduardo, Rider walked over and peered inside. Herald was sitting in the back seat. He had discovered a new feature of his refurbished wand. In the air quivered an image of Candy Crush, Level 6. Herald beamed at him. "Brilliant! Rumpbuckle installed it for me. It's given me ever so many ideas." He swished his wand and crushed a whole line of candies.

The aftershock of a tough but successful day hit Rider and he sagged. "Mind if I join you?"

"I can show you how it works, if you like." Despite the grey hair and beard, Herald was still really a big kid. Rider flopped down next to him, amused.

"So you didn't desert us again?"

"No! Of course not. I *am* sorry for the mess I made. I just didn't know how to undo it."

"But you know how to now?" Rider crossed fingers.

"Oh, yes. Rumpbuckle worked it out for me, once I explained the original spell I was going for. So that's all sorted."

"Except . . . I'm still a werewolf. Or will be again in a few weeks."

"No, no. I'll have you back to yourself good as new by then. Just have to round up a couple of ingredients."

Rider squeezed his eyes shut, praying. "Please tell me these ingredients have nothing to do with your GMOs."

"What? Oh. Goodness, no! They were absolute rubbish. Don't know what I was thinking. No, this is proper stuff Rumpbuckle's getting me."

Rider sat back against the cushions, thanking God and picturing his old life returning to him.

"Er. There's just one thing."

Rider tensed and sat up. "And what's that?" he scowled.

"Only . . . Rumpbuckle said he wasn't positive how much of it he could lay his hands on. There'll be enough for you, so no worries there! But the other two . . . he was a bit doubtful. They might end up having to take the bullet. The silver one."

Rider flopped back again, grinning ear to ear. "I wouldn't worry about those two." *They have what's coming to them.* Life was good.

CHAPTER 29

Crowned with Comeuppance

The following Friday morning, at Castle Crossmenot a royal courtier in pantalooned livery came forward into the throne room and banged his staff on the ancient parquet floor. “Her Royal Majesty, Queen Eleanor.”

Her full name was Marian Eleanor Loveanger Crossmenot. In her youth, she’d been more than a bit of a Maid Marian, but now the name Eleanor suited her best. Tall and elegantly slim, she was artlessly regal. A crown of intertwined mayflowers, violets and roses worked in gold sat on her burnished auburn hair, pulled back in a simple chignon at the nape of her neck. A matching gold necklace encircled her throat. Her gown of brushed-gold satin was worn just off her shoulders, its neckline and front panel embroidered in gold and russet garlands of autumn berries and leaves and beaded with tiny garnets.

From her serene and queenly visage, one would never know just how cheesed off she was.

Her audience was divided into two halves; one half was shackled and under stern scrutiny of the royal guards. Both sides were obliged to bow as Queen Eleanor passed between them and ascended the richly canopied dais, to sit on the centre-most throne of three.

The staff banged again. “Her Royal Highness, Princess Verisimila.” Millie walked in next, now dressed traditionally in plum-coloured velvet, a regulation diamond coronet and a lavender sash. Reluctantly, she’d replaced the hob-nailed slippers with burgundy heels.

As the audience again bowed, she joined her mother on the dais, taking the smaller throne to the queen's left.

Once more the staff banged. "Her Royal Highness, the Queen Mother, Boadicea Gertrude Loveanger."

Rider leaned over to Rumpbuckle, expressing his surprise. "I did wonder who would sit on the third throne."

"I, on the other hand, did not." Rumpbuckle inclined his head with a wink, smoothing the placket on his green velvet jacket. Rider saw that the earring was back. And Wolfgang was again adorned with his red bow and medal. Their whole group looked wonderful. Even the film crew had donned their best, even swapping their trainers for dress shoes. Alice and Dinah were looking particularly toothsome in becoming frocks and large, fetching hats.

Ignoring their bows, Granny Loveanger ascended the dais and sat on the third throne, to her daughter's right. Rumpbuckle looked fit to burst with pride. She looked absolutely splendid. Few of them had ever seen her wearing jewellery, but the gorgeous silver necklace of rubies and pearls was just right, as was the unusual design of her silver crown. Embossed at its base with a constellation of stars interspersed with borage blossoms set with sapphires, it supported a graceful fan of interlocking silver hazel twigs. Rider'd wager she'd chosen the design herself. Like her daughter's, her hair was drawn back, but in a business-like bun, the lavender streak creating an intriguing glimmer among the silver strands.

Granny's gown was a bit higher in the neckline, but equally sumptuous: pearl-grey satin embroidered with silver garlands of thistle, chamomile and currants—both berries and blossoms. It suited her: prickly, but sweetly healing and deliciously tart.

As she sat, however, one shod toe escaped the hem of her skirts. It was booted in black. Granny saw no sense in suffering pinched toes. Rider, Rumpbuckle and Wolfgang creased up, sneaking glances at one another.

A new courtier came forward in different livery, banging his staff.

"Baron and Baroness Heinrich and Elisabetta von Intermittierend Allianzen unter Landadels." Heinrich and Betty entered at a stately pace, resplendent in their official 19th century finery, and joined the group on the left.

"Countess Veronica von . . ." (There was dwindling mumbling, followed by an embarrassed cough). Ronny exhaled evenly, then sashayed in undaunted, joining her confederates.

"Count Vladimir Dracula." There was a hush at the announcement of his name. He was escorted by a guard to the group on the right, Queen's left. Being nobility, he was unshackled (they knew where he resurrected) and had been permitted to wear his cape.

"All be seated. This tribunal is in session. God save the Queen!" The courtier turned and marched off smartly to the side of the room.

The accused were brought forward and the charges were listed: trespassing, illegal use and appropriation of protected property, falsifying documents, falsifying soil and water sample reports, mining without a permit, vandalism and damage to property . . .

The list went on and on. A volume of well-documented evidence (thanks to Nigel et al.) was then duly produced.

One by one, each was asked, "How plead you, guilty or innocent?" And one by one, with chagrin, each responded, "Guilty, Your Highness."

During the three preceding days (and four preceding nights), the prisoners had had ample opportunity to do some hard thinking, consider their options (few) and reconsider their actions. Their thinking was aided by the graphic persuasions of Rider, Rumpbuckle, Sidney and Granny, each making use of his or her individual talents and methods, in case the perpetrators couldn't imagine the consequences well enough on their own.

Tyrone had, by this time, once more been airlifted, by dual capes, to Castle Crossmenot to join his fellow felons.

When they weren't down in the cells persuading, the four defenders of the forest had spent long hours upstairs with the queen, princess and their cousin, Herald. The problem, of course, was what to do with the miscreants, and with their corporation, so they wouldn't do it again. Ever. Not even the teensiest temptation. And whatever the sentence, it needed to be well and spectacularly publicized so that any other buggers with a similar idea would be likewise dissuaded (in quaking corporate boots and damp corporate drawers).

The documents Sidney, Rider and his dad had bashed out remotely in the wee hours. Rumpbuckle's wand transferred them, in perfect copperplate, to the castle's printers.

The courtier was back with a bang. "All rise. This tribunal will recess for one hour. Bailiffs, remove the prisoners." Bang! Bang!

Rider's group waited until the others had filed out. Princess Millie came over to them, Granny and Eleanor following in her wake. "How are you all bearing up? Mum's got some eats laid on in the next room. Golly, my stomach was rumbling so loudly, I was afraid people could hear it down where you are!"

Eleanor held out her hand to each of them, smiling. "Terrific work, all of you. I'm afraid it's just a cold luncheon, but as soon as this is over, we can dine more properly. You all are staying over, aren't you? Countess? Baron and Baroness? I should be hurt if you didn't stay a day or two. One so rarely gets to have a good chat with friends these days."

"It's not like we don't have loads of room," added the princess.

"That's very gracious of you, Your Majesty." Rider bowed. "I'll be happy to accept, but only for one night. I'm much overdue at the office and have some personal things to attend to, as well." He eyed Herald.

They all agreed to stay. And why not?

"Wolfie can bunk with me," Granny offered. "We have some catching up to do." Her stare skewered Wolfgang.

"I can explain," he began.

"I'm sure you will. Come along. We only have an hour to eat before this crowd comes back." Granny led the way into the dining room.

Over a hurried luncheon, the members of the tribunal again discussed the sentencing they'd worked out in the preceding days. Was everyone still agreed? They were.

First and foremost, the corporation would be required to replace every tree felled on a same-size, same-species basis.

The two executive werewolves would continue to suffer the change indefinitely, but henceforth be incapable of satisfying their offal lust. Rumpbuckle had devised a fiendish spell, ensuring they be denied any flesh, not so much as a fish finger, at "that time of the month." Whatever the market, kitchen, or restaurant appealed to, a vegetarian substitute would be all that was on offer. The juicy steak the wife left in the fridge would sadly be soy.

The were-kahunas would also be prohibited from mauling innocent members of the public. Fat chance of that, any road. Their appearances would be so hairy and laughably fangy, they'd be forced to retire from public life (at least monthly), fed up with fabrications: Yes, they *were en route* to another fancy dress ball; *yes*, it was the same bloody costume as the last dozen times, and; no, it was *not* a gorilla suit with tusks stuck on.

The queen permitted her mother to caution them sternly not to whinge about it or their faces would stick that way; then they would have to be put in a zoo.

After a 90-day staycation in their local county prisons, they could return home but would be forever banned from hunting: anywhere and anything, or any*one*. Poor Cyril would have to resign his membership in the Hounds Club.

Police agencies around the globe would be sent their full descriptions, complete with unflattering colour photos, to ensure compliance. Millie imagined all the lovely dart boards those would make in various constabularies.

However, the hunting season for *them* would remain permanently open. Their compliance would be enforced by the simple threat, in the alternative, of being run down as prey by the real wolf population. Then they would know what it was to be dismissed as mere sport.

The workmen would receive sentences that were less severe, but still fully binding. All of the convicted, including their various governing corporations, companies, and subsidiaries, as well as assignees, licensees and heirs (blah, blah, blah), would be enjoined in perpetuity from any activity whatsoever involving the felling of trees, or mining, or from entering into any business arrangement with an entity, organization, etc., etc. engaged in same. This would extend to their own private properties; if a tree fell on one of their houses, so be it. Natural justice, pure and simple. Granny's Affidavit and Agreement, signed by all of the work crew, would be entered in the royal injunction as a cautionary precedent, labelled Exhibit A.

When the big-wigs returned to their company, they'd be stripped of title and privilege and re-assigned to PR to liaise with the newly mandated Land Restoration Department, where they'd have the joy of answering complaints and fielding bad press, of which there was expected to be plenty.

One week of community service would also be required monthly at a nature preserve, educating the public on the importance of protecting wild places. Snarl as they might, if they didn't perform their duties convincingly, they'd hear about it (so help them, Granny). And, yes, they *would* have to wear the silly hats and had better not frighten the children.

Picturing Tyrone dressed as Smokey the Bear made Rider's day.

In ten years, the former execs could resign or retire, but could not look forward to severance packages or pensions. They would receive compensation for service at the same level as regular staff. Addison saw the light at the end of his tunnel retreating.

The final humiliation would be relinquishing the keys to the executive washroom.

That was Millie's brainwave. "Can you imagine them in the staff washroom, shaving off the face fur, with file clerks and mailroom boys going in and out?" she giggled.

"What about appeals?" Rider had asked.

"Or parole?" Sidney added.

"Eleanor doesn't believe in any of that." Granny winked. The queen smiled at her mum. "And neither do I. Once we Loveangers get angry, good and proper, gods help the wicked sods who got our dander up."

Sometimes a benevolent monarchy wasn't such a bad thing, Rider considered. *It certainly reduced a lot of red tape and aggravation.*

"We do believe in fairness," Millie interjected earnestly. "But that goes both ways. All ways, really. We truly listen to all sides and consider all the arguments, when they're not total rot. And Mum doesn't believe in physical torture or capital punishment."

"Nor did your father." Turning from her daughter, Eleanor continued, "Our hope and our goal was always to mete out a punishment that would, in the end, turn the criminal's heart and mind around to a kind, just and sensible way of living. Failing that, we simply incorporated into the sentence a method by which the unrepentant would be hoisted on his or her own petard."

Rider straightened his face. "I believe you've done that nicely, Your Majesty."

The door opened and the courtier approached. "It's time, Your Highness."

"Thank you." Eleanor blotted her lips on her napkin and rose. She gazed around the large table at her guests. Such a diverse group: a countess, a baron and baroness (Heinrich was looking especially smashing), a wizard (no, make that two—Cousin Herald finally deserved the title), her mother (warrior witch and healer), two valiant attorneys, the resourceful film crew and their director, Dinah the kitchen maid (what an agent of espionage that one had become!), the reliable Manuel, and Cedric (one could never forget *him*). And Wolfgang, their beloved "homeboy." What a rogue he was, but with such a good heart. She was quite glad they'd adopted him, despite his penchant for tall tales. Eleanor had no doubt that the "catching up" her mother mentioned would be giving him the what-for about that whopper he'd told about her daughter and mother. Threatening to serve him on a platter? As if! He knew perfectly well he was beloved. Eleanor beamed at her champions.

"Ladies, gentlemen, shall we go forth and smite?"

Bang! "All rise! The Crown's tribunal is resumed."

As the prisoners were herded in, with a clanking of hardware, the unshackled members returned to their places.

"Prisoners, remain standing. Plaintiffs and members of the tribunal, be seated."

They sat.

"The prisoners will approach the dais, each as his name is called."

A heavy folio was presented to the queen and, addressing her prisoners, she read the terms of their sentencing. Eleanor had the pleasure of seeing their faces redden one by one like a faulty string of rosy fairy lights.

After receiving his sentence, each prisoner was escorted back to his seat by a liveried bailiff and thrust into it. At last it was Count D.'s turn.

"Vladimir Dracula, you may approach the throne."

"Count Dracula, what defence do you offer for your involvement in this unlawful endeavour?" Eleanor had never appeared more regal or more stern. But that was nothing compared to Gertrude Loveanger to her right, simmering just beneath the boil.

"Your Gracious Majesty, I most humbly offer my apologies und beg your forgiveness und clemency. I vuz not avare zat ze corporation mit vhich I have made ze agreement vould be encroaching upon my neighbours' land or taking ze trees." Wolfgang spotted the count's crossed fingers behind his back. "Zey zaid zey vould only be removing some minerals from ze water, vich, as you know, springs from my own estate. Und zey assured me nobody owns ze vater, zo . . ." He shrugged and offered his best self-effacing smile.

"Indeed? We have scrutinized every article of Global Advanced Management's sales agreement you have signed, before witnesses I might add, and the terms and details of their intended work were quite clearly set out. How is it you did not understand?"

"Ze language barrier?" he suggested, hopefully.

"We do not find that to be a sound defence. You have been in this country for more than 400 years, an ample amount of time in which to learn and perfect the language of your neighbours and your sovereign. Whatever the passage of time, however, ignorance is never an excuse for lawlessness.

"Further, we find it exceedingly interesting that it was you who raised the alarm about the werewolves, who were in fact the very men you were doing business with."

"But I did not know zey were ze verwolves!" the count pleaded.

"Hmph. Seems like a red herring to me!" Granny narrowed her eyes at the count.

"Vas is zis red herrink?" he asked, bewildered. "If I had seen a herrink, I vould have et him."

"Be that as it may," Queen Eleanor resumed, "Count Dracula, I sentence you to house arrest for a period of five years, except for such times when your presence may be requested or authorized by the Crown, such as the royal bonfire on All Hallow's Eve." (The queen did hate to disappoint the children.) "Then, and only on such occasions we deem fit, may you leave your castle and attend the authorized events.

"In addition, your light-proof, hermetically sealed carriage will be confiscated until we agree to restore it to you. Such restoration will be based solely upon review of your behaviour.

"Further, all invitations, whether anticipated, presumed, implied or spoken, received by you within this realm from persons as yet unknown to enter their residences will be considered null and will be refused by you, or you will face deportation and seizure of your estate and assets. We will let stand all current social arrangements and understandings with your peers and may permit you to attend such social gatherings as we see fit, once the period of confinement has concluded.

"In consideration of your . . . diet, we will make arrangements within the next fortnight to deliver to you, on a rationed monthly basis, your accustomed sustenance. In the meantime, if you find you are running short, you may appeal to the baroness's blood bank for any supplies you may require. If granted, such supplies will be distributed on a limited, one-time basis, and will not be 'refillable,' except in case of fire, theft, loss, or non-delivery, to be documented in writing.

"Renovations you wish to make to your castle and outbuildings, including all materials and their source, must be approved and authorized by the Crown."

There was some whispering in her ear from her daughter next to her, as the count began to sputter.

"My daughter reminds me of our final condition. The collection of pointed sticks you have stored in your cellars and outbuildings will be removed and put to good use by the Crown."

Here, the count turned quite pale.

"We have determined they will make an excellent fence, which will be erected between the bottom boundary of your land and that of the countess and baroness. Points planted in, of course."

"But zey are antiques!" the count objected.

"Then they should be well cured." She signalled her bailiffs, who came forward and removed the count, along with the other accused.

Bang! Bang! The chief bailiff cried, "The accused have been sentenced, according to sovereign law. The Crown's tribunal has concluded. Plaintiffs are dismissed. God save the Queen!"

CHAPTER 30

A Great and Righteous Day

"Gosh! The look on that tall fellow's face! What was his name again? Mr. Upman?" As Millie sipped her sherry, stockinged feet up on a hassock in the family's private lounge, a footman passed around trays of elegant morsels. Another was plying them with drink. She chortled merrily and grabbed a crab Rangoon off the salver. "As slimy a character as I've ever seen! Bet you anything he'll try to squirm out of it."

"Besides the stringent terms of the injunction, you forget how publicized his face and name will be within the next few weeks, Princess," reminded Sidney. "He'll be so universally loathed by the time we're through with him, he'll be quite lucky if his milkman leaves him a pint."

"Even his own company will want to be shed of him," Rider agreed.

"They won't be happy they can't, you know, which will be a bit of a giggle." Millie demonstrated.

Rider beamed at the princess. "Yes. Normally, that might seem a bit unfair, as these clandestine projects usually get approved by the top echelon before being forced on some luckless minions to carry out. However, in this case, the nasty scheme originated with Mr. Upman. It was he who talked his superiors into doing something so risky."

"But there are heaps of precedents of underhanded rottenness in that corporation. Even in our little realm, we've heard plenty about their shoddy goings-on," Sidney objected. "Birds of a feather."

"True. Global's vultures have been doing dodgy deals for some time, camouflaged as various sorts of crusades—allegedly to protect the public—falsifying samples and tests run by their payrolled 'scientists,' " (Rider gestured with sarcastic air quotes) "to give them an excuse for wading in and making off with larger 'samples.' " (More air quotes.) "We're just lucky this time they bit off more than they could chew."

The countess chuckled. "That sounds more like something in our line."

"Going after ancient forest protected by the Crown just shows how complacent they'd become," Rider continued, "how persuaded they were of being beyond the reach of the law. It'll be a good lesson for others. I can't wait to read the lurid headlines."

"Hear! Hear!" Heiny raised his glass to them.

The gong went. The queen rose and offered her arm to Sidney. "I believe dinner is served. Will you take me in, Mr. van der Chase?"

"With great pleasure, Your Majesty."

The dining room was beautiful, quietly furnished with gleaming mahogany and cherry antiques, white linens, and tasteful displays of flowers and silver. In the glow of so many candles, the room was dazzling without aid of electricity. Above, stars were picked out in gold leaf against the midnight blue background of the ancient coffered ceiling. Tranquil landscapes framed in muted gold and painted by masters adorned the walls.

The queen sat at the head, with Herald opposite—a kindness and a deserved one; he had done his part, quite an important part, as it happened. In gratitude, Herald had smartened himself up. His beard had been tamed into neat braids, and he wore a new, dark blue, spangled robe.

Granny's chair, vacant so far, was, unsurprisingly, next to Rumpbuckle's, with Millie across from her, among the film crew. Millie was mad keen on talking shop with them. In typical form, Ronny eyed Nigel proprietarily. Dinah had been seated next to Rider, which was a bit awkward after their words at the baroness's. But Rider nodded to her gamely. He smiled, though, when he saw that Alice was between Derek and Ian. His smile widened when he realized Wolfgang would be sitting next to Herald. *Where* is *Wolfgang?* Granny and he were both missing.

Cedric and Manuel were below stairs so they could get caught up on gossip. Outside the kitchen, Eduardo was enjoying a manger full of new-mown hay and sweet herbs. Cook even left the Dutch door open so that he'd be able to listen in.

Upstairs, as the waitstaff came round with choice of beverage, Granny entered with a subdued Wolfgang in tow.

"Everything all right?" Rider asked.

"Quite satisfactory, thank you." Granny held up her wineglass to be filled. "Wolfie and I have just been discussing the importance of truth and when not to bend it. Haven't we, Wolfie?"

He nodded and looked down at his empty plate.

"Now, Granny. Don't be so hard on him," Millie said. "It was a funny story. Even Brie allowed a chuckle, once she got over her huff. Mind you, she has renounced runny cheeses since then."

"I don't doubt it was quite entertaining," Granny replied. "But it is important that he understands that it's not good to bite, as it were, the very hands that feed him."

"Undoubtedly, Wolfgang is extremely sorry about it," Rider defended. Wolfgang nodded sorrowfully. "And you all know what an important role he played in bringing the crooks to ground."

A round of "Hear! Hear!" volleyed, glasses held high.

"Which is why I let him keep his bow and medal." Granny's eyes crinkled as she relented, gazing fondly at Wolfie. "Tall tales aside, he *has* been a very good boy." She raised her own glass to her Wolfie.

"A toast to Wolfgang!" Heinrich stood. "To the noblest heart that e'er beat in a wolf, or in many a man, come to that!"

"To Wolfgang!" they all chorused.

Just in time, Herald saw Wolfgang's rear leg quivering to scratch an embarrassed ear and put a calming hand on it. The quivering subsided. "Think where you are, man," Herald whispered.

"Thanks, dude." Wolfgang ran a claw under his bow, happy he didn't have to wear it often, though he was even happier to keep that medal. A footman approached.

"And what would sir like to drink?"

"Oh, whatever y'all are havin'. Unless you happen to have some cider on you. Kinda partial to that."

"Of course, sir. The very thing to go with the roast pork, I feel." His glass was filled and he took a big swallow. *Boy,* that *was good stuff!* A large plate of pork and potatoes lashed with gravy was next set before him. Herald leaned over to him. "Granny's recipe, of course. There is none better."

"You know, you all right, little dude." He smiled at Herald. "Just don't lead me on any more of them wild goose chases!"

"Wouldn't dream of it." Herald touched his glass to Wolfgang's.

Rider heard a female throat's being cleared to his right.

"Um. I'm glad it turned out the way it did," began Dinah.

He considered her, eyebrows raised, waiting.

"I, um . . . I just wanted to say that I'm sorry for any . . ." She was having trouble finding the least incriminating word.

"Aggravation? Inconvenience? Bother?" he suggested.

"Yes." Her shoulders drooped. "All of the above. Maisie and the girls seemed so dead cert it was you. Only it wasn't. I'm sorry, that's all."

She really was cute. And smart, as well as resourceful. He smiled at her.

"It's all right. Truly."

She looked up at him in grateful relief. "Thanks. Not that I deserve it, but, thanks."

Hmmmm. Smart, resourceful, damned good at research and willing to admit her mistakes. We could do with someone like her in the firm. Maybe I'll mention it to Dad, when I get back.

As dessert was passed around, Rumpbuckle stood up. Glasses were pinged to halt the boisterous conversations. Heads raised expectantly.

"I have an announcement to make." He cleared his throat. "I know I am somewhat aged and probably much too set in my ways, but I have asked Gerty to be my wife." A mutual gasp escaped. "And she has accepted. To my bride to be, Boadicea Gertrude Loveanger, the one and only!"

Applause erupted. Hands pounded his shoulder, others shook his free hand. Glasses raised all round to the two of them.

"Well done, you two!" they shouted. Gerty smiled back at him and at them all. She'd start tearing up if she wasn't careful.

"She'll keep her surname, of course. I'm sure you can understand why! Gerty'll be needing to keep some folks on their toes. The name of Loveanger still strikes terror in the hearts it's meant to."

More cheers and congratulations, toasts and speeches.

They all adjourned to the library for the prescribed brandies and cordials. Excited chatter hummed as new alliances were being forged. In the middle of the room, surrounded by impossibly high bookshelves on two sides and lit at intervals by shaded lamps, was a long refectory table around which normally were placed reading chairs. Tonight they were pulled back into several rows facing the table, upon which a small, silver casket sat. An antique, high-backed chair was positioned on the far end of the table, near the French windows. At this, Eleanor took her place, still standing. Granny chose a wing-backed armchair to one side of the fireplace, with Millie standing nearby.

Footmen passed around more drinks. When everyone had a glass, Eleanor addressed them.

"I wanted to take this opportunity to address each of you and give you our heartfelt thanks for the courageous part every one of you has played in preserving what is so dear to us all. My mother has told me a great deal regarding your heroic feats. I know several of you need to return to your homes and businesses as soon as possible, so I thought it best to do this tonight. I hope you don't mind the informality of holding my little ceremony in the library."

Murmurs of dismissal mingled with glances of bewilderment.

"It is such a very pretty room and I felt it was appropriate in this instance, as it is a symbol of learning and wisdom, is it not?"

Heads nodded.

"It was my late husband's favourite room. Perhaps you did not know, but his Christian name was not Percy. It was Perseus—a name he lived up to. He was very much a man committed to vanquishing the monsters of our time to benefit others. I do so wish he were alive today to witness what you have done. I know he would have seen you all as heroes, every bit as do I, my mother and my daughter. Goodness! I think I'm getting a bit weepy. Queens aren't supposed to, you know." Eleanor cleared her throat.

"So it is my great pleasure to present to you each a memento, as testimony of our eternal gratitude."

A footman went to the windows and opened them.

"Some of our heroes are outside, too shy to come in, but they are not less included, I assure you."

Several sets of eyes were seen approaching the open windows, three golden lights floating among them.

Opening the silver casket, she held up the first medal. It was exquisitely wrought in silver and hung on a scarlet and black ribbon with gilt edging. She called forth Rider.

"Esmond Rippon the Third, as a measure of your tenacity and valour, I hereby bestow upon you this token of our esteem and gratitude and appoint you Knight of the Scarlet Fang and Defender of the Realm." There was a small, red velvet stool before her upon which he knelt. As she fastened the medal around his neck, Millie handed her mother the monarch's ceremonial sword, which the queen laid gently on each of Rider's shoulders.

One by one she called them all up or inside. Each medal was engraved with the name of the recipient as well as the date. Alice, Dinah, Ronny and Betty were each made Ladies of the Scarlet Fang and, likewise, Defenders.

As Rider resumed his seat, Wolfgang leaned over and whispered, "So what's the short name for Esmond?"

Rider hesitated. "It's 'Essy.' " Which is why he preferred to be called Rider.

Wolfgang grinned, slapping his leg. "Essy, huh? Sounds pretty much like 'Easy' don't it? See, I *knew* you was 'Easy Rider'!"

Finally, it was Wolfgang's turn to be knighted.

"To our most loyal friend, raconteur and watchdog, Wolfgang, who, from humble beginnings, grew in stature to become a formidable foe of those who attempt to destroy the woodlands and wild places, we make this bestowal with great and lasting affection."

She placed the medal around his neck and fondled his ears. Wolfgang held his head high and kept himself from bolting when the sword came down on his shoulders.

There was an outburst of cheers and more applause. Tongue lolling, he grinned back at them. He rather liked the jingle of the two medals against each other.

About midnight, Granny stood up, taking Rumpbuckle's arm.

The others also stood. "No, no. You young'uns carry on, if you have the stamina. It's past my bedtime. G'night all. Rumpy, lead the way. I'll leave the door ajar for you, Wolfie. Your bed's just inside."

Wolfie nodded. He'd give them some time to themselves.

Eleanor yawned behind a hand and likewise excused herself. "I'm also for bed. But please don't feel you have to follow suit. The night staff will see to any of your needs."

They said their goodnights and thanks to Queen Eleanor. Then, one by one, the rest drifted off to their rooms, as well.

Outside, on an ancient elm growing by the side of the library, an owl, a rat and a crow sat, enjoying the bounty of a basket hanging in the boughs: nuts, berries, seeds and two dressed voles. When they'd had sufficient, the crow lit up a pipe, blowing the smoke thoughtfully away from his friends. Below, a rabbit and an orange tabby cat hunkered companionably over their food bowls. Several wolves were bedding down after a succulent dinner of roasted meats.

A gleam of silver glinted from each collared neck under the glow shed by three lights that swarmed above. Eduardo and Wolfgang came over to give their bros a blow-by-blow account of the tribunal's proceedings.

“Now that truly is a wrap!” Brain declared.

It had been a great and righteous day: the good guys of all species had prevailed.

In a bedroom above, Gerty Loveanger leaned her head out the open casement. “All right, boys?”

Their voices called up to her. “Better than all right. Ta, Granny.”

CHAPTER 31

Departures and Revivals

T*he following day,* there was a small, private ceremony in the throne room in which Herald was made the Royal Acquisitor and Defender of Intellectual Property, in acknowledgement and gratitude for his skills in wizardry. An honorary DT (Doctorate of Thaumaturgy) was also bestowed upon him by the fellows of Voodoo U, presenting him with a diploma and star-embellished mortarboard. (His outstanding loans had been forgiven.)

Last, the baron and baroness presented to Herald their own beribboned medal, embossed with the family crest.

"In gratitude for your services in matters magical, I hereby appoint you a member of the Royal Order of Lupo and bestow upon you, Herald Fetidston, this token of our own esteem." Betty hung the medal on its ribbon around his neck and vouchsafed a smile. "Had it not been for you, as well as Granny, we would never have arrived in time to save our forest or apprehend the criminals. Whenever you're in the area, please do look us up and let us know how you are getting on."

Herald bowed to her and thanked her.

Rumpbuckle came forward with Rider. "And now, Fetidston, I believe it is time to right a wrong. Have you your wand with you?"

Herald produced his wand.

"And I have the required ingredients. You do remember the words? The correct ones?"

"Yes," Herald said, blinking sheepishly. "I think I have them well memorized now."

"Then let us begin."

Wolfbane and heartsease were sprinkled around Rider in a circle and he was given a bouquet of them to hold. The incantations were surprisingly short and to the point, and recited in tandem (just in case). In a shuddering flicker of images, Rider's body underwent a fast-forward transformation from man to wolf and back. Then a wisp of something like smoke poured from the region of Rider's solar plexus, carrying the transparent image of a wolf with it. For a moment, Rider was surrounded by a silver aura.

"How do you feel?" Rumpbuckle asked him, when the aura had dissipated.

Rider looked at his hands that had been briefly furry and clawed but which were now smooth and human. He seemed a bit stunned. "Fine. I think. So . . . is that it?"

"Yes. You should have no further troubles with wolfishness."

"What a relief! Thank you. Thank you both!" Rider grasped both their hands. "Would it be too much to ask you to help Eduardo, also?"

"We had already planned on that. I believe you're referring to his wind problem."

"Indeed."

"Do you wish to reverse his ability to converse as well?"

"No, I think we'd both prefer maintaining our channels of communication, at least telepathically. I've gotten so that I enjoy his humorous observations."

And it was done. (With thanks from Eduardo's friends.)

As the party then got ready to leave in their various conveyances, the queen and princess came out to see them off. "Although we've known most of you for only a short time, I truly feel that we have gained good friends. My castle and home will always be open to you. And I will be very interested, Nigel, in seeing this documentary when it is released."

"You will be the first to know—after the baroness, of course," Nigel replied.

"Thank you. I wish you all safe journeys." Giving a fond rub underneath Eduardo's forelock, the queen thanked him once again for the major part he'd played and gave him an apple. His medal jingled, as he nuzzled her hand.

The parties descended the winding streets and were back on the road toward Slaughter's End. A lot of light-hearted banter went back and forth among the carriage, cars and Rider on Eduardo.

Betty prevailed upon Rider to stop over at her castle one more night and he yielded. Rider hadn't had a true holiday in a long while.

CHAPTER 32

Epilogue

A ***few months later,*** Rider was sitting in his office going through the latest brief, when his email pinged the arrival of a new message. It was from Wolfie@grannysgang.org. Struggling through the typos, he read Wolfgang's news. Besides the welcome catch-up on gossip, Rider was glad to learn that the hapless poodle who'd whizzed through the bank windows during the wizard chase had miraculously survived. The dog had landed on a plump bank deposit and now enjoyed new status as the bank's mascot (*sans* the pink bows), a symbol of solvent indomitability.

Creasing up, Rider was about to reply when Dinah knocked on the open door before coming in with a cup of coffee. Upon Rider's recommendation, his father had sent an offer of employment to Dinah Clarkson, former *sous chef* in the baroness's kitchen. She had accepted and was quite enjoying training as a paralegal, as well as the stimulation of city life and increased circulation among eligible bachelors.

She set the cup down on a clear space of his desk.

"Thanks, Dinah. But you know you don't have to do that. It is *not* part of your job description, nor one of the skills we hired you for."

"I know," she said. "I suppose it's just become habit, after working in the kitchens. Besides, my coffee is a *bit* better than the usual office swill, don't you think?"

"Swill is being kind. Yes, quite an improvement."

She handed him the morning paper. "Have you seen the latest on GAM?"

"Not yet."

Rider gave the paper a cursory glance, but his mind was on too many other things to give it much notice. As predicted, there had been weeks of juicy scandal, concerning GAM's illicit activities, in the national dailies as well as *The Sun* and the *Daily Mirror,* among the sensationalist tabloids, and on prime time news. Prominently displayed were unflattering photos of the executives as well as the work crew. Most articles were syndicated and had reached international newscasts. World news was now teeming with exposés of the corporation and its sleazy subsidiaries.

On the home front, there had been more legal indictments of the corporation, with convictions speedily won by Rippon, Rippon and Magnus. Crowned with glory, the firm enjoyed an almost equal share of publicity. Their plaintiff client base had nearly doubled, which is why Rider hadn't had time to see the latest, entertaining headline. As he was reaching for the paper, there was a knock on the doorjamb.

"Ian! Good to see you, man!" Rider arose and came around his desk to shake Ian's hand. "What are you doing in our neck of the woods?"

"We've been meeting in town with the producers. They really like our documentary, especially the unexpected departure in plot line. They're going to release it in a few weeks. I've brought you a bunch of tickets for the premier."

"Good show! And thanks. I know Dad will want to come and I'll be there definitely. Would you care to join us, Dinah? You were in on the activities, too."

She dimpled at both of them. "That would be fab! Thanks, Ian. And Mr. Rippon."

Rider pulled a face. "I can't get her to call me by my first name, Ian. I *have* tried."

"So what did you end up calling the film?" Dinah asked Ian.

"*Blood Will Out (With the Proper Solvent)*," Ian told her solemnly.

Dinah laughed. "An interesting title. What made you choose it, other than the vampire slant, of course?"

"It was Rider's idea, actually," Ian told her.

Dinah regarded Rider quizzically.

"It's an old family joke." Rider explained, "When my father was a young barrister, he was prosecuting counsel on a murder case and in the heat of his dramatic summation to the jury, he misquoted the Bard, 'Blood will out!' Which provoked the accused, who was a dry cleaner, to comment, 'Well, yars. Given the proper solvent.'

"Too late, the man realized his mistake. The trial was neatly turned around and the accused was convicted. But my dad got untold amounts of ribbing from his peers, naturally, as well as congratulations."

"You know, I think I like it," Dinah laughed. "And I do like your father. He's been so kind and has such a wonderful sense of humour."

"Dad has his points," agreed Rider.

"Oh, before I forget! Have you heard the latest from *der Schwarzwald*?" Ian asked them.

"From the baroness?"

"Well, not from the baroness. From Granny et al."

"Aside from helping us with further evidence for the case, no. What's up?"

"Well, I'm told our Wolfgang has a girlfriend."

Rider folded his arms and sat on the edge of his desk, smirking. "Really? That's great news! May I ask what . . . er . . . species she is?"

"The same, you rascal, what else? The story goes when he was a stowaway on the ship that came over from New York, he hid out in cargo where he made 'friends' with a lovely Siberian she-wolf being transported back to the Moscow zoo. They shared a crate, you understand." Ian's eyebrows jiggled. "Well, somehow she managed to escape from the zoo. Couldn't stand the long, cold, lonely winters anymore, it seems. Word had gotten round via the howl-wire about Wolfgang. And she tracked him down! Granny told us all about it.

"She's kipping at Wolfgang's now, and he's got a big smile on his muzzle, apparently."

Rider scratched his chin. "That really is too bad,"

"How so?"

"It's just that I was looking forward to visiting and now I suppose the guest room will be unavailable." Rider's face remained deadpan.

Ian smiled. "Oh, I wouldn't worry about that, chum. Although you might have to put up with some late-night howling."

" 'Nudge, nudge, wink, wink,' " said Dinah.

" 'Say no more'!" they all carolled.

"I *am* glad to hear it," Rider admitted. "I'll have to send him an email with congrats."

Ian glanced at the clock on the wall. "Shite! I have to go. Another meeting. Give us a ring for drinks some time before the show."

"I'll do that. Thanks for the tickets!" Rider clapped Ian on the shoulder.

"No prob. See you two soon."

Rider sighed and took a sip of his coffee. "Ah, well. Back to the grind." He sat back at his desk, eyeing the mountain of material he had to get through.

"Aren't you going to read the paper, first?" Dinah prodded.

He looked up from a deposition, eyebrows raised. "All right. If you insist." He picked up the newspaper and saw the enlarged photo of Tyrone Upman on the front page with the headline:

"GAM EXEC CHOMPED AND SHREDDED"

Rider set down his cup and read, Dinah perching on the edge of his desk reading over his shoulder:

> At two a.m. Tuesday morning, Tyrone P. Upman, former Chief Development Officer of Global Advanced Management, LLP (GAM), was found in his office, slain by unknown assailants. Mr. Upman's body was discovered by the janitor, Bernard T. Scrubbs of Slough, who vowed he'd never seen such blood and carnage. The victim's throat was found torn out and a couple of limbs had been ripped from his body. These appeared to have been masticated by two different sets of teeth. From the bite marks, the teeth did not appear to have been human. The coroner commented that the marks more resembled canine dentation. There was a good deal of coarse hair found on the deceased's body and clothes,

which is being tested, but at cursory inspection it also appears to be that of a canid species.

When questioned, co-workers revealed that there had been a lot of tension between the deceased and former co-executives, Cyril B. Stonewall, previously VP Business Development, and Addison T. Brickheart, the corporation's former Chief Compliance Officer. For reasons that are as yet forthcoming, the two latter gentlemen were prohibited from eating meat during the period of the full moon. Mr. Upman was under no such prohibition, and co-workers told detectives that he often took great delight in eating rare steaks in front of the other two gentlemen. These actions were generally seen to be of a goading nature and the cause of considerable friction.

Brian Smithson, the office manager, was alerted to the problem by in-house counsel, Barton Woodge. Mr. Woodge stated that Messrs. Stonewall and Brickheart had come to him in the past week, asking to see the exact terms of the ban. Specifically, they wished to know if the term "flesh" included that of all species, or merely referred to that of animals raised for food. Mr. Woodge advised the two men of the terms, as was his duty to do but, alarmed by their questioning, alerted Mr. Smithson late last Friday. Although Mr. Upman was never popular among his subordinates, being allegedly infamous for his biting sarcasm and unkind remarks, Mr. Smithson nevertheless planned to take any disciplinary steps deemed necessary. However, as it was closing time and the weekend, he would have to wait until Monday to approach the men. On Monday, an urgent meeting and press conference intervened, making impossible a meeting with Messrs. Stonewall and Brickheart who have now been reported missing and are wanted for questioning.

Mr. Scrubbs noted that on Monday night the full moon was at its zenith, and further disclosed that he'd found complete suits of clothes lying apparently abandoned in each of the suspects' offices. Sargent Detective Jacobson said that the clothes appeared to have been recently occupied, and that the shirt buttons had popped off and the seams at the armholes had burst. He made no supposition as to the cause.

We expect to know more in the coming weeks.

One of the grisliest details of the crime scene was the presence of a brown substance upon the deceased's severed limbs. The substance is presumed to have come from the open bottle of HP sauce found on the victim's desk.

Mr. Scrubbs, in the manner of janitors everywhere, gave the appearance of knowing more than most about the corporate goings-on, and is reported to have made the following comment: "Well, looks like, after all, it *is* a dog-eat-dog world."

Rider was wiping down a file folder that had received the main thrust of coffee that had spewed from his mouth as he read the concluding quote. His chest was heaving. Dinah was biting her lip, trying not to laugh until she thought it safe. He next wiped his eyes, choking back his own laughter. Then he checked the clock.

Sod it, the files can wait. "Miss Clarkson, it's a beautiful day and I do believe it's lunch time. I rather think this calls for a good nosh-up at the local." He rose and offered his arm to Dinah. "Shall we?"

Her smile was broad as she took his arm in hers. "Let's, Mr. Rippon."

As they waited for the elevator, he asked her, "Anything in particular you fancy?"

"I'm not fussed, so long as it's not CDO with HP sauce!"

Acknowledgements

My heartfelt thanks go to the following:

Ruth Haber, my long-time friend, all-suffering editor and English authority *extraordinaire*, who gamely braved four readings of my book without expiring or resorting to defenestration. The latter would be difficult, at any rate, with loose pages, unless you had a really still day. But she's never been one to litter. Forgive me for (mostly) eschewing the Oxford comma, among other transgressions;

Kathleen O'Shell, my wonderful sister and head cheerleader, who read my book with joy, but nevertheless with a discerning eye;

Virginia Young, my canny, seasoned author friend and beta reader, who read my book and even forced husband Ed to do so, although they don't usually read fantasy. I give them both my condolences and gratitude for sticking with it, and even laughing along the way;

Joanne Cavatorta, another talented writing friend and beta reader, who found a bunch of typos yet forgave me, and laughed throughout (or so she said); and

BG Callahan for permission to use her exotic culinary term, "flapioca." It may never be served at an IHOP, but the loss, I'm sure, is theirs.

About the Author

Native Californian and survivor of U.C. Santa Barbara, **LAUREN STOKER** moved to New England for the thrill of skiing on ice and owning a snow blower. She lives in Plymouth, Massachusetts with her cat and Chief Shreditor, Sam. Lauren enjoys playing loud music, ranting about anti-environmentalists, and collecting beer coasters, while drinking a fine British ale. Since the tender age of 15, she has struggled with the written word (and sometimes won). Lauren's short stories have been published throughout the U.S. and in the U.K.

Her book of satirical Christmas carol parodies, *A MOST PECULIAR CHRISTMAS (Songs of [J]Oy or Mirth),* was released in October of 2020. Links to her publications may be found at: https://LaurenHStoker.com.

Made in the USA
Monee, IL
19 September 2021